W9-AKU-655

The frontispiece illustration by George Kerr from the second (1908) edition of *American Fairy Tales.*

AMERICAN FAIRY TALES

by

L. Frank Baum

Illustrated by

N. P. Hall, Harry Kennedy, Ike Morgan
and Ralph Fletcher Seymour

With a New Introduction by

Martin Gardner

DOVER PUBLICATIONS, INC.
NEW YORK

This Dover edition,, first published in 1978, is an unabridged and unaltered republication of the work first published by the George M. Hill Company, Chicago, in 1901. A new introduction by Martin Gardner has been prepared especially for this edition.

International Standard Book Number: 0486-23643-9
Library of Congress Catalog Card Number:
77-94153

Manufactured in the United States by Courier Corporation
23643910
www.doverpublications.com

INTRODUCTION

The title of this book is something of a misnomer. Not all its stories occur in America, and not all are about fairies. Most of them, however, have native settings, and all are "fairy tales" in the broader sense of being fantasies. In a preface to a later edition, Lyman Frank Baum maintained that never before had a book contained "fairy tales" that take place, for the most part, in the United States. I do not know if this is true or not. But if there were earlier books of this sort for children, they were by now-forgotten writers.

In 1901 when *American Fairy Tales* first went on sale, Baum had a well-established reputation. Two of his books, *Father Goose: His Book* (1899) and *The Wonderful Wizard of Oz* (1900) had been excellent sellers. Both were preceded by a less successful collection of short fantasies, *Mother Goose in Prose* (1897), and in 1900 another book of short stories, *A New Wonderland,* had been published. (The second book was later retitled *The Magical Monarch of Mo,* and is currently in print as a Dover edition.) It is true that Dorothy and Toto came from Kansas, and the Wizard from Omaha; but their adventures take place in Oz, all the characters of *The Magical Monarch* live in Mo, and most of the settings of the Mother Goose tales are in England, as they should be. None of the stories in this last collection is clearly identified as taking place in this country, although the

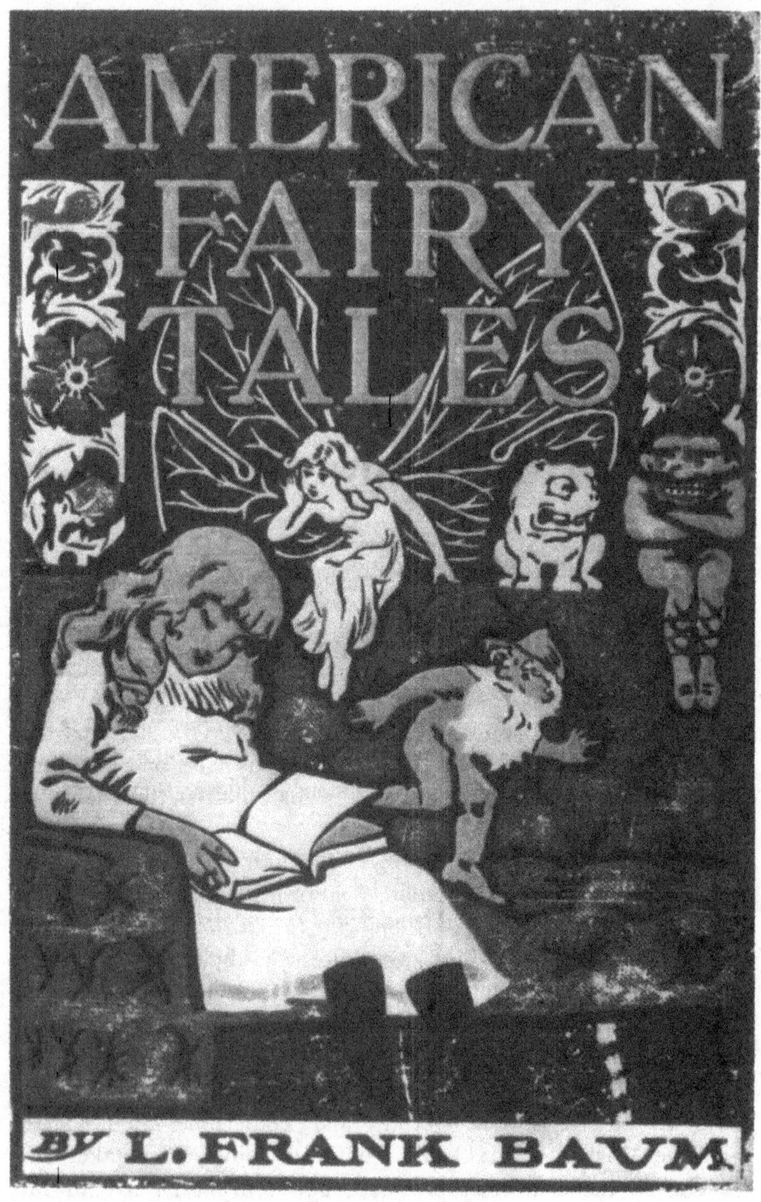

Cover of the original 1901 Hill edition of *American Fairy Tales*—the edition used in this facsimile reprint (illustration by Ralph Fletcher Seymour).

final story, about a little farm girl named Dorothy, is surely American because it speaks of Santa Claus instead of Father Christmas.

The twelve stories of *American Fairy Tales* were first syndicated weekly in at least five newspapers during the first half of 1901. Four of these papers are named by the newsboy on page 173 when he calls out: "Chronicle, 'Quirer, R'public 'n' 'Spatch! Wot'll ye 'ave?" (The Chicago *Chronicle,* Cincinnati *Enquirer,* St. Louis *Republic,* and Pittsburgh *Dispatch.*) The stories also ran in the Boston *Post.* The book's illustrations, by Ike Morgan, Harry Kennedy, N. P. Hall and Ralph Fletcher Seymour (who did the cover, title page and border pictures) were the basis of most of the drawings that accompanied the stories in the *Enquirer, Dispatch* and *Post.* Pictures in the *Chronicle* and the *Republic* by staff artists were, I am told, quite different.

George M. Hill, who handled newspaper syndication rights and printed the book's first edition in 1901,[1] was the small Chicago house that had earlier published *Father Goose* and *Wizard.* In the same year that *American Fairy Tales* appeared, Hill also issued Baum's second full-length fantasy, *Dot and Tot of Merryland.* It would be several years before Baum's readers, and the great success of the 1902 stage version of *Wizard,* persuaded him to return to Oz.

A completely new edition of *American Fairy Tales* was published by Bobbs-Merrill in 1908. All the illustrations from the Hill edition were replaced with sixteen two-color plates by George Kerr, a cartoonist for the New York *Herald.* The twelve stories were rearranged—for the worse, because the weakest story, "The King of the Polar Bears," was shifted to the end, thus destroying the lovely ending of the first edition. All the stories were revised

[1] It is this edition that is here reprinted in facsimile. Three full pages of advertisements for other Baum titles published by Hill have been dropped from the end of book; page numbers have been added, along with page references in the table of contents (the original had neither), but no attempt has been made to correct uneven lines and other instances of careless printing. On page 176, between lines 11 and 12 from the bottom, an entire line of type has been lost. The book was also poorly copy-edited; if indeed any attempt was made. David Greene points out that on page 119 Mr. Bostwick's wife calls him John, and on the next page she calls him William. Was his full name John William Bostwick? And what is a Yale professor (again page 119) doing in Boston? Greene suspects that Baum confused Yale and Harvard.

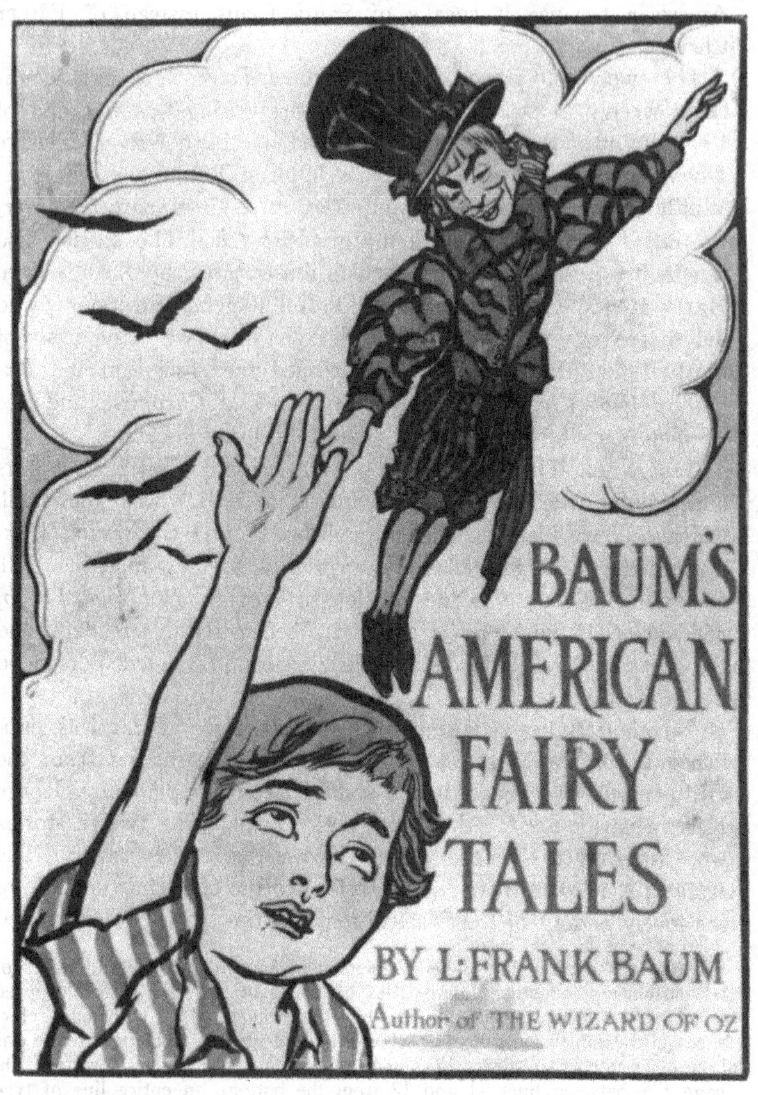

Cover of the second edition of *American Fairy Tales,* published by Bobbs-Merrill in 1908 (illustration by George Kerr).

in numerous minor ways, and three entirely new tales were added. Baum also added the following "Author's Note":

> This is the first time, I believe, that a book has been printed containing Fairy Tales that relate mainly to American boys and girls and their adventures with real fairies in the United States and other American countries.
>
> If fairies exist at all—and no one has yet been able to prove that they do *not* exist—then there is no good reason why they should not inhabit our favored land as well as the forest glades and flowery dales of the older world across the water. For fairies are not peculiar to any one locality, and every race has its own fairy legends.
>
> Yet, we must consider that the beautiful and well-known tales of Andersen and the Brothers Grimm, as well as those of Hauff, Perault [sic], Caballero and Andrew Lang, date many long years ago, and such histories would never do for American Fairy Tales, because our country has no great age to boast of. So I am obliged to offer our wide-awake youngsters modern tales about modern fairies, and while my humble efforts must not be compared with the classic stories of my masters, they at least bear the stamp of our own times and depict the progressive fairies of to-day.
>
> My friends, the children, will find these stories quite as astonishing as if they had been written hundreds of years ago, for ours is the age of astonishing things. They are not too serious in purpose, but aim to amuse and entertain, yet I trust the more thoughtful of my readers will find a wholesome lesson hidden beneath each extravagant notion and humorous incident.
>
> L. FRANK BAUM.
>
> Macatawa, 1908.

Sometime around 1924 Bobbs-Merrill issued a third edition with a new pictorial label on the cover and Kerr's color plates reduced to eight. It is not known how often this edition was reprinted, but it was in print until 1942. Four stories from the 1901 edition are in *The Purple Dragon and Other Fantasies,* a collection of Baum short stories edited and annotated by David L. Greene (Fictioneer Books, Ltd., 1976).

Children seemed not to care much for *American Fairy Tales,* though it is hard to tell because only grown-ups buy children's books and write reviews. Is fantasy at its best only when it takes place in a far-off region or long ago? J. M. Barrie wrote a dull

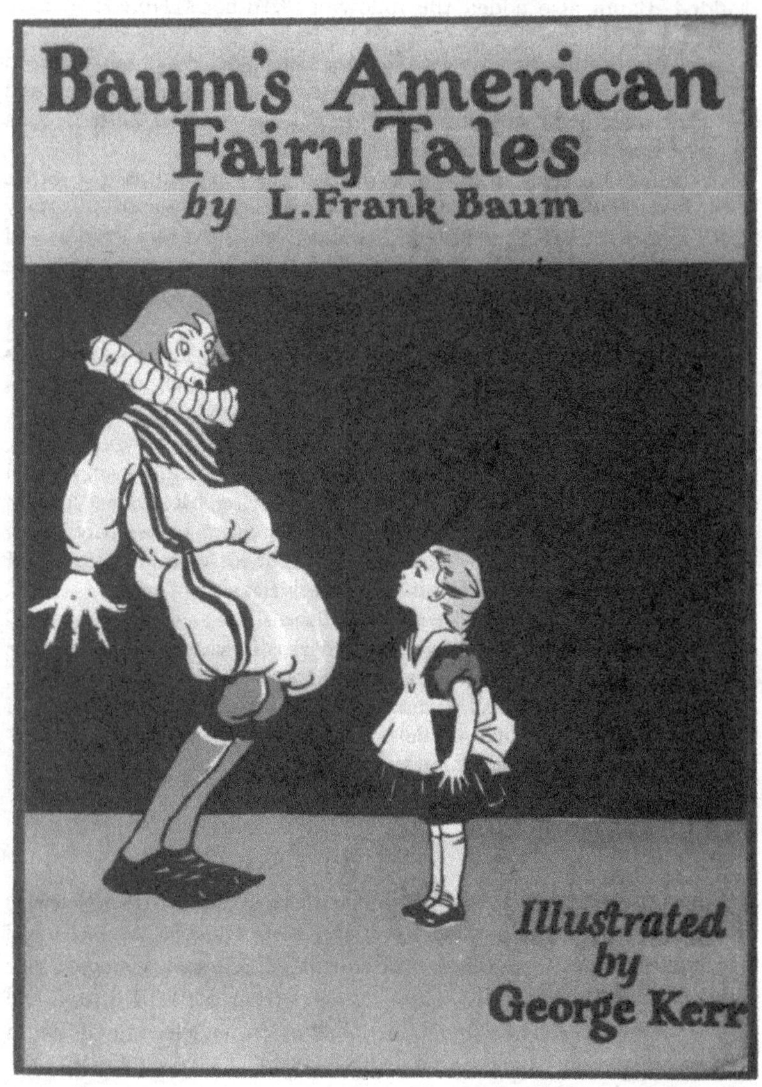

Cover of the third edition of *American Fairy Tales,* published by Bobbs-Merrill in 1923 or 1924 (illustration by George Kerr).

book about Peter Pan in Kensington Gardens; it was only when Peter took Wendy to Neverland that Peter became famous. Of course there are exceptions (Mary Poppins!). Classics such as *The Wind in the Willows* and *Charlotte's Web* are not exceptions, because talking animals alone do not a fantasy make—they are merely devices for disguising real people.

"*American Fairy Tales,* I am sorry to tell you," wrote James Thurber in a short essay on Baum, "are not good fairy tales. The scene of the first one is the attic of a house 'on Prairie Avenue, in Chicago.' It never leaves there for any wondrous, far-away realm." Russel B. Nye, in an appreciation of Baum, elaborates the same point:

> The *American Fairy Tales* were good stories, far better than most run-of-the-mill "educational" tales for children, but in the majority of them Baum failed to observe the first rule of the wonder-tale—that it must create a never-never land in which all laws of probability may be credibly contravened or suspended. When in the first story the little girl (Dorothy by another name) replies to a puzzled, lost genie, "You are on Prairie Avenue in Chicago," the heart goes out of the story. It is only in Quok, or in Baum's zany version of the African Congo, or among the Ryls, that the book captures the fine free spirit of Oz. The child could see Chicago (or a city much like it) with his eyes; Oz he could see much more distinctly and believably with his imagination. Baum nevertheless clung for a few years to the belief that he could make the United States an authentic fairyland. "There's lots of magic in all nature," he remarked in *Tik-Tok of Oz,* "and you may see it as well in the United States, where you and I once lived, as you can here." But children could not. They saw magic only in Oz, which never was nor could be Chicago or Omaha or California or Kansas.

To this criticism we may add that Baum injected into the stories more than his usual quota of adult farce—witticisms that few young readers could appreciate. The Women's Anti-Gambling League sponsors a weekly card party. An Italian bandit, tightly packed for a long time in a chest with two of his comrades, refers to one of them as his "nearest friend for years." When one of the bandits tells Martha that his business is to rob, the girl informs him that jobs with the gas company are hard to get, but he might consider becoming a politician. A wealthy crone, who is the highest bidder for the right to marry the ten-year-old King of Quok, pays $3,900,624.16 "in cash and on the spot, which proves this is a fairy story." As Michael Hearn points out, only adult readers would perceive this story as a satire on a common practice of the time, the marriage of wealthy American women to younger and destitute Europeans with royal titles.

In spite of Baum's cynical attitude (his irrelevant "morals" at the end of many of the stories are obviously tongue-in-cheek), most of the stories are excellent yarns, and alert children can appreciate much of the humor. Particularly amusing are the dialog about the pie that got packed into the chest with the bandits; the senator's compulsive ballet dance after he has just declared it to be "a most impressive and important occasion"; the merry laugh ("Guk-uk-uk-uk!") of Gouie, the hippopotamus, and the surprise ending of the story about him; the dress that is reduced from $20 to the great bargain of "only $19.98." Judging by its many reprints, "The Magic Bon Bons" was the book's most popular story. It was even made into a movie by Baum's Oz Film Company.

Science-fiction buffs will find "The Capture of Father Time" of special interest. There have been endless stories about time speeding up or slowing down—H. G. Wells's "The New Accelerator," for example—but stories about the world's gyrations coming to a total halt (except for the observer) are not common. Baum handles the theme skillfully. "The Wonderful Pump" is a well-constructed imitation of a traditional fairy tale. And who can read "The Enchanted Types," a biting satire on female fashions—especially the outlandish turn-of-the-century fad of wearing stuffed real birds on hats—without instantly becoming a disciple of Thorstein Veblen?

Baum enthusiasts will find many parallels with ideas in other Baum books. The notion of a glass animal was used again in *The Patchwork Girl of Oz* when Dr. Pipt brings to life a transparent glass cat named Bungle. The butterfly, who has such a tender heart but no soul or conscience, recalls the Tin Woodman of *Wizard,* taking great pains to be kind because he lacks a heart.

Knooks and Ryls inhabit the Forest of Burzee in *The Life and Adventures of Santa Claus* (now also back in print as a Dover edition), and along with Santa they attend Ozma's birthday party at the close of *The Road to Oz.* A Ryl is prominent in three other Baum stories. One is "The Ryl," a tale added to the 1908 edition of *American Fairy Tales.* Another, "The Runaway Shadows," was a newspaper story intended to be part of the 1901 serialization, although it did not appear until much later. It was reprinted for the first time in *The Baum Bugle* for April 1962. Tanko-Mankie, the Yellow Ryl in "The Dummy That Lived," reappears in "The Yellow Ryl," a story apparently first published in two parts in the August and September 1925 issues of a children's magazine called *A Child's Garden.* The story was perhaps intended for the 1908 edition of *American Fairy Tales. The Baum Bugle* reprinted it in 1964 in its Spring and Autumn numbers.

Although Baum's style is sometimes pedestrian, his narratives move along briskly, seldom flagging in interest and Ozzy invention. There are spots where his sentences have a spare, concise beauty. "He tossed and tumbled around upon his hard bed until the moonlight came in at the window and lay like a great white sheet upon the bare floor." The book's final sentence startles with the abruptness, brevity and elemental poetry of a *haiku.*

When Jim releases Father Time, "with a rustle and rumble and roar of activity the world came to life again and jogged along as it always had before." This is Baum writing with his usual carelessness, but creating vivid images that jog his tale along for the delight of all of us, old and young, who have fallen under the Royal Historian's magic spell.[2]

MARTIN GARDNER

[2] As usual, I must thank David Greene, James Haff, Michael Hearn, Dick Martin, and Fred Meyer for their astute criticisms of this introduction's first draft. *The Baum Bugle,* official periodical of the International Wizard of Oz Club, Inc., goes free to all members. Anyone wishing to join should write to the secretary, Fred Meyer, 220 North Eleventh Street, Escanaba, Michigan 49829.

American Fairy Tales
by L. FRANK BAUM
The Original
"Father Goose"

COVER, Title Page, & Borders designed *by* Ralph Fletcher Seymour — Illustrations *by* Ike Morgan, Harry Kennedy & N. P. Hall.

AMERICAN FAIRYTALES

By

L. FRANK BAUM

Author of

FATHER GOOSE; HIS BOOK,
THE WONDERFUL WIZARD OF OZ, ETC.

CHICAGO NEW YORK
GEORGE M. HILL COMPANY
1901

Copyright, 1901,
By
Geo. M. Hill Co.,
Chicago

CONTENTS

CONTENTS

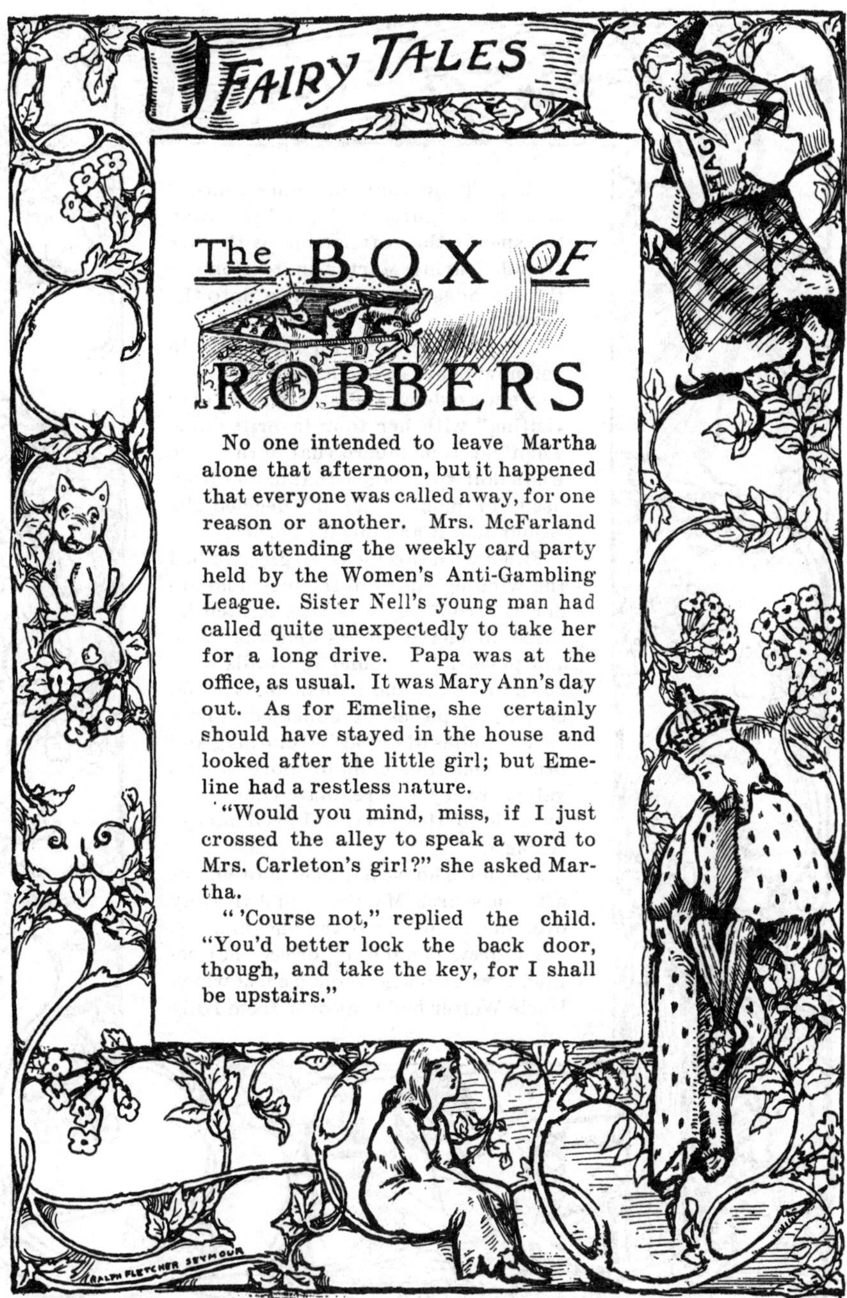

The BOX OF ROBBERS

No one intended to leave Martha alone that afternoon, but it happened that everyone was called away, for one reason or another. Mrs. McFarland was attending the weekly card party held by the Women's Anti-Gambling League. Sister Nell's young man had called quite unexpectedly to take her for a long drive. Papa was at the office, as usual. It was Mary Ann's day out. As for Emeline, she certainly should have stayed in the house and looked after the little girl; but Emeline had a restless nature.

"Would you mind, miss, if I just crossed the alley to speak a word to Mrs. Carleton's girl?" she asked Martha.

"'Course not," replied the child. "You'd better lock the back door, though, and take the key, for I shall be upstairs."

"Oh, I'll do that, of course, miss," said the delighted maid, and ran away to spend the afternoon with her friend, leaving Martha quite alone in the big house, and locked in, into the bargain.

The little girl read a few pages in her new book, sewed a few stitches in her embroidery and started to "play visiting" with her four favorite dolls. Then she rememberd that in the attic was a doll's playhouse that hadn't been used for months, so she decided she would dust it and put it in order.

Filled with this idea, the girl climbed the winding stairs to the big room under the roof. It was well lighted by three dormer windows and was warm and pleasant. Around the walls were rows of boxes and trunks, piles of old carpeting, pieces of damaged furniture, bundles of discarded clothing and other odds and ends of more or less value. Every well-regulated house has an attic of this sort, so I need not describe it.

The doll's house had been moved, but after a search Martha found it away over in a corner near the big chimney.

She drew it out and noticed that behind it was a black wooden chest which Uncle Walter had sent over from Italy

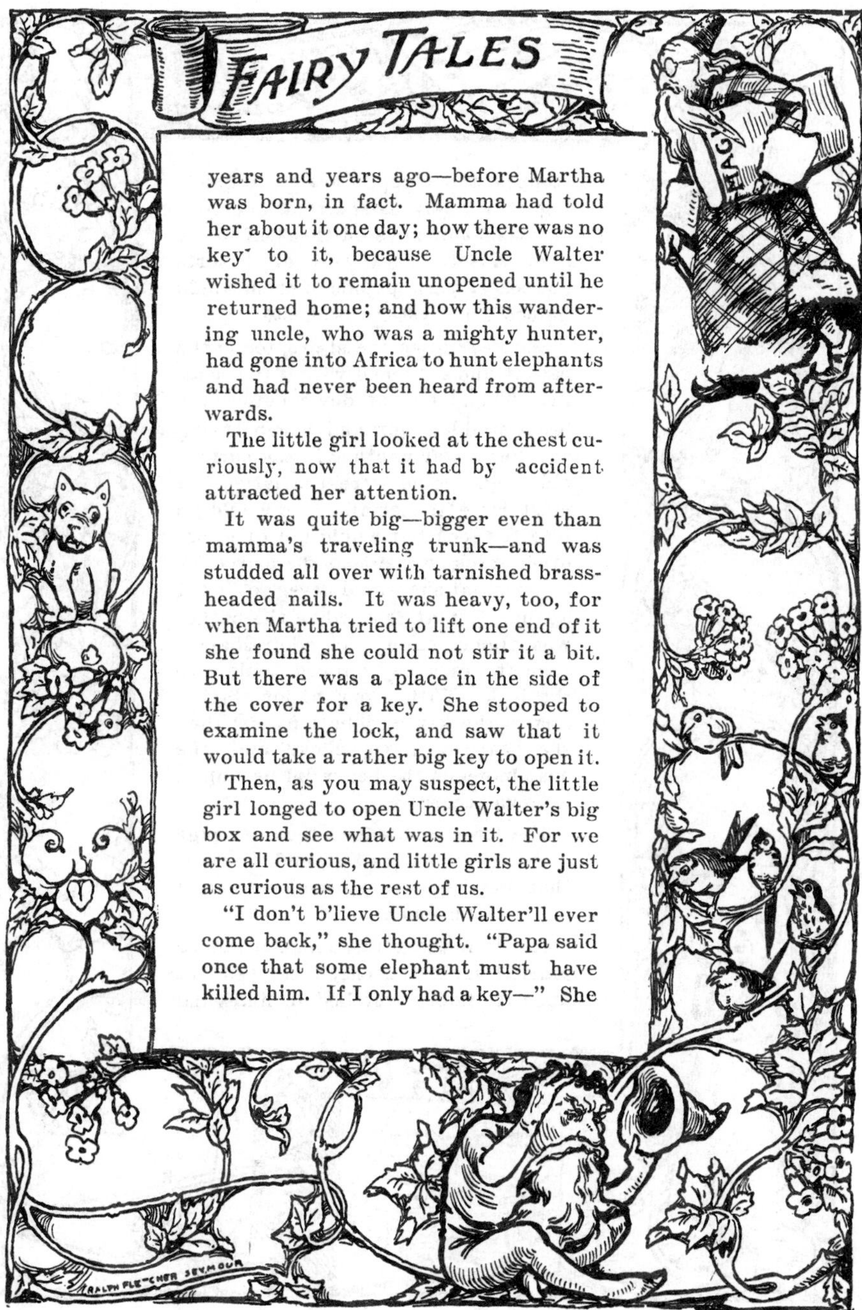

years and years ago—before Martha was born, in fact. Mamma had told her about it one day; how there was no key to it, because Uncle Walter wished it to remain unopened until he returned home; and how this wandering uncle, who was a mighty hunter, had gone into Africa to hunt elephants and had never been heard from afterwards.

The little girl looked at the chest curiously, now that it had by accident attracted her attention.

It was quite big—bigger even than mamma's traveling trunk—and was studded all over with tarnished brass-headed nails. It was heavy, too, for when Martha tried to lift one end of it she found she could not stir it a bit. But there was a place in the side of the cover for a key. She stooped to examine the lock, and saw that it would take a rather big key to open it.

Then, as you may suspect, the little girl longed to open Uncle Walter's big box and see what was in it. For we are all curious, and little girls are just as curious as the rest of us.

"I don't b'lieve Uncle Walter'll ever come back," she thought. "Papa said once that some elephant must have killed him. If I only had a key—" She

stopped and clapped her little hands together gayly as she remembered a big basket of keys on the shelf in the linen closet. They were of all sorts and sizes; perhaps one of them would unlock the mysterious chest!

She flew down the stairs, found the basket and returned with it to the attic. Then she sat down before the brass-studded box and began trying one key after another in the curious old lock. Some were too large, but most were too small. One would go into the lock but would not turn; another stuck so fast that she feared for a time that she would never get it out again. But at last, when the basket was almost empty, an oddly-shaped, ancient brass key slipped easily into the lock. With a cry of joy Martha turned the key with both hands; then she heard a sharp "click," and the next moment the heavy lid flew up of its own accord!

The little girl leaned over the edge of the chest an instant, and the sight that met her eyes caused her to start back in amazement.

Slowly and carefully a man unpacked himself from the chest, stepped out upon the floor, stretched his limbs and

The bandits unpack themselves from the box.

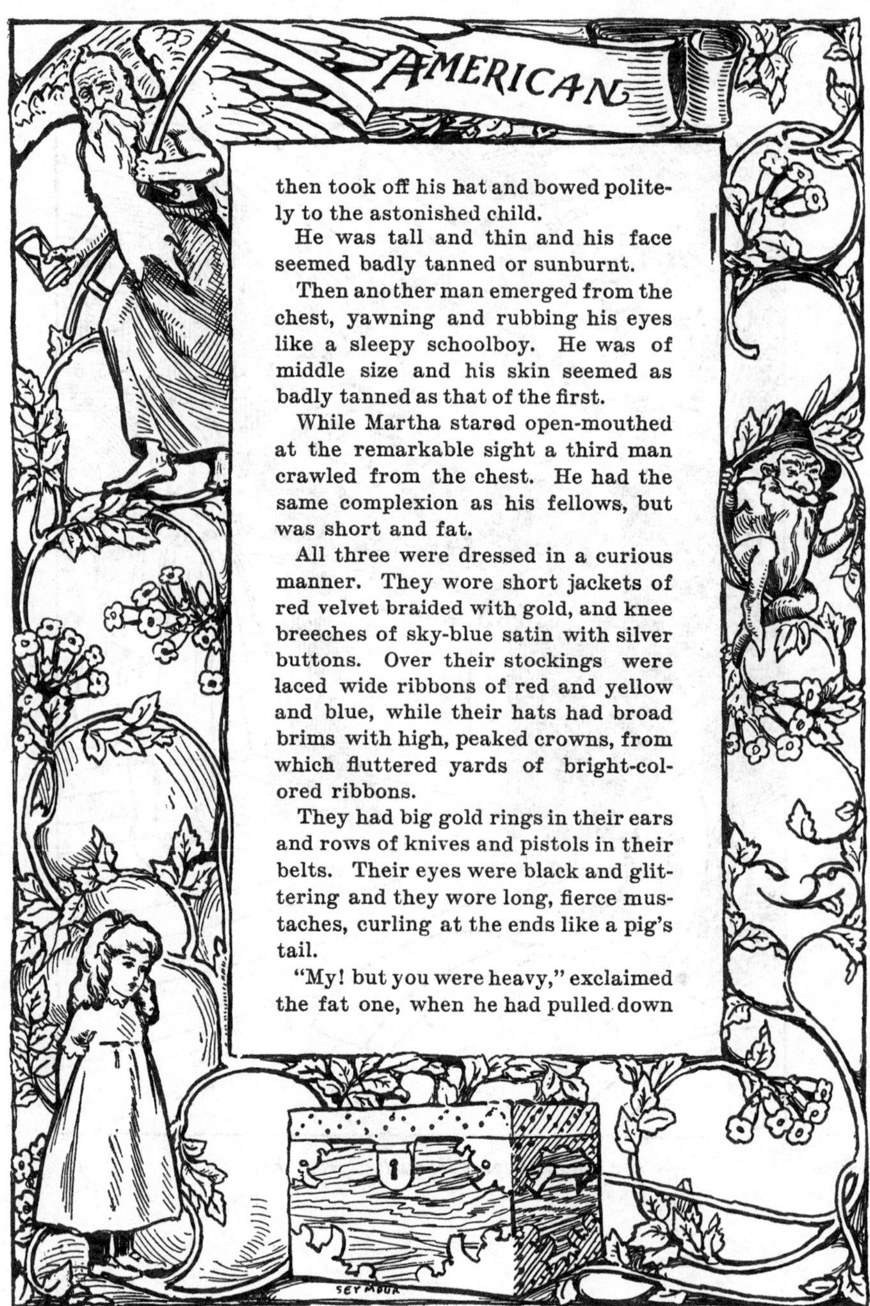

then took off his hat and bowed politely to the astonished child.

He was tall and thin and his face seemed badly tanned or sunburnt.

Then another man emerged from the chest, yawning and rubbing his eyes like a sleepy schoolboy. He was of middle size and his skin seemed as badly tanned as that of the first.

While Martha stared open-mouthed at the remarkable sight a third man crawled from the chest. He had the same complexion as his fellows, but was short and fat.

All three were dressed in a curious manner. They wore short jackets of red velvet braided with gold, and knee breeches of sky-blue satin with silver buttons. Over their stockings were laced wide ribbons of red and yellow and blue, while their hats had broad brims with high, peaked crowns, from which fluttered yards of bright-colored ribbons.

They had big gold rings in their ears and rows of knives and pistols in their belts. Their eyes were black and glittering and they wore long, fierce mustaches, curling at the ends like a pig's tail.

"My! but you were heavy," exclaimed the fat one, when he had pulled down

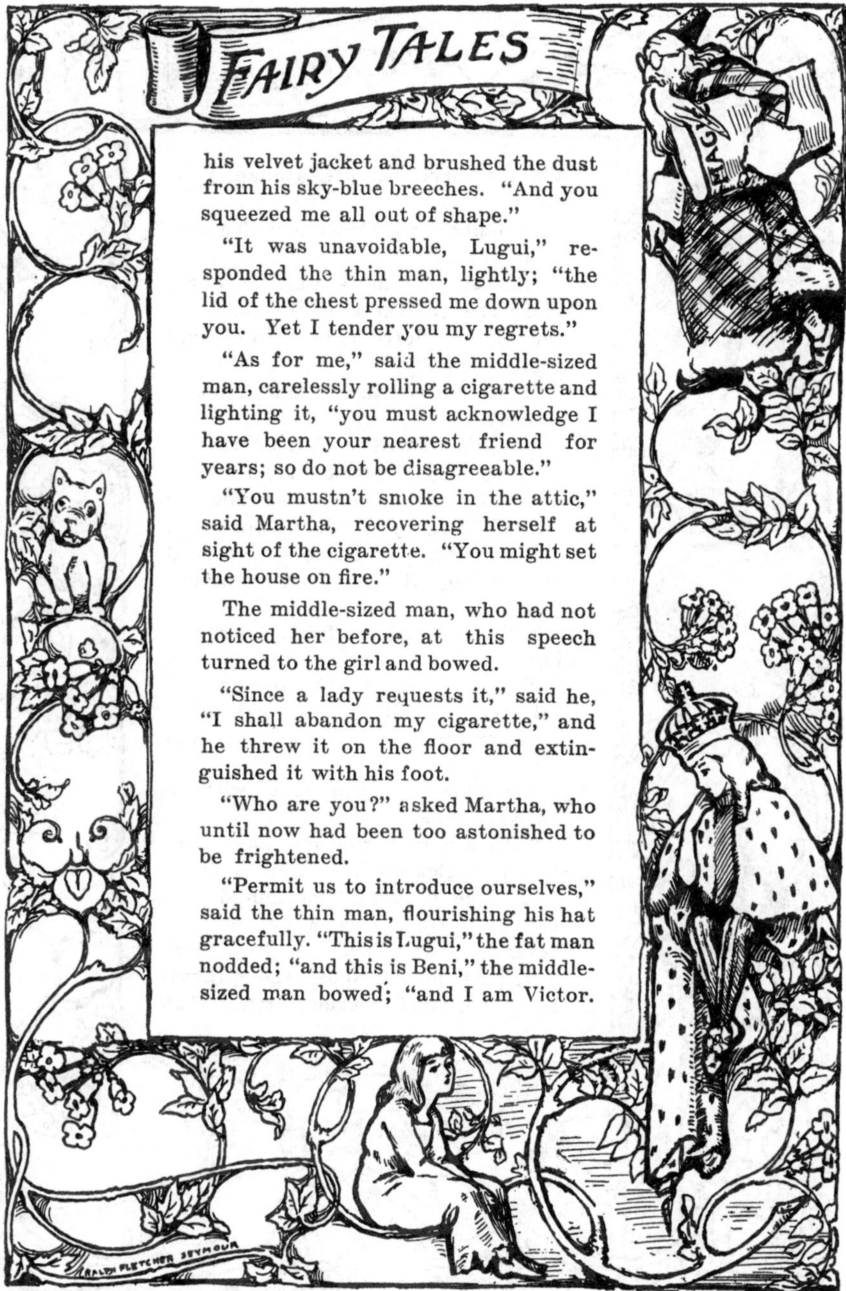

his velvet jacket and brushed the dust from his sky-blue breeches. "And you squeezed me all out of shape."

"It was unavoidable, Lugui," responded the thin man, lightly; "the lid of the chest pressed me down upon you. Yet I tender you my regrets."

"As for me," said the middle-sized man, carelessly rolling a cigarette and lighting it, "you must acknowledge I have been your nearest friend for years; so do not be disagreeable."

"You mustn't smoke in the attic," said Martha, recovering herself at sight of the cigarette. "You might set the house on fire."

The middle-sized man, who had not noticed her before, at this speech turned to the girl and bowed.

"Since a lady requests it," said he, "I shall abandon my cigarette," and he threw it on the floor and extinguished it with his foot.

"Who are you?" asked Martha, who until now had been too astonished to be frightened.

"Permit us to introduce ourselves," said the thin man, flourishing his hat gracefully. "This is Lugui," the fat man nodded; "and this is Beni," the middle-sized man bowed; "and I am Victor.

2

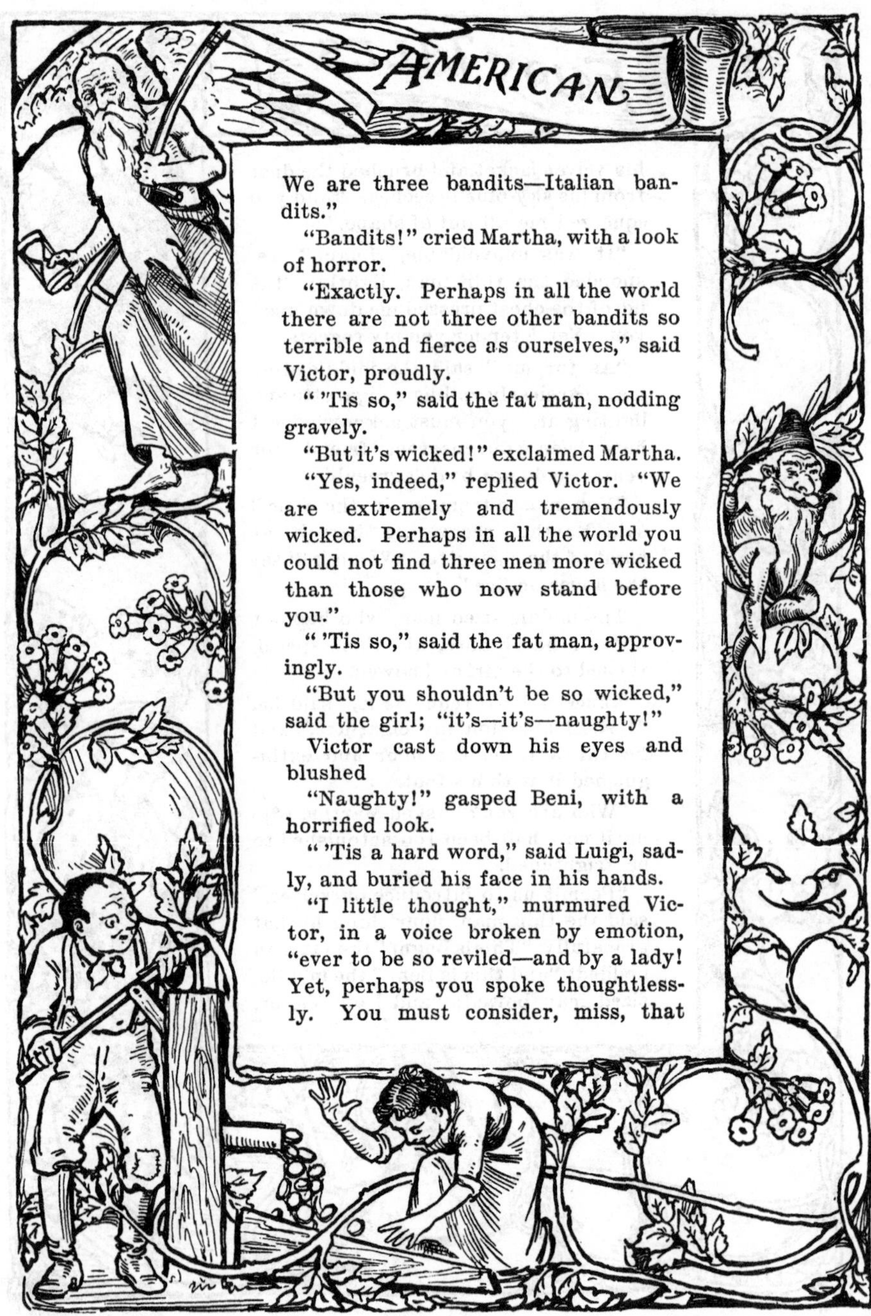

We are three bandits—Italian bandits."

"Bandits!" cried Martha, with a look of horror.

"Exactly. Perhaps in all the world there are not three other bandits so terrible and fierce as ourselves," said Victor, proudly.

" 'Tis so," said the fat man, nodding gravely.

"But it's wicked!" exclaimed Martha.

"Yes, indeed," replied Victor. "We are extremely and tremendously wicked. Perhaps in all the world you could not find three men more wicked than those who now stand before you."

" 'Tis so," said the fat man, approvingly.

"But you shouldn't be so wicked," said the girl; "it's—it's—naughty!"

Victor cast down his eyes and blushed

"Naughty!" gasped Beni, with a horrified look.

" 'Tis a hard word," said Luigi, sadly, and buried his face in his hands.

"I little thought," murmured Victor, in a voice broken by emotion, "ever to be so reviled—and by a lady! Yet, perhaps you spoke thoughtlessly. You must consider, miss, that

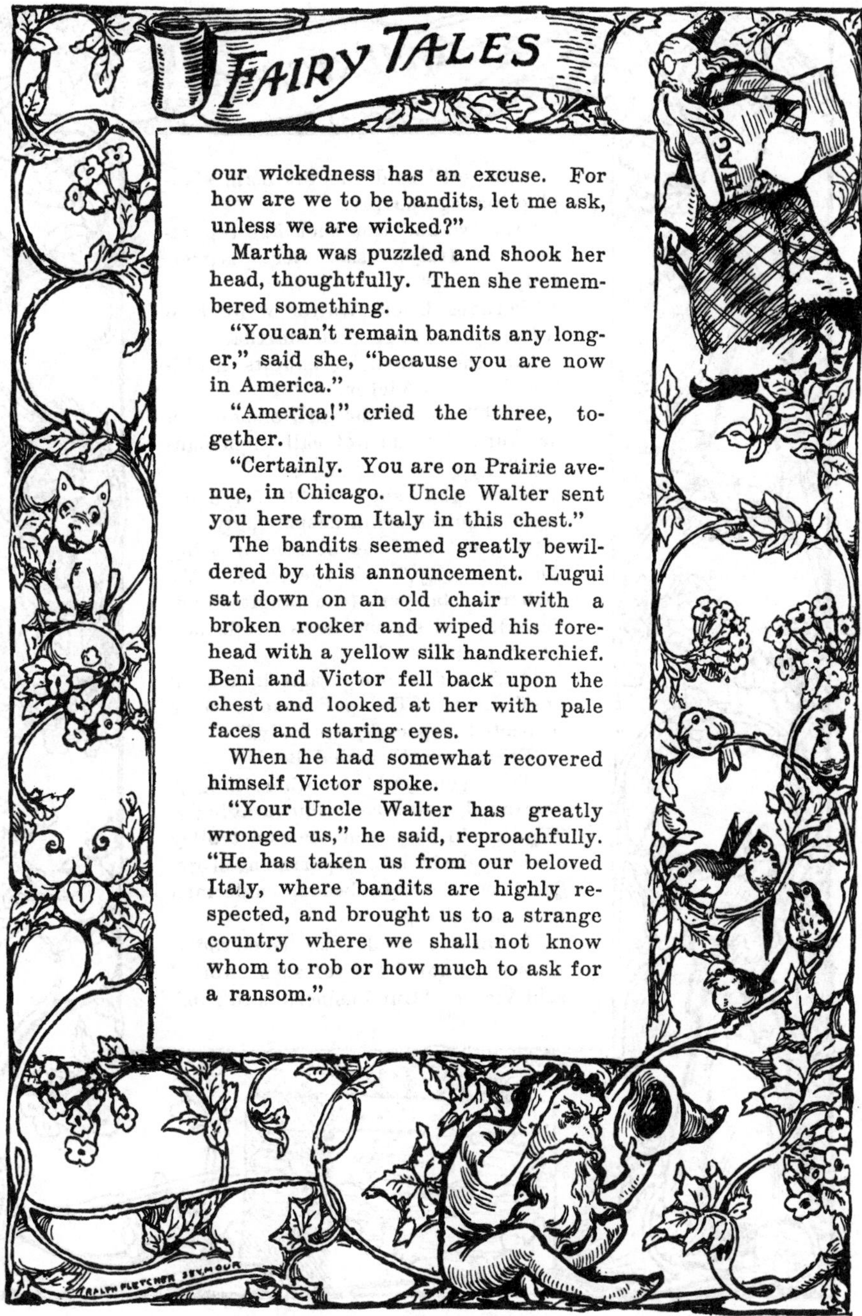

our wickedness has an excuse. For how are we to be bandits, let me ask, unless we are wicked?"

Martha was puzzled and shook her head, thoughtfully. Then she remembered something.

"You can't remain bandits any longer," said she, "because you are now in America."

"America!" cried the three, together.

"Certainly. You are on Prairie avenue, in Chicago. Uncle Walter sent you here from Italy in this chest."

The bandits seemed greatly bewildered by this announcement. Lugui sat down on an old chair with a broken rocker and wiped his forehead with a yellow silk handkerchief. Beni and Victor fell back upon the chest and looked at her with pale faces and staring eyes.

When he had somewhat recovered himself Victor spoke.

"Your Uncle Walter has greatly wronged us," he said, reproachfully. "He has taken us from our beloved Italy, where bandits are highly respected, and brought us to a strange country where we shall not know whom to rob or how much to ask for a ransom."

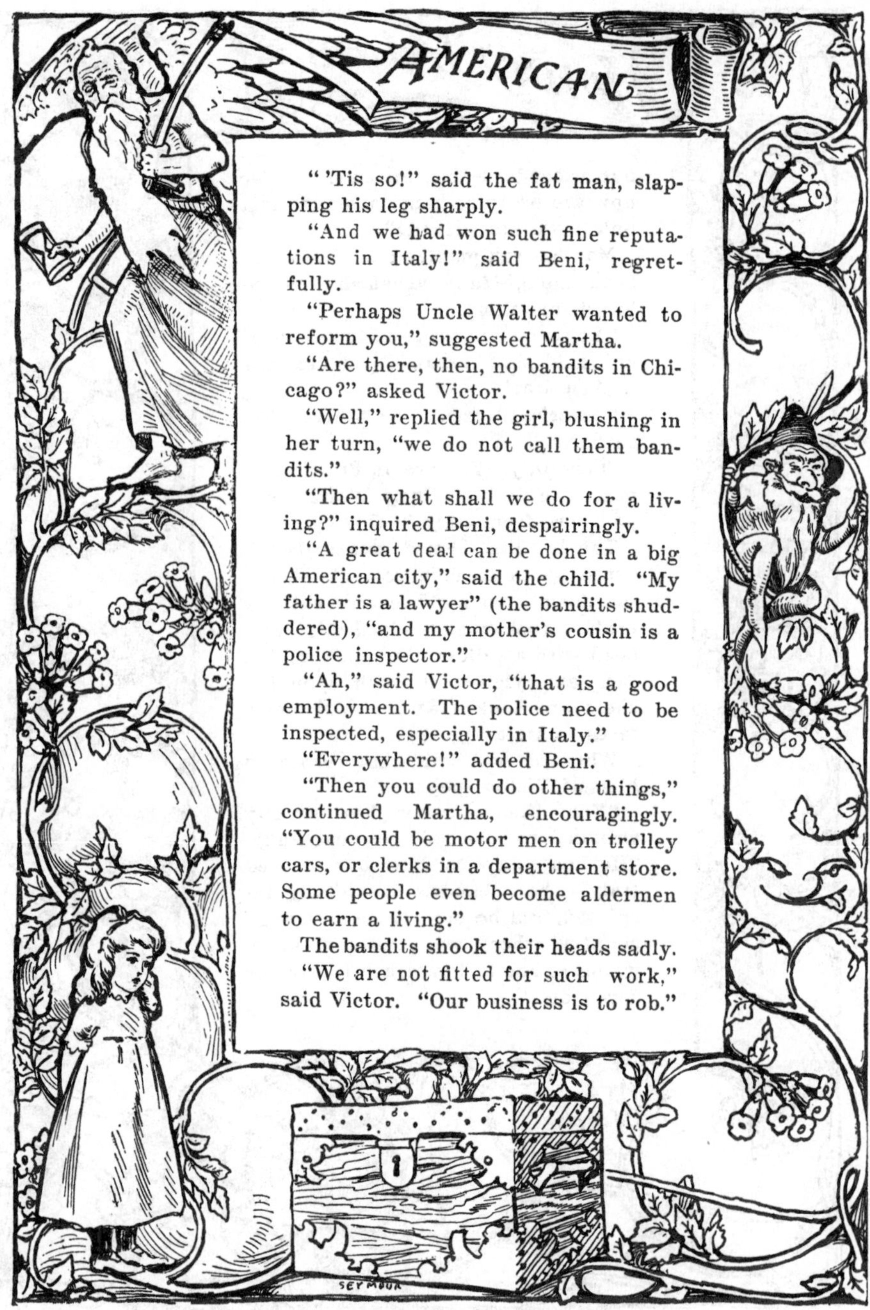

" 'Tis so!" said the fat man, slapping his leg sharply.

"And we had won such fine reputations in Italy!" said Beni, regretfully.

"Perhaps Uncle Walter wanted to reform you," suggested Martha.

"Are there, then, no bandits in Chicago?" asked Victor.

"Well," replied the girl, blushing in her turn, "we do not call them bandits."

"Then what shall we do for a living?" inquired Beni, despairingly.

"A great deal can be done in a big American city," said the child. "My father is a lawyer" (the bandits shuddered), "and my mother's cousin is a police inspector."

"Ah," said Victor, "that is a good employment. The police need to be inspected, especially in Italy."

"Everywhere!" added Beni.

"Then you could do other things," continued Martha, encouragingly. "You could be motor men on trolley cars, or clerks in a department store. Some people even become aldermen to earn a living."

The bandits shook their heads sadly.

"We are not fitted for such work," said Victor. "Our business is to rob."

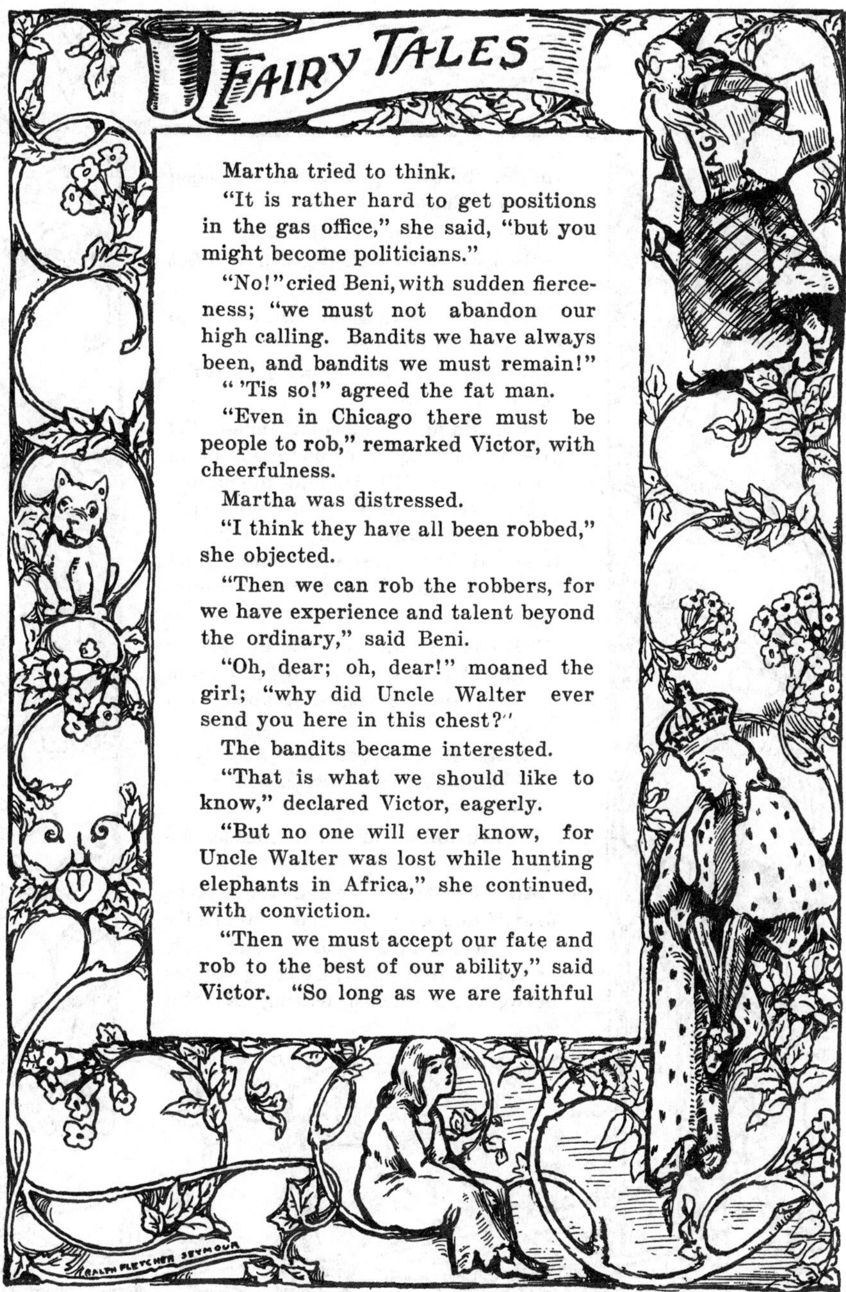

Martha tried to think.

"It is rather hard to get positions in the gas office," she said, "but you might become politicians."

"No!" cried Beni, with sudden fierceness; "we must not abandon our high calling. Bandits we have always been, and bandits we must remain!"

" 'Tis so!" agreed the fat man.

"Even in Chicago there must be people to rob," remarked Victor, with cheerfulness.

Martha was distressed.

"I think they have all been robbed," she objected.

"Then we can rob the robbers, for we have experience and talent beyond the ordinary," said Beni.

"Oh, dear; oh, dear!" moaned the girl; "why did Uncle Walter ever send you here in this chest?"

The bandits became interested.

"That is what we should like to know," declared Victor, eagerly.

"But no one will ever know, for Uncle Walter was lost while hunting elephants in Africa," she continued, with conviction.

"Then we must accept our fate and rob to the best of our ability," said Victor. "So long as we are faithful

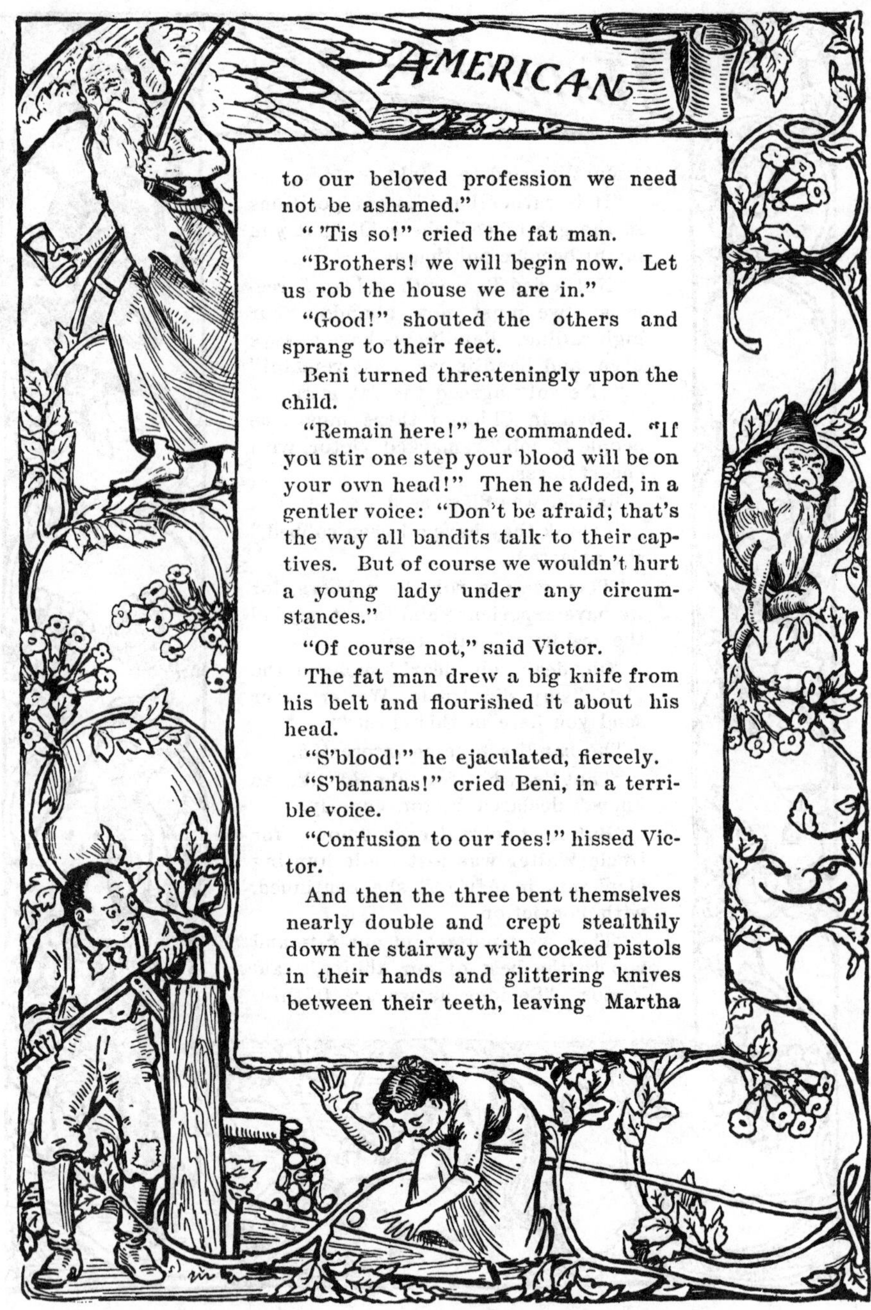

to our beloved profession we need not be ashamed."

"'Tis so!" cried the fat man.

"Brothers! we will begin now. Let us rob the house we are in."

"Good!" shouted the others and sprang to their feet.

Beni turned threateningly upon the child.

"Remain here!" he commanded. "If you stir one step your blood will be on your own head!" Then he added, in a gentler voice: "Don't be afraid; that's the way all bandits talk to their captives. But of course we wouldn't hurt a young lady under any circumstances."

"Of course not," said Victor.

The fat man drew a big knife from his belt and flourished it about his head.

"S'blood!" he ejaculated, fiercely.

"S'bananas!" cried Beni, in a terrible voice.

"Confusion to our foes!" hissed Victor.

And then the three bent themselves nearly double and crept stealthily down the stairway with cocked pistols in their hands and glittering knives between their teeth, leaving Martha

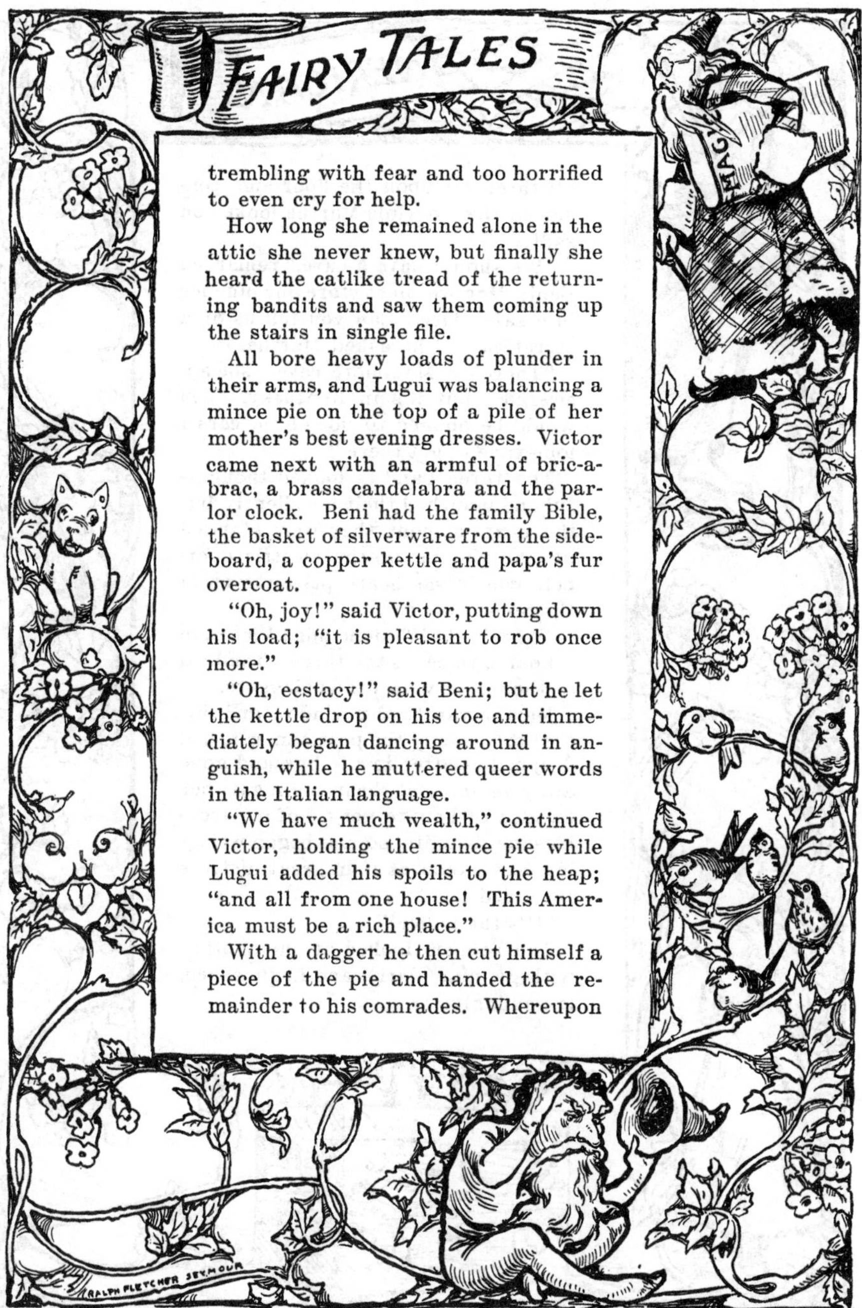

trembling with fear and too horrified to even cry for help.

How long she remained alone in the attic she never knew, but finally she heard the catlike tread of the returning bandits and saw them coming up the stairs in single file.

All bore heavy loads of plunder in their arms, and Lugui was balancing a mince pie on the top of a pile of her mother's best evening dresses. Victor came next with an armful of bric-a-brac, a brass candelabra and the parlor clock. Beni had the family Bible, the basket of silverware from the sideboard, a copper kettle and papa's fur overcoat.

"Oh, joy!" said Victor, putting down his load; "it is pleasant to rob once more."

"Oh, ecstacy!" said Beni; but he let the kettle drop on his toe and immediately began dancing around in anguish, while he muttered queer words in the Italian language.

"We have much wealth," continued Victor, holding the mince pie while Lugui added his spoils to the heap; "and all from one house! This America must be a rich place."

With a dagger he then cut himself a piece of the pie and handed the remainder to his comrades. Whereupon

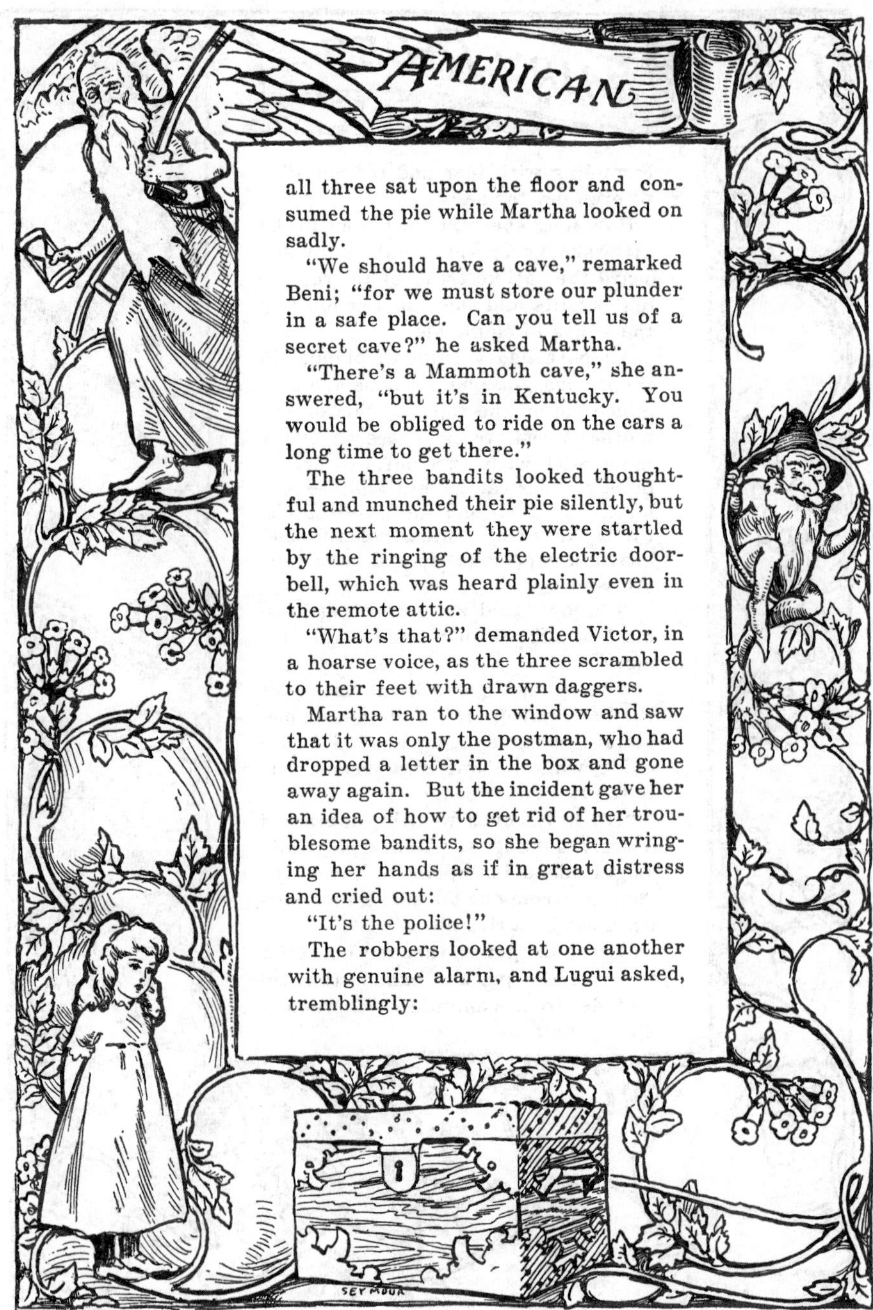

all three sat upon the floor and consumed the pie while Martha looked on sadly.

"We should have a cave," remarked Beni; "for we must store our plunder in a safe place. Can you tell us of a secret cave?" he asked Martha.

"There's a Mammoth cave," she answered, "but it's in Kentucky. You would be obliged to ride on the cars a long time to get there."

The three bandits looked thoughtful and munched their pie silently, but the next moment they were startled by the ringing of the electric doorbell, which was heard plainly even in the remote attic.

"What's that?" demanded Victor, in a hoarse voice, as the three scrambled to their feet with drawn daggers.

Martha ran to the window and saw that it was only the postman, who had dropped a letter in the box and gone away again. But the incident gave her an idea of how to get rid of her troublesome bandits, so she began wringing her hands as if in great distress and cried out:

"It's the police!"

The robbers looked at one another with genuine alarm, and Lugui asked, tremblingly:

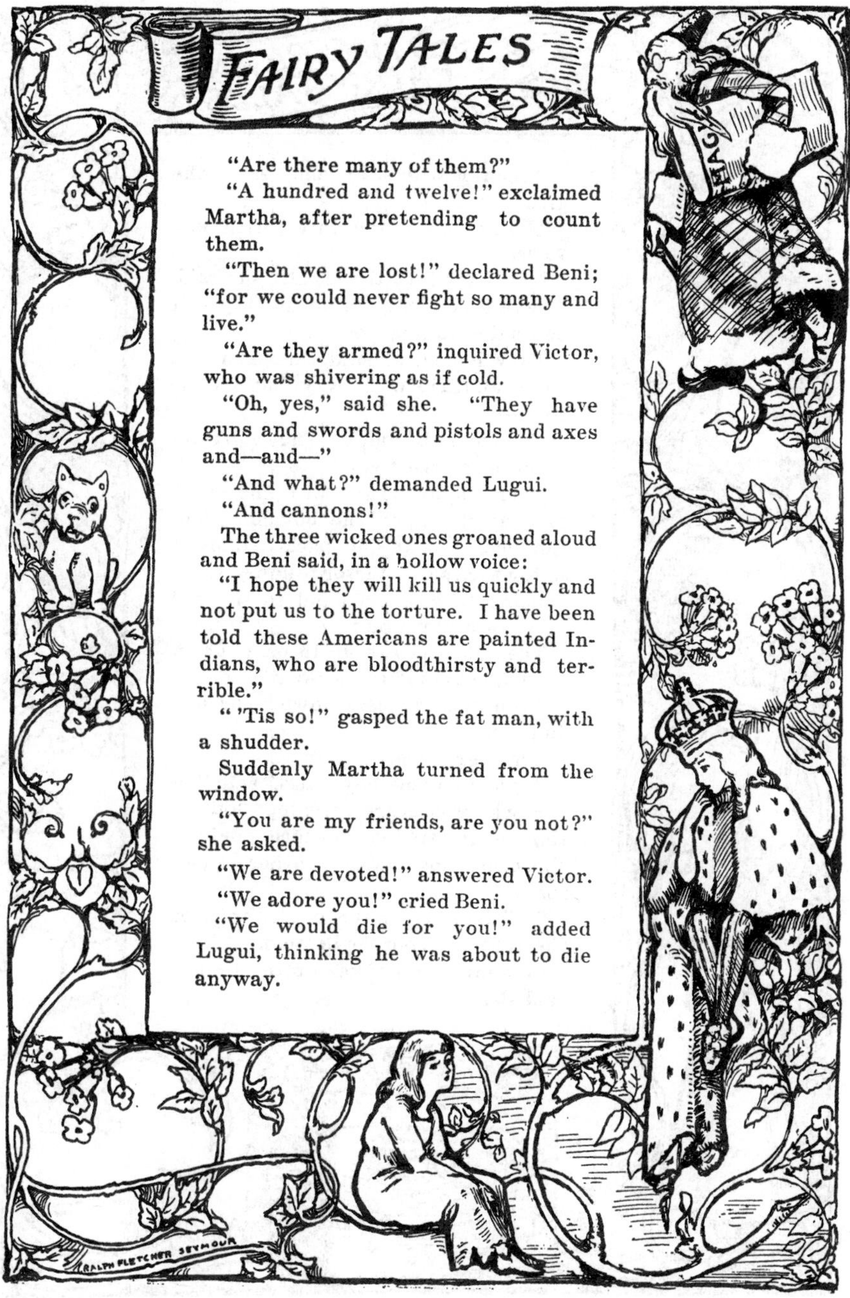

"Are there many of them?"

"A hundred and twelve!" exclaimed Martha, after pretending to count them.

"Then we are lost!" declared Beni; "for we could never fight so many and live."

"Are they armed?" inquired Victor, who was shivering as if cold.

"Oh, yes," said she. "They have guns and swords and pistols and axes and—and—"

"And what?" demanded Lugui.

"And cannons!"

The three wicked ones groaned aloud and Beni said, in a hollow voice:

"I hope they will kill us quickly and not put us to the torture. I have been told these Americans are painted Indians, who are bloodthirsty and terrible."

" 'Tis so!" gasped the fat man, with a shudder.

Suddenly Martha turned from the window.

"You are my friends, are you not?" she asked.

"We are devoted!" answered Victor.

"We adore you!" cried Beni.

"We would die for you!" added Lugui, thinking he was about to die anyway.

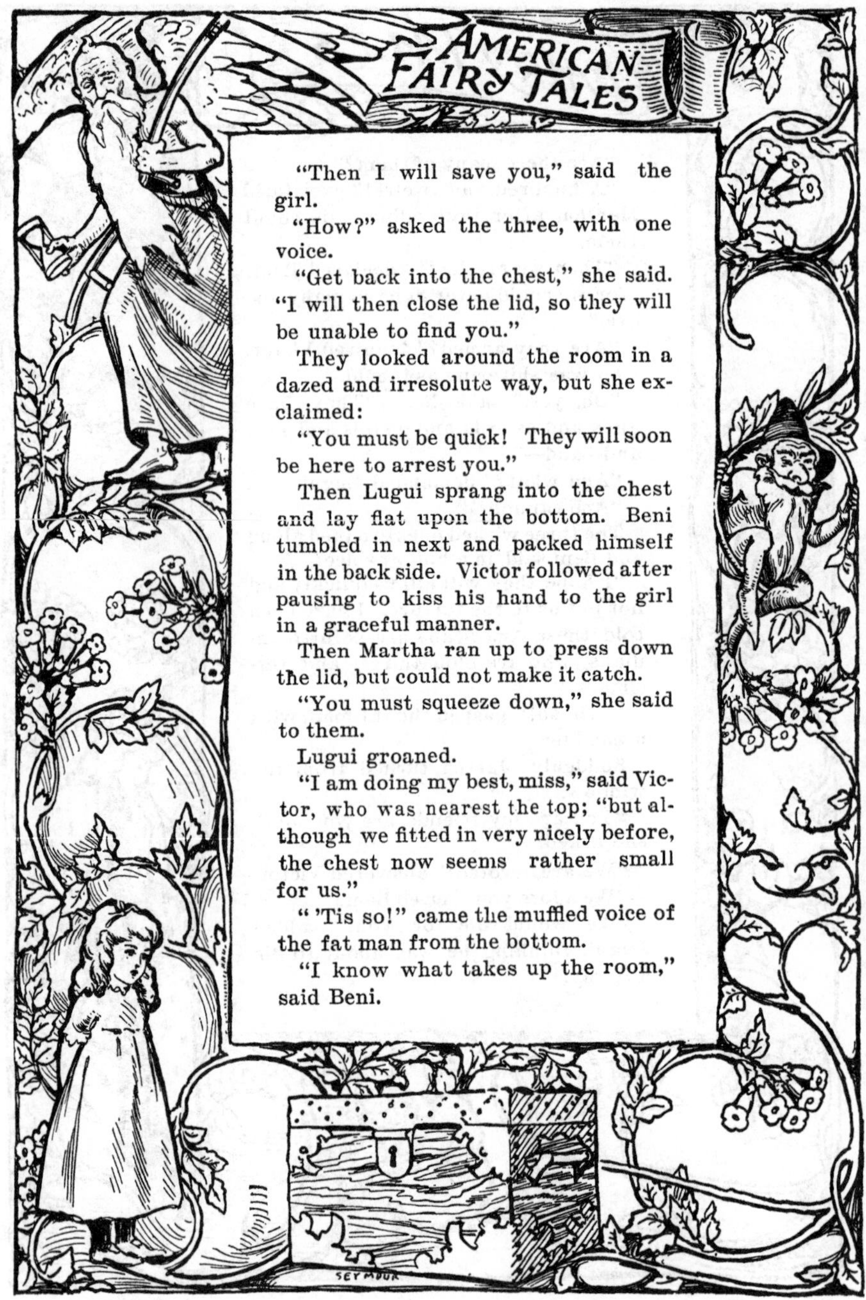

"Then I will save you," said the girl.

"How?" asked the three, with one voice.

"Get back into the chest," she said. "I will then close the lid, so they will be unable to find you."

They looked around the room in a dazed and irresolute way, but she exclaimed:

"You must be quick! They will soon be here to arrest you."

Then Lugui sprang into the chest and lay flat upon the bottom. Beni tumbled in next and packed himself in the back side. Victor followed after pausing to kiss his hand to the girl in a graceful manner.

Then Martha ran up to press down the lid, but could not make it catch.

"You must squeeze down," she said to them.

Lugui groaned.

"I am doing my best, miss," said Victor, who was nearest the top; "but although we fitted in very nicely before, the chest now seems rather small for us."

" 'Tis so!" came the muffled voice of the fat man from the bottom.

"I know what takes up the room," said Beni.

Locking the box after repacking the robbers.

"What?" inquired Victor, anxiously.

"The pie," returned Beni.

" 'Tis so!" came from the bottom, in faint accents.

Then Martha sat upon the lid and pressed it down with all her weight. To her great delight the lock caught, and, springing down, she exerted all her strength and turned the key.

* * * * *

This story should teach us not to interfere in matters that do not concern us. For had Martha refrained from opening Uncle Walter's mysterious chest she would not have been obliged to carry downstairs all the plunder the robbers had brought into the attic.

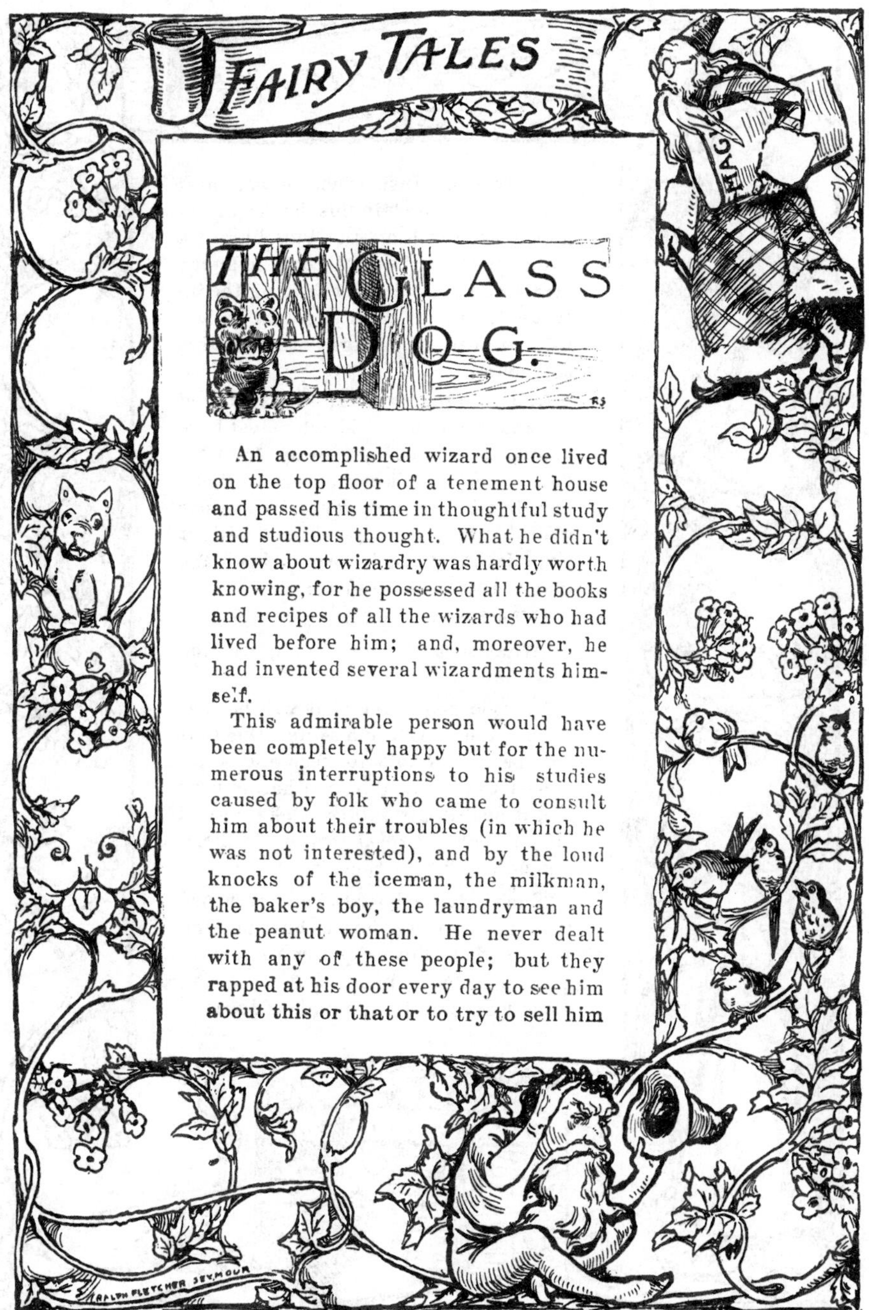

An accomplished wizard once lived on the top floor of a tenement house and passed his time in thoughtful study and studious thought. What he didn't know about wizardry was hardly worth knowing, for he possessed all the books and recipes of all the wizards who had lived before him; and, moreover, he had invented several wizardments himself.

This admirable person would have been completely happy but for the numerous interruptions to his studies caused by folk who came to consult him about their troubles (in which he was not interested), and by the loud knocks of the iceman, the milkman, the baker's boy, the laundryman and the peanut woman. He never dealt with any of these people; but they rapped at his door every day to see him about this or that or to try to sell him

their wares. Just when he was most deeply interested in his books or engaged in watching the bubbling of a cauldron there would come a knock at his door. And after sending the intruder away he always found he had lost his train of thought or ruined his compound.

At length these interruptions aroused his anger, and he decided he must have a dog to keep people away from his door. He didn't know where to find a dog, but in the next room lived a poor glass-blower with whom he had a slight acquaintance; so he went into the man's apartment and asked:

"Where can I find a dog?"

"What sort of a dog?" inquired the glass-blower.

"A good dog. One that will bark at people and drive them away. One that will be no trouble to keep and won't expect to be fed. One that has no fleas and is neat in his habits. One that will obey me when I speak to him. In short, a good dog," said the wizard.

"Such a dog is hard to find," returned the glass-blower, who was busy making a blue glass flower pot with a pink glass rosebush in it, having green glass leaves and yellow glass roses.

The wizard watched him thoughtfully.

"Why cannot you blow me a dog out of glass?" he asked, presently.

"I can," declared the glass-blower; "but it would not bark at people, you know."

"Oh, I'll fix that easily enough," replied the other. "If I could not make a glass dog bark I would be a mighty poor wizard."

"Very well; if you can use a glass dog I'll be pleased to blow one for you. Only, you must pay for my work."

"Certainly," agreed the wizard. "But I have none of that horrid stuff you call money. You must take some of my wares in exchange."

The glass-blower considered the matter for a moment.

"Could you give me something to cure my rheumatism?" he asked.

"Oh, yes; easily."

"Then it's a bargain. I'll start the dog at once. What color of glass shall I use?"

"Pink is a pretty color," said the wizard, "and it's unusual for a dog, isn't it?"

"Very," answered the glass-blower; "but it shall be pink."

So the wizard went back to his stud-

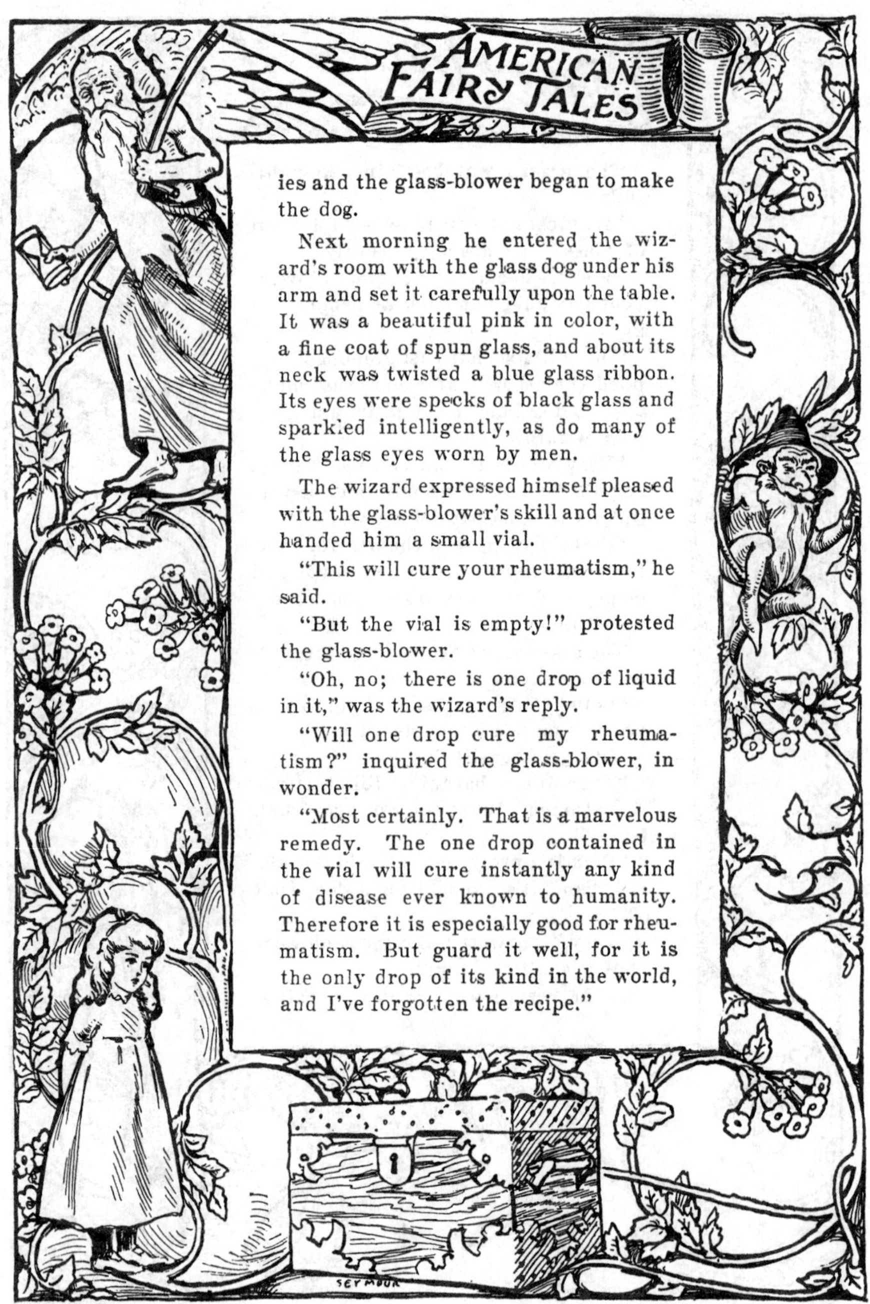

ies and the glass-blower began to make the dog.

Next morning he entered the wizard's room with the glass dog under his arm and set it carefully upon the table. It was a beautiful pink in color, with a fine coat of spun glass, and about its neck was twisted a blue glass ribbon. Its eyes were specks of black glass and sparkled intelligently, as do many of the glass eyes worn by men.

The wizard expressed himself pleased with the glass-blower's skill and at once handed him a small vial.

"This will cure your rheumatism," he said.

"But the vial is empty!" protested the glass-blower.

"Oh, no; there is one drop of liquid in it," was the wizard's reply.

"Will one drop cure my rheumatism?" inquired the glass-blower, in wonder.

"Most certainly. That is a marvelous remedy. The one drop contained in the vial will cure instantly any kind of disease ever known to humanity. Therefore it is especially good for rheumatism. But guard it well, for it is the only drop of its kind in the world, and I've forgotten the recipe."

The glass dog was a beautiful pink in color.

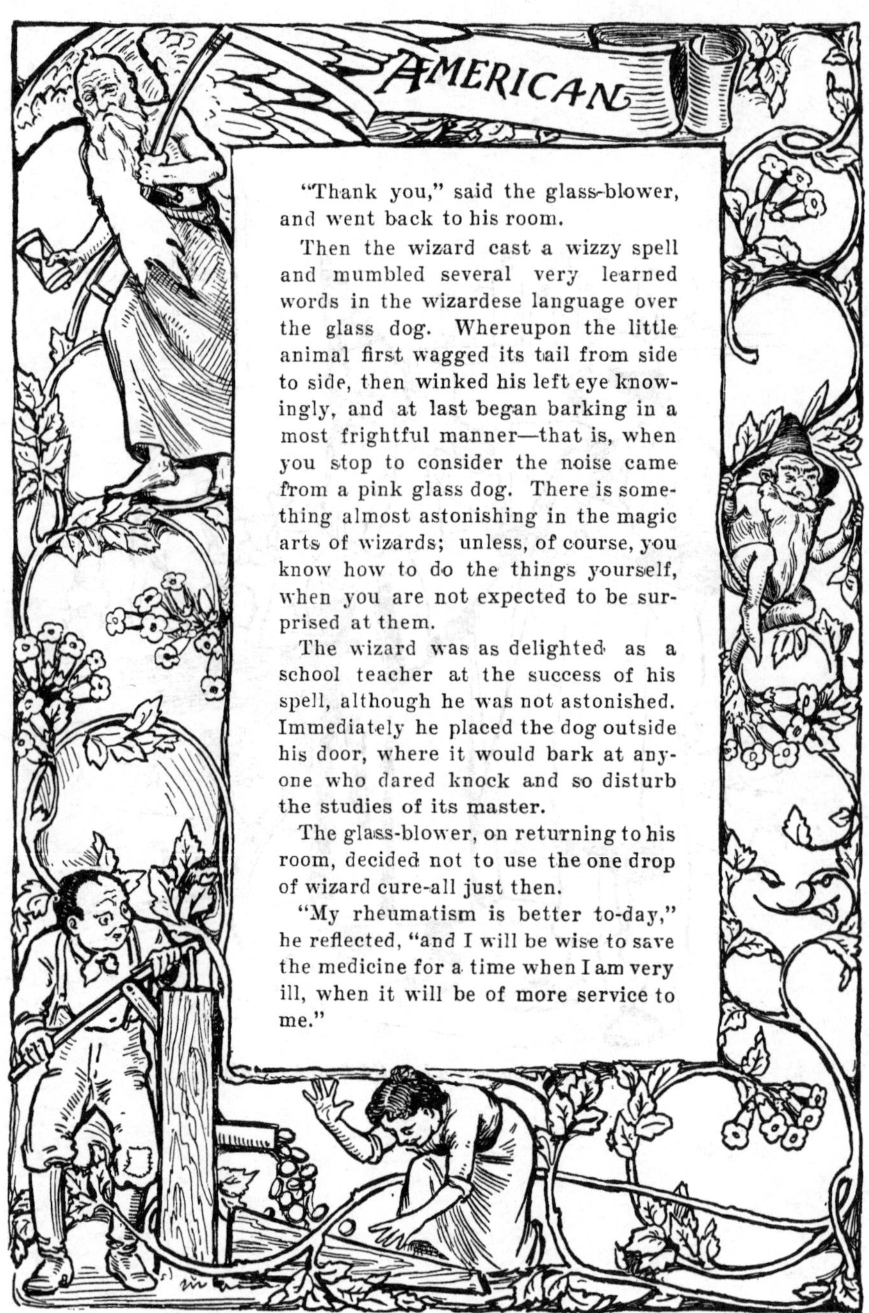

"Thank you," said the glass-blower, and went back to his room.

Then the wizard cast a wizzy spell and mumbled several very learned words in the wizardese language over the glass dog. Whereupon the little animal first wagged its tail from side to side, then winked his left eye knowingly, and at last began barking in a most frightful manner—that is, when you stop to consider the noise came from a pink glass dog. There is something almost astonishing in the magic arts of wizards; unless, of course, you know how to do the things yourself, when you are not expected to be surprised at them.

The wizard was as delighted as a school teacher at the success of his spell, although he was not astonished. Immediately he placed the dog outside his door, where it would bark at anyone who dared knock and so disturb the studies of its master.

The glass-blower, on returning to his room, decided not to use the one drop of wizard cure-all just then.

"My rheumatism is better to-day," he reflected, "and I will be wise to save the medicine for a time when I am very ill, when it will be of more service to me."

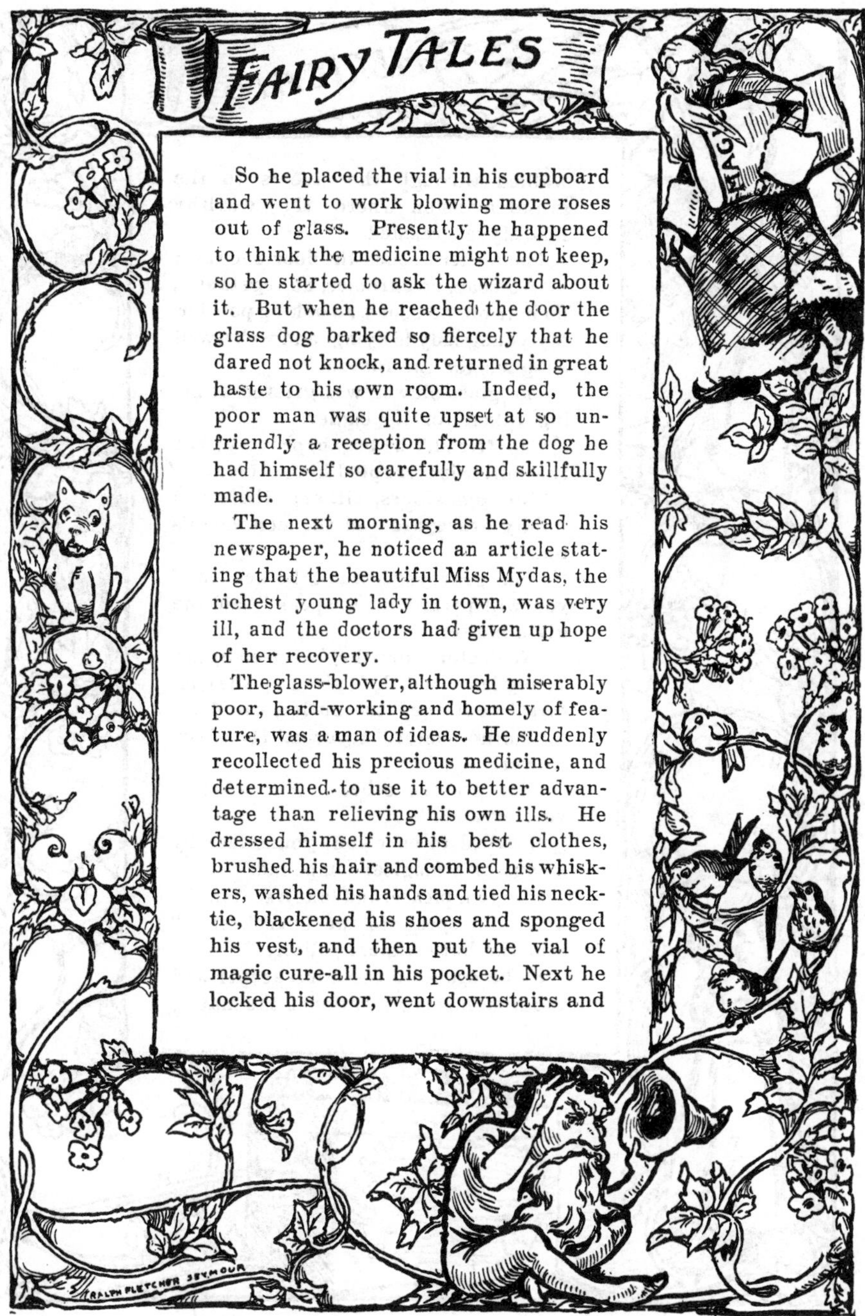

So he placed the vial in his cupboard and went to work blowing more roses out of glass. Presently he happened to think the medicine might not keep, so he started to ask the wizard about it. But when he reached the door the glass dog barked so fiercely that he dared not knock, and returned in great haste to his own room. Indeed, the poor man was quite upset at so unfriendly a reception from the dog he had himself so carefully and skillfully made.

The next morning, as he read his newspaper, he noticed an article stating that the beautiful Miss Mydas, the richest young lady in town, was very ill, and the doctors had given up hope of her recovery.

The glass-blower, although miserably poor, hard-working and homely of feature, was a man of ideas. He suddenly recollected his precious medicine, and determined to use it to better advantage than relieving his own ills. He dressed himself in his best clothes, brushed his hair and combed his whiskers, washed his hands and tied his necktie, blackened his shoes and sponged his vest, and then put the vial of magic cure-all in his pocket. Next he locked his door, went downstairs and

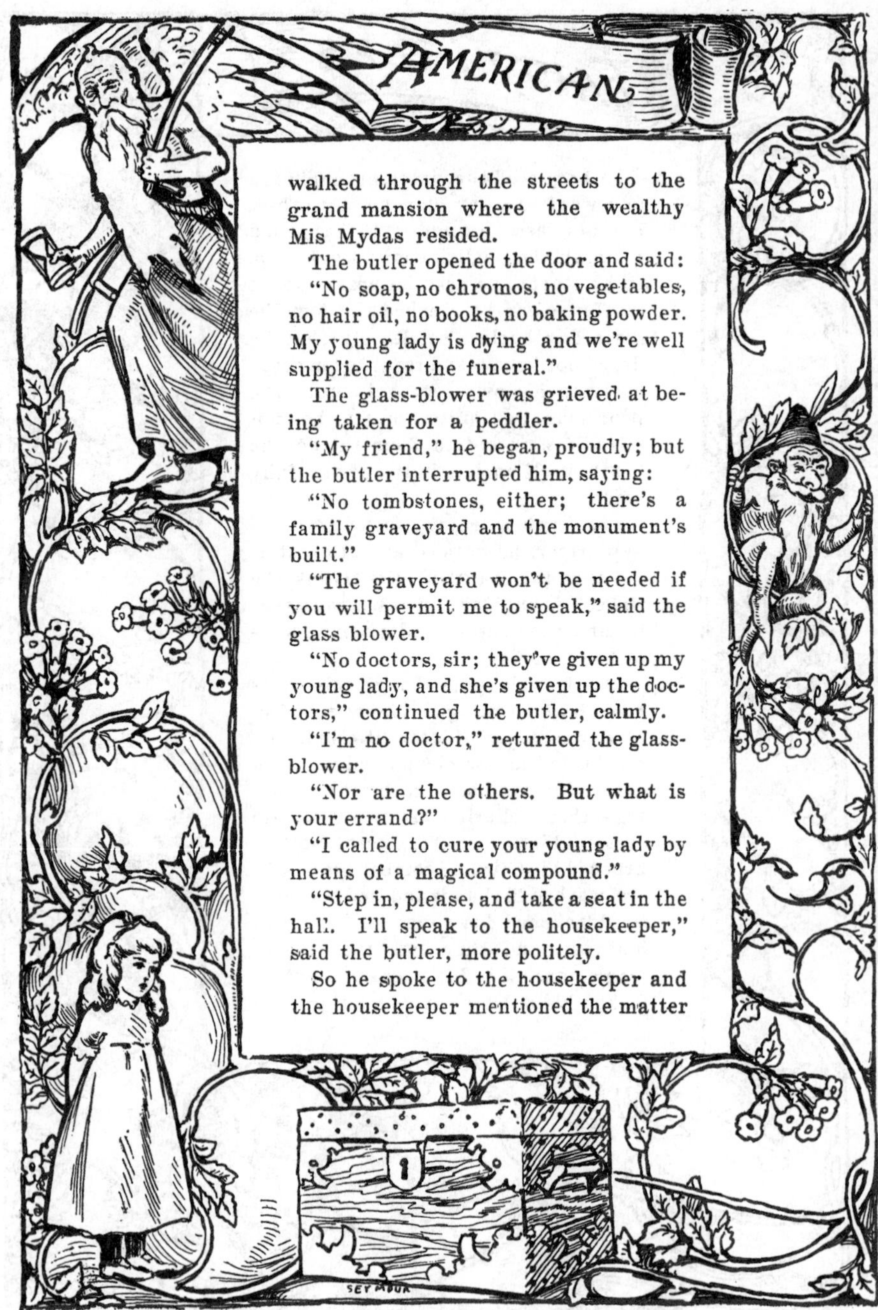

walked through the streets to the grand mansion where the wealthy Mis Mydas resided.

The butler opened the door and said:

"No soap, no chromos, no vegetables, no hair oil, no books, no baking powder. My young lady is dying and we're well supplied for the funeral."

The glass-blower was grieved at being taken for a peddler.

"My friend," he began, proudly; but the butler interrupted him, saying:

"No tombstones, either; there's a family graveyard and the monument's built."

"The graveyard won't be needed if you will permit me to speak," said the glass blower.

"No doctors, sir; they've given up my young lady, and she's given up the doctors," continued the butler, calmly.

"I'm no doctor," returned the glass-blower.

"Nor are the others. But what is your errand?"

"I called to cure your young lady by means of a magical compound."

"Step in, please, and take a seat in the hall. I'll speak to the housekeeper," said the butler, more politely.

So he spoke to the housekeeper and the housekeeper mentioned the matter

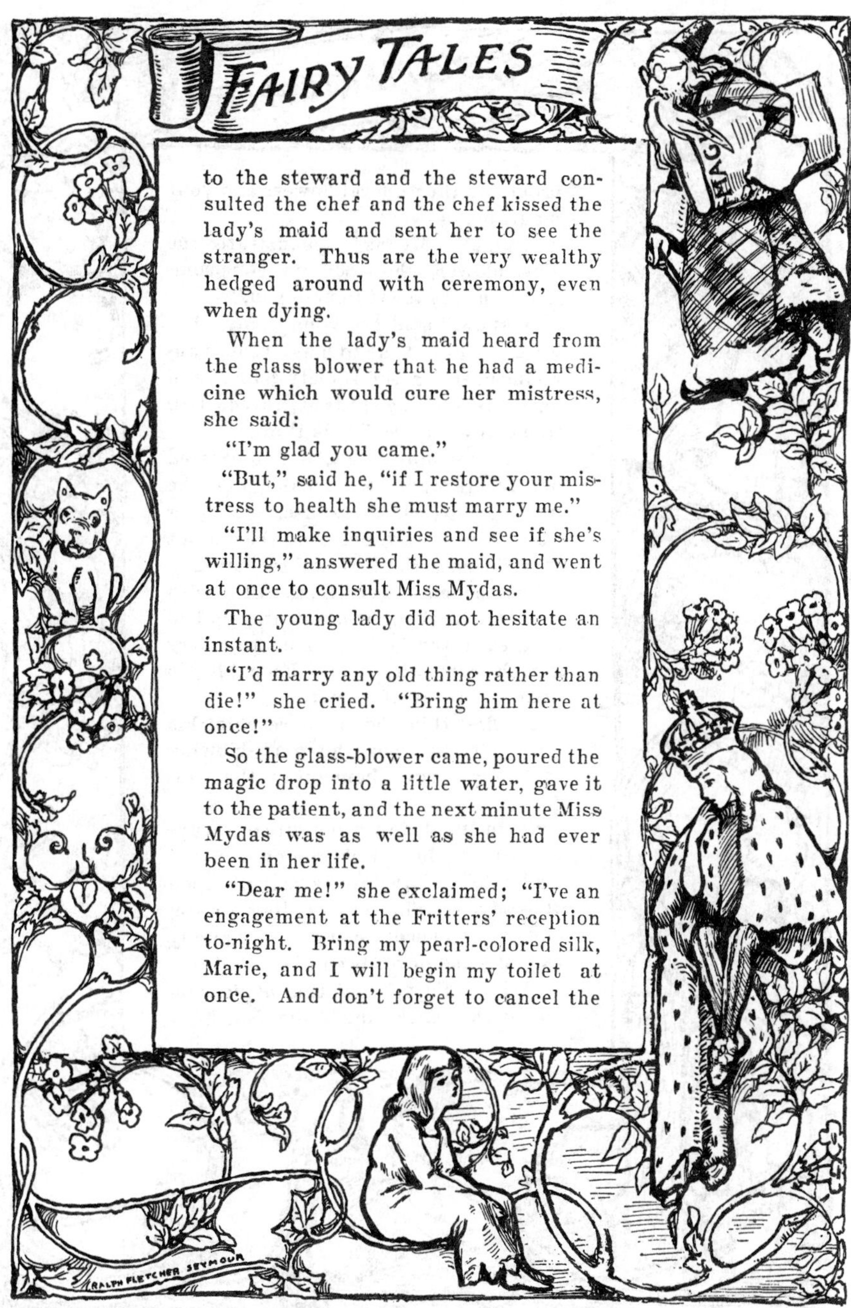

to the steward and the steward consulted the chef and the chef kissed the lady's maid and sent her to see the stranger. Thus are the very wealthy hedged around with ceremony, even when dying.

When the lady's maid heard from the glass blower that he had a medicine which would cure her mistress, she said:

"I'm glad you came."

"But," said he, "if I restore your mistress to health she must marry me."

"I'll make inquiries and see if she's willing," answered the maid, and went at once to consult Miss Mydas.

The young lady did not hesitate an instant.

"I'd marry any old thing rather than die!" she cried. "Bring him here at once!"

So the glass-blower came, poured the magic drop into a little water, gave it to the patient, and the next minute Miss Mydas was as well as she had ever been in her life.

"Dear me!" she exclaimed; "I've an engagement at the Fritters' reception to-night. Bring my pearl-colored silk, Marie, and I will begin my toilet at once. And don't forget to cancel the

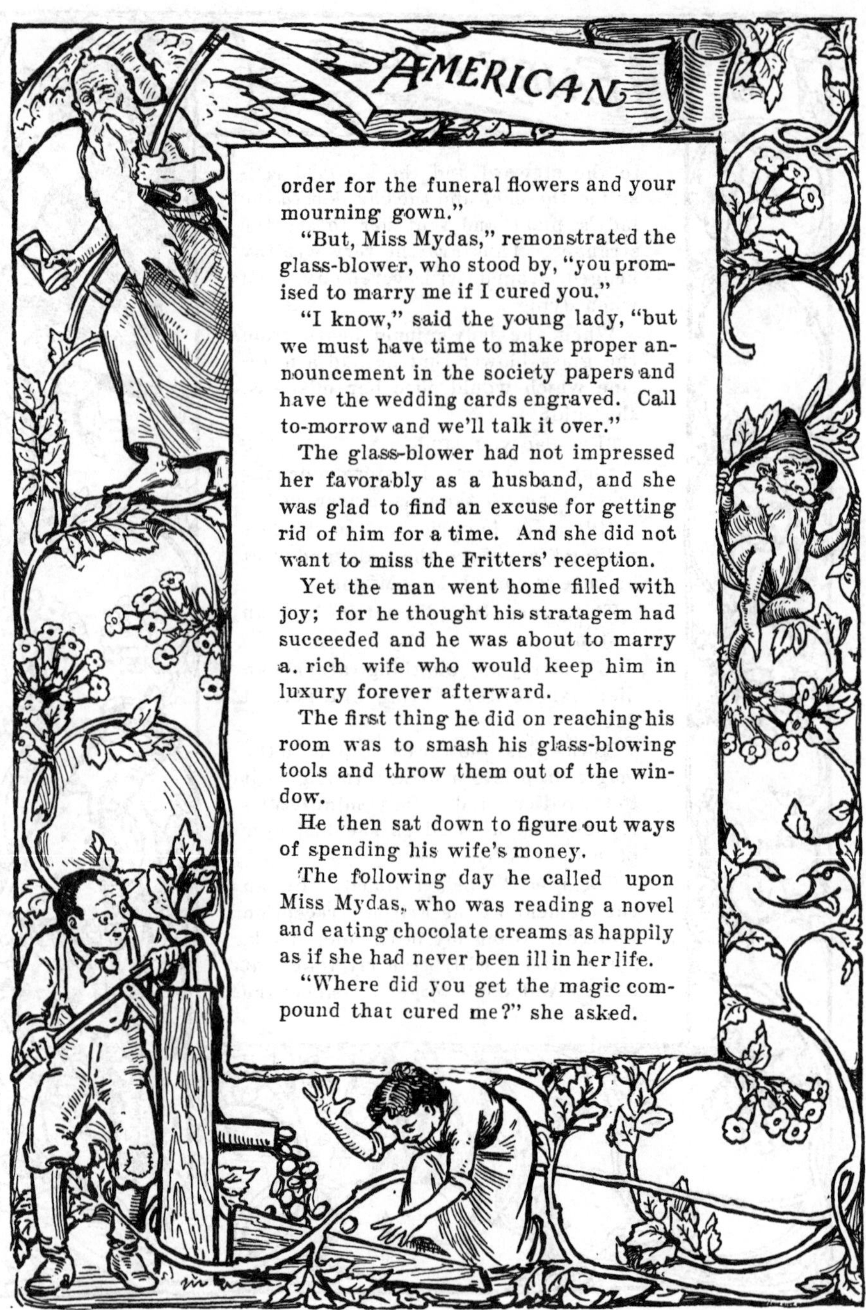

order for the funeral flowers and your mourning gown."

"But, Miss Mydas," remonstrated the glass-blower, who stood by, "you promised to marry me if I cured you."

"I know," said the young lady, "but we must have time to make proper announcement in the society papers and have the wedding cards engraved. Call to-morrow and we'll talk it over."

The glass-blower had not impressed her favorably as a husband, and she was glad to find an excuse for getting rid of him for a time. And she did not want to miss the Fritters' reception.

Yet the man went home filled with joy; for he thought his stratagem had succeeded and he was about to marry a. rich wife who would keep him in luxury forever afterward.

The first thing he did on reaching his room was to smash his glass-blowing tools and throw them out of the window.

He then sat down to figure out ways of spending his wife's money.

The following day he called upon Miss Mydas, who was reading a novel and eating chocolate creams as happily as if she had never been ill in her life.

"Where did you get the magic compound that cured me?" she asked.

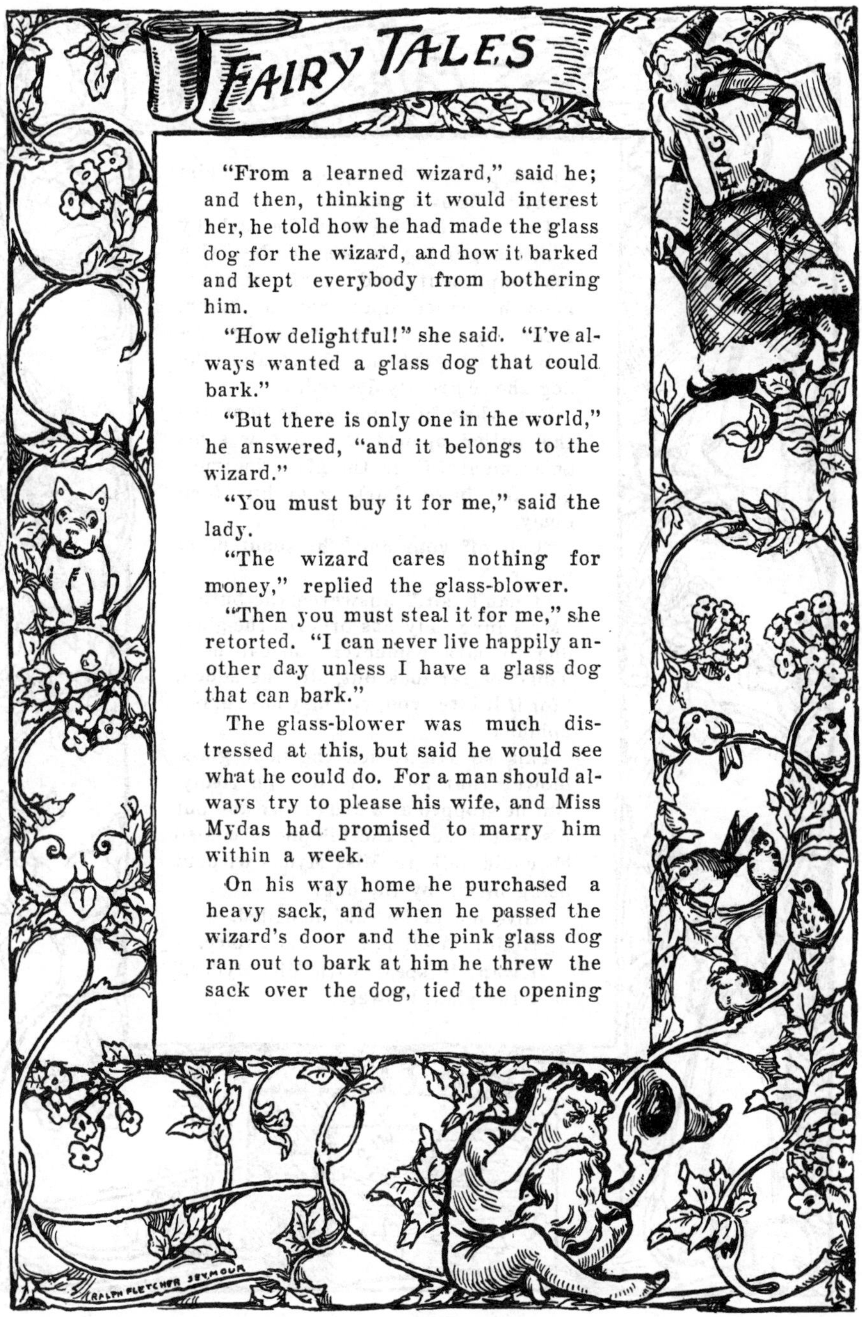

"From a learned wizard," said he; and then, thinking it would interest her, he told how he had made the glass dog for the wizard, and how it barked and kept everybody from bothering him.

"How delightful!" she said. "I've always wanted a glass dog that could bark."

"But there is only one in the world," he answered, "and it belongs to the wizard."

"You must buy it for me," said the lady.

"The wizard cares nothing for money," replied the glass-blower.

"Then you must steal it for me," she retorted. "I can never live happily another day unless I have a glass dog that can bark."

The glass-blower was much distressed at this, but said he would see what he could do. For a man should always try to please his wife, and Miss Mydas had promised to marry him within a week.

On his way home he purchased a heavy sack, and when he passed the wizard's door and the pink glass dog ran out to bark at him he threw the sack over the dog, tied the opening

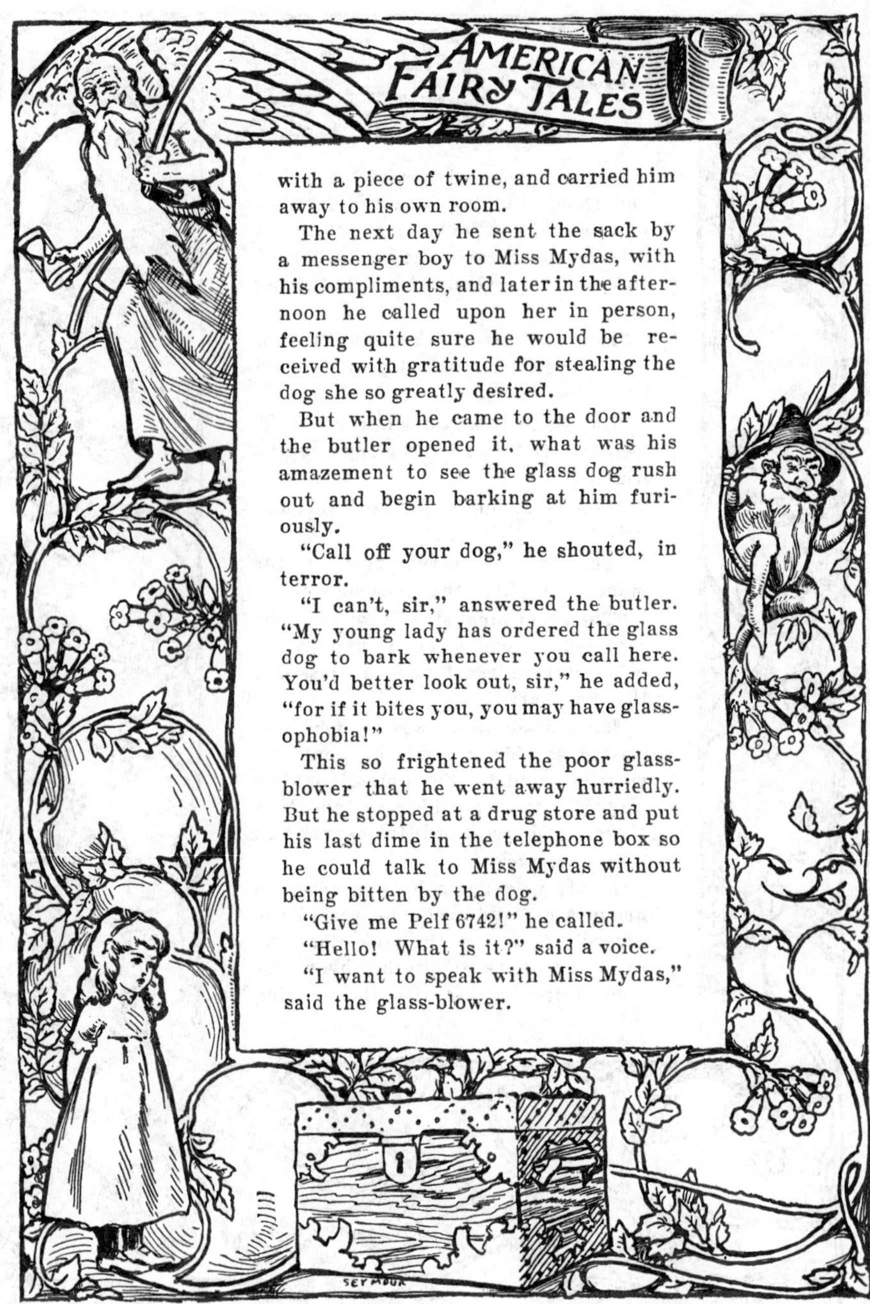

with a piece of twine, and carried him away to his own room.

The next day he sent the sack by a messenger boy to Miss Mydas, with his compliments, and later in the afternoon he called upon her in person, feeling quite sure he would be received with gratitude for stealing the dog she so greatly desired.

But when he came to the door and the butler opened it, what was his amazement to see the glass dog rush out and begin barking at him furiously.

"Call off your dog," he shouted, in terror.

"I can't, sir," answered the butler. "My young lady has ordered the glass dog to bark whenever you call here. You'd better look out, sir," he added, "for if it bites you, you may have glassophobia!"

This so frightened the poor glass-blower that he went away hurriedly. But he stopped at a drug store and put his last dime in the telephone box so he could talk to Miss Mydas without being bitten by the dog.

"Give me Pelf 6742!" he called.

"Hello! What is it?" said a voice.

"I want to speak with Miss Mydas," said the glass-blower.

"Call off your dog!"

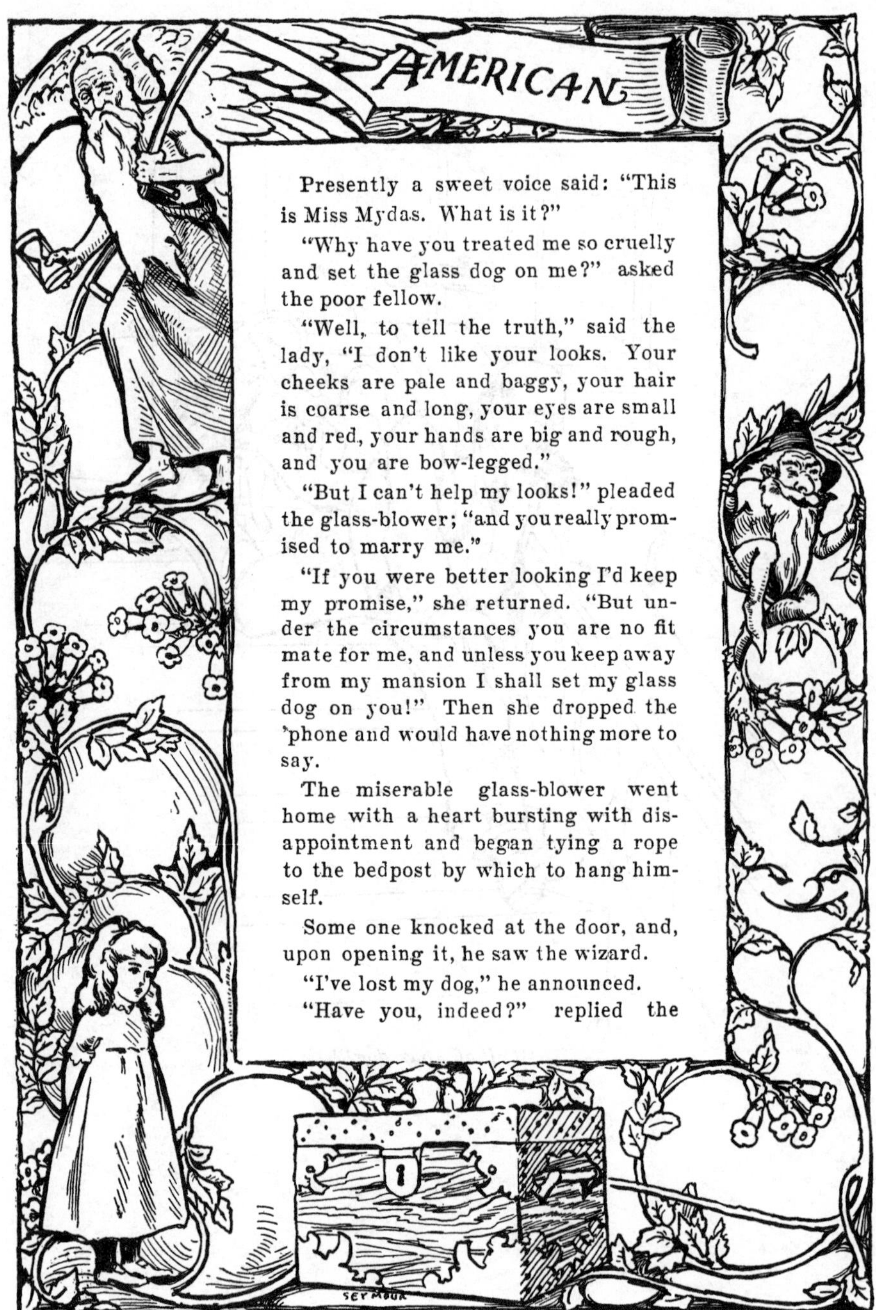

Presently a sweet voice said: "This is Miss Mydas. What is it?"

"Why have you treated me so cruelly and set the glass dog on me?" asked the poor fellow.

"Well, to tell the truth," said the lady, "I don't like your looks. Your cheeks are pale and baggy, your hair is coarse and long, your eyes are small and red, your hands are big and rough, and you are bow-legged."

"But I can't help my looks!" pleaded the glass-blower; "and you really promised to marry me."

"If you were better looking I'd keep my promise," she returned. "But under the circumstances you are no fit mate for me, and unless you keep away from my mansion I shall set my glass dog on you!" Then she dropped the 'phone and would have nothing more to say.

The miserable glass-blower went home with a heart bursting with disappointment and began tying a rope to the bedpost by which to hang himself.

Some one knocked at the door, and, upon opening it, he saw the wizard.

"I've lost my dog," he announced.

"Have you, indeed?" replied the

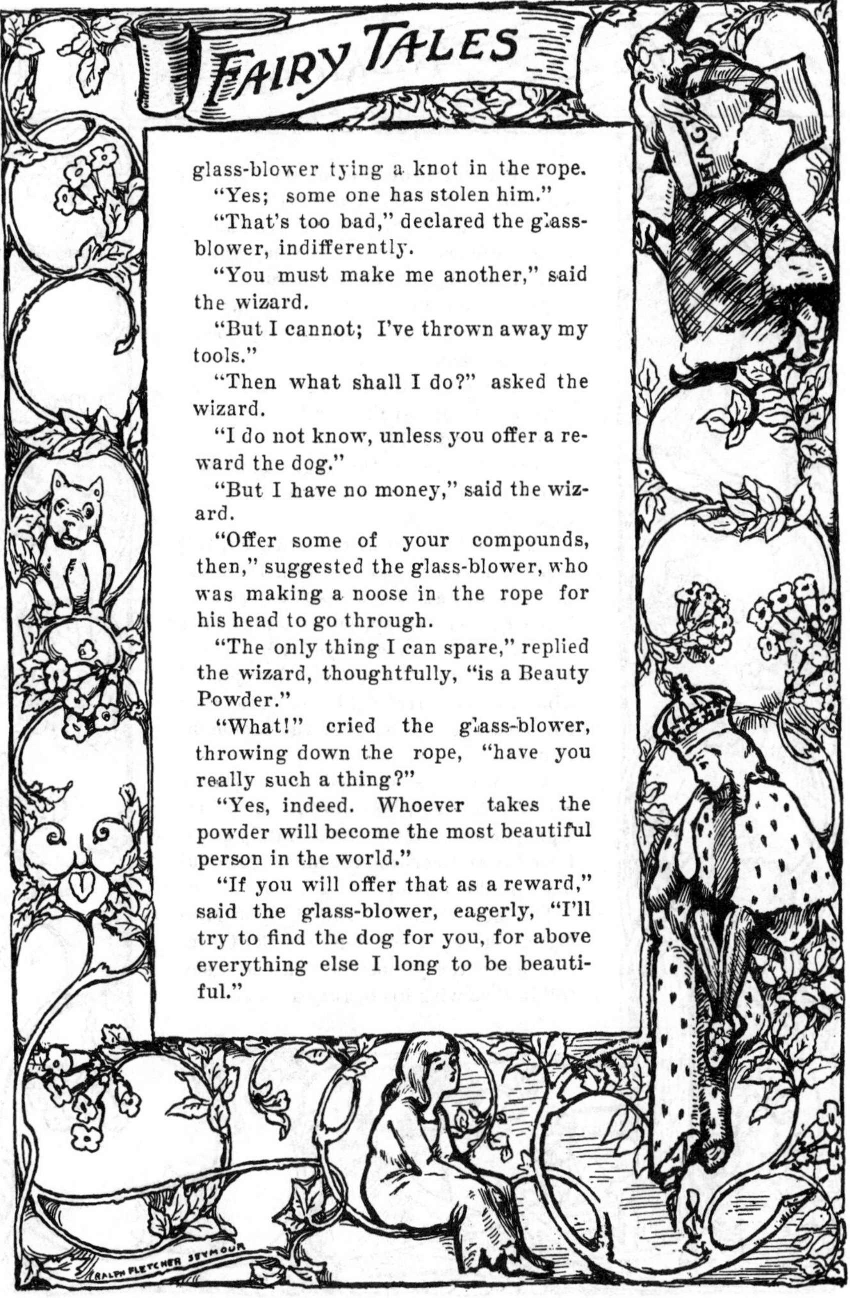

glass-blower tying a knot in the rope.

"Yes; some one has stolen him."

"That's too bad," declared the glass-blower, indifferently.

"You must make me another," said the wizard.

"But I cannot; I've thrown away my tools."

"Then what shall I do?" asked the wizard.

"I do not know, unless you offer a reward the dog."

"But I have no money," said the wizard.

"Offer some of your compounds, then," suggested the glass-blower, who was making a noose in the rope for his head to go through.

"The only thing I can spare," replied the wizard, thoughtfully, "is a Beauty Powder."

"What!" cried the glass-blower, throwing down the rope, "have you really such a thing?"

"Yes, indeed. Whoever takes the powder will become the most beautiful person in the world."

"If you will offer that as a reward," said the glass-blower, eagerly, "I'll try to find the dog for you, for above everything else I long to be beautiful."

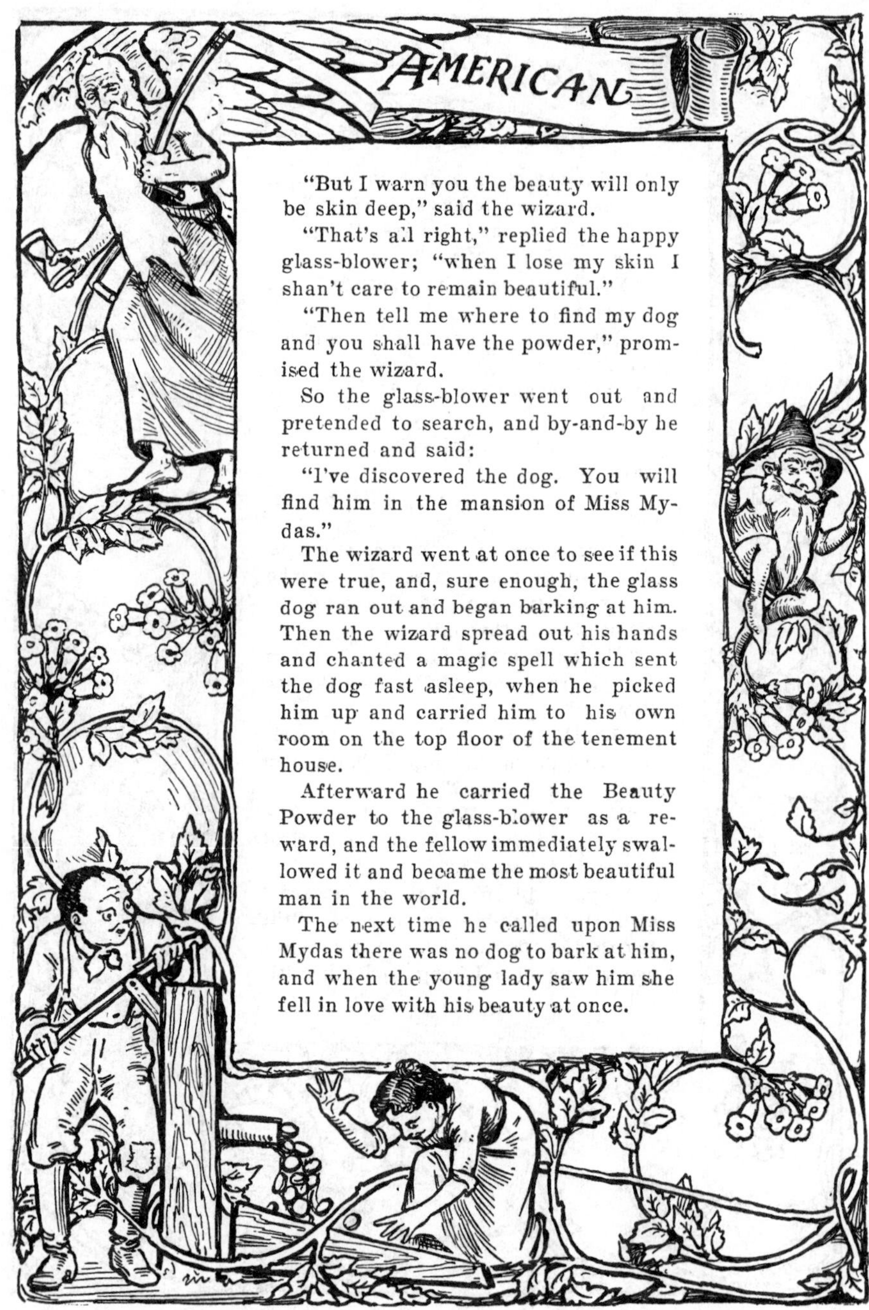

"But I warn you the beauty will only be skin deep," said the wizard.

"That's all right," replied the happy glass-blower; "when I lose my skin I shan't care to remain beautiful."

"Then tell me where to find my dog and you shall have the powder," promised the wizard.

So the glass-blower went out and pretended to search, and by-and-by he returned and said:

"I've discovered the dog. You will find him in the mansion of Miss Mydas."

The wizard went at once to see if this were true, and, sure enough, the glass dog ran out and began barking at him. Then the wizard spread out his hands and chanted a magic spell which sent the dog fast asleep, when he picked him up and carried him to his own room on the top floor of the tenement house.

Afterward he carried the Beauty Powder to the glass-blower as a reward, and the fellow immediately swallowed it and became the most beautiful man in the world.

The next time he called upon Miss Mydas there was no dog to bark at him, and when the young lady saw him she fell in love with his beauty at once.

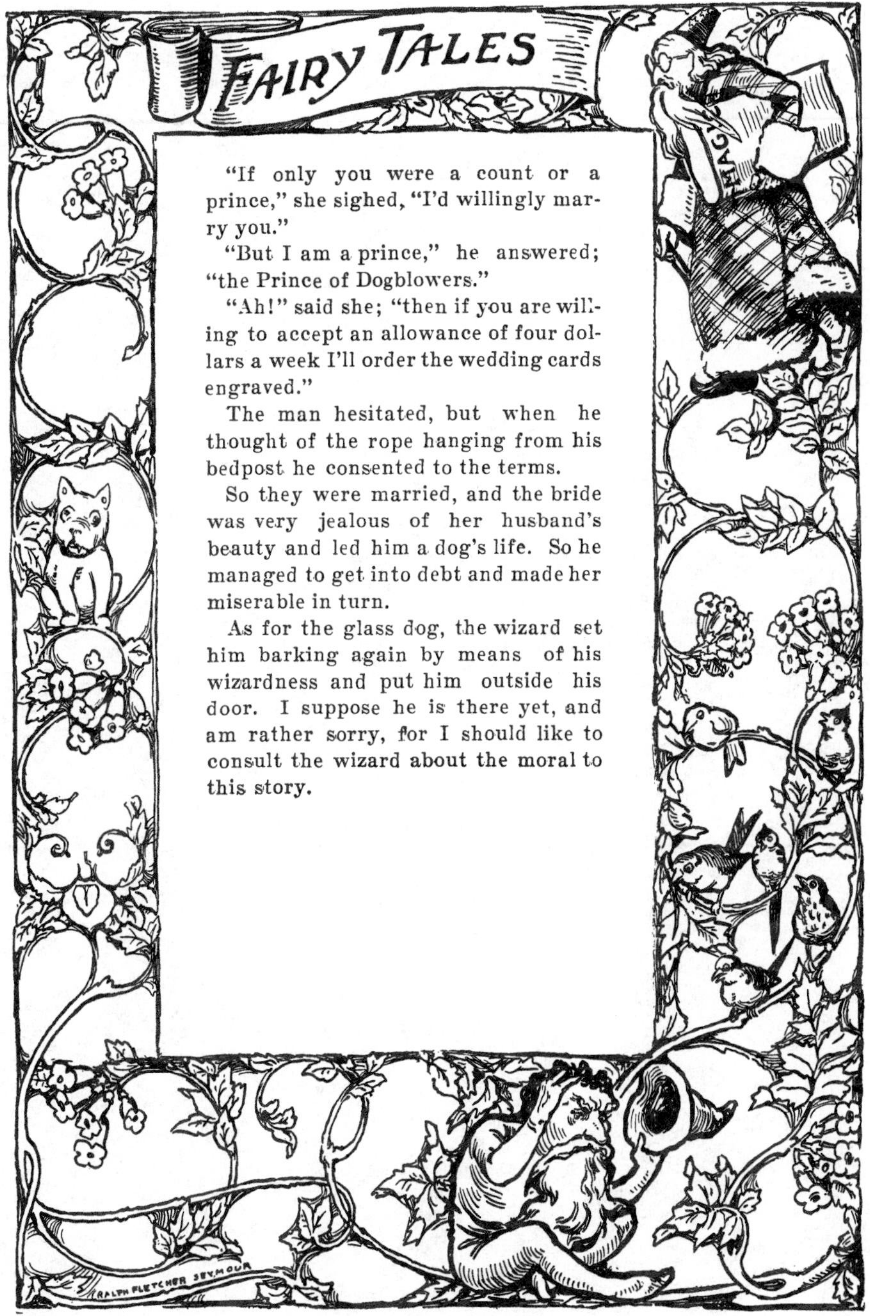

"If only you were a count or a prince," she sighed, "I'd willingly marry you."

"But I am a prince," he answered; "the Prince of Dogblowers."

"Ah!" said she; "then if you are willing to accept an allowance of four dollars a week I'll order the wedding cards engraved."

The man hesitated, but when he thought of the rope hanging from his bedpost he consented to the terms.

So they were married, and the bride was very jealous of her husband's beauty and led him a dog's life. So he managed to get into debt and made her miserable in turn.

As for the glass dog, the wizard set him barking again by means of his wizardness and put him outside his door. I suppose he is there yet, and am rather sorry, for I should like to consult the wizard about the moral to this story.

THE QUEEN of QUOK

A king once died, as kings are apt to do, being as liable to shortness of breath as other mortals.

It was high time this king abandoned his earth life, for he had lived in a sadly extravagant manner, and his subjects could spare him without the slightest inconvenience.

His father had left him a full treasury, both money and jewels being in abundance. But the foolish king just deceased had squandered every penny in riotous living. He had then taxed his subjects until most of them became paupers, and this money vanished in more riotous living. Next he sold all the grand old furniture in the palace; all the silver and gold plate and bric-a-brac; all the rich carpets and furnishings and even his own kingly wardrobe, reserving only a soiled and moth-eaten ermine robe to fold over his

threadbare raiment. And he spent the money in further riotous living.

Don't ask me to explain what riotous living is. I only know, from hearsay, that it is an excellent way to get rid of money. And so this spendthrift king found it.

He now picked all the magnificent jewels from his kingly crown and from the round ball on the top of his scepter, and sold them and spent the money. Riotous living, of course. But at last he was at the end of his resources. He couldn't sell the crown itself, because no one but the king had the right to wear it. Neither could he sell the royal palace, because only the king had the right to live there.

So, finally, he found himself reduced to a bare palace, containing only a big mahogany bedstead that he slept in, a small stool on which he sat to pull off his shoes and the moth-eaten ermine robe.

In this straight he was reduced to the necessity of borrowing an occasional dime from his chief counselor, with which to buy a ham sandwich. And the chief counselor hadn't many dimes. One who counseled his king so foolishly was likely to ruin his own prospects as well.

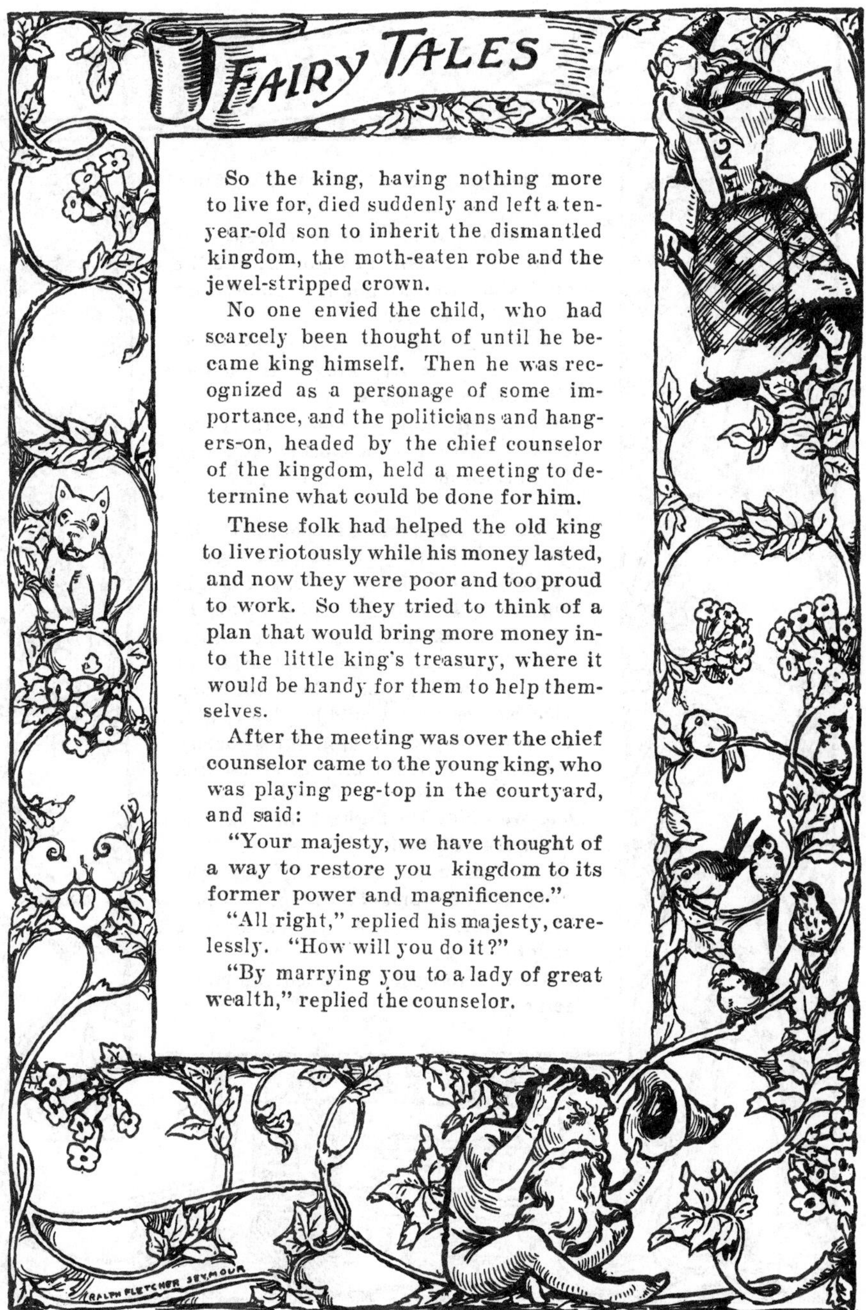

So the king, having nothing more to live for, died suddenly and left a ten-year-old son to inherit the dismantled kingdom, the moth-eaten robe and the jewel-stripped crown.

No one envied the child, who had scarcely been thought of until he became king himself. Then he was recognized as a personage of some importance, and the politicians and hangers-on, headed by the chief counselor of the kingdom, held a meeting to determine what could be done for him.

These folk had helped the old king to live riotously while his money lasted, and now they were poor and too proud to work. So they tried to think of a plan that would bring more money into the little king's treasury, where it would be handy for them to help themselves.

After the meeting was over the chief counselor came to the young king, who was playing peg-top in the courtyard, and said:

"Your majesty, we have thought of a way to restore you kingdom to its former power and magnificence."

"All right," replied his majesty, carelessly. "How will you do it?"

"By marrying you to a lady of great wealth," replied the counselor.

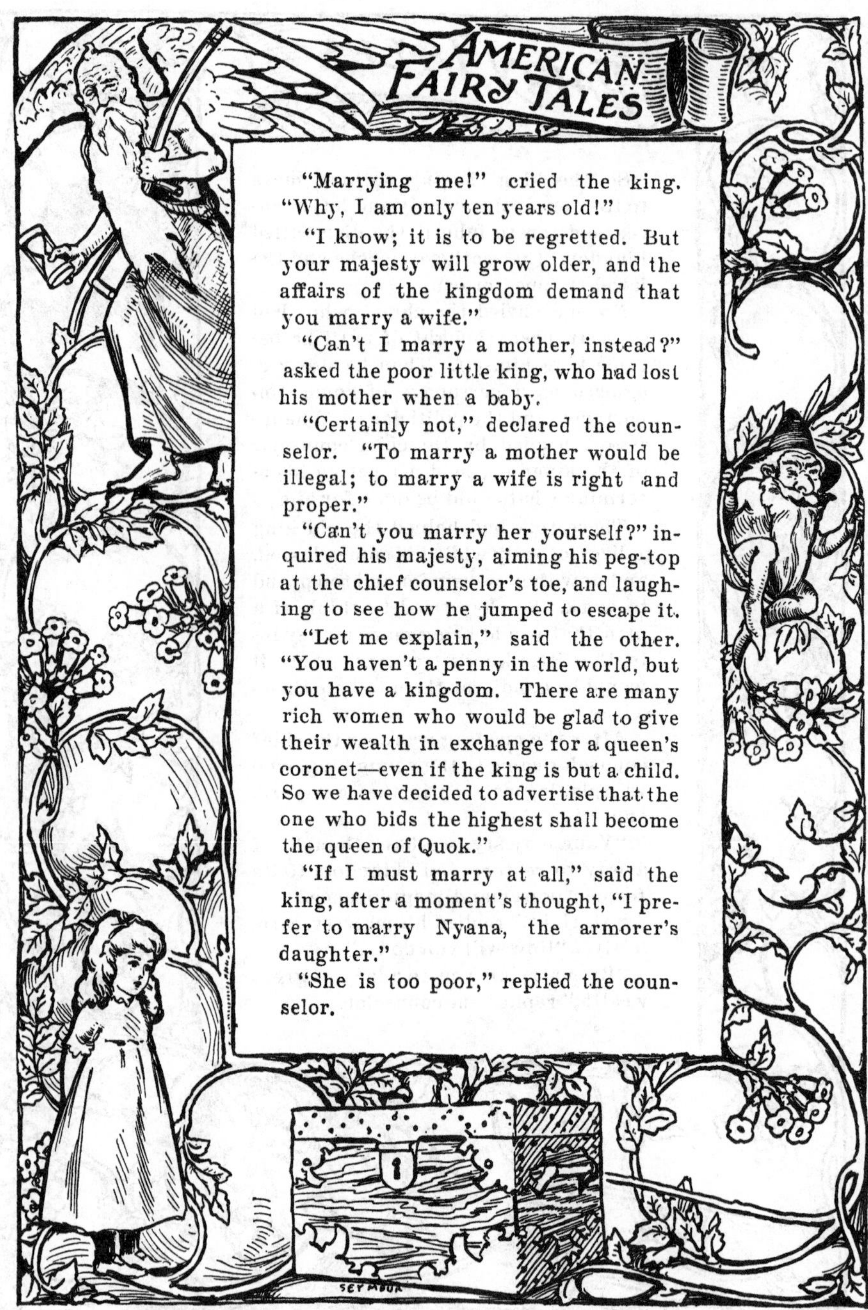

"Marrying me!" cried the king. "Why, I am only ten years old!"

"I know; it is to be regretted. But your majesty will grow older, and the affairs of the kingdom demand that you marry a wife."

"Can't I marry a mother, instead?" asked the poor little king, who had lost his mother when a baby.

"Certainly not," declared the counselor. "To marry a mother would be illegal; to marry a wife is right and proper."

"Can't you marry her yourself?" inquired his majesty, aiming his peg-top at the chief counselor's toe, and laughing to see how he jumped to escape it.

"Let me explain," said the other. "You haven't a penny in the world, but you have a kingdom. There are many rich women who would be glad to give their wealth in exchange for a queen's coronet—even if the king is but a child. So we have decided to advertise that the one who bids the highest shall become the queen of Quok."

"If I must marry at all," said the king, after a moment's thought, "I prefer to marry Nyana, the armorer's daughter."

"She is too poor," replied the counselor.

The boy king and the chief counselor.

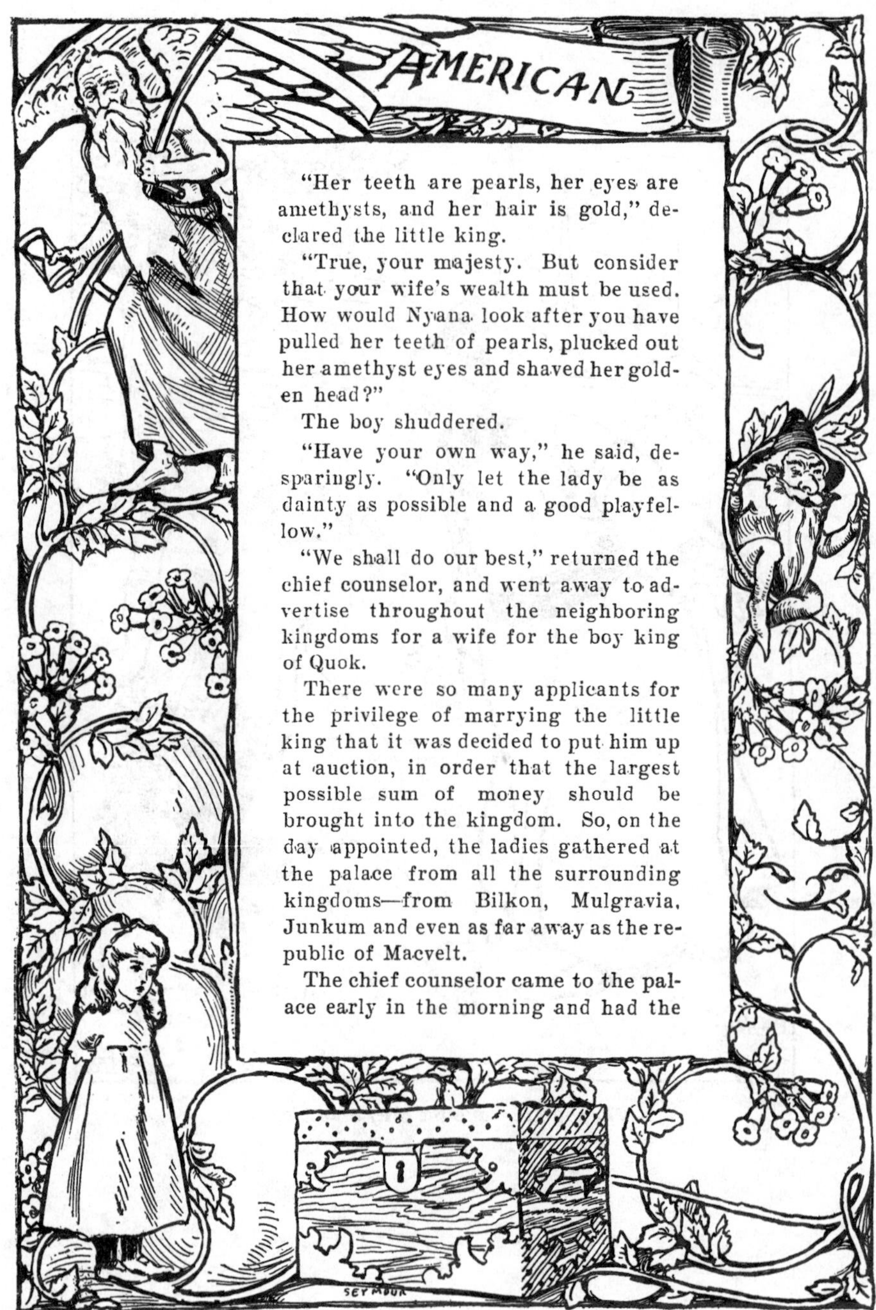

"Her teeth are pearls, her eyes are amethysts, and her hair is gold," declared the little king.

"True, your majesty. But consider that your wife's wealth must be used. How would Nyana look after you have pulled her teeth of pearls, plucked out her amethyst eyes and shaved her golden head?"

The boy shuddered.

"Have your own way," he said, desparingly. "Only let the lady be as dainty as possible and a good playfellow."

"We shall do our best," returned the chief counselor, and went away to advertise throughout the neighboring kingdoms for a wife for the boy king of Quok.

There were so many applicants for the privilege of marrying the little king that it was decided to put him up at auction, in order that the largest possible sum of money should be brought into the kingdom. So, on the day appointed, the ladies gathered at the palace from all the surrounding kingdoms—from Bilkon, Mulgravia, Junkum and even as far away as the republic of Macvelt.

The chief counselor came to the palace early in the morning and had the

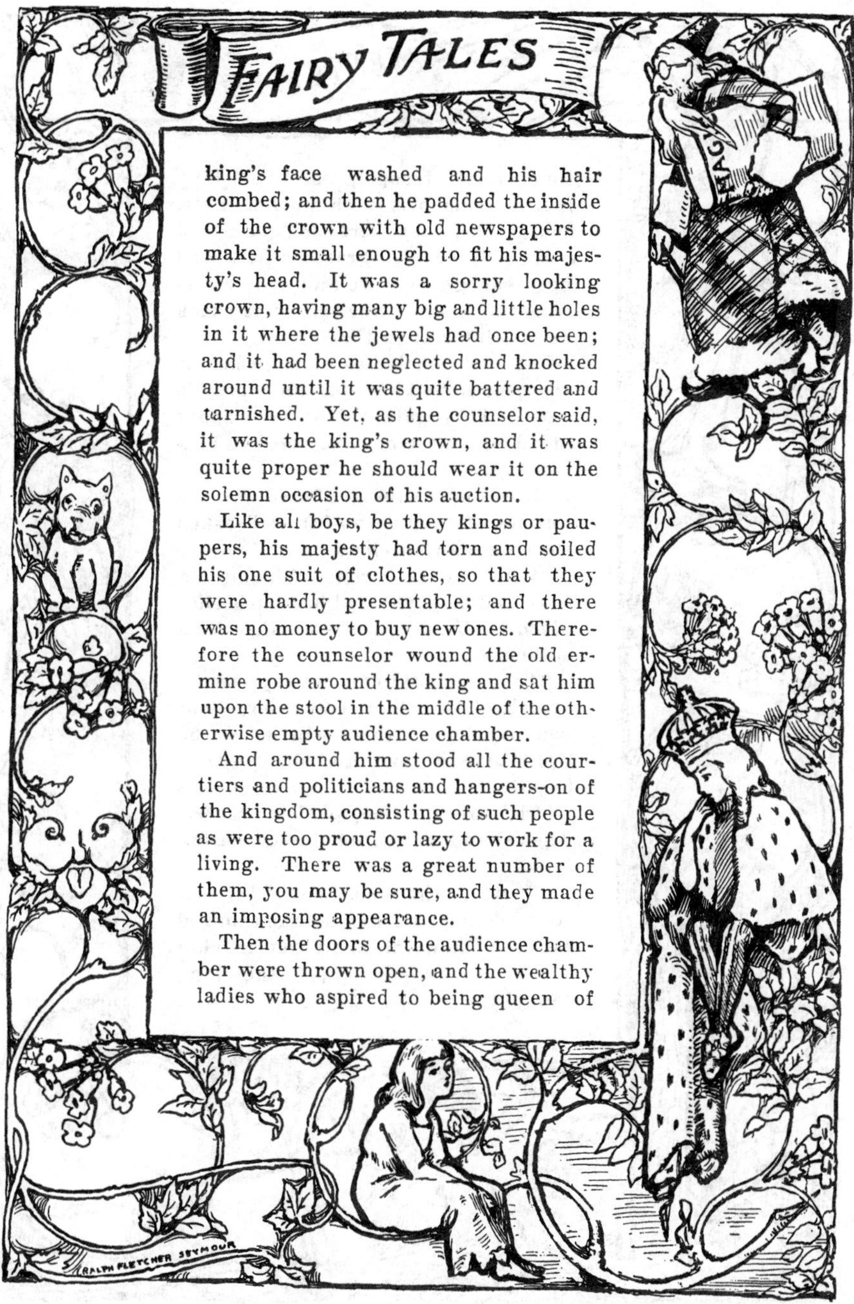

king's face washed and his hair combed; and then he padded the inside of the crown with old newspapers to make it small enough to fit his majesty's head. It was a sorry looking crown, having many big and little holes in it where the jewels had once been; and it had been neglected and knocked around until it was quite battered and tarnished. Yet, as the counselor said, it was the king's crown, and it was quite proper he should wear it on the solemn occasion of his auction.

Like all boys, be they kings or paupers, his majesty had torn and soiled his one suit of clothes, so that they were hardly presentable; and there was no money to buy new ones. Therefore the counselor wound the old ermine robe around the king and sat him upon the stool in the middle of the otherwise empty audience chamber.

And around him stood all the courtiers and politicians and hangers-on of the kingdom, consisting of such people as were too proud or lazy to work for a living. There was a great number of them, you may be sure, and they made an imposing appearance.

Then the doors of the audience chamber were thrown open, and the wealthy ladies who aspired to being queen of

Quok came trooping in. The king looked them over with much anxiety, and decided they were each and all old enough to be his grandmother, and ugly enough to scare away the crows from the royal cornfields. After which he lost interest in them.

But the rich ladies never looked at the poor little king squatting upon his stool. They gathered at once about the chief counselor, who acted as auctioneer.

"How much am I offered for the coronet of the queen of Quok?" asked the counselor, in a loud voice.

"Where is the coronet?" inquired a fussy old lady who had just buried her ninth husband and was worth several millions.

"There isn't any coronet at present," explained the chief counselor, "but whoever bids highest will have the right to wear one, and she can then buy it."

"Oh," said the fussy old lady, "I see." Then she added: "I'll bid fourteen dollars."

"Fourteen thousand dollars!" cried a sour-looking woman who was thin and tall and had wrinkles all over her skin —"like a frosted apple," the king thought.

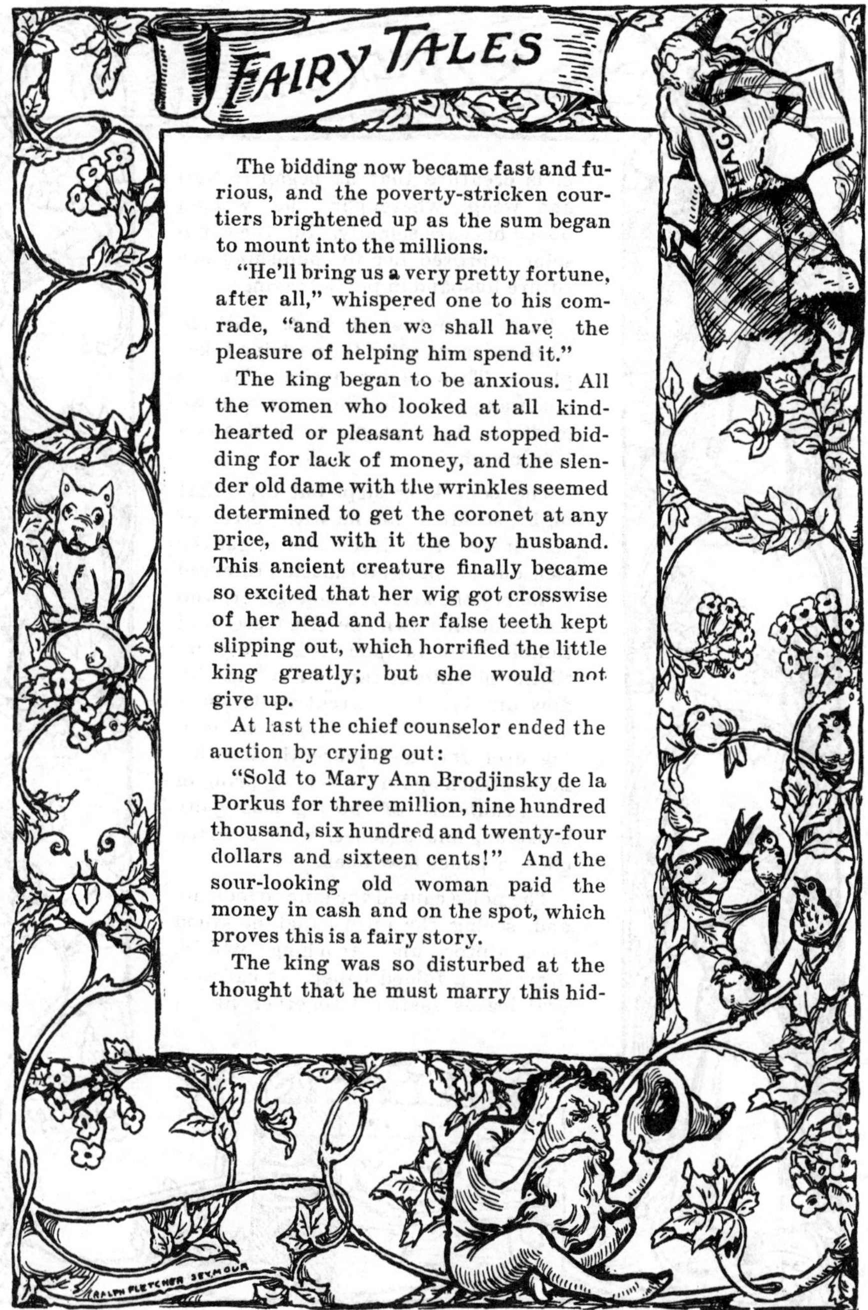

The bidding now became fast and furious, and the poverty-stricken courtiers brightened up as the sum began to mount into the millions.

"He'll bring us a very pretty fortune, after all," whispered one to his comrade, "and then we shall have the pleasure of helping him spend it."

The king began to be anxious. All the women who looked at all kind-hearted or pleasant had stopped bidding for lack of money, and the slender old dame with the wrinkles seemed determined to get the coronet at any price, and with it the boy husband. This ancient creature finally became so excited that her wig got crosswise of her head and her false teeth kept slipping out, which horrified the little king greatly; but she would not give up.

At last the chief counselor ended the auction by crying out:

"Sold to Mary Ann Brodjinsky de la Porkus for three million, nine hundred thousand, six hundred and twenty-four dollars and sixteen cents!" And the sour-looking old woman paid the money in cash and on the spot, which proves this is a fairy story.

The king was so disturbed at the thought that he must marry this hid-

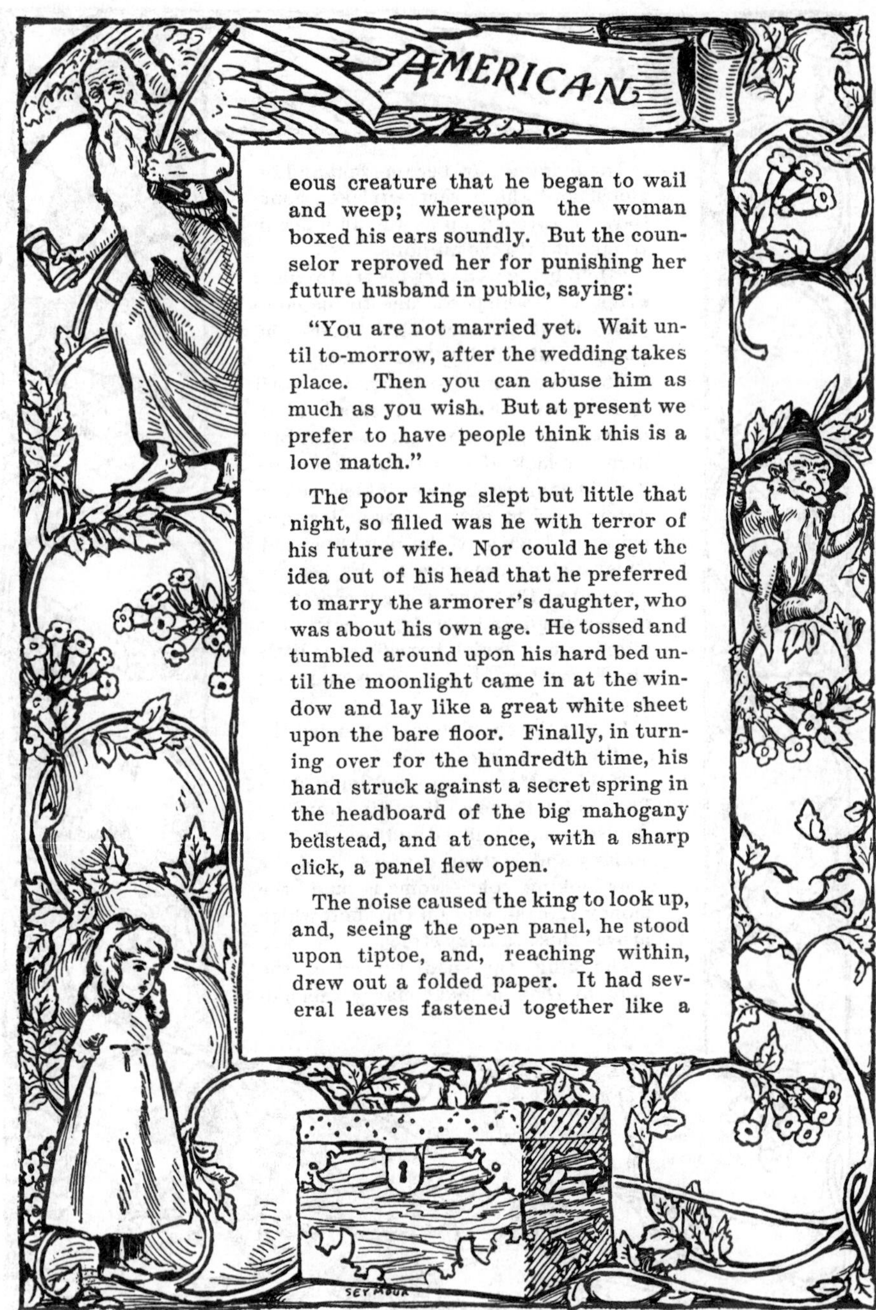

eous creature that he began to wail and weep; whereupon the woman boxed his ears soundly. But the counselor reproved her for punishing her future husband in public, saying:

"You are not married yet. Wait until to-morrow, after the wedding takes place. Then you can abuse him as much as you wish. But at present we prefer to have people think this is a love match."

The poor king slept but little that night, so filled was he with terror of his future wife. Nor could he get the idea out of his head that he preferred to marry the armorer's daughter, who was about his own age. He tossed and tumbled around upon his hard bed until the moonlight came in at the window and lay like a great white sheet upon the bare floor. Finally, in turning over for the hundredth time, his hand struck against a secret spring in the headboard of the big mahogany bedstead, and at once, with a sharp click, a panel flew open.

The noise caused the king to look up, and, seeing the open panel, he stood upon tiptoe, and, reaching within, drew out a folded paper. It had several leaves fastened together like a

book, and upon the first page was written:

> "When the king is in trouble
> This leaf he must double
> And set it on fire
> To obtain his desire."

This was not very good poetry, but when the king had spelled it out in the moonlight he was filled with joy.

"There's no doubt about my being in trouble," he exclaimed; "so I'll burn it at once, and see what happens."

He tore off the leaf and put the rest of the book in its secret hiding place. Then, folding the paper double, he placed it on the top of his stool, lighted a match and set fire to it.

It made a horrid smudge for so small a paper, and the king sat on the edge of the bed and watched it eagerly.

When the smoke cleared away he was surprised to see, sitting upon the stool, a round little man, who, with folded arms and crossed legs, sat calmly facing the king and smoking a black briarwood pipe.

"Well, here I am," said he.

"So I see," replied the little king. "But how did you get here?"

"Didn't you burn the paper?" demanded the round man, by way of answer.

"Yes, I did," acknowledged the king.

"Then you are in trouble, and I've come to help you out of it. I'm the Slave of the Royal Bedstead."

"Oh!" said the king. "I didn't know there was one."

"Neither did your father, or he would not have been so foolish as to sell everything he had for money. By the way, it's lucky for you he did not sell this bedstead. Now, then, what do you want?"

"I'm not sure what I want," replied the king; "but I know what I don't want, and that is the old woman who is going to marry me."

"That's easy enough," said the Slave of the Royal Bedstead. "All you need do is to return her the money she paid the chief counselor and declare the match off. Don't be afraid. You are the king, and your word is law."

"To be sure," said his majesty. "But I am in great need of money. How am I going to live if the chief counselor returns to Mary Ann Brodjinski her millions?"

"Phoo! that's easy enough," again answered the man, and, putting his hand in his pocket, he drew out and tossed to the king an old-fashioned leather purse. "Keep that with you," said he, "and you will always be rich,

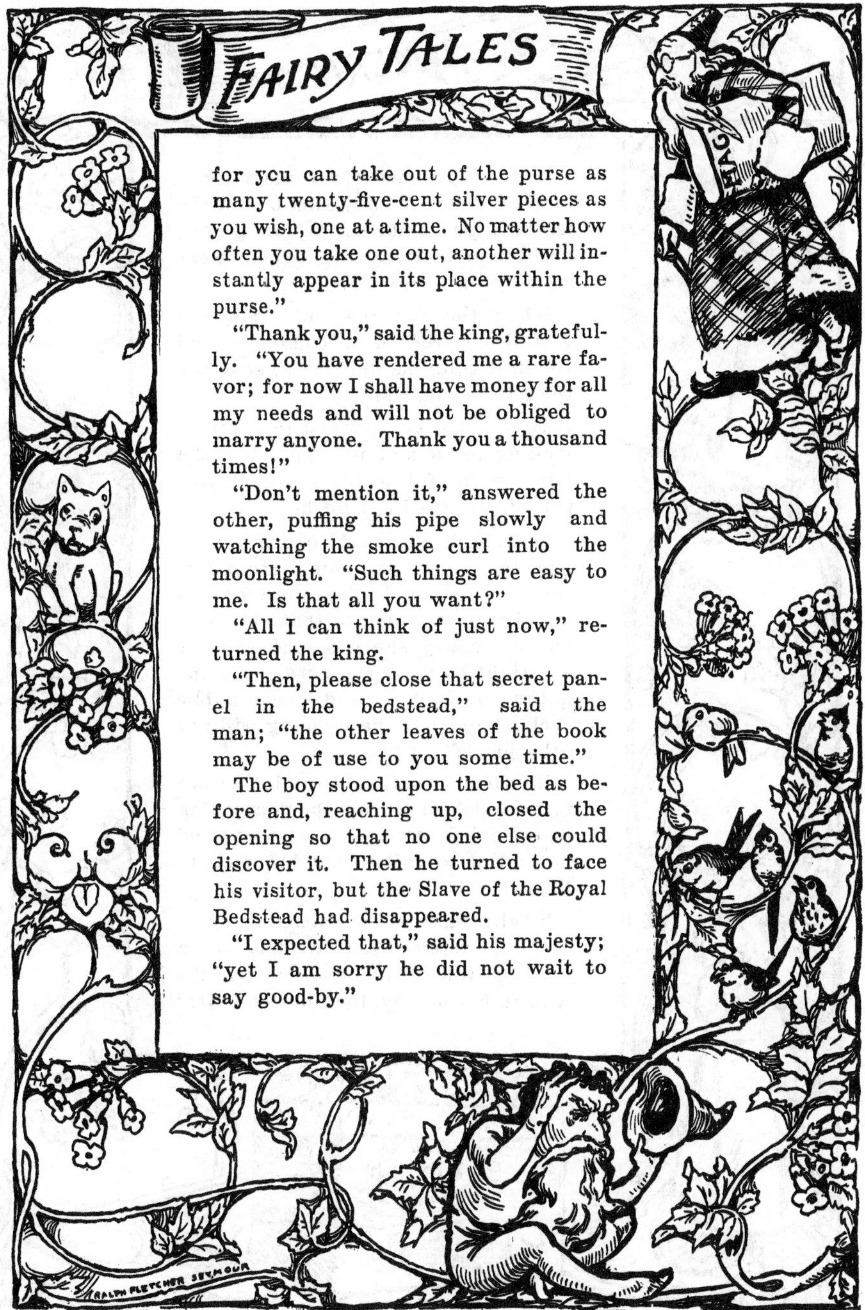

for ycu can take out of the purse as many twenty-five-cent silver pieces as you wish, one at a time. No matter how often you take one out, another will instantly appear in its place within the purse."

"Thank you," said the king, gratefully. "You have rendered me a rare favor; for now I shall have money for all my needs and will not be obliged to marry anyone. Thank you a thousand times!"

"Don't mention it," answered the other, puffing his pipe slowly and watching the smoke curl into the moonlight. "Such things are easy to me. Is that all you want?"

"All I can think of just now," returned the king.

"Then, please close that secret panel in the bedstead," said the man; "the other leaves of the book may be of use to you some time."

The boy stood upon the bed as before and, reaching up, closed the opening so that no one else could discover it. Then he turned to face his visitor, but the Slave of the Royal Bedstead had disappeared.

"I expected that," said his majesty; "yet I am sorry he did not wait to say good-by."

With a lightened heart and a sense of great relief the boy king placed the leathern purse underneath his pillow, and climbing into bed again slept soundly until morning.

When the sun rose his majesty rose also, refreshed and comforted, and the first thing he did was to send for the chief counselor.

That mighty personage arrived looking glum and unhappy, but the boy was too full of his own good fortune to notice it. Said he:

"I have decided not to marry anyone, for I have just come into a fortune of my own. Therefore I command you to return to that old woman the money she has paid you for the right to wear the coronet of the queen of Quok. And make public declaration that the wedding will not take place."

Hearing this the counselor began to tremble, for he saw the young king had decided to reign in earnest; and he looked so guilty that his majesty inquired:

"Well! what is the matter now?"

"Sire," replied the wretch, in a shaking voice, "I cannot return the woman her money, for I have lost it!"

"Lost it!" cried the king, in mingled astonishment and anger.

"Even so, your majesty. On my way home from the auction last night I stopped at the drug store to get some potash lozenges for my throat, which was dry and hoarse with so much loud talking; and your majesty will admit it was through my efforts the woman was induced to pay so great a price. Well, going into the drug store I carelessly left the package of money lying on the seat of my carriage, and when I came out again it was gone. Nor was the thief anywhere to be seen."

"Did you call the police?" asked the king.

"Yes, I called; but they were all on the next block, and although they have promised to search for the robber I have little hope they will ever find him."

The king sighed.

"What shall we do now?" he asked.

"I fear you must marry Mary Ann Brodjinski," answered the chief counselor; "unless, indeed, you order the executioner to cut her head off."

"That would be wrong," declared the king. "The woman must not be harmed. And it is just that we re-

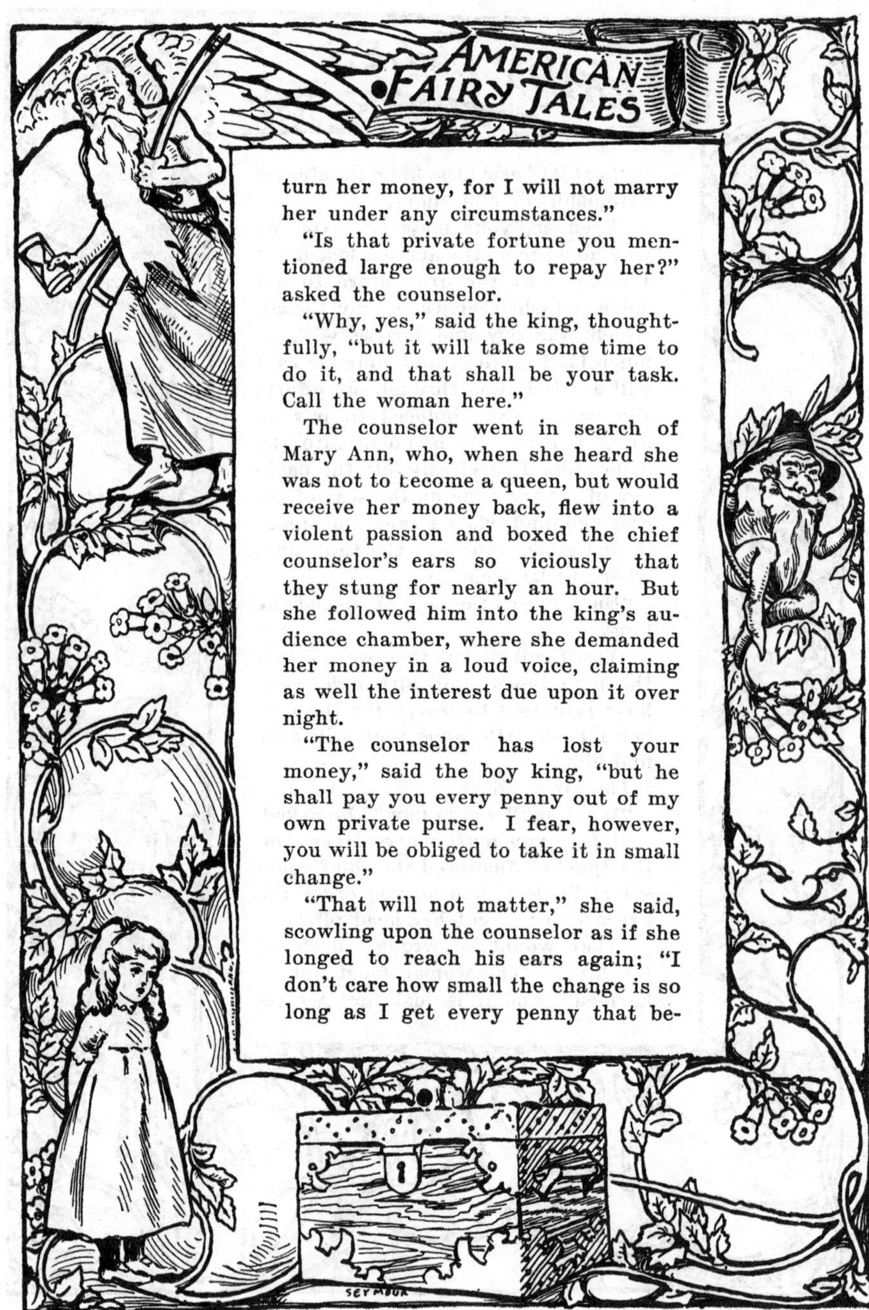

turn her money, for I will not marry her under any circumstances."

"Is that private fortune you mentioned large enough to repay her?" asked the counselor.

"Why, yes," said the king, thoughtfully, "but it will take some time to do it, and that shall be your task. Call the woman here."

The counselor went in search of Mary Ann, who, when she heard she was not to become a queen, but would receive her money back, flew into a violent passion and boxed the chief counselor's ears so viciously that they stung for nearly an hour. But she followed him into the king's audience chamber, where she demanded her money in a loud voice, claiming as well the interest due upon it over night.

"The counselor has lost your money," said the boy king, "but he shall pay you every penny out of my own private purse. I fear, however, you will be obliged to take it in small change."

"That will not matter," she said, scowling upon the counselor as if she longed to reach his ears again; "I don't care how small the change is so long as I get every penny that be-

Counting the money from the magic purse.

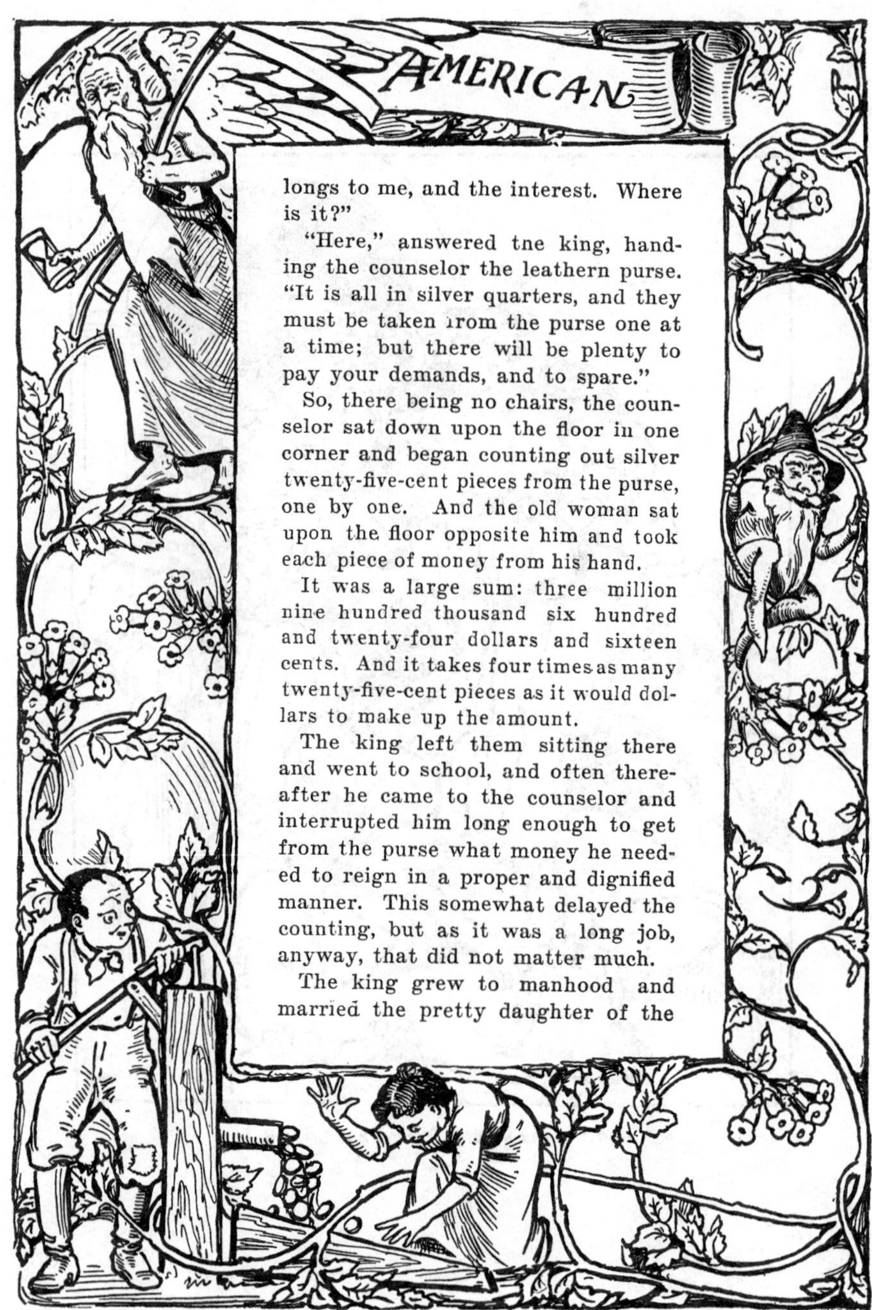

longs to me, and the interest. Where is it?"

"Here," answered tne king, handing the counselor the leathern purse. "It is all in silver quarters, and they must be taken from the purse one at a time; but there will be plenty to pay your demands, and to spare."

So, there being no chairs, the counselor sat down upon the floor in one corner and began counting out silver twenty-five-cent pieces from the purse, one by one. And the old woman sat upon the floor opposite him and took each piece of money from his hand.

It was a large sum: three million nine hundred thousand six hundred and twenty-four dollars and sixteen cents. And it takes four times as many twenty-five-cent pieces as it would dollars to make up the amount.

The king left them sitting there and went to school, and often thereafter he came to the counselor and interrupted him long enough to get from the purse what money he needed to reign in a proper and dignified manner. This somewhat delayed the counting, but as it was a long job, anyway, that did not matter much.

The king grew to manhood and married the pretty daughter of the

armorer, and they now have two lovely children of their own. Once in awhile they go into the big audience chamber of the palace and let the little ones watch the aged, hoary-headed counselor count out silver twenty-five-cent pieces to a withered old woman, who watches his every movement to see that he does not cheat her.

It is a big sum, three million, nine hundred thousand, six hundred and twenty-four dollars and sixteen cents in twenty-five-cent pieces.

But this is how the counselor was punished for being so careless with the woman's money. And this is how Mary Ann Brodjinski de la Porkus was also punished for wishing to marry a ten-year-old king in order that she might wear the coronet of the queen of Quok.

5

The GIRL WHO OWNED A BEAR

Mamma had gone down-town to shop. She had asked Nora to look after Jane Gladys, and Nora promised she would. But it was her afternoon for polishing the silver, so she stayed in the pantry and left Jane Gladys to amuse herself alone in the big sitting-room upstairs.

The little girl did not mind being alone, for she was working on her first piece of embroidery—a sofa pillow for papa's birthday present. So she crept into the big bay window and curled herself up on the broad sill while she bent her brown head over her work.

Soon the door opened and closed again, quietly. Jane Gladys thought it was Nora, so she didn't look up until she had taken a couple more stitches on a forget-me-not. Then she raised her eyes and was astonished to find a strange man in the middle of the room, who regarded her earnestly.

He was short and fat, and seemed to be breathing heavily from his climb up the stairs. He held a worn silk hat in one hand and underneath his other elbow was tucked a good-sized book. He was dressed in a black suit that looked old and rather shabby, and his head was bald upon the top.

"Excuse me," he said, while the child gazed at him in solemn surprise. "Are you Jane Gladys Brown?"

"Yes, sir," she answered.

"Very good; very good, indeed!" he remarked, with a queer sort of smile. "I've had quite a hunt to find you, but I've succeeded at last."

"How did you get in?" inquired Jane Gladys, with a growing distrust of her visitor.

"That is a secret," he said, mysteriously.

This was enough to put the girl on her guard. She looked at the man and the man looked at her, and both looks were grave and somewhat anxious.

"What do you want?" she asked, straightening herself up with a dignified air.

"Ah!—now we are coming to business," said the man, briskly. "I'm going to be quite frank with you. To be-

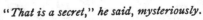

"That is a secret," he said, mysteriously.

gin with, your father has abused me in a most ungentlemanly manner."

Jane Gladys got off the window sill and pointed her small finger at the door.

"Leave this room 'meejitly!" she cried, her voice trembling with indignation. "My papa is the best man in the world. He never 'bused anybody!"

"Allow me to explain, please," said the visitor, without paying any attention to her request to go away. "Your father may be very kind to you, for you are his little girl, you know. But when he's down-town in his office he's inclined to be rather severe, especially on book agents. Now, I called on him the other day and asked him to buy the 'Complete Works of Peter Smith,' and what do you suppose he did?"

She said nothing.

"Why," continued the man, with growing excitement, "he ordered me from his office, and had me put out of the building by the janitor! What do you think of such treatment as that from the 'best papa in the world,' eh?"

"I think he was quite right," said Jane Gladys.

"Oh, you do? Well," said the man, "I resolved to be revenged for the insult. So, as your father is big and

strong and a dangerous man, I have decided to be revenged upon his little girl."

Jane Gladys shivered.

"What are you going to do?" she asked.

"I'm going to present you with this book," he answered, taking it from under his arm. Then he sat down on the edge of a chair, placed his hat on the rug and drew a fountain pen from his vest pocket.

"I'll write your name in it," said he. "How do you spell Gladys?"

"G-l-a-d-y-s," she spelled.

"Thank you. Now this," he continued, rising and handing her the book with a bow, "is my revenge for your father's treatment of me. Perhaps he'll be sorry he didn't buy the 'Complete Works of Peter Smith.' Good-by, my dear."

He walked to the door, gave her another bow, and left the room, and Jane Gladys could see that he was laughing to himself as if very much amused.

When the door had closed behind the queer little man the child sat down in the window again and glanced at the book. It had a red and yellow cover and the word "Thingamajigs" was across the front in big letters.

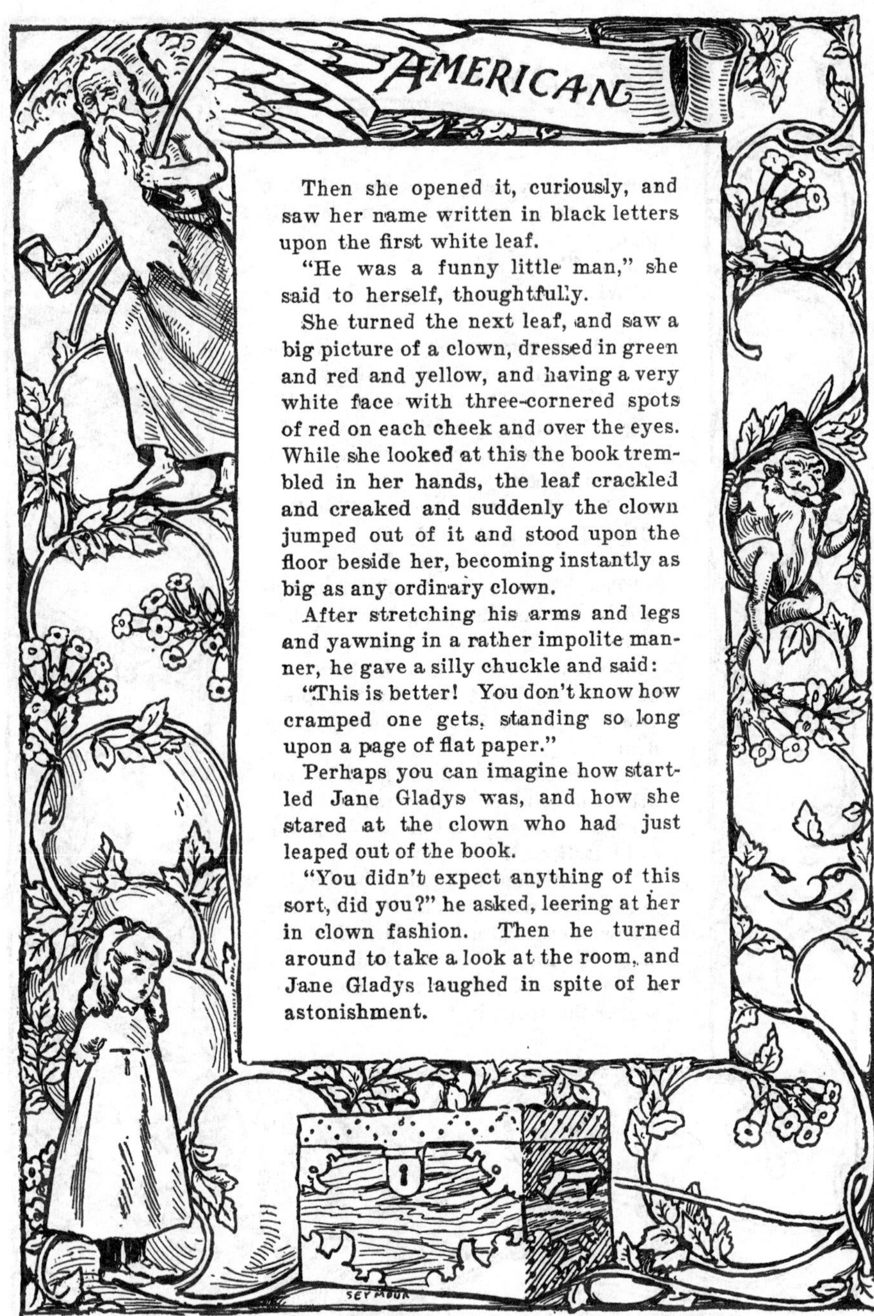

Then she opened it, curiously, and saw her name written in black letters upon the first white leaf.

"He was a funny little man," she said to herself, thoughtfully.

She turned the next leaf, and saw a big picture of a clown, dressed in green and red and yellow, and having a very white face with three-cornered spots of red on each cheek and over the eyes. While she looked at this the book trembled in her hands, the leaf crackled and creaked and suddenly the clown jumped out of it and stood upon the floor beside her, becoming instantly as big as any ordinary clown.

After stretching his arms and legs and yawning in a rather impolite manner, he gave a silly chuckle and said:

"This is better! You don't know how cramped one gets, standing so long upon a page of flat paper."

Perhaps you can imagine how startled Jane Gladys was, and how she stared at the clown who had just leaped out of the book.

"You didn't expect anything of this sort, did you?" he asked, leering at her in clown fashion. Then he turned around to take a look at the room, and Jane Gladys laughed in spite of her astonishment.

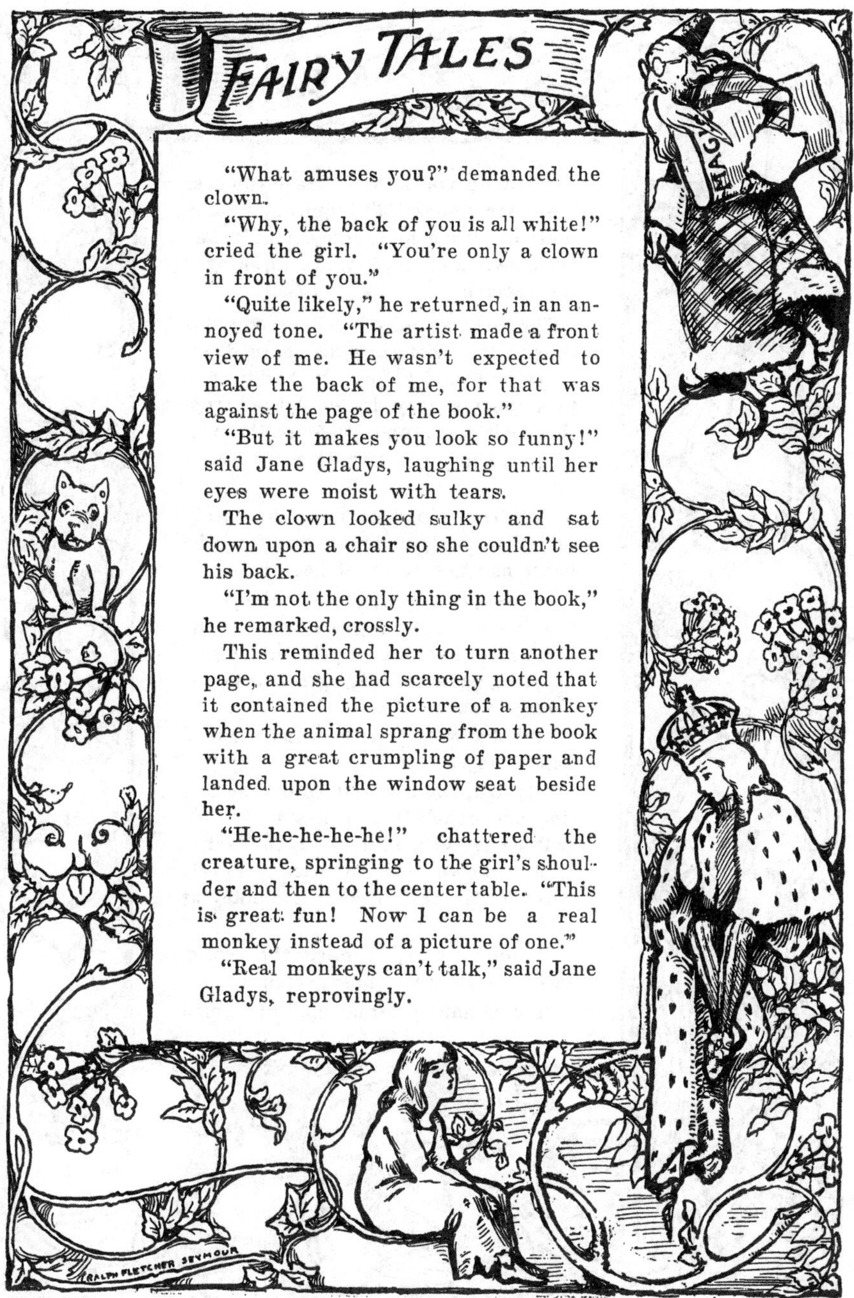

"What amuses you?" demanded the clown.

"Why, the back of you is all white!" cried the girl. "You're only a clown in front of you."

"Quite likely," he returned, in an annoyed tone. "The artist made a front view of me. He wasn't expected to make the back of me, for that was against the page of the book."

"But it makes you look so funny!" said Jane Gladys, laughing until her eyes were moist with tears.

The clown looked sulky and sat down upon a chair so she couldn't see his back.

"I'm not the only thing in the book," he remarked, crossly.

This reminded her to turn another page, and she had scarcely noted that it contained the picture of a monkey when the animal sprang from the book with a great crumpling of paper and landed upon the window seat beside her.

"He-he-he-he-he!" chattered the creature, springing to the girl's shoulder and then to the center table. "This is great fun! Now I can be a real monkey instead of a picture of one."

"Real monkeys can't talk," said Jane Gladys, reprovingly.

"How do you know? Have you ever been one yourself?" inquired the animal; and then he laughed loudly, and the clown laughed, too, as if he enjoyed the remark.

The girl was quite bewildered by this time. She thoughtlessly turned another leaf, and before she had time to look twice a gray donkey leaped from the book and stumbled from the window seat to the floor with a great clatter.

"You're clumsy enough, I'm sure!" said the child, indignantly, for the beast had nearly upset her.

"Clumsy! And why not?" demanded the donkey, with angry voice. "If the fool artist had drawn you out of perspective, as he did me, I guess you'd be clumsy yourself."

"What's wrong with you?" asked Jane Gladys.

"My front and rear legs on the left side are nearly six inches too short, that's what's the matter! If that artist didn't known how to draw properly why did he try to make a donkey at all?"

"I don't know," replied the child, seeing an answer was expected.

"I can hardly stand up," grumbled

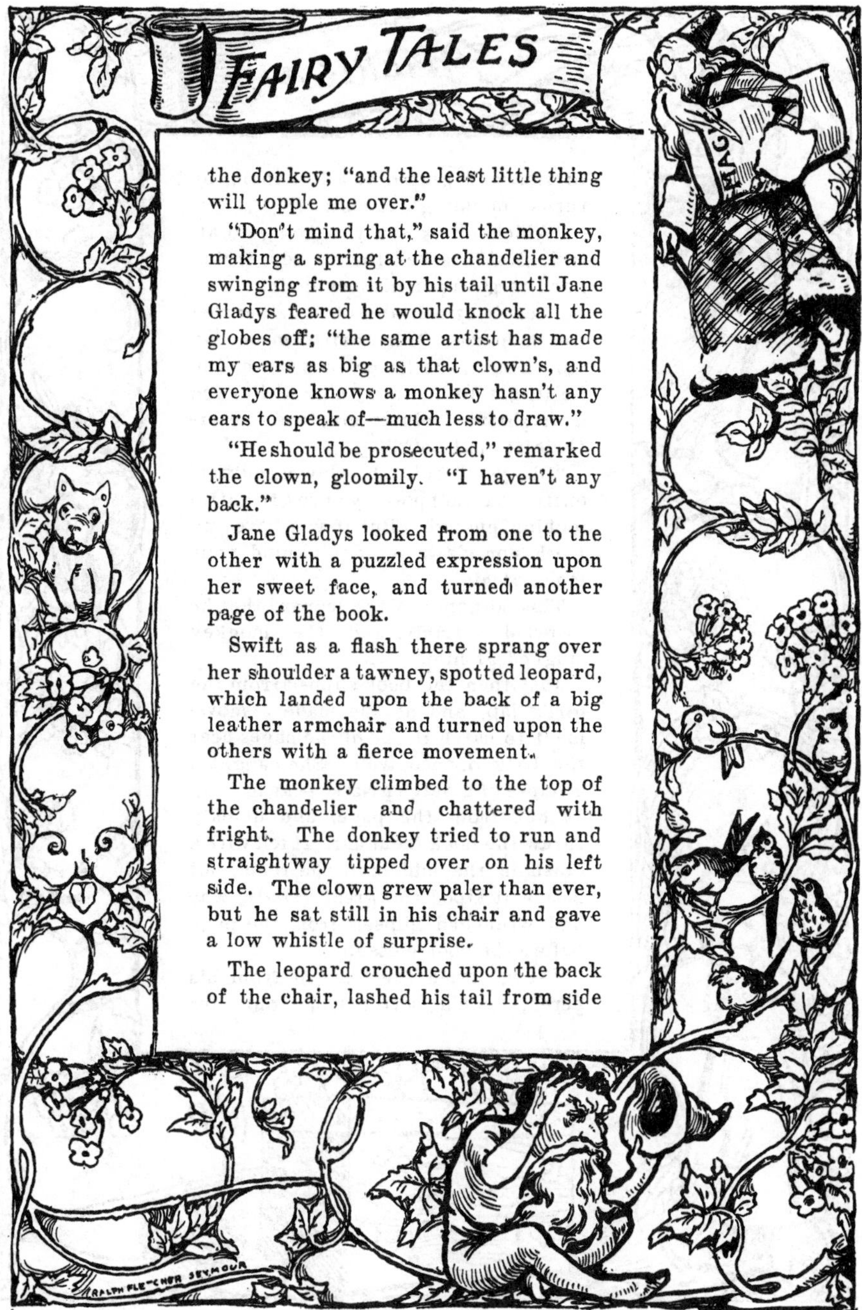

the donkey; "and the least little thing will topple me over."

"Don't mind that," said the monkey, making a spring at the chandelier and swinging from it by his tail until Jane Gladys feared he would knock all the globes off; "the same artist has made my ears as big as that clown's, and everyone knows a monkey hasn't any ears to speak of—much less to draw."

"He should be prosecuted," remarked the clown, gloomily. "I haven't any back."

Jane Gladys looked from one to the other with a puzzled expression upon her sweet face, and turned another page of the book.

Swift as a flash there sprang over her shoulder a tawney, spotted leopard, which landed upon the back of a big leather armchair and turned upon the others with a fierce movement.

The monkey climbed to the top of the chandelier and chattered with fright. The donkey tried to run and straightway tipped over on his left side. The clown grew paler than ever, but he sat still in his chair and gave a low whistle of surprise.

The leopard crouched upon the back of the chair, lashed his tail from side

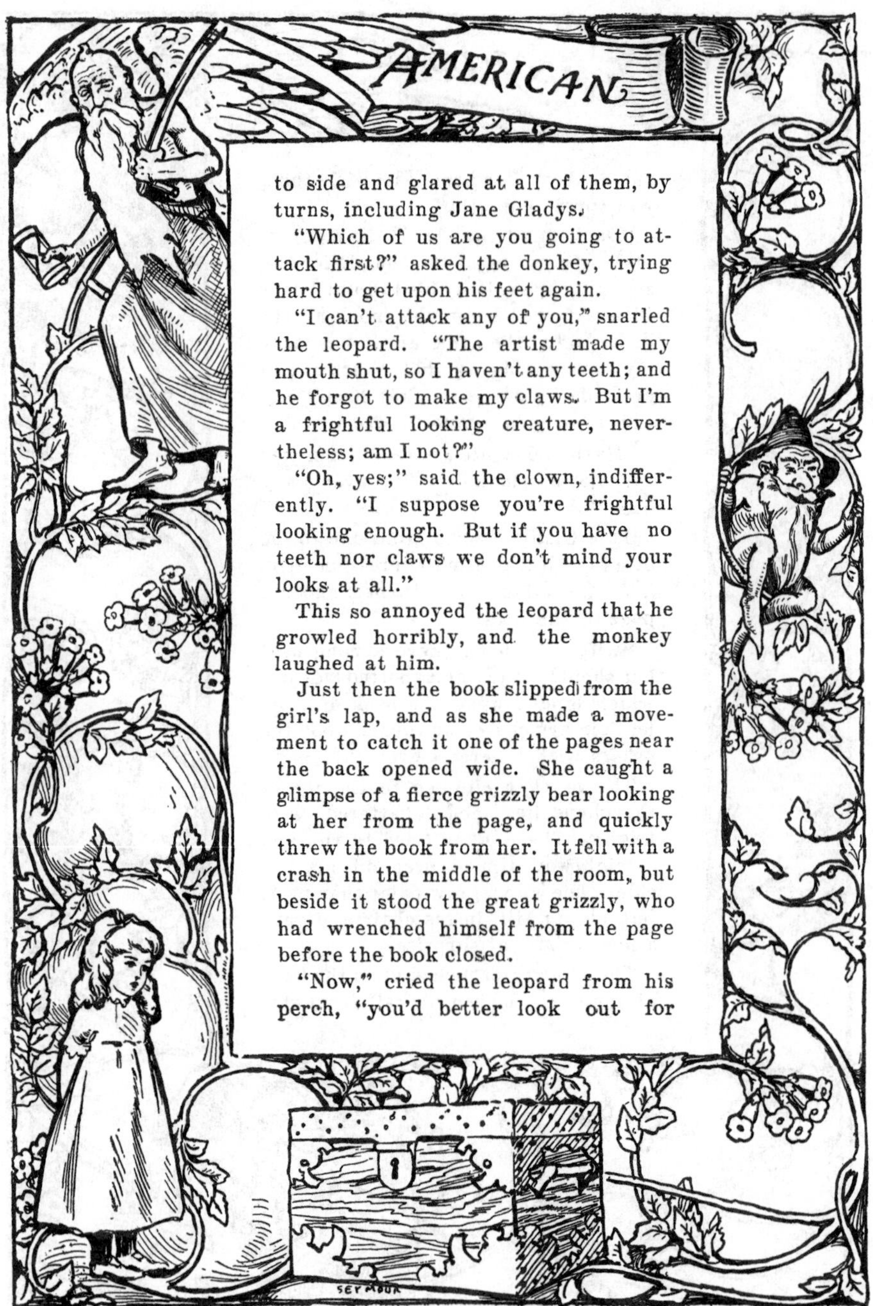

to side and glared at all of them, by turns, including Jane Gladys.

"Which of us are you going to attack first?" asked the donkey, trying hard to get upon his feet again.

"I can't attack any of you," snarled the leopard. "The artist made my mouth shut, so I haven't any teeth; and he forgot to make my claws. But I'm a frightful looking creature, nevertheless; am I not?"

"Oh, yes;" said the clown, indifferently. "I suppose you're frightful looking enough. But if you have no teeth nor claws we don't mind your looks at all."

This so annoyed the leopard that he growled horribly, and the monkey laughed at him.

Just then the book slipped from the girl's lap, and as she made a movement to catch it one of the pages near the back opened wide. She caught a glimpse of a fierce grizzly bear looking at her from the page, and quickly threw the book from her. It fell with a crash in the middle of the room, but beside it stood the great grizzly, who had wrenched himself from the page before the book closed.

"Now," cried the leopard from his perch, "you'd better look out for

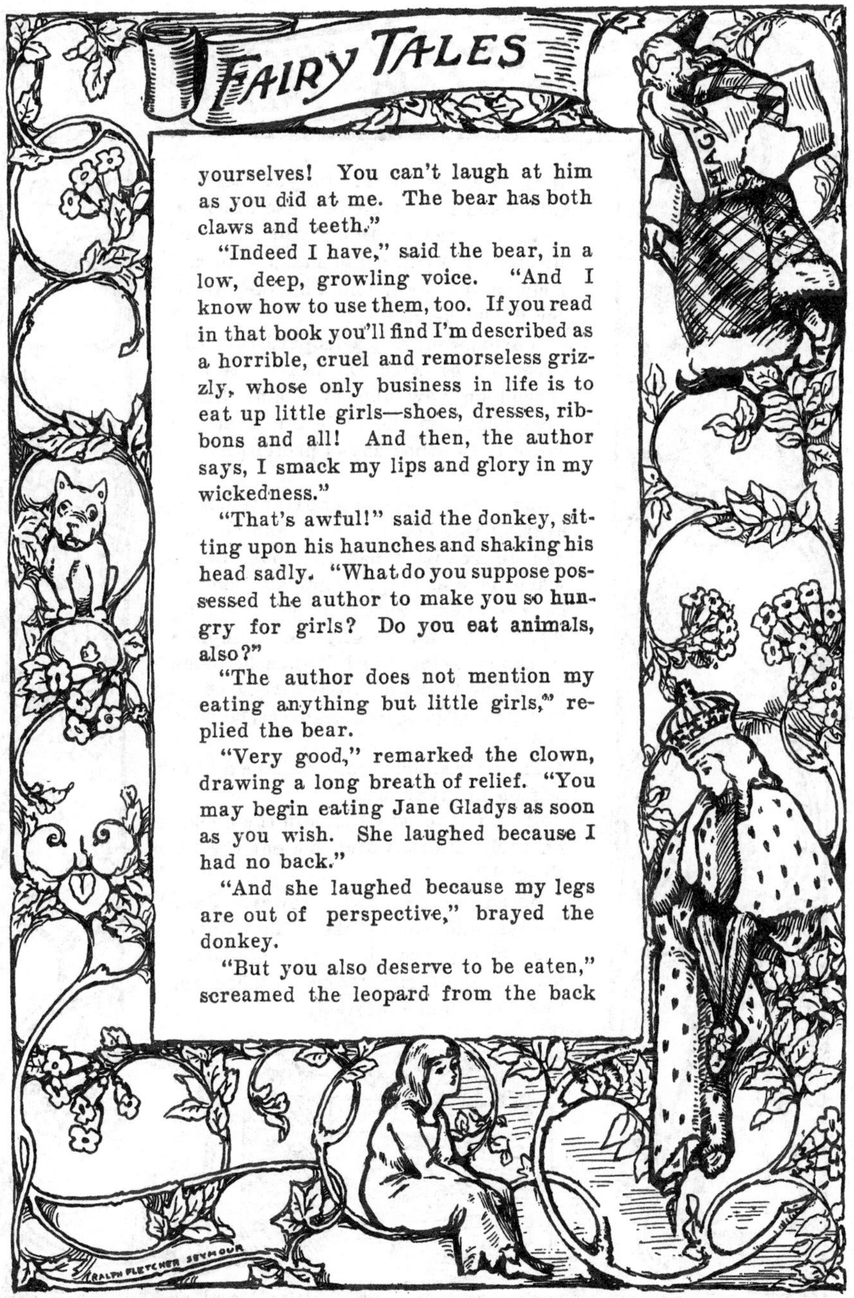

yourselves! You can't laugh at him as you did at me. The bear has both claws and teeth."

"Indeed I have," said the bear, in a low, deep, growling voice. "And I know how to use them, too. If you read in that book you'll find I'm described as a horrible, cruel and remorseless grizzly, whose only business in life is to eat up little girls—shoes, dresses, ribbons and all! And then, the author says, I smack my lips and glory in my wickedness."

"That's awful!" said the donkey, sitting upon his haunches and shaking his head sadly. "What do you suppose possessed the author to make you so hungry for girls? Do you eat animals, also?"

"The author does not mention my eating anything but little girls," replied the bear.

"Very good," remarked the clown, drawing a long breath of relief. "You may begin eating Jane Gladys as soon as you wish. She laughed because I had no back."

"And she laughed because my legs are out of perspective," brayed the donkey.

"But you also deserve to be eaten," screamed the leopard from the back

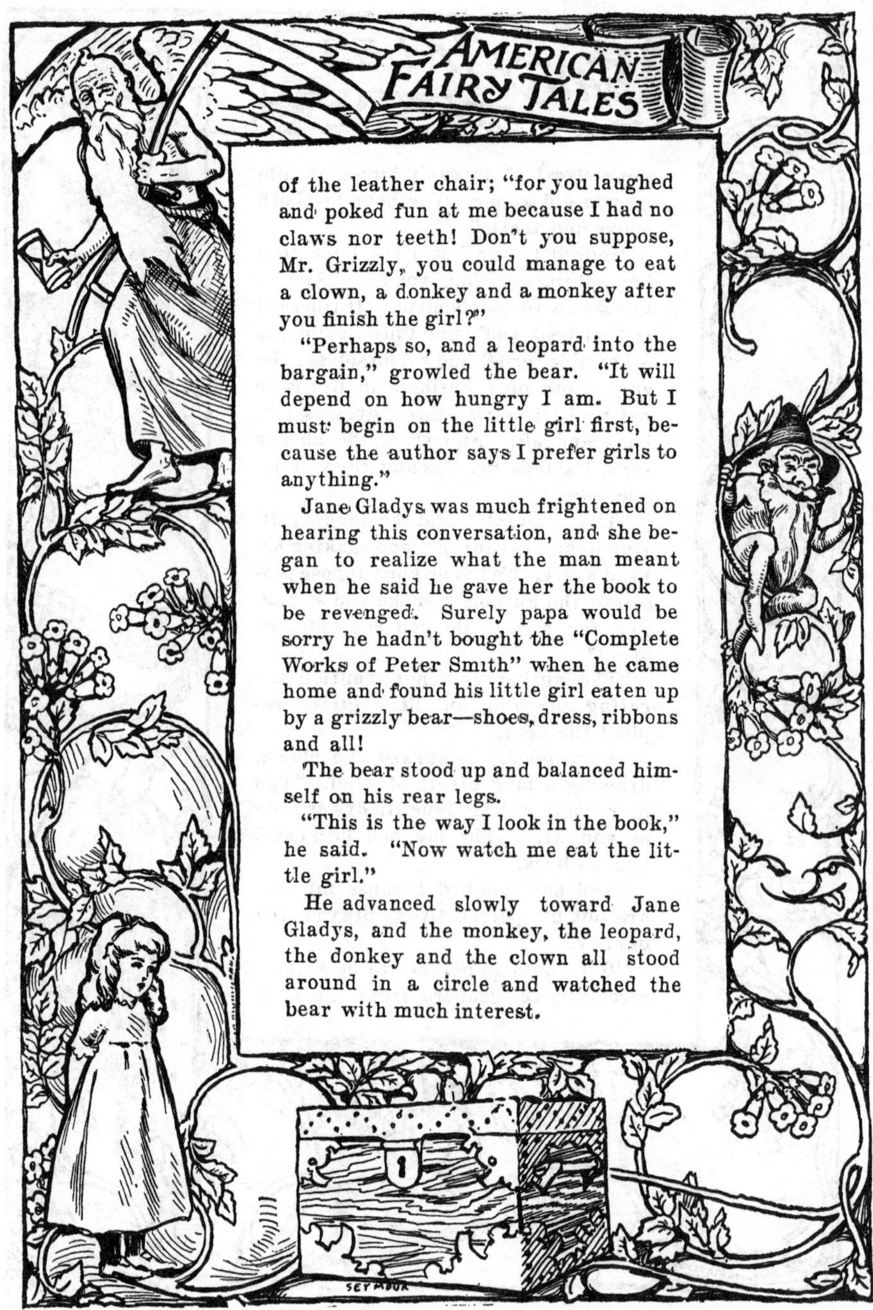

of the leather chair; "for you laughed and poked fun at me because I had no claws nor teeth! Don't you suppose, Mr. Grizzly, you could manage to eat a clown, a donkey and a monkey after you finish the girl?"

"Perhaps so, and a leopard into the bargain," growled the bear. "It will depend on how hungry I am. But I must begin on the little girl first, because the author says I prefer girls to anything."

Jane Gladys was much frightened on hearing this conversation, and she began to realize what the man meant when he said he gave her the book to be revenged. Surely papa would be sorry he hadn't bought the "Complete Works of Peter Smith" when he came home and found his little girl eaten up by a grizzly bear—shoes, dress, ribbons and all!

The bear stood up and balanced himself on his rear legs.

"This is the way I look in the book," he said. "Now watch me eat the little girl."

He advanced slowly toward Jane Gladys, and the monkey, the leopard, the donkey and the clown all stood around in a circle and watched the bear with much interest.

"Now watch me eat the little girl," said the bear.

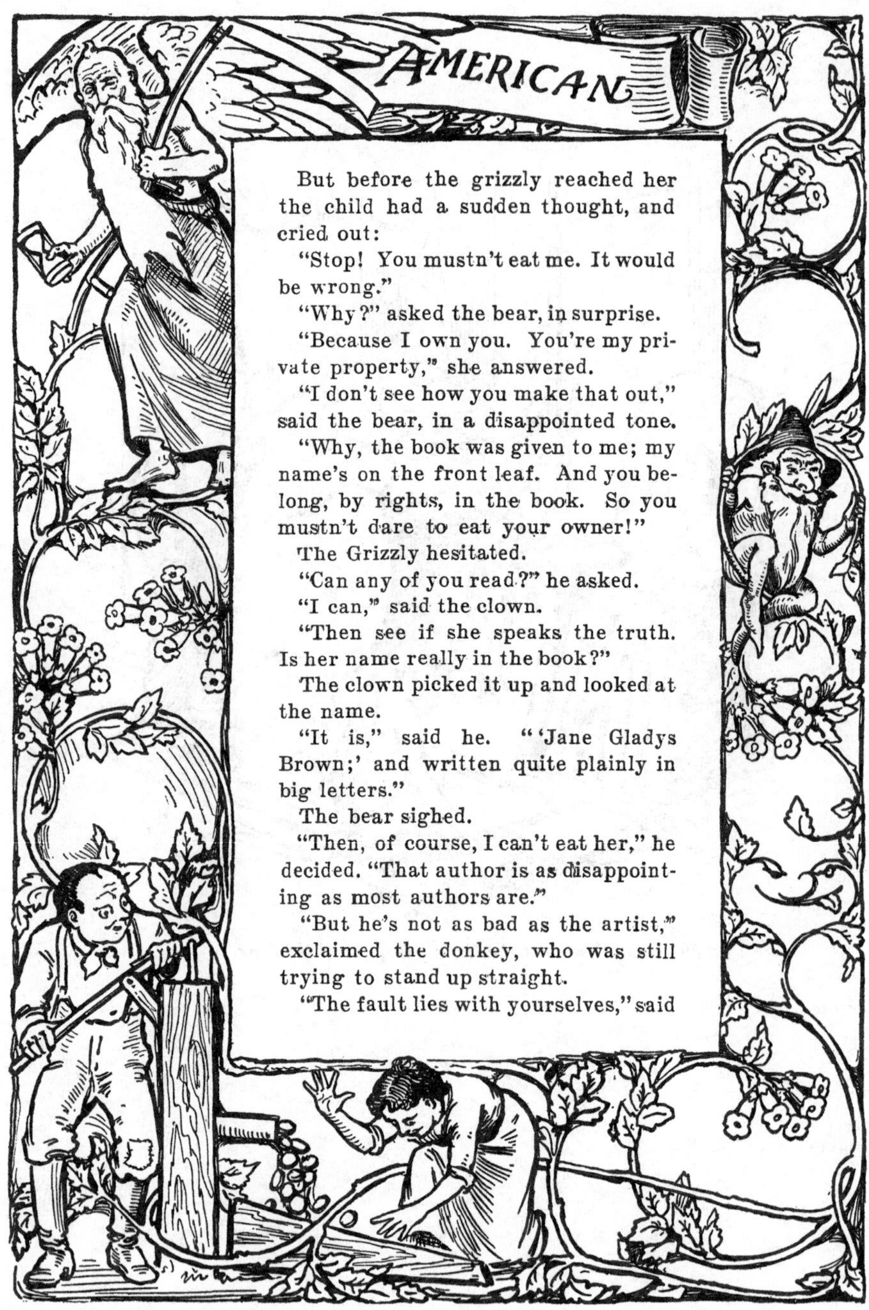

But before the grizzly reached her the child had a sudden thought, and cried out:

"Stop! You mustn't eat me. It would be wrong."

"Why?" asked the bear, in surprise.

"Because I own you. You're my private property," she answered.

"I don't see how you make that out," said the bear, in a disappointed tone.

"Why, the book was given to me; my name's on the front leaf. And you belong, by rights, in the book. So you mustn't dare to eat your owner!"

The Grizzly hesitated.

"Can any of you read?" he asked.

"I can," said the clown.

"Then see if she speaks the truth. Is her name really in the book?"

The clown picked it up and looked at the name.

"It is," said he. "'Jane Gladys Brown;' and written quite plainly in big letters."

The bear sighed.

"Then, of course, I can't eat her," he decided. "That author is as disappointing as most authors are."

"But he's not as bad as the artist," exclaimed the donkey, who was still trying to stand up straight.

"The fault lies with yourselves," said

Jane Gladys, severely. "Why didn't you stay in the book, where you were put?"

The animals looked at each other in a foolish way, and the clown blushed under his white paint.

"Really—" began the bear, and then he stopped short.

The door bell rang loudly.

"It's mamma!" cried Jane Gladys, springing to her feet. "She's come home at last. Now, you stupid creatures—"

But she was interrupted by them all making a rush for the book. There was a swish and a whirr and a rustling of leaves, and an instant later the book lay upon the floor looking just like any other book, while Jane Gladys' strange companions had all disappeared.

* * * * *

This story should teach us to think quickly and clearly upon all occasions; for had Jane Gladys not remembered that she owned the bear he probably would have eaten her before the bell rang.

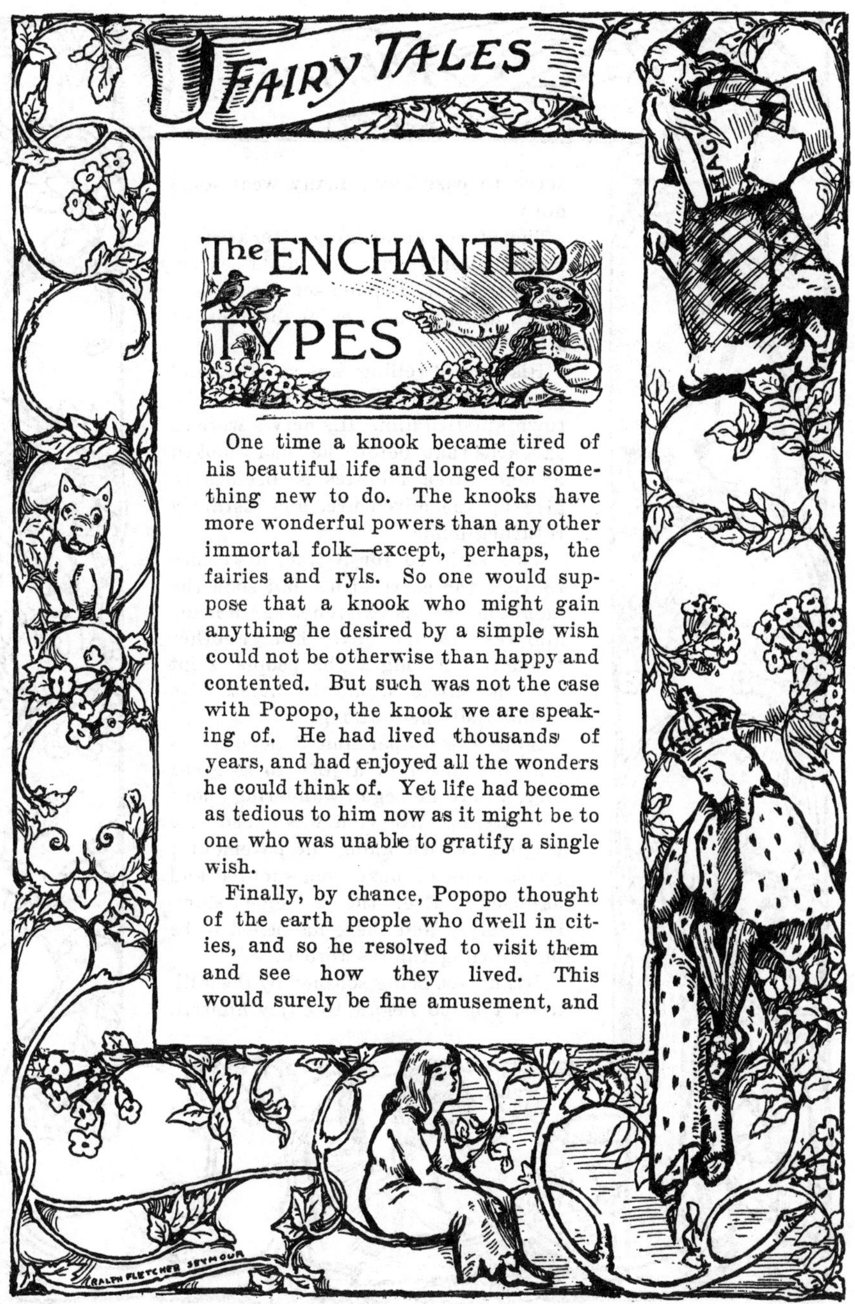

The ENCHANTED TYPES

One time a knook became tired of his beautiful life and longed for something new to do. The knooks have more wonderful powers than any other immortal folk—except, perhaps, the fairies and ryls. So one would suppose that a knook who might gain anything he desired by a simple wish could not be otherwise than happy and contented. But such was not the case with Popopo, the knook we are speaking of. He had lived thousands of years, and had enjoyed all the wonders he could think of. Yet life had become as tedious to him now as it might be to one who was unable to gratify a single wish.

Finally, by chance, Popopo thought of the earth people who dwell in cities, and so he resolved to visit them and see how they lived. This would surely be fine amusement, and

serve to pass away many wearisome hors.

Therefore one morning, after a breakfast so dainty that you could scarcely imagine it, Popopo set out for the earth and at once was in the midst of a big city.

His own dwelling was so quiet and peaceful that the roaring noise of the town startled him. His nerves were so shocked that before he had looked around three minutes he decided to give up the adventure, and instantly returned home.

This satisfied for a time his desire to visit the earth cities, but soon the monotony of his existence again made him restless and gave him another thought. At night the people slept and the cities would be quiet. He would visit them at night.

So at the proper time Popopo transported himself in a jiffy to a great city, where he began wandering about the streets. Everyone was in bed. No wagons rattled along the pavements; no throngs of busy men shouted and halloaed. Even the policemen slumbered slyly and there happened to be no prowling thieves abroad.

His nerves being soothed by the stillness, Popopo began to enjoy himself.

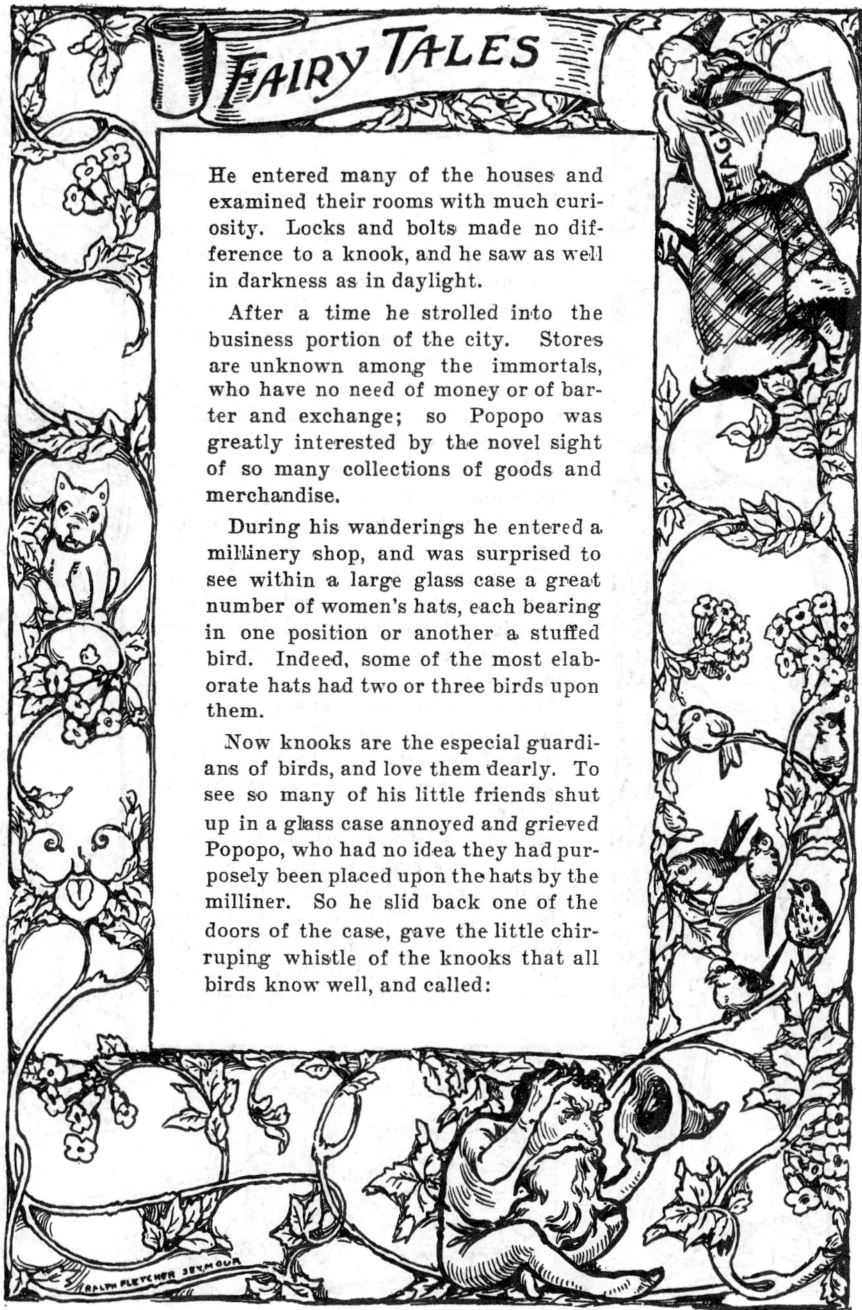

He entered many of the houses and examined their rooms with much curiosity. Locks and bolts made no difference to a knook, and he saw as well in darkness as in daylight.

After a time he strolled into the business portion of the city. Stores are unknown among the immortals, who have no need of money or of barter and exchange; so Popopo was greatly interested by the novel sight of so many collections of goods and merchandise.

During his wanderings he entered a millinery shop, and was surprised to see within a large glass case a great number of women's hats, each bearing in one position or another a stuffed bird. Indeed, some of the most elaborate hats had two or three birds upon them.

Now knooks are the especial guardians of birds, and love them dearly. To see so many of his little friends shut up in a glass case annoyed and grieved Popopo, who had no idea they had purposely been placed upon the hats by the milliner. So he slid back one of the doors of the case, gave the little chirruping whistle of the knooks that all birds know well, and called:

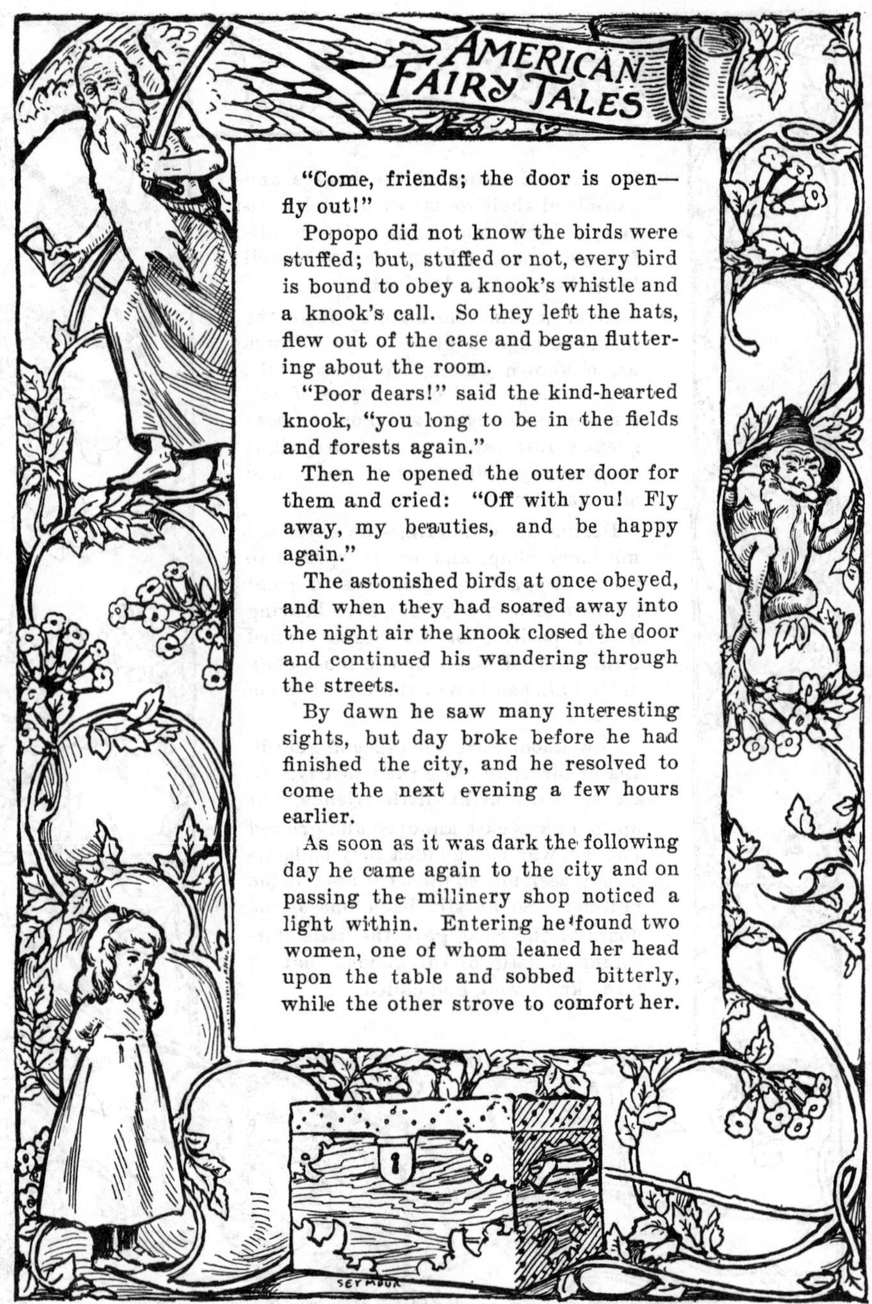

"Come, friends; the door is open—fly out!"

Popopo did not know the birds were stuffed; but, stuffed or not, every bird is bound to obey a knook's whistle and a knook's call. So they left the hats, flew out of the case and began fluttering about the room.

"Poor dears!" said the kind-hearted knook, "you long to be in the fields and forests again."

Then he opened the outer door for them and cried: "Off with you! Fly away, my beauties, and be happy again."

The astonished birds at once obeyed, and when they had soared away into the night air the knook closed the door and continued his wandering through the streets.

By dawn he saw many interesting sights, but day broke before he had finished the city, and he resolved to come the next evening a few hours earlier.

As soon as it was dark the following day he came again to the city and on passing the millinery shop noticed a light within. Entering he found two women, one of whom leaned her head upon the table and sobbed bitterly, while the other strove to comfort her.

"Come, friends, the door is open—fly out!"

Of course Popopo was invisible to mortal eyes, so he stood by and listened to their conversation.

"Cheer up, sister," said one. "Even though your pretty birds have all been stolen the hats themselves remain."

"Alas!" cried the other, who was the milliner, "no one will buy my hats partly trimmed, for the fashion is to wear birds upon them. And if I cannot sell my goods I shall be utterly ruined."

Then she renewed her sobbing and the knook stole away, feeling a little ashamed to realize that in his love for the birds he had unconsciously wronged one of the earth people and made her unhappy.

This thought brought him back to the millinery shop later in the night, when the two women had gone home. He wanted, in some way, to replace the birds upon the hats, that the poor woman might be happy again. So he searched until he came upon a nearby cellar full of little gray mice, who lived quite undisturbed and gained a livelihood by gnawing through the walls into neighboring houses and stealing food from the pantries.

"Here are just the creatures,"

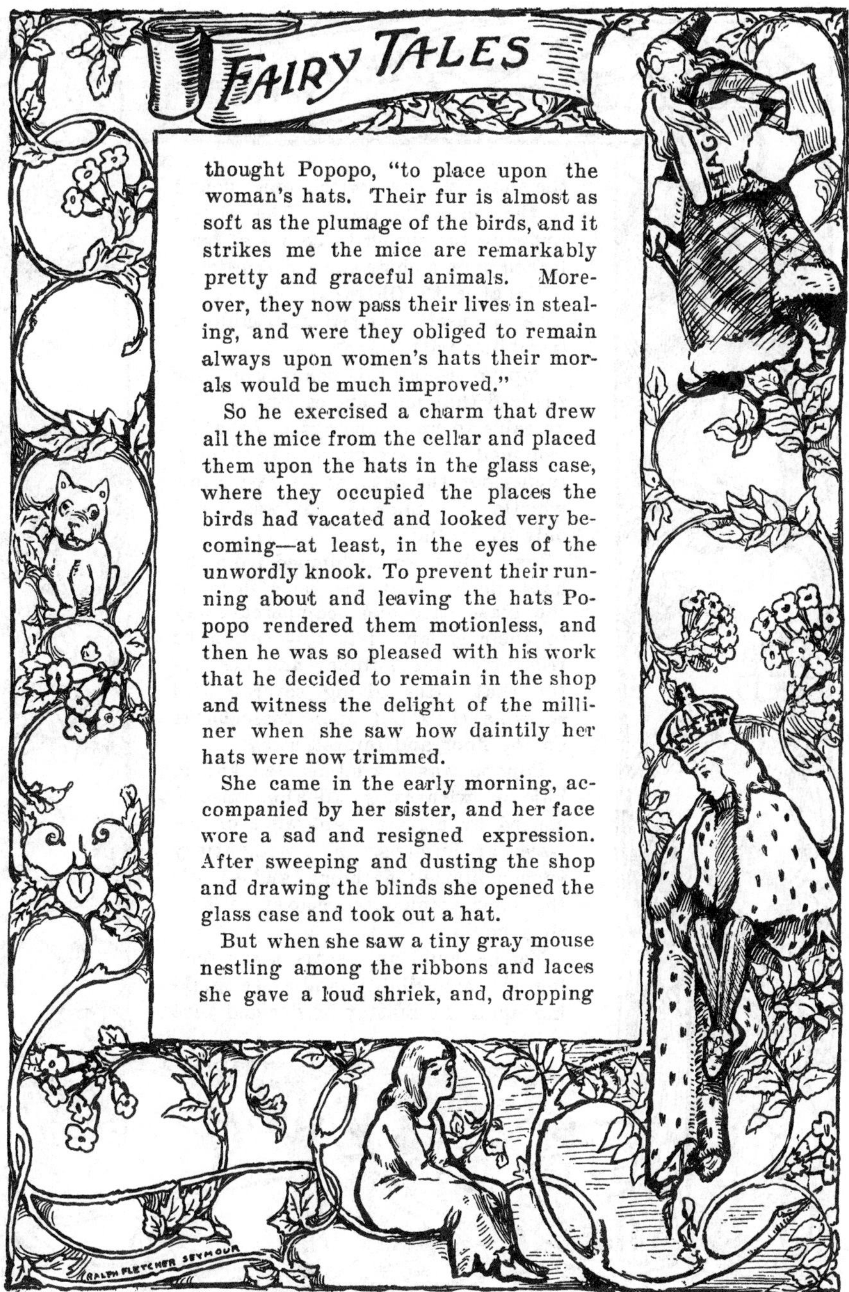

thought Popopo, "to place upon the woman's hats. Their fur is almost as soft as the plumage of the birds, and it strikes me the mice are remarkably pretty and graceful animals. Moreover, they now pass their lives in stealing, and were they obliged to remain always upon women's hats their morals would be much improved."

So he exercised a charm that drew all the mice from the cellar and placed them upon the hats in the glass case, where they occupied the places the birds had vacated and looked very becoming—at least, in the eyes of the unwordly knook. To prevent their running about and leaving the hats Popopo rendered them motionless, and then he was so pleased with his work that he decided to remain in the shop and witness the delight of the milliner when she saw how daintily her hats were now trimmed.

She came in the early morning, accompanied by her sister, and her face wore a sad and resigned expression. After sweeping and dusting the shop and drawing the blinds she opened the glass case and took out a hat.

But when she saw a tiny gray mouse nestling among the ribbons and laces she gave a loud shriek, and, dropping

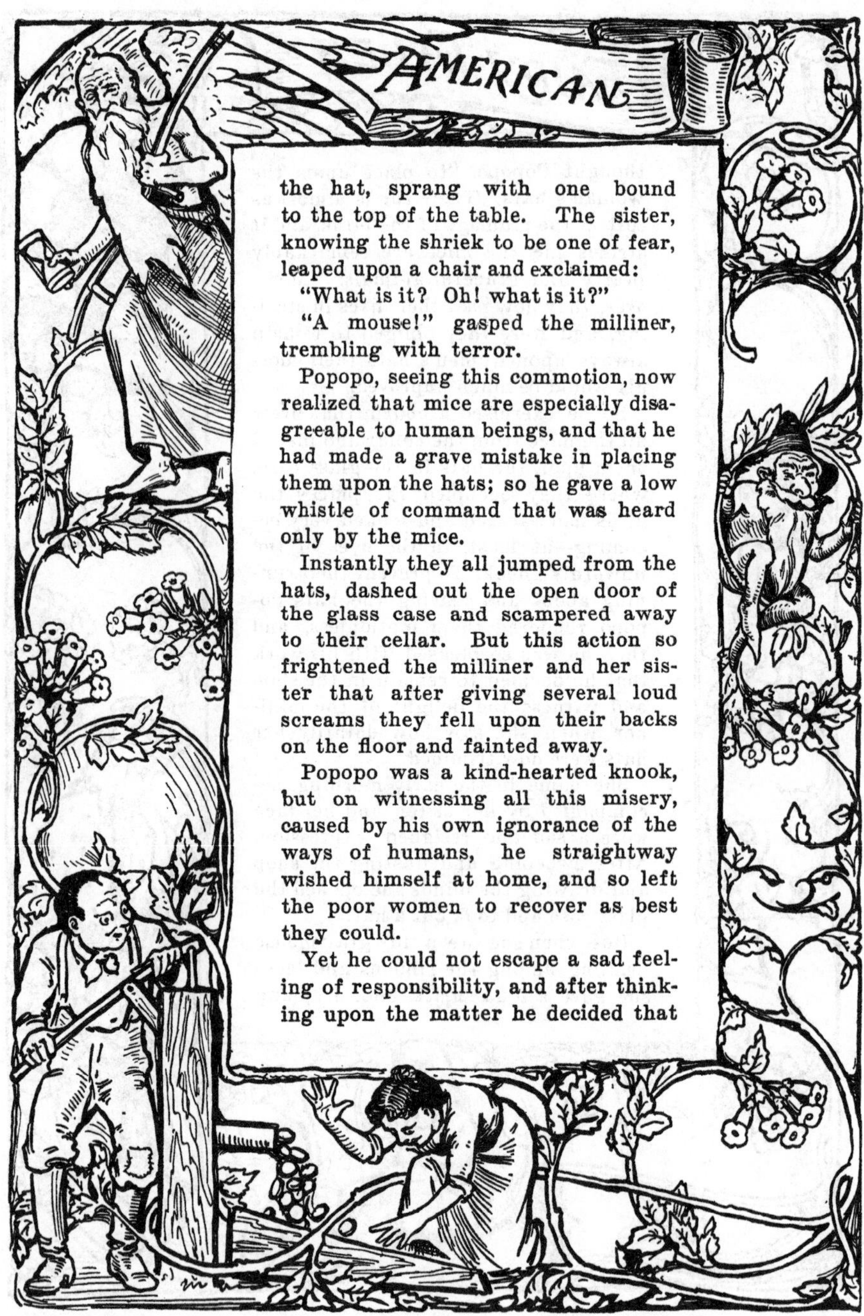

the hat, sprang with one bound to the top of the table. The sister, knowing the shriek to be one of fear, leaped upon a chair and exclaimed:

"What is it? Oh! what is it?"

"A mouse!" gasped the milliner, trembling with terror.

Popopo, seeing this commotion, now realized that mice are especially disagreeable to human beings, and that he had made a grave mistake in placing them upon the hats; so he gave a low whistle of command that was heard only by the mice.

Instantly they all jumped from the hats, dashed out the open door of the glass case and scampered away to their cellar. But this action so frightened the milliner and her sister that after giving several loud screams they fell upon their backs on the floor and fainted away.

Popopo was a kind-hearted knook, but on witnessing all this misery, caused by his own ignorance of the ways of humans, he straightway wished himself at home, and so left the poor women to recover as best they could.

Yet he could not escape a sad feeling of responsibility, and after thinking upon the matter he decided that

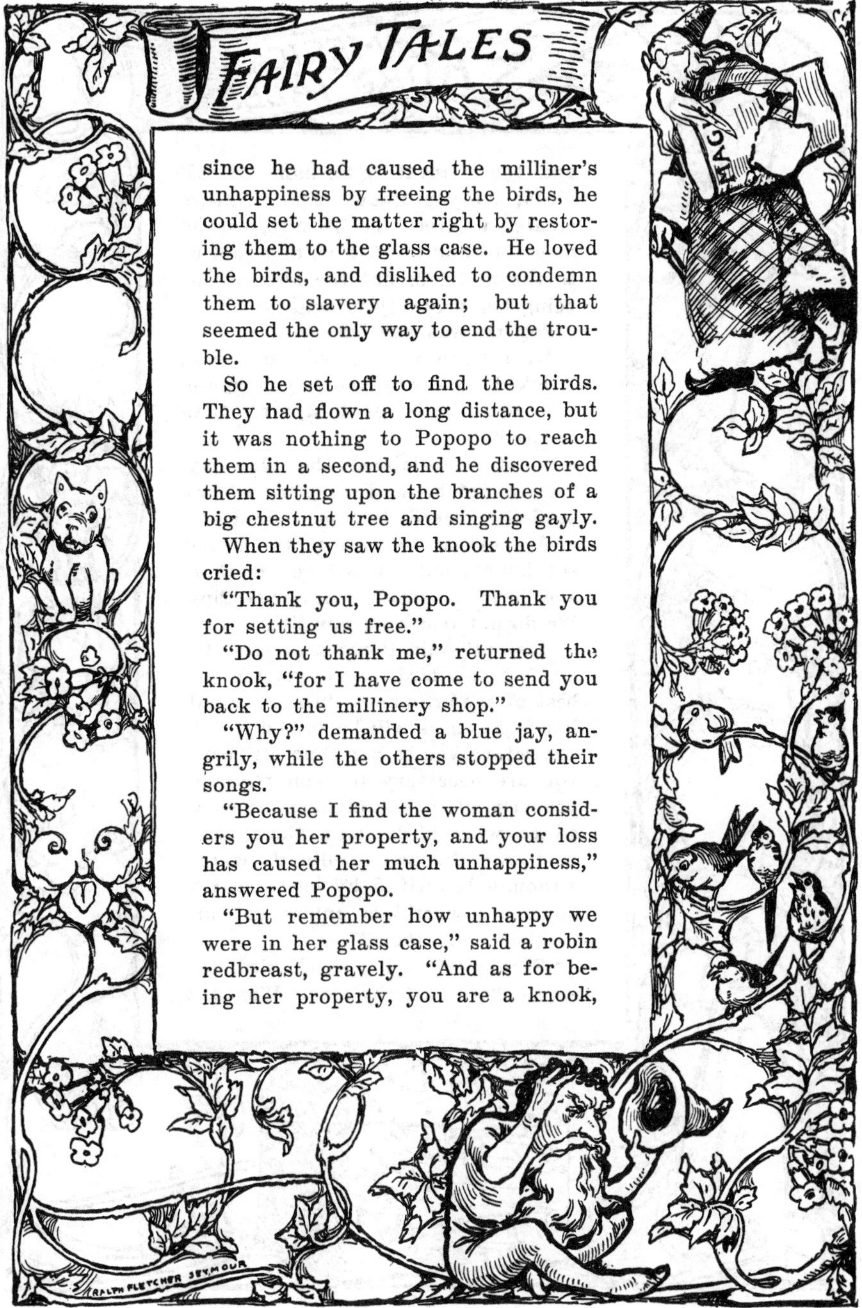

since he had caused the milliner's unhappiness by freeing the birds, he could set the matter right by restoring them to the glass case. He loved the birds, and disliked to condemn them to slavery again; but that seemed the only way to end the trouble.

So he set off to find the birds. They had flown a long distance, but it was nothing to Popopo to reach them in a second, and he discovered them sitting upon the branches of a big chestnut tree and singing gayly.

When they saw the knook the birds cried:

"Thank you, Popopo. Thank you for setting us free."

"Do not thank me," returned the knook, "for I have come to send you back to the millinery shop."

"Why?" demanded a blue jay, angrily, while the others stopped their songs.

"Because I find the woman considers you her property, and your loss has caused her much unhappiness," answered Popopo.

"But remember how unhappy we were in her glass case," said a robin redbreast, gravely. "And as for being her property, you are a knook,

and the natural guardian of all birds; so you know that Nature created us free. To be sure, wicked men shot and stuffed us, and sold us to the milliner; but the idea of our being her property is nonsense!"

Popopo was puzzled.

"If I leave you free," he said, "wicked men will shoot you again, and you will be no better off than before."

"Pooh!" exclaimed the blue jay, "we cannot be shot now, for we are stuffed. Indeed, two men fired several shots at us this morning, but the bullets only ruffled our feathers and buried themselves in our stuffing. We do not fear men now."

"Listen!" said Popopo, sternly, for he felt the birds were getting the best of the argument; "the poor milliner's business will be ruined if I do not return you to her shop. It seems you are necessary to trim the hats properly. It is the fashion for women to wear birds upon their headgear. So the poor milliner's wares, although beautified by lace and ribbons, are worthless unless you are perched upon them."

"Fashions," said a black bird, solemnly, "are made by men. What law

"We do not fear men now."

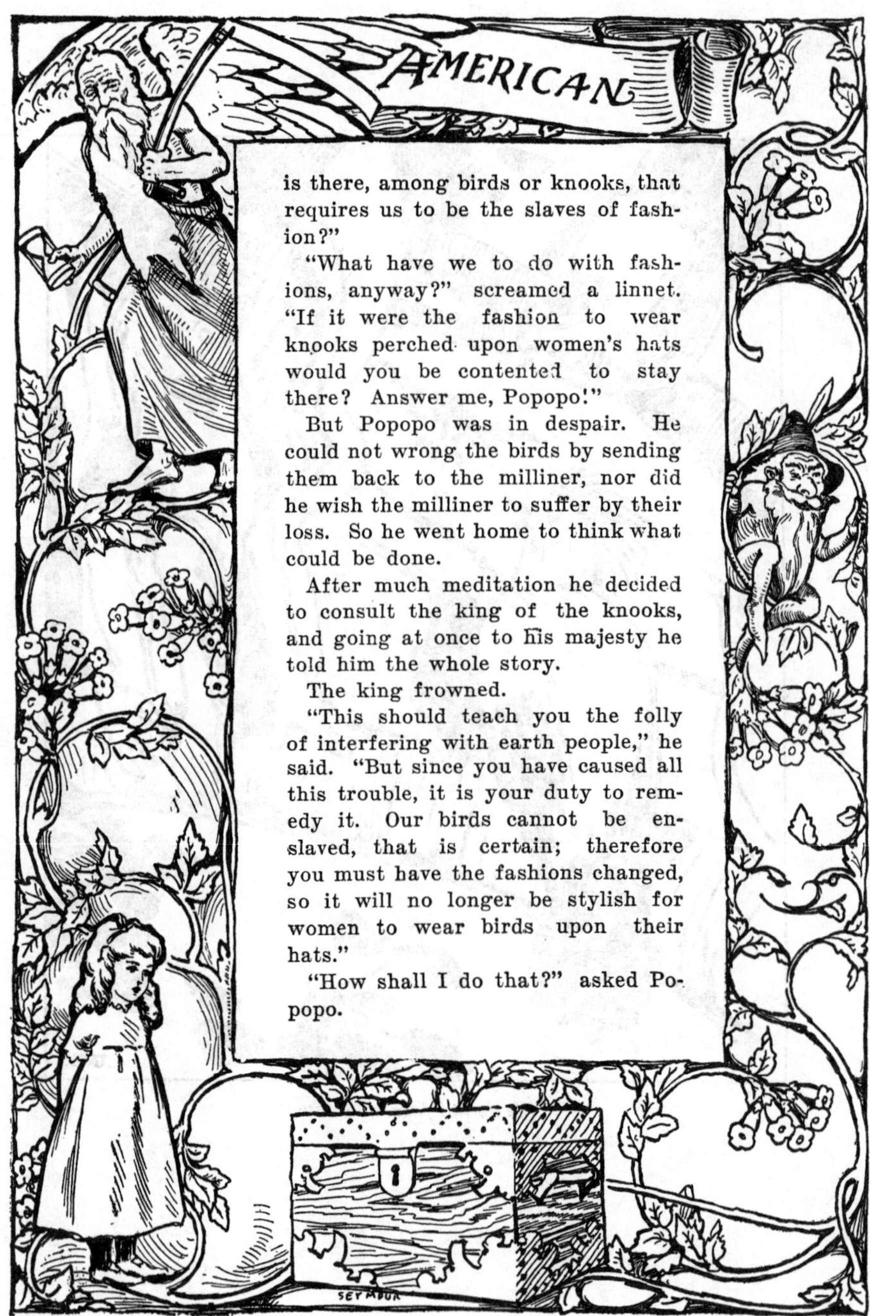

is there, among birds or knooks, that requires us to be the slaves of fashion?"

"What have we to do with fashions, anyway?" screamed a linnet. "If it were the fashion to wear knooks perched upon women's hats would you be contented to stay there? Answer me, Popopo!"

But Popopo was in despair. He could not wrong the birds by sending them back to the milliner, nor did he wish the milliner to suffer by their loss. So he went home to think what could be done.

After much meditation he decided to consult the king of the knooks, and going at once to his majesty he told him the whole story.

The king frowned.

"This should teach you the folly of interfering with earth people," he said. "But since you have caused all this trouble, it is your duty to remedy it. Our birds cannot be enslaved, that is certain; therefore you must have the fashions changed, so it will no longer be stylish for women to wear birds upon their hats."

"How shall I do that?" asked Popopo.

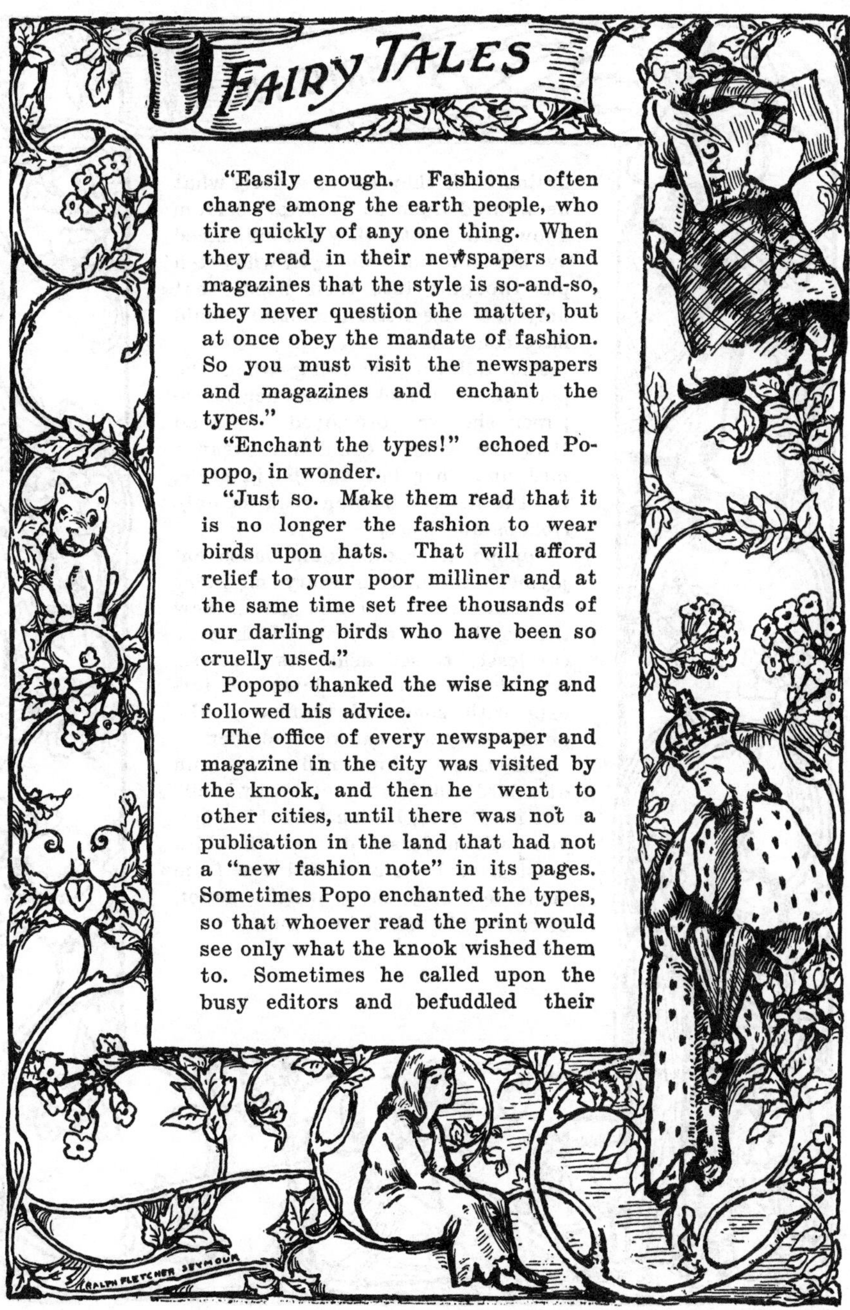

"Easily enough. Fashions often change among the earth people, who tire quickly of any one thing. When they read in their newspapers and magazines that the style is so-and-so, they never question the matter, but at once obey the mandate of fashion. So you must visit the newspapers and magazines and enchant the types."

"Enchant the types!" echoed Popopo, in wonder.

"Just so. Make them read that it is no longer the fashion to wear birds upon hats. That will afford relief to your poor milliner and at the same time set free thousands of our darling birds who have been so cruelly used."

Popopo thanked the wise king and followed his advice.

The office of every newspaper and magazine in the city was visited by the knook, and then he went to other cities, until there was not a publication in the land that had not a "new fashion note" in its pages. Sometimes Popo enchanted the types, so that whoever read the print would see only what the knook wished them to. Sometimes he called upon the busy editors and befuddled their

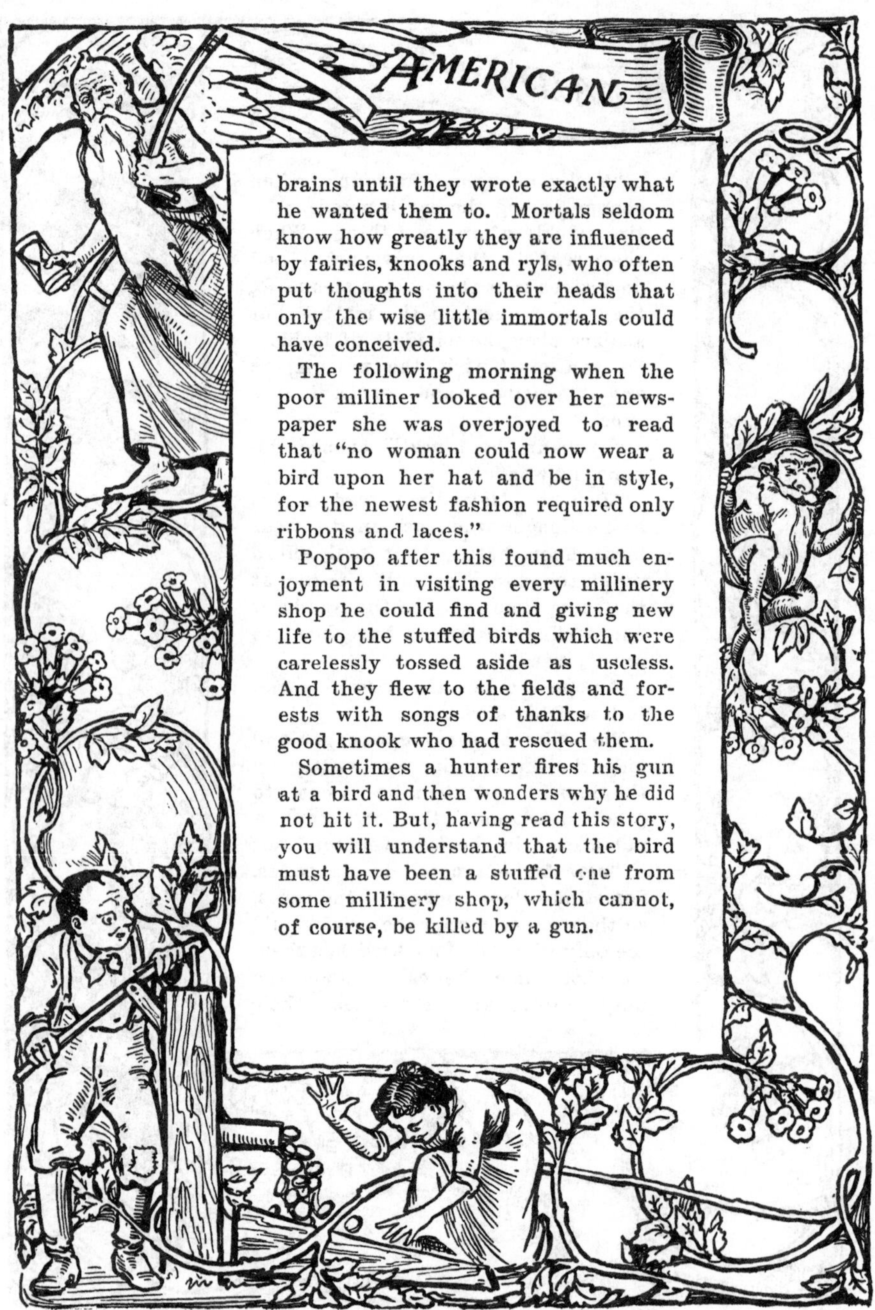

brains until they wrote exactly what he wanted them to. Mortals seldom know how greatly they are influenced by fairies, knooks and ryls, who often put thoughts into their heads that only the wise little immortals could have conceived.

The following morning when the poor milliner looked over her newspaper she was overjoyed to read that "no woman could now wear a bird upon her hat and be in style, for the newest fashion required only ribbons and laces."

Popopo after this found much enjoyment in visiting every millinery shop he could find and giving new life to the stuffed birds which were carelessly tossed aside as useless. And they flew to the fields and forests with songs of thanks to the good knook who had rescued them.

Sometimes a hunter fires his gun at a bird and then wonders why he did not hit it. But, having read this story, you will understand that the bird must have been a stuffed one from some millinery shop, which cannot, of course, be killed by a gun.

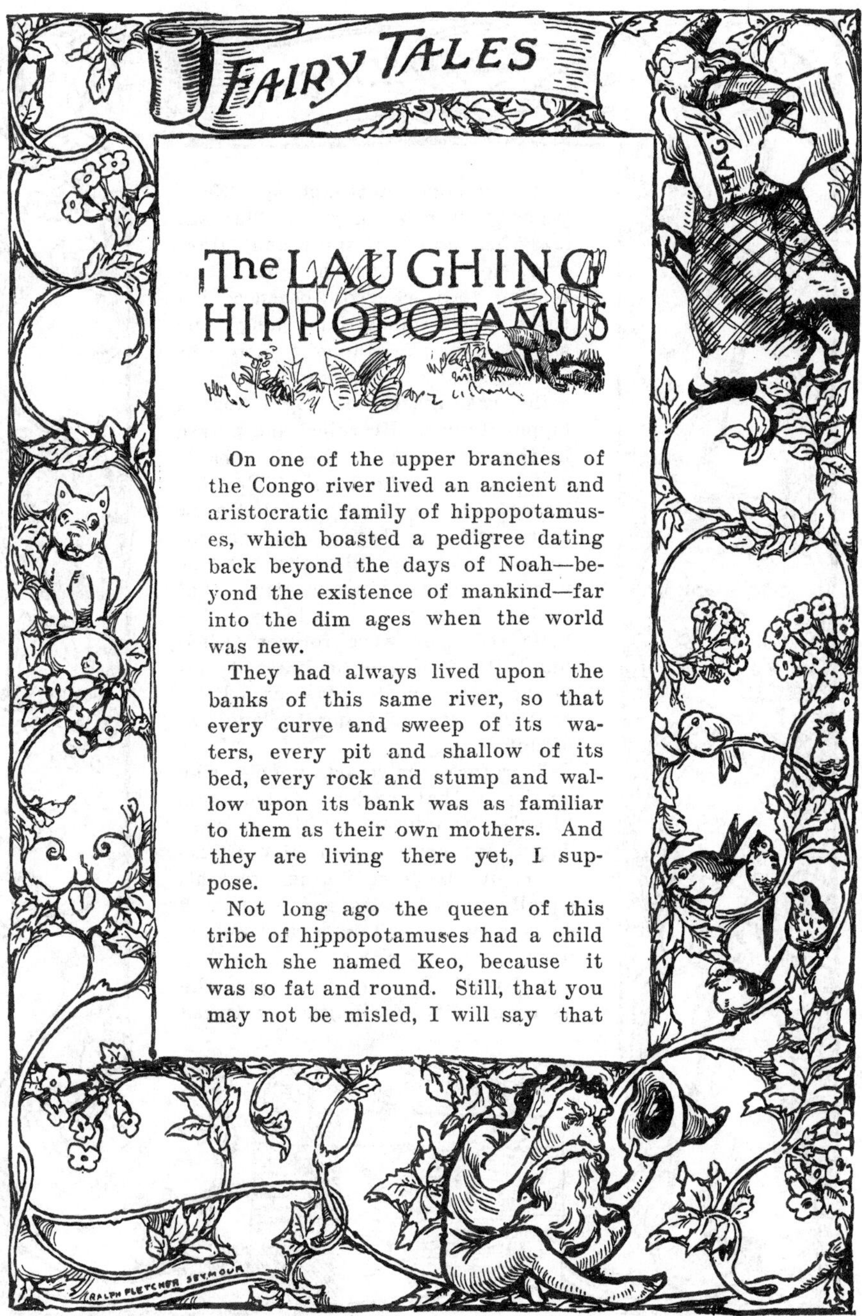

The LAUGHING HIPPOPOTAMUS

On one of the upper branches of the Congo river lived an ancient and aristocratic family of hippopotamuses, which boasted a pedigree dating back beyond the days of Noah—beyond the existence of mankind—far into the dim ages when the world was new.

They had always lived upon the banks of this same river, so that every curve and sweep of its waters, every pit and shallow of its bed, every rock and stump and wallow upon its bank was as familiar to them as their own mothers. And they are living there yet, I suppose.

Not long ago the queen of this tribe of hippopotamuses had a child which she named Keo, because it was so fat and round. Still, that you may not be misled, I will say that

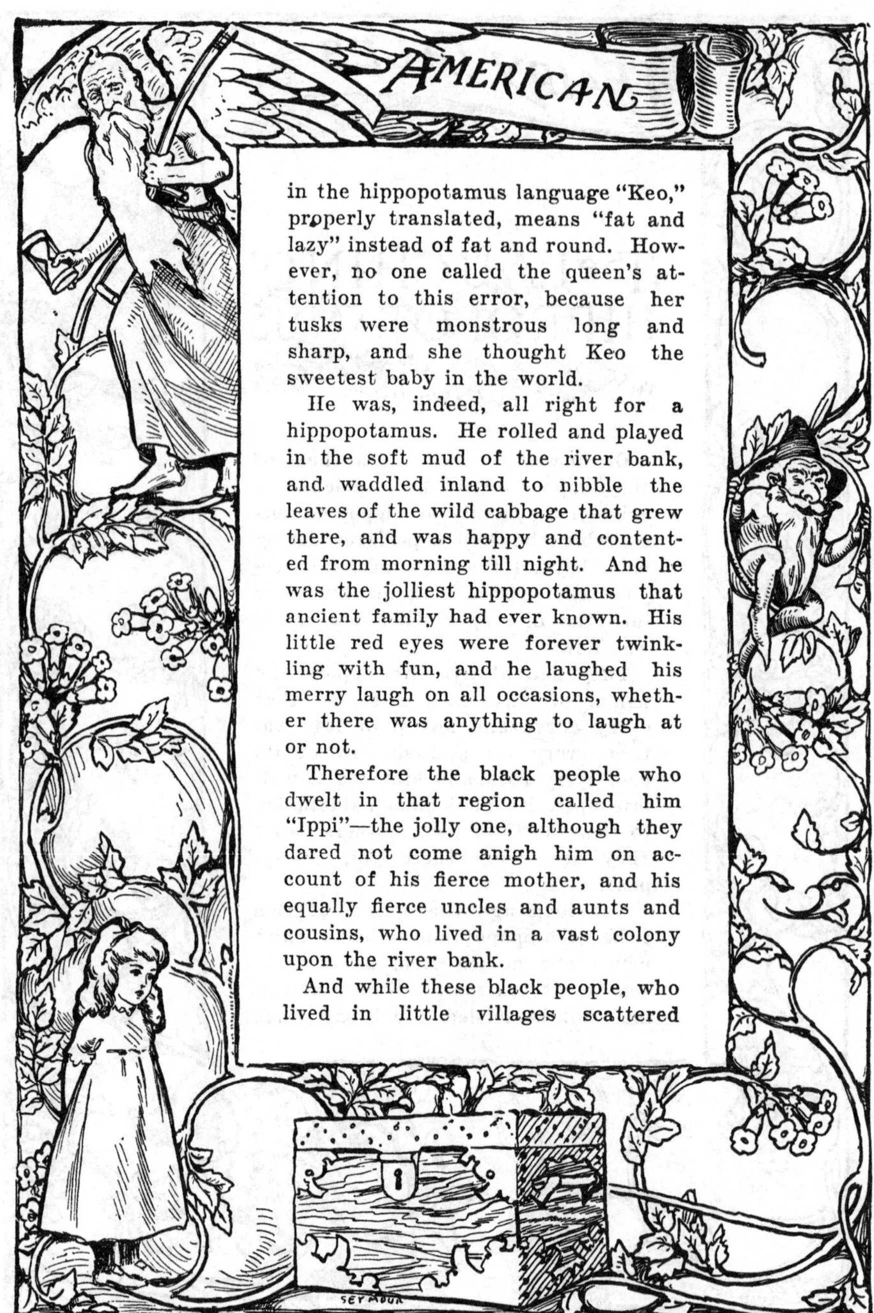

in the hippopotamus language "Keo," properly translated, means "fat and lazy" instead of fat and round. However, no one called the queen's attention to this error, because her tusks were monstrous long and sharp, and she thought Keo the sweetest baby in the world.

He was, indeed, all right for a hippopotamus. He rolled and played in the soft mud of the river bank, and waddled inland to nibble the leaves of the wild cabbage that grew there, and was happy and contented from morning till night. And he was the jolliest hippopotamus that ancient family had ever known. His little red eyes were forever twinkling with fun, and he laughed his merry laugh on all occasions, whether there was anything to laugh at or not.

Therefore the black people who dwelt in that region called him "Ippi"—the jolly one, although they dared not come anigh him on account of his fierce mother, and his equally fierce uncles and aunts and cousins, who lived in a vast colony upon the river bank.

And while these black people, who lived in little villages scattered

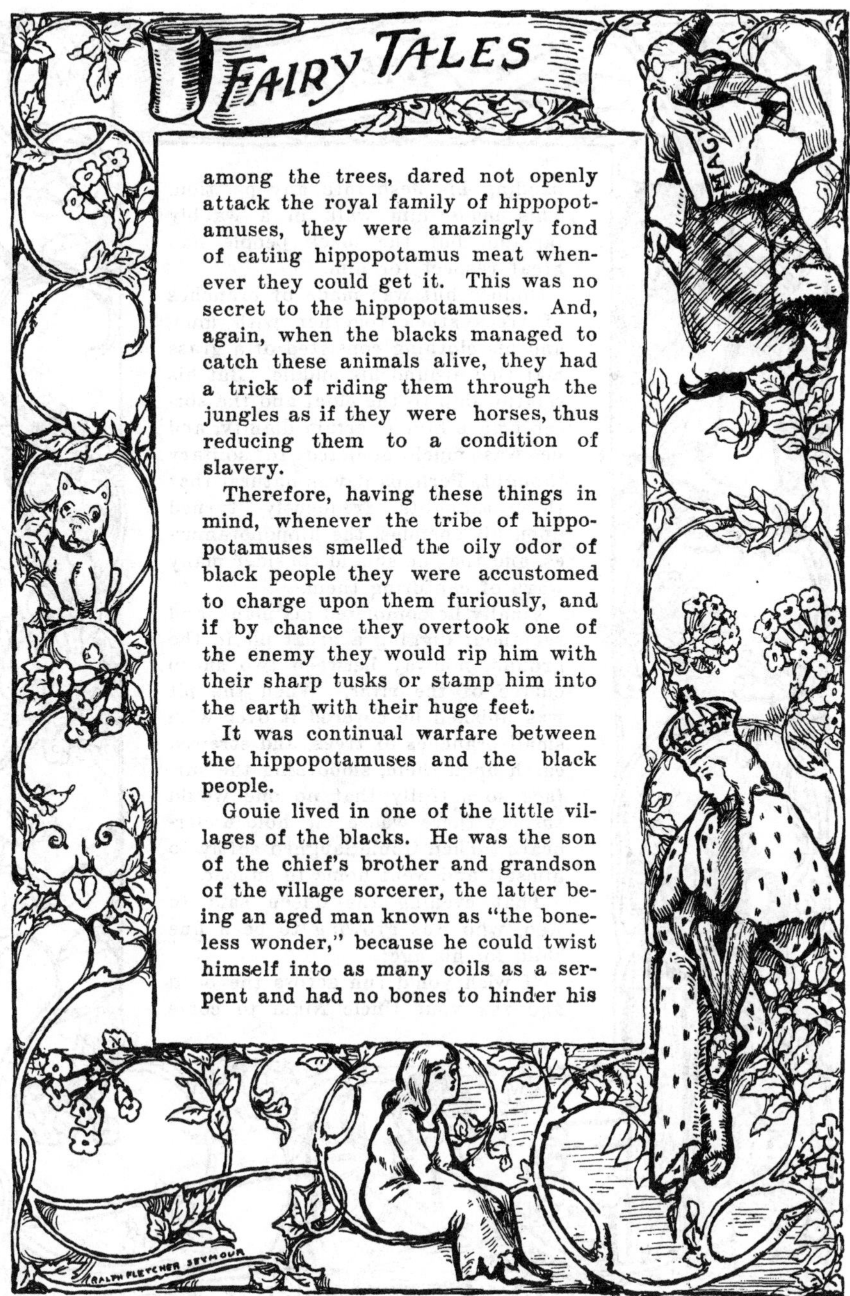

among the trees, dared not openly attack the royal family of hippopotamuses, they were amazingly fond of eating hippopotamus meat whenever they could get it. This was no secret to the hippopotamuses. And, again, when the blacks managed to catch these animals alive, they had a trick of riding them through the jungles as if they were horses, thus reducing them to a condition of slavery.

Therefore, having these things in mind, whenever the tribe of hippopotamuses smelled the oily odor of black people they were accustomed to charge upon them furiously, and if by chance they overtook one of the enemy they would rip him with their sharp tusks or stamp him into the earth with their huge feet.

It was continual warfare between the hippopotamuses and the black people.

Gouie lived in one of the little villages of the blacks. He was the son of the chief's brother and grandson of the village sorcerer, the latter being an aged man known as "the boneless wonder," because he could twist himself into as many coils as a serpent and had no bones to hinder his

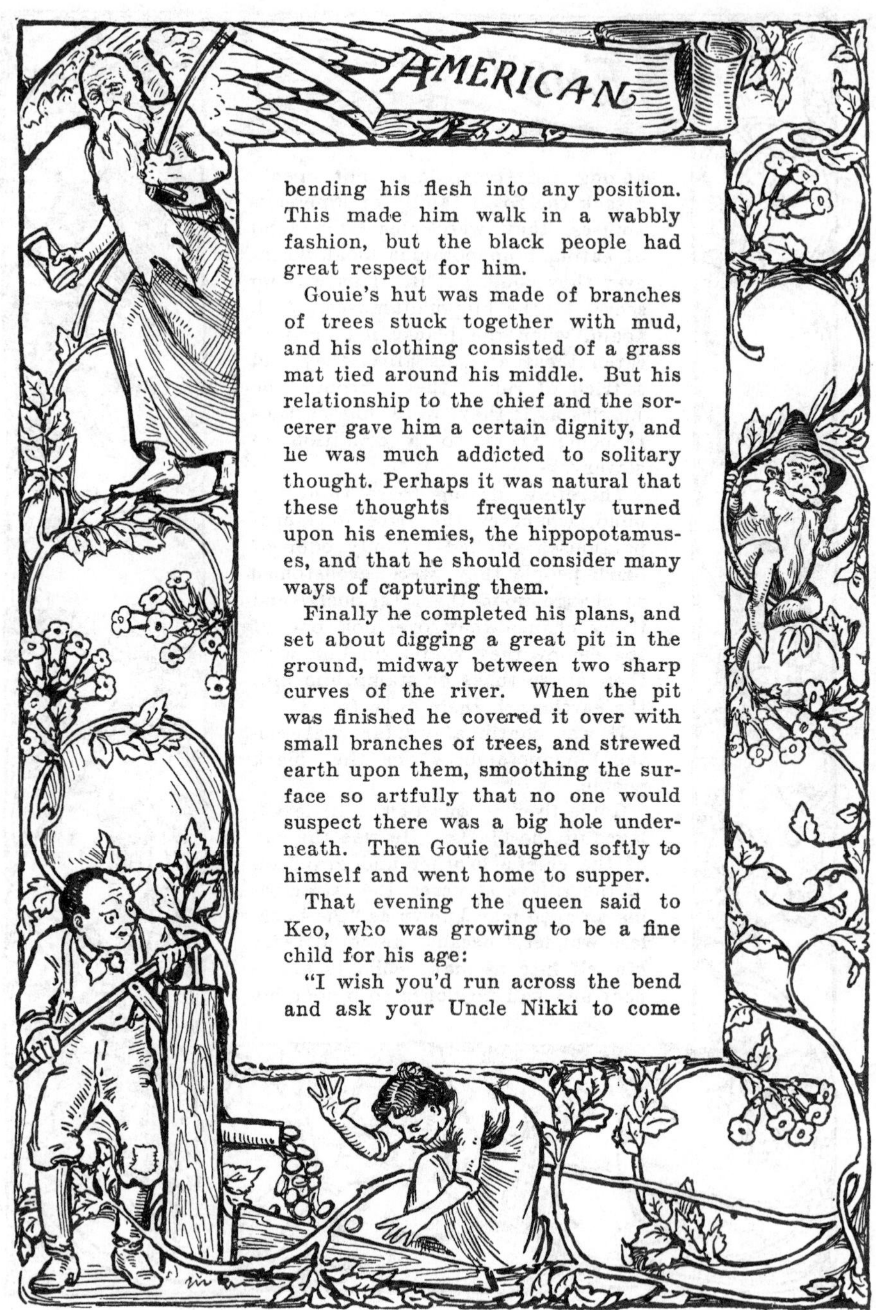

bending his flesh into any position. This made him walk in a wabbly fashion, but the black people had great respect for him.

Gouie's hut was made of branches of trees stuck together with mud, and his clothing consisted of a grass mat tied around his middle. But his relationship to the chief and the sorcerer gave him a certain dignity, and he was much addicted to solitary thought. Perhaps it was natural that these thoughts frequently turned upon his enemies, the hippopotamuses, and that he should consider many ways of capturing them.

Finally he completed his plans, and set about digging a great pit in the ground, midway between two sharp curves of the river. When the pit was finished he covered it over with small branches of trees, and strewed earth upon them, smoothing the surface so artfully that no one would suspect there was a big hole underneath. Then Gouie laughed softly to himself and went home to supper.

That evening the queen said to Keo, who was growing to be a fine child for his age:

"I wish you'd run across the bend and ask your Uncle Nikki to come

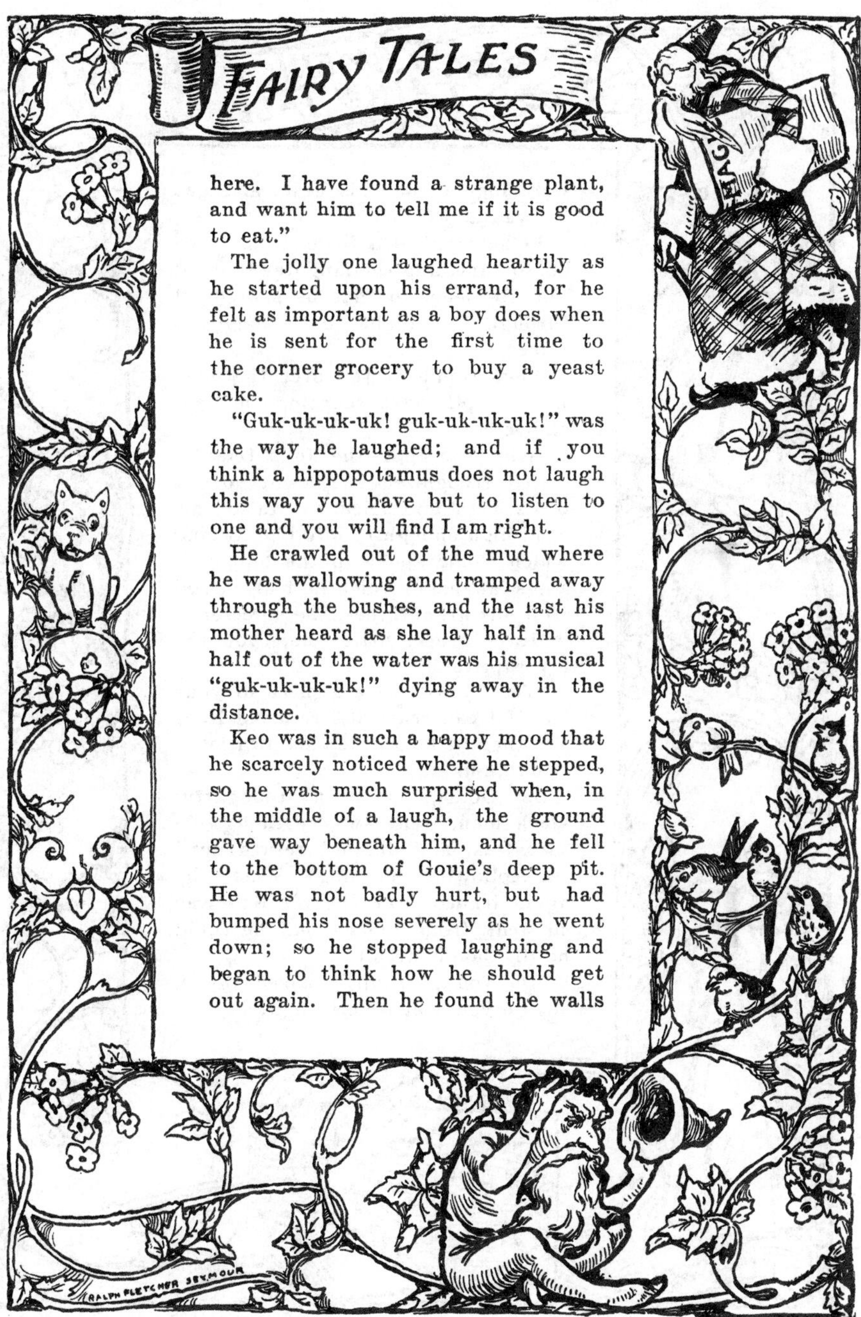

here. I have found a strange plant, and want him to tell me if it is good to eat."

The jolly one laughed heartily as he started upon his errand, for he felt as important as a boy does when he is sent for the first time to the corner grocery to buy a yeast cake.

"Guk-uk-uk-uk! guk-uk-uk-uk!" was the way he laughed; and if you think a hippopotamus does not laugh this way you have but to listen to one and you will find I am right.

He crawled out of the mud where he was wallowing and tramped away through the bushes, and the last his mother heard as she lay half in and half out of the water was his musical "guk-uk-uk-uk!" dying away in the distance.

Keo was in such a happy mood that he scarcely noticed where he stepped, so he was much surprised when, in the middle of a laugh, the ground gave way beneath him, and he fell to the bottom of Gouie's deep pit. He was not badly hurt, but had bumped his nose severely as he went down; so he stopped laughing and began to think how he should get out again. Then he found the walls

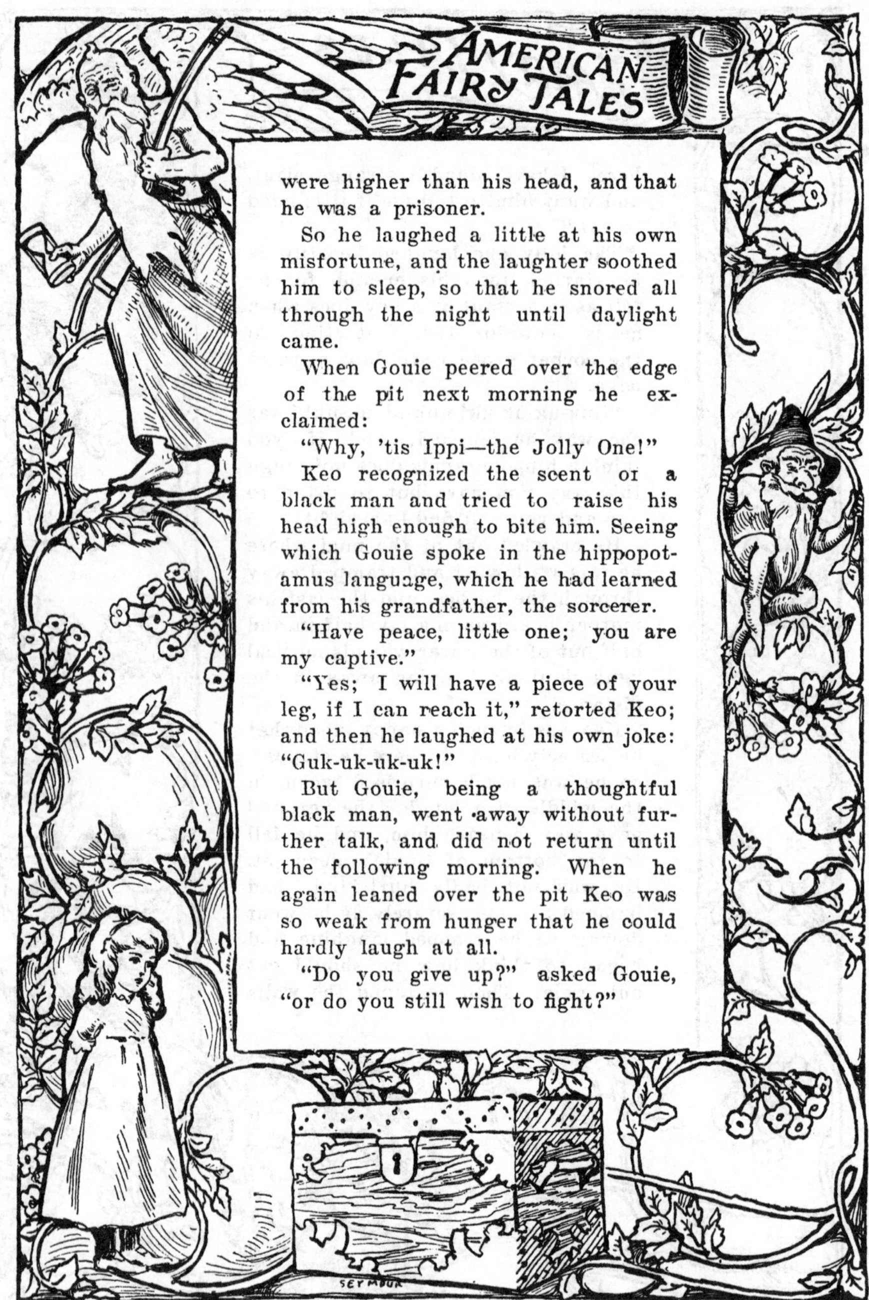

were higher than his head, and that he was a prisoner.

So he laughed a little at his own misfortune, and the laughter soothed him to sleep, so that he snored all through the night until daylight came.

When Gouie peered over the edge of the pit next morning he exclaimed:

"Why, 'tis Ippi—the Jolly One!"

Keo recognized the scent or a black man and tried to raise his head high enough to bite him. Seeing which Gouie spoke in the hippopotamus language, which he had learned from his grandfather, the sorcerer.

"Have peace, little one; you are my captive."

"Yes; I will have a piece of your leg, if I can reach it," retorted Keo; and then he laughed at his own joke: "Guk-uk-uk-uk!"

But Gouie, being a thoughtful black man, went away without further talk, and did not return until the following morning. When he again leaned over the pit Keo was so weak from hunger that he could hardly laugh at all.

"Do you give up?" asked Gouie, "or do you still wish to fight?"

"Why, 'tis Ippi—the Jolly One."

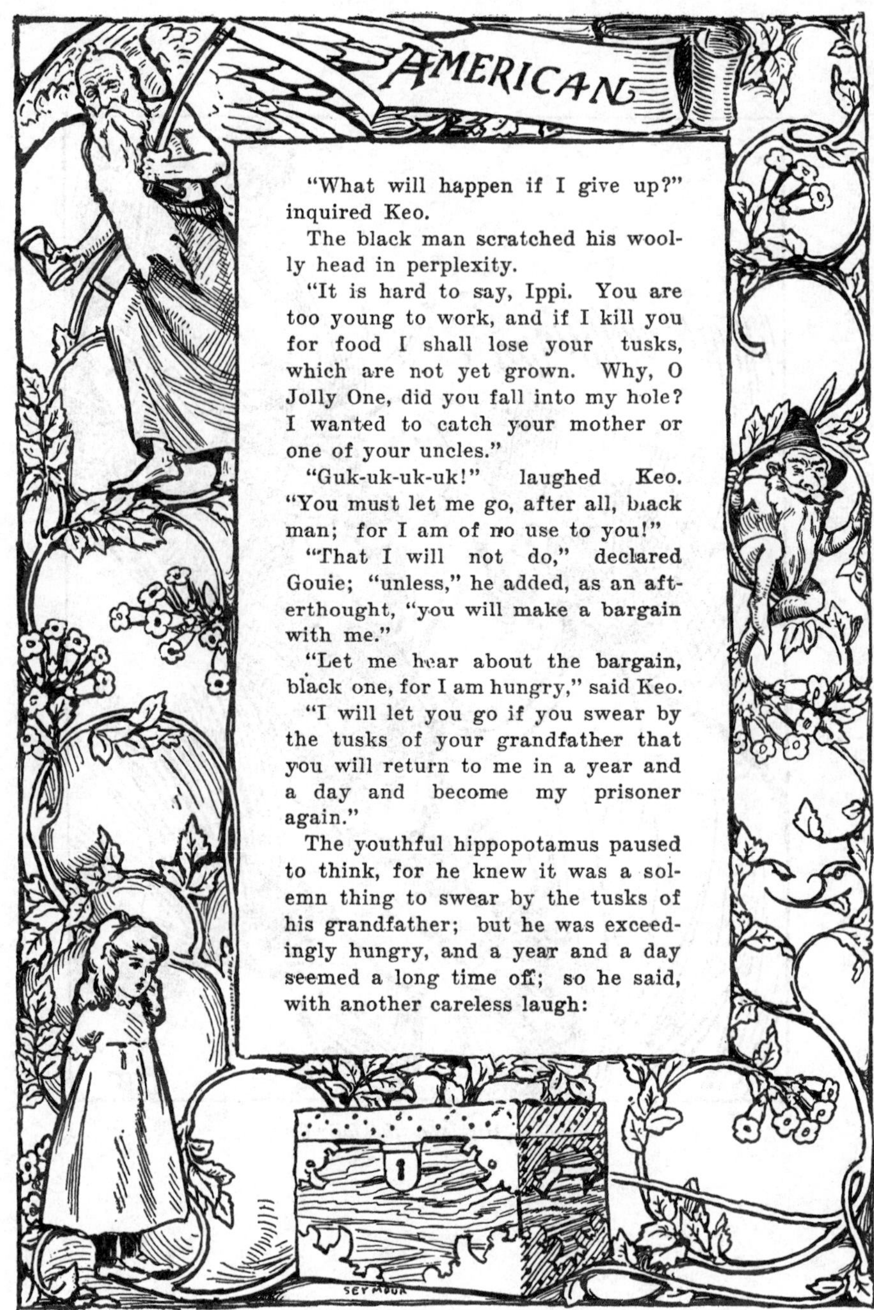

"What will happen if I give up?" inquired Keo.

The black man scratched his woolly head in perplexity.

"It is hard to say, Ippi. You are too young to work, and if I kill you for food I shall lose your tusks, which are not yet grown. Why, O Jolly One, did you fall into my hole? I wanted to catch your mother or one of your uncles."

"Guk-uk-uk-uk!" laughed Keo. "You must let me go, after all, black man; for I am of no use to you!"

"That I will not do," declared Gouie; "unless," he added, as an afterthought, "you will make a bargain with me."

"Let me hear about the bargain, black one, for I am hungry," said Keo.

"I will let you go if you swear by the tusks of your grandfather that you will return to me in a year and a day and become my prisoner again."

The youthful hippopotamus paused to think, for he knew it was a solemn thing to swear by the tusks of his grandfather; but he was exceedingly hungry, and a year and a day seemed a long time off; so he said, with another careless laugh:

"Very well; if you will now let me go I swear by the tusks of my grandfather to return to you in a year and a day and become your prisoner."

Gouie was much pleased, for he knew that in a year and a day Keo would be almost full grown. So he began digging away one end of the pit and filling it up with the earth until he had made an incline which would allow the hippopotamus to climb out.

Keo was so pleased when he found himself upon the surface of the earth again that he indulged in a merry fit of laughter, after which he said:

"Good-by, Gouie; in a year and a day you will see me again."

Then he waddled away toward the river to see his mother and get his breakfast, and Gouie returned to his village.

During the months that followed, as the black man lay in his hut or hunted in the forest, he heard at times the faraway "Guk-uk-uk-uk!" of the laughing hippopotamus. But he only smiled to himself and thought: "A year and a day will soon pass away!"

Now when Keo returned to his mother safe and well every member of his tribe was filled with joy, for the Jolly One was a general favorite. But when he told them that in a year and a day he must again become the slave of the black man, they began to wail and weep, and so many were their tears that the river rose several inches.

Of course Keo only laughed at their sorrow; but a great meeting of the tribe was called and the matter discussed seriously.

"Having sworn by the tusks of his grandfather," said Uncle Nikki, "he must keep his promise. But it is our duty to try in some way to rescue him from death or a life of slavery."

To this all agreed, but no one could think of any method of saving Keo from his fate. So months passed away, during which all the royal hippopotamuses were sad and gloomy except the Jolly One himself.

Finally but a week of freedom remained to Keo, and his mother, the queen, became so nervous and worried that another meeting of the tribe was called. By this time the laughing hippopotamus had grown

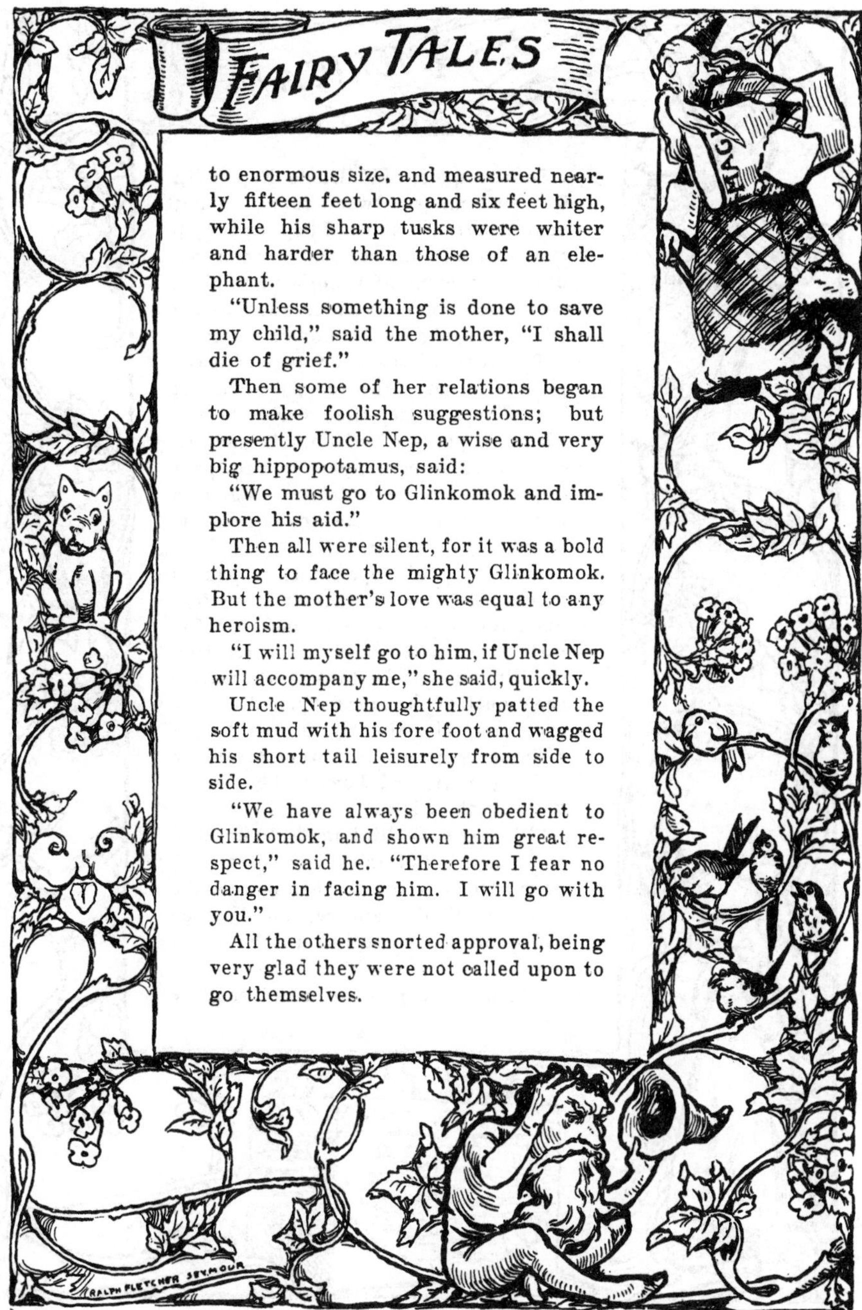

to enormous size, and measured nearly fifteen feet long and six feet high, while his sharp tusks were whiter and harder than those of an elephant.

"Unless something is done to save my child," said the mother, "I shall die of grief."

Then some of her relations began to make foolish suggestions; but presently Uncle Nep, a wise and very big hippopotamus, said:

"We must go to Glinkomok and implore his aid."

Then all were silent, for it was a bold thing to face the mighty Glinkomok. But the mother's love was equal to any heroism.

"I will myself go to him, if Uncle Nep will accompany me," she said, quickly.

Uncle Nep thoughtfully patted the soft mud with his fore foot and wagged his short tail leisurely from side to side.

"We have always been obedient to Glinkomok, and shown him great respect," said he. "Therefore I fear no danger in facing him. I will go with you."

All the others snorted approval, being very glad they were not called upon to go themselves.

So the queen and Uncle Nep, with Keo swimming between them, set out upon their journey. They swam up the river all that day and all the next, until they came at sundown to a high, rocky wall, beneath which was the cave where the mighty Glinkomok dwelt.

This fearful creature was part beast, part man, part fowl and part fish. It had lived since the world began. Through years of wisdom it had become part sorcerer, part wizard, part magician and part fairy. Mankind knew it not, but the ancient beasts knew and feared it.

The three hippopotamuses paused before the cave, with their front feet upon the bank and their bodies in the water, and called in chorus a greeting to Glinkomok. Instantly thereafter the mouth of the cave darkened and the creature glided silently toward them.

The hippopotamuses were afraid to look upon it, and bowed their heads between their legs.

"We come, O Glinkomok, to implore your mercy and friendly assistance!" began Uncle Nep; and then he told the story of Keo's capture, and how he had promised to return to the black man.

"He must keep his promise," said the

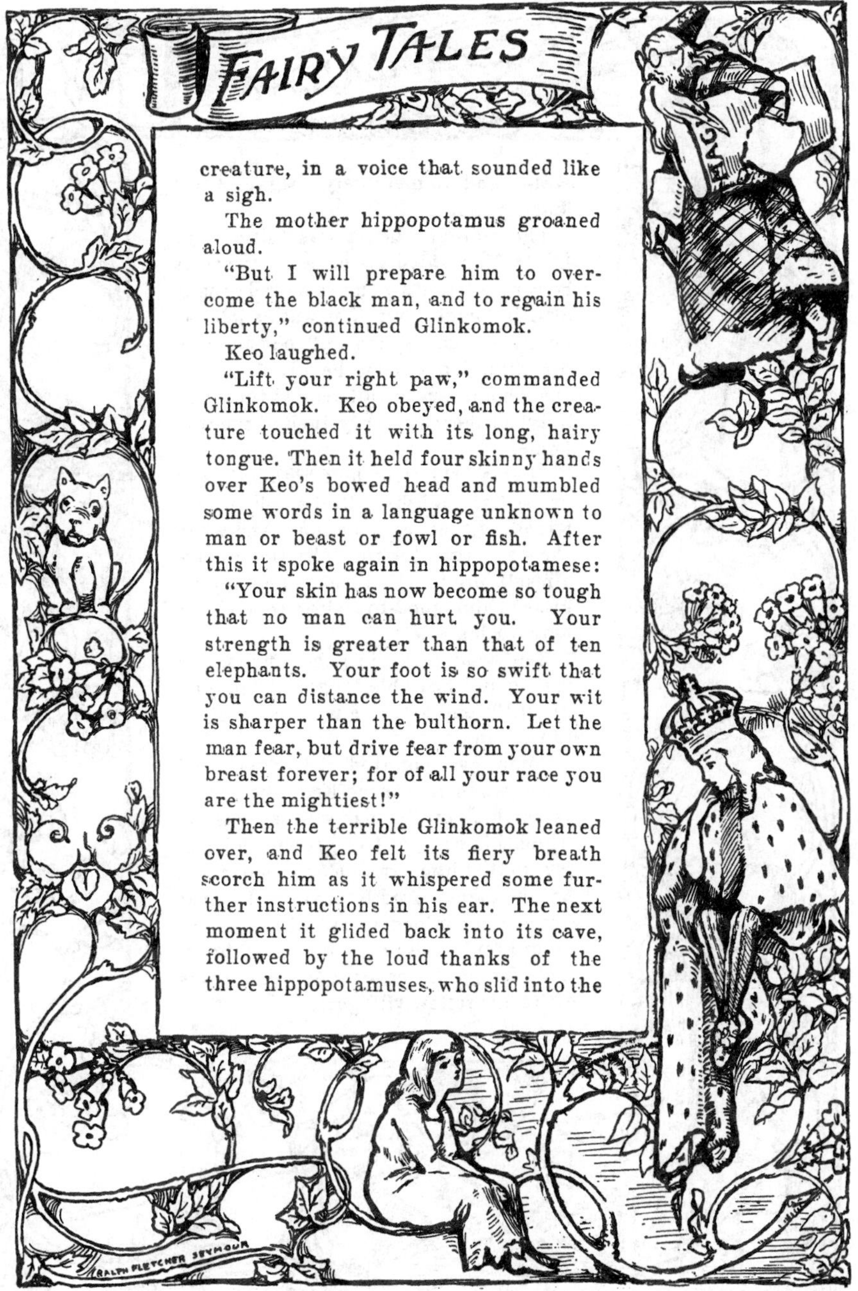

creature, in a voice that sounded like a sigh.

The mother hippopotamus groaned aloud.

"But I will prepare him to overcome the black man, and to regain his liberty," continued Glinkomok.

Keo laughed.

"Lift your right paw," commanded Glinkomok. Keo obeyed, and the creature touched it with its long, hairy tongue. Then it held four skinny hands over Keo's bowed head and mumbled some words in a language unknown to man or beast or fowl or fish. After this it spoke again in hippopotamese:

"Your skin has now become so tough that no man can hurt you. Your strength is greater than that of ten elephants. Your foot is so swift that you can distance the wind. Your wit is sharper than the bulthorn. Let the man fear, but drive fear from your own breast forever; for of all your race you are the mightiest!"

Then the terrible Glinkomok leaned over, and Keo felt its fiery breath scorch him as it whispered some further instructions in his ear. The next moment it glided back into its cave, followed by the loud thanks of the three hippopotamuses, who slid into the

water and immediately began their journey home.

The mother's heart was full of joy; Uncle Nep shivered once or twice as he remembered a glimpse he had caught of Glinkomok; but Keo was as jolly as possible, and, not content to swim with his dignified elders, he dived under their bodies, raced all around them and laughed merrily every inch of the way home.

Then all the tribe held high jinks and praised the mighty Glinkomok for befriending their queen's son. And when the day came for the Jolly One to give himself up to the black man they all kissed him good-by without a single fear for his safety.

Keo went away in good spirits, and they could hear his laughing "guk-uk-uk-uk!" long after he was lost to sight in the jungle.

Gouie had counted the days and knew when to expect Keo; but he was astonished at the monstrous size to which his captive had grown, and congratulated himself on the wise bargain he had made. And Keo was so fat that Gouie determined to eat him—that is, all of him he possibly could, and the remainder of the carcass he would trade off to his fellow villagers.

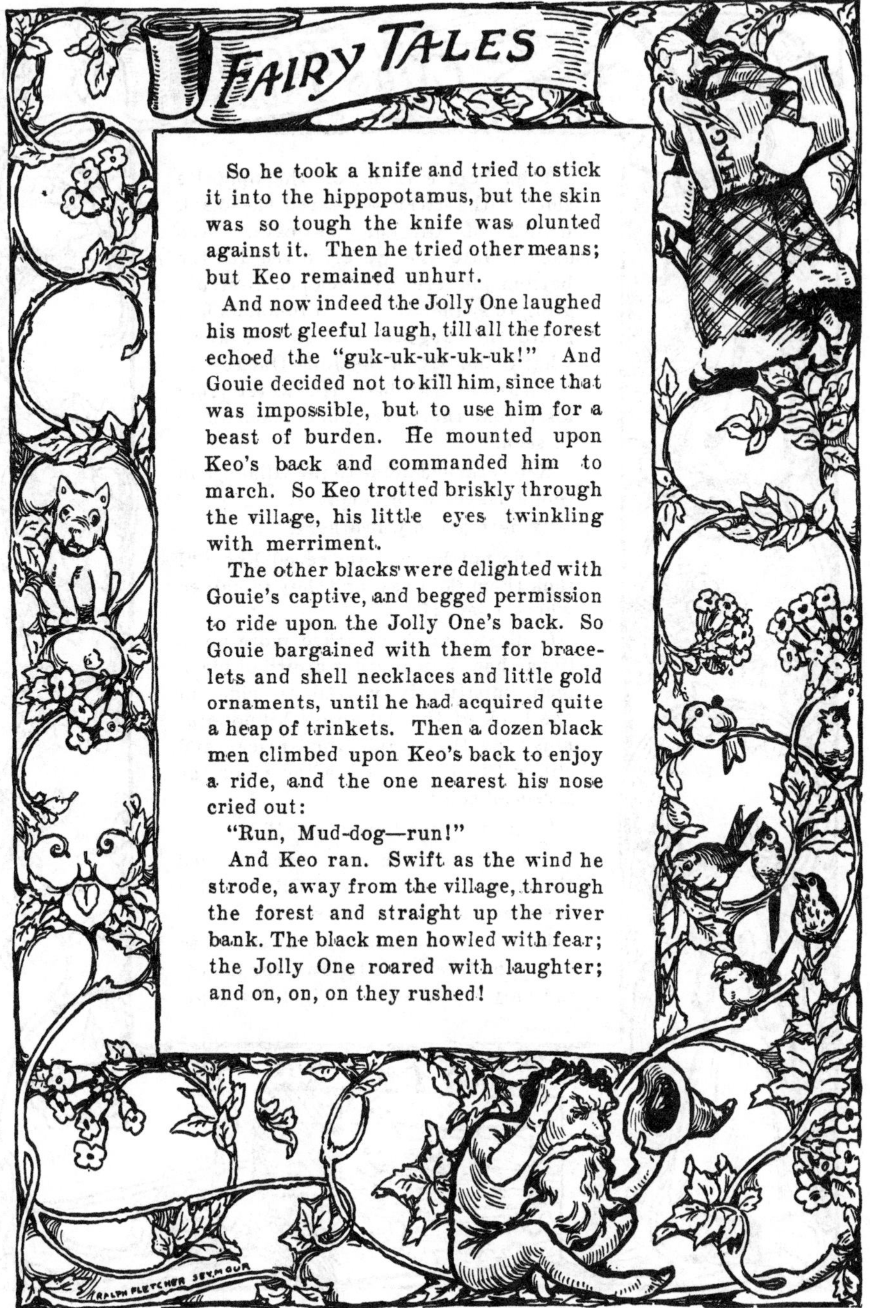

So he took a knife and tried to stick it into the hippopotamus, but the skin was so tough the knife was blunted against it. Then he tried other means; but Keo remained unhurt.

And now indeed the Jolly One laughed his most gleeful laugh, till all the forest echoed the "guk-uk-uk-uk-uk!" And Gouie decided not to kill him, since that was impossible, but to use him for a beast of burden. He mounted upon Keo's back and commanded him to march. So Keo trotted briskly through the village, his little eyes twinkling with merriment.

The other blacks were delighted with Gouie's captive, and begged permission to ride upon the Jolly One's back. So Gouie bargained with them for bracelets and shell necklaces and little gold ornaments, until he had acquired quite a heap of trinkets. Then a dozen black men climbed upon Keo's back to enjoy a ride, and the one nearest his nose cried out:

"Run, Mud-dog—run!"

And Keo ran. Swift as the wind he strode, away from the village, through the forest and straight up the river bank. The black men howled with fear; the Jolly One roared with laughter; and on, on, on they rushed!

Then before them, on the opposite side of the river, appeared the black mouth of Glinkomok's cave. Keo dashed into the water, dived to the bottom and left the black people struggling to swim out. But Glinkomok had heard the laughter of Keo and knew what to do. When the Jolly One rose to the surface and blew the water from his throat there was no black man to be seen.

Keo returned alone to the village, and Gouie asked, with surprise:

"Where are my brothers:

"I do not know," answered Keo. "I took them far away, and they remained where I left them."

Gouie would have asked more questions then, but another crowd of black men impatiently waited to ride on the back of the laughing hippopotamus. So they paid the price and climbed to their seats, after which the foremost said:

"Run, mud-wallower—run!"

And Keo ran as before and carried them to the mouth of Glinkomok's cave, and returned alone.

But now Gouie became anxious to know the fate of his fellows, for he was the only black man left in his village.

"Save me, Keo! Save me!"

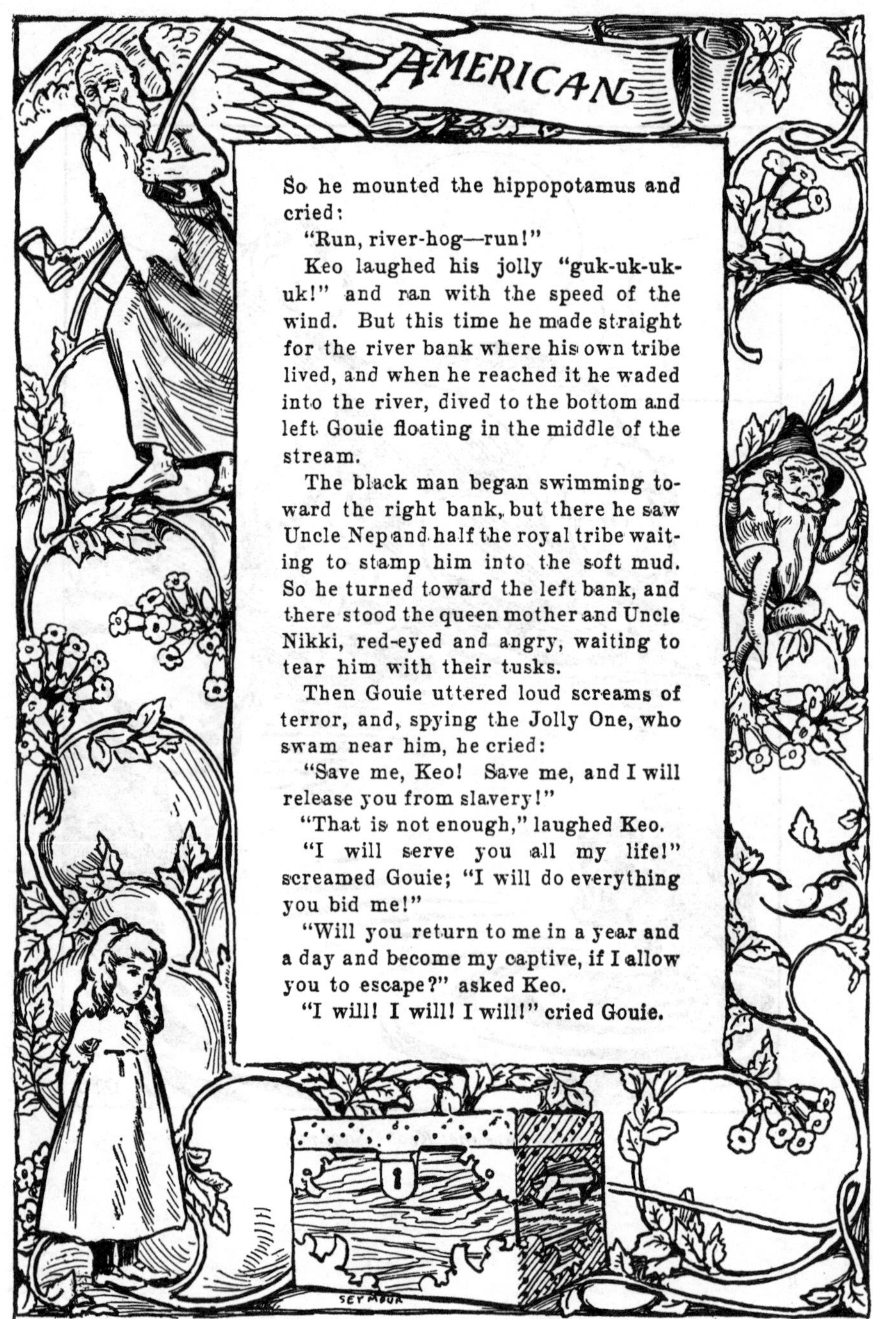

So he mounted the hippopotamus and cried:

"Run, river-hog—run!"

Keo laughed his jolly "guk-uk-uk-uk!" and ran with the speed of the wind. But this time he made straight for the river bank where his own tribe lived, and when he reached it he waded into the river, dived to the bottom and left Gouie floating in the middle of the stream.

The black man began swimming toward the right bank, but there he saw Uncle Nep and half the royal tribe waiting to stamp him into the soft mud. So he turned toward the left bank, and there stood the queen mother and Uncle Nikki, red-eyed and angry, waiting to tear him with their tusks.

Then Gouie uttered loud screams of terror, and, spying the Jolly One, who swam near him, he cried:

"Save me, Keo! Save me, and I will release you from slavery!"

"That is not enough," laughed Keo.

"I will serve you all my life!" screamed Gouie; "I will do everything you bid me!"

"Will you return to me in a year and a day and become my captive, if I allow you to escape?" asked Keo.

"I will! I will! I will!" cried Gouie.

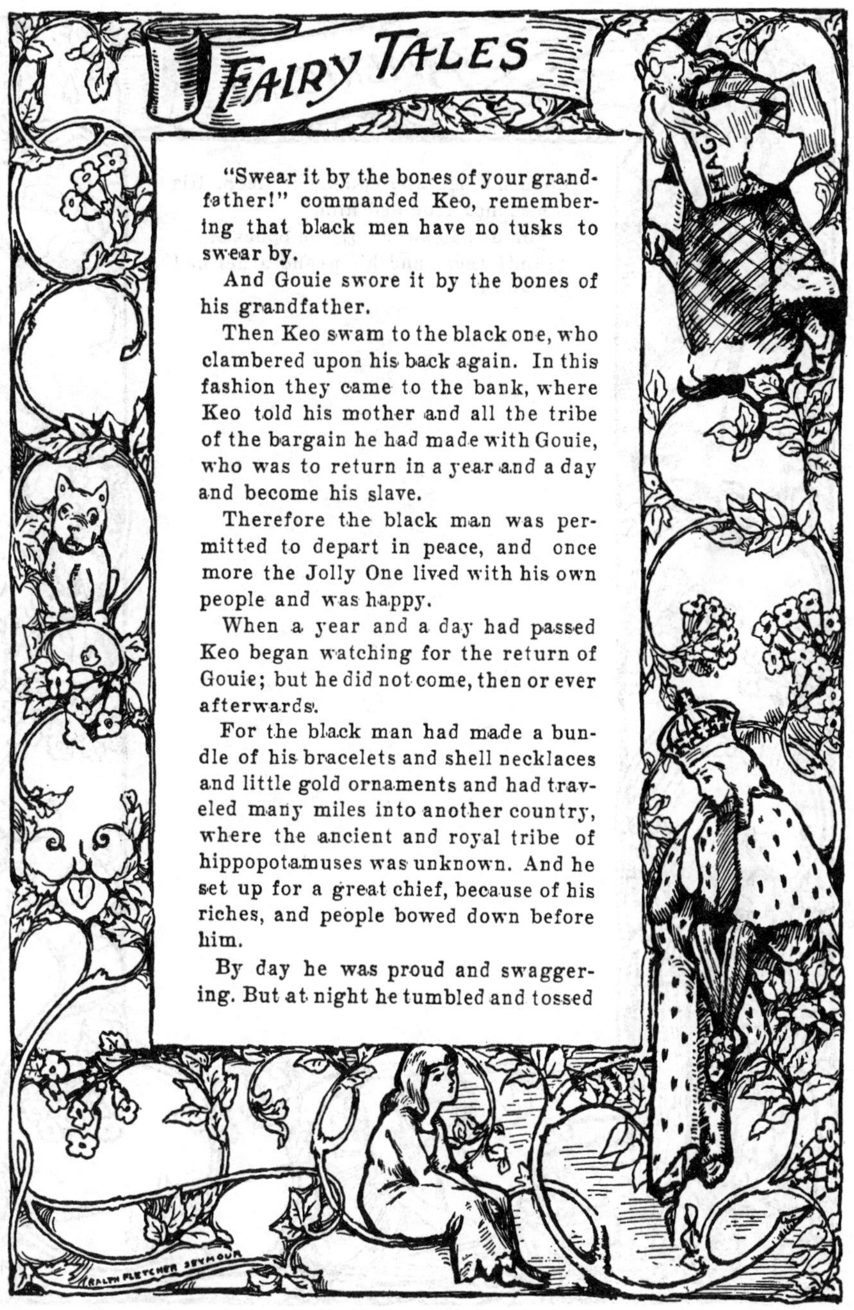

"Swear it by the bones of your grandfather!" commanded Keo, remembering that black men have no tusks to swear by.

And Gouie swore it by the bones of his grandfather.

Then Keo swam to the black one, who clambered upon his back again. In this fashion they came to the bank, where Keo told his mother and all the tribe of the bargain he had made with Gouie, who was to return in a year and a day and become his slave.

Therefore the black man was permitted to depart in peace, and once more the Jolly One lived with his own people and was happy.

When a year and a day had passed Keo began watching for the return of Gouie; but he did not come, then or ever afterwards.

For the black man had made a bundle of his bracelets and shell necklaces and little gold ornaments and had traveled many miles into another country, where the ancient and royal tribe of hippopotamuses was unknown. And he set up for a great chief, because of his riches, and people bowed down before him.

By day he was proud and swaggering. But at night he tumbled and tossed

upon his bed and could not sleep. His conscience troubled him.

For he had sworn by the bones of his grandfather; and his grandfather had no bones.

The MAGIC BON BONS

There lived in Boston a wise and ancient chemist by the name of Dr. Daws, who dabbled somewhat in magic. There also lived in Boston a young lady by the name of Claribel Sudds, who was possessed of much money, little wit and an intense desire to go upon the stage.

So Claribel went to Dr. Daws and said:

"I can neither sing nor dance; I cannot recite verse nor play upon the piano; I am no acrobat nor leaper nor high kicker; yet I wish to go upon the stage. What shall I do?"

"Are you willing to pay for such accomplishments?" asked the wise chemist.

"Certainly," answered Claribel, jingling her purse.

"Then come to me to-morrow at two o'clock," said he.

All that night he practiced what is known as chemical sorcery; so that when Claribel Sudds came next day at two o'clock he showed her a small box filled with compounds that closely resembled French bonbons.

"This is a progressive age," said the old man, "and I flatter myself your Uncle Daws keeps right along with the procession. Now, one of your old-fashioned sorcerers would have made you some nasty, bitter pills to swallow; but I have consulted your taste and convenience. Here are some magic bonbons. If you eat this one with the lavender color you can dance thereafter as lightly and gracefully as if you had been trained a lifetime. After you consume the pink confection you will sing like a nightingale. Eating the white one will enable you to become the finest elocutionist in the land. The chocolate piece will charm you into playing the piano better than Rubenstein, while after eating the lemon-yellow bonbon you can easily kick six feet above your head."

"How delightful!" exclaimed Claribel, who was truly enraptured. "You are certainly a most clever sorcerer as well as a considerate compounder,"

"Here are some magic bonbons."

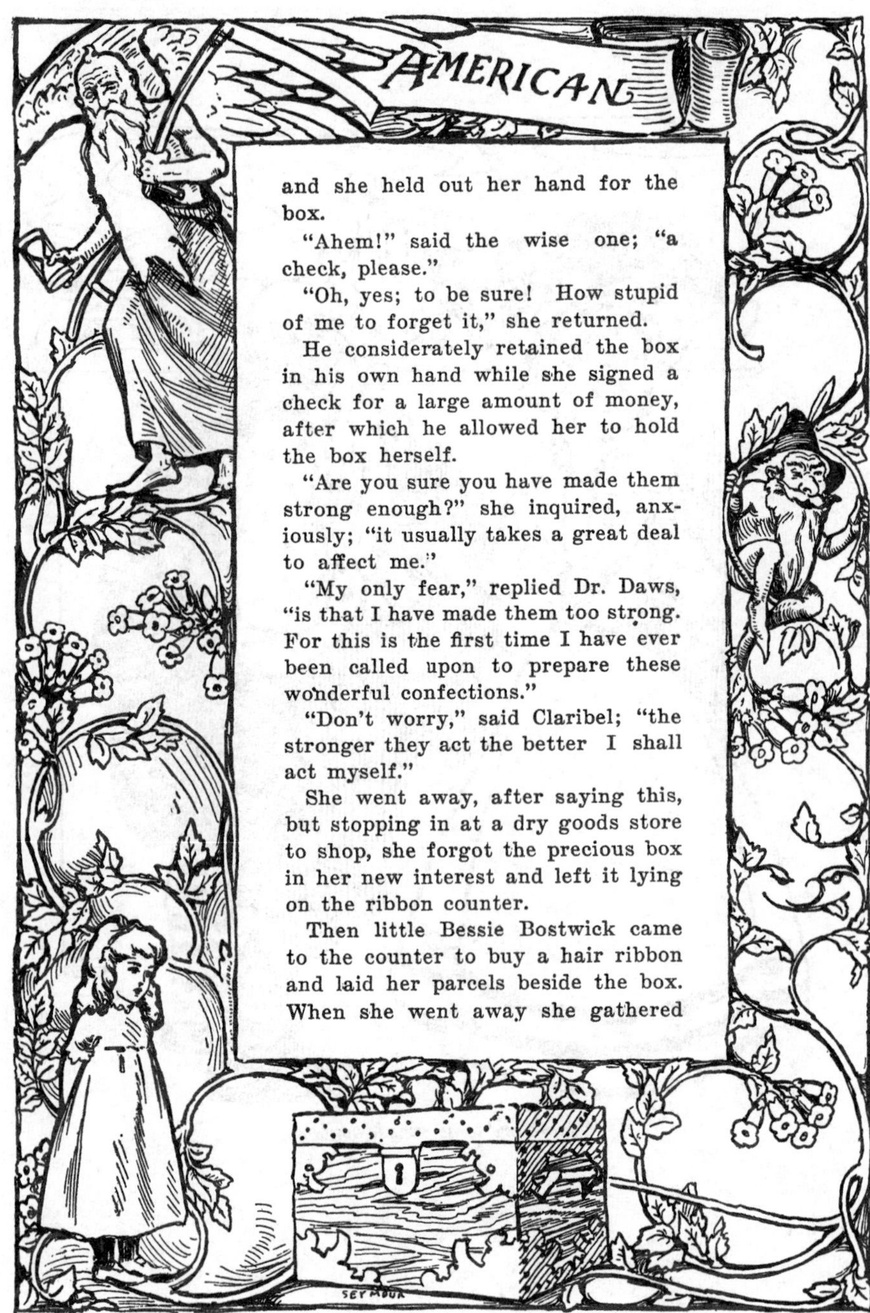

and she held out her hand for the box.

"Ahem!" said the wise one; "a check, please."

"Oh, yes; to be sure! How stupid of me to forget it," she returned.

He considerately retained the box in his own hand while she signed a check for a large amount of money, after which he allowed her to hold the box herself.

"Are you sure you have made them strong enough?" she inquired, anxiously; "it usually takes a great deal to affect me."

"My only fear," replied Dr. Daws, "is that I have made them too strong. For this is the first time I have ever been called upon to prepare these wonderful confections."

"Don't worry," said Claribel; "the stronger they act the better I shall act myself."

She went away, after saying this, but stopping in at a dry goods store to shop, she forgot the precious box in her new interest and left it lying on the ribbon counter.

Then little Bessie Bostwick came to the counter to buy a hair ribbon and laid her parcels beside the box. When she went away she gathered

up the box with her other bundles and trotted off home with it.

Bessie never knew, until after she had hung her coat in the hall closet and counted up her parcels, that she had one too many. Then she opened it and exclaimed:

"Why, it's a box of candy! Someone must have mislaid it. But it is too small a matter to worry about; there are only a few pieces." So she dumped the contents of the box into a bonbon dish that stood upon the hall table and picking out the chocolate piece—she was fond of chocolates—ate it daintily while she examined her purchases.

These were not many, for Bessie was only twelve years old and was not yet trusted by her parents to expend much money at the stores. But while she tried on the hair ribbon she suddenly felt a great desire to play upon the piano, and the desire at last became so overpowering that she went into the parlor and opened the instrument.

The little girl had, with infinite pains, contrived to learn two "pieces" which she usually executed with a jerky movement of her right hand and a left hand that forgot to keep

up and so made dreadful discords. But under the influence of the chocolate bonbon she sat down and ran her fingers lightly over the keys producing such exquisite harmony that she was filled with amazement at her own performance.

That was the prelude, however. The next moment she dashed into Beethoven's seventh sonata and played it magnificently.

Her mother, hearing the unusual burst of melody, came downstairs to see what musical guest had arrived; but when she discovered it was her own little daughter who was playing so divinely she had an attack of palpitation of the heart (to which she was subject) and sat down upon a sofa until it should pass away.

Meanwhile Bessie played one piece after another with untiring energy. She loved music, and now found that all she need do was to sit at the piano and listen and watch her hands twinkle over the keyboard.

Twilight deepened in the room and Bessie's father came home and hung up his hat and overcoat and placed his umbrella in the rack. Then he peeped into the parlor to see who was playing.

"Great Caesar!" he exclaimed. But

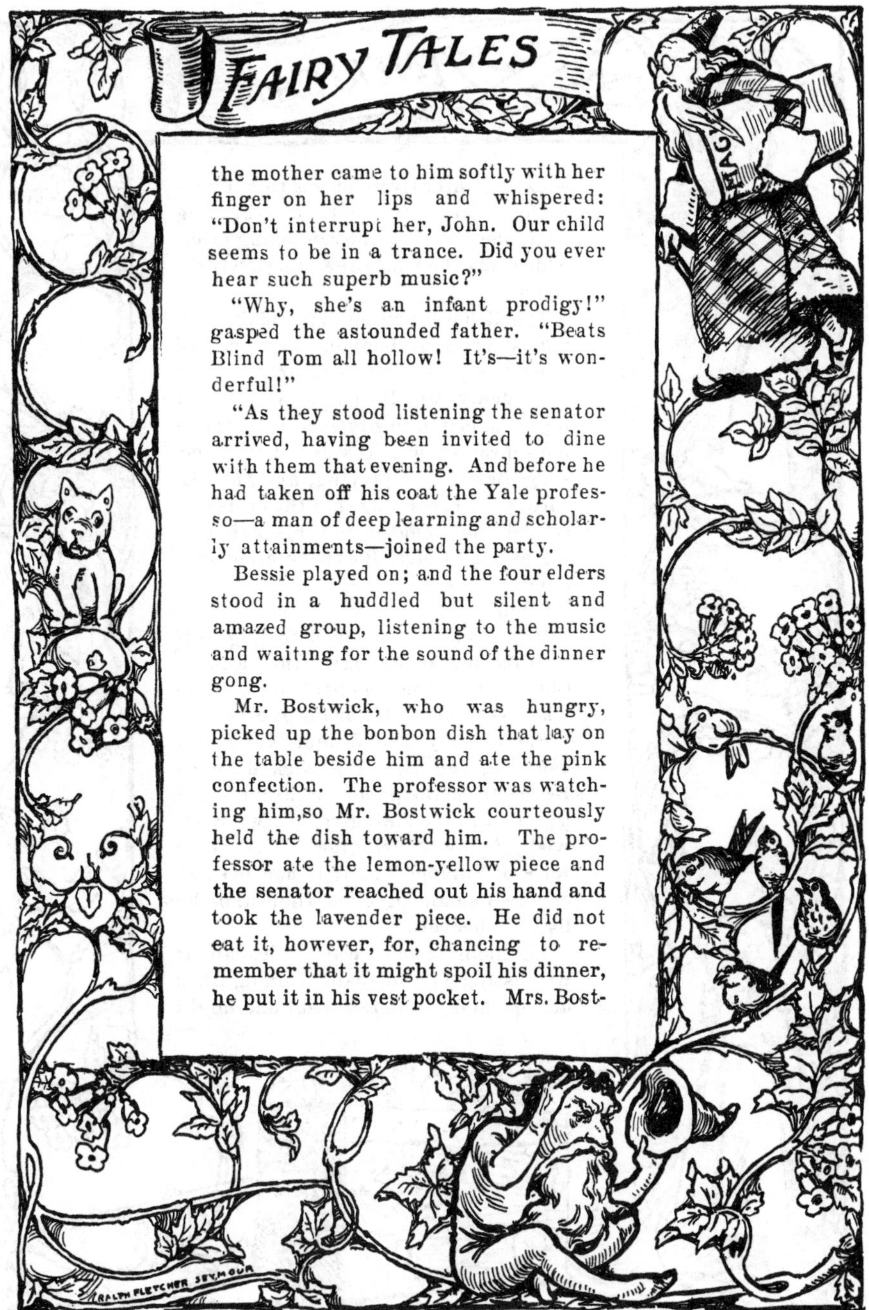

the mother came to him softly with her finger on her lips and whispered: "Don't interrupt her, John. Our child seems to be in a trance. Did you ever hear such superb music?"

"Why, she's an infant prodigy!" gasped the astounded father. "Beats Blind Tom all hollow! It's—it's wonderful!"

"As they stood listening the senator arrived, having been invited to dine with them that evening. And before he had taken off his coat the Yale professo—a man of deep learning and scholarly attainments—joined the party.

Bessie played on; and the four elders stood in a huddled but silent and amazed group, listening to the music and waiting for the sound of the dinner gong.

Mr. Bostwick, who was hungry, picked up the bonbon dish that lay on the table beside him and ate the pink confection. The professor was watching him,so Mr. Bostwick courteously held the dish toward him. The professor ate the lemon-yellow piece and the senator reached out his hand and took the lavender piece. He did not eat it, however, for, chancing to remember that it might spoil his dinner, he put it in his vest pocket. Mrs. Bost-

wick, still intently listening to her precocious daughter, without thinking what she did, took the remaining piece, which was the white one, and slowly devoured it.

The dish was now empty, and Claribel Sudds' precious bonbons had passed from her possession forever!

Suddenly Mr. Bostwick, who was a big man, began to sing in a shrill, tremolo soprano voice. It was not the same song Bessie was playing, and the discord was so shocking that the professor smiled, the senator put his hands to his ears and Mrs. Bostwick cried in a horrified voice:

"William!"

Her husband continued to sing as if endeavoring to emulate the famous Christine Nillson, and paid no attention whatever to his wife or his guests.

Fortunately the dinner gong now sounded, and Mrs. Bostwick dragged Bessie from the piano and ushered her guests into the dining-room. Mr. Bostwick followed, singing "The Last Rose of Summer" as if it had been an encore demanded by a thousand delighted hearers.

The poor woman was in despair at witnessing her husband's undignified actions and wondered what she might

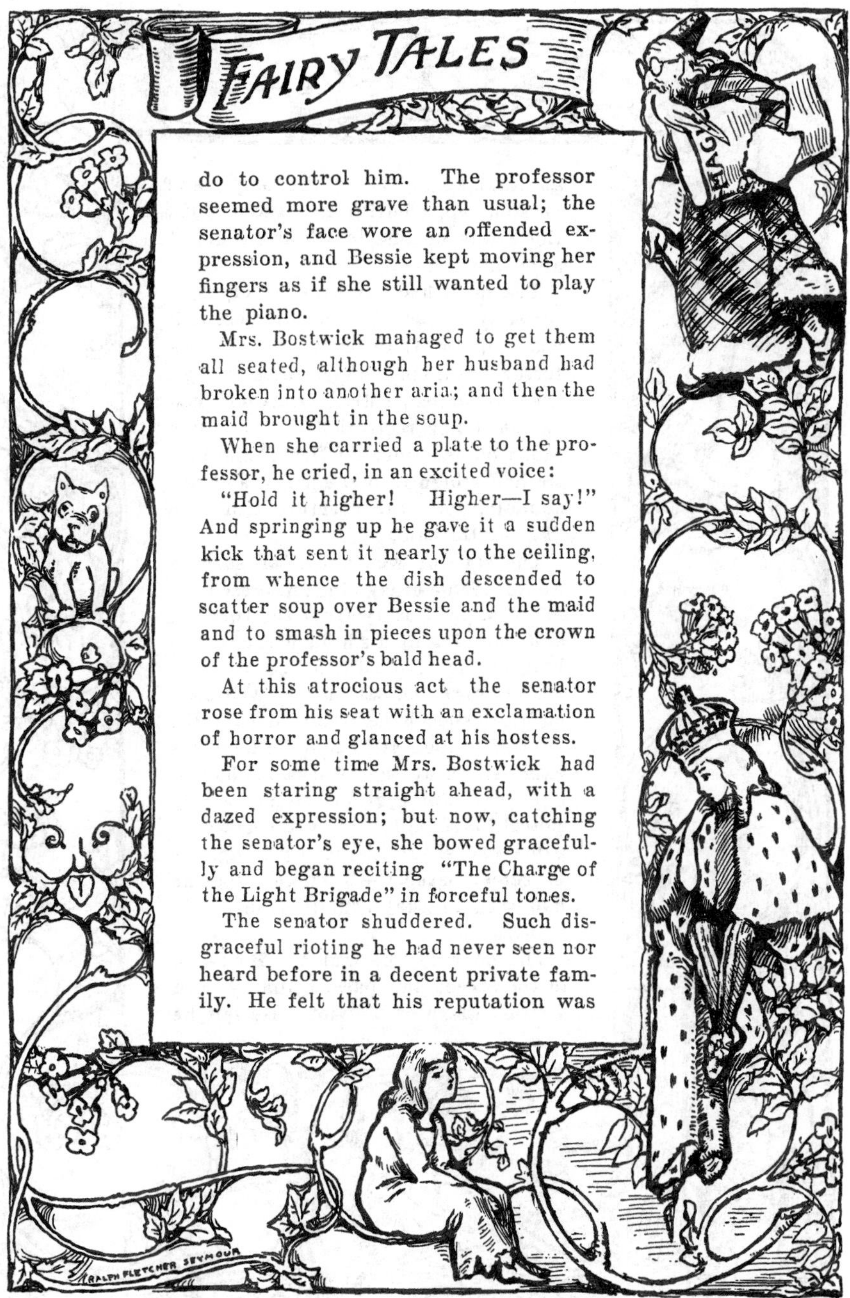

do to control him. The professor seemed more grave than usual; the senator's face wore an offended expression, and Bessie kept moving her fingers as if she still wanted to play the piano.

Mrs. Bostwick managed to get them all seated, although her husband had broken into another aria; and then the maid brought in the soup.

When she carried a plate to the professor, he cried, in an excited voice:

"Hold it higher! Higher—I say!" And springing up he gave it a sudden kick that sent it nearly to the ceiling, from whence the dish descended to scatter soup over Bessie and the maid and to smash in pieces upon the crown of the professor's bald head.

At this atrocious act the senator rose from his seat with an exclamation of horror and glanced at his hostess.

For some time Mrs. Bostwick had been staring straight ahead, with a dazed expression; but now, catching the senator's eye, she bowed gracefully and began reciting "The Charge of the Light Brigade" in forceful tones.

The senator shuddered. Such disgraceful rioting he had never seen nor heard before in a decent private family. He felt that his reputation was

at stake, and, being the only sane person, apparently, in the room, there was no one to whom he might appeal.

The maid had run away to cry hysterically in the kitchen; Mr. Bostwick was singing "O Promise Me;" the professor was trying to kick the globes off the chandelier; Mrs. Bostwick had switched her recitation to "The Boy Stood on the Burning Deck," and Bessie had stolen into the parlor and was pounding out the overture from the "Flying Dutchman."

The senator was not at all sure he would not go crazy himself, presently; so he slipped away from the turmoil, and, catching up his hat and coat in the hall, hurried from the house.

That night he sat up late writing a political speech he was to deliver the next afternoon at Faneuil hall, but his experiences at the Bostwicks' had so unnerved him that he could scarcely collect his thoughts, and often he would pause and shake his head pityingly as he remembered the strange things he had seen in that usually respectable home.

The next day he met Mr. Bostwick in the street, but passed him by with a stony glare of oblivion. He felt he

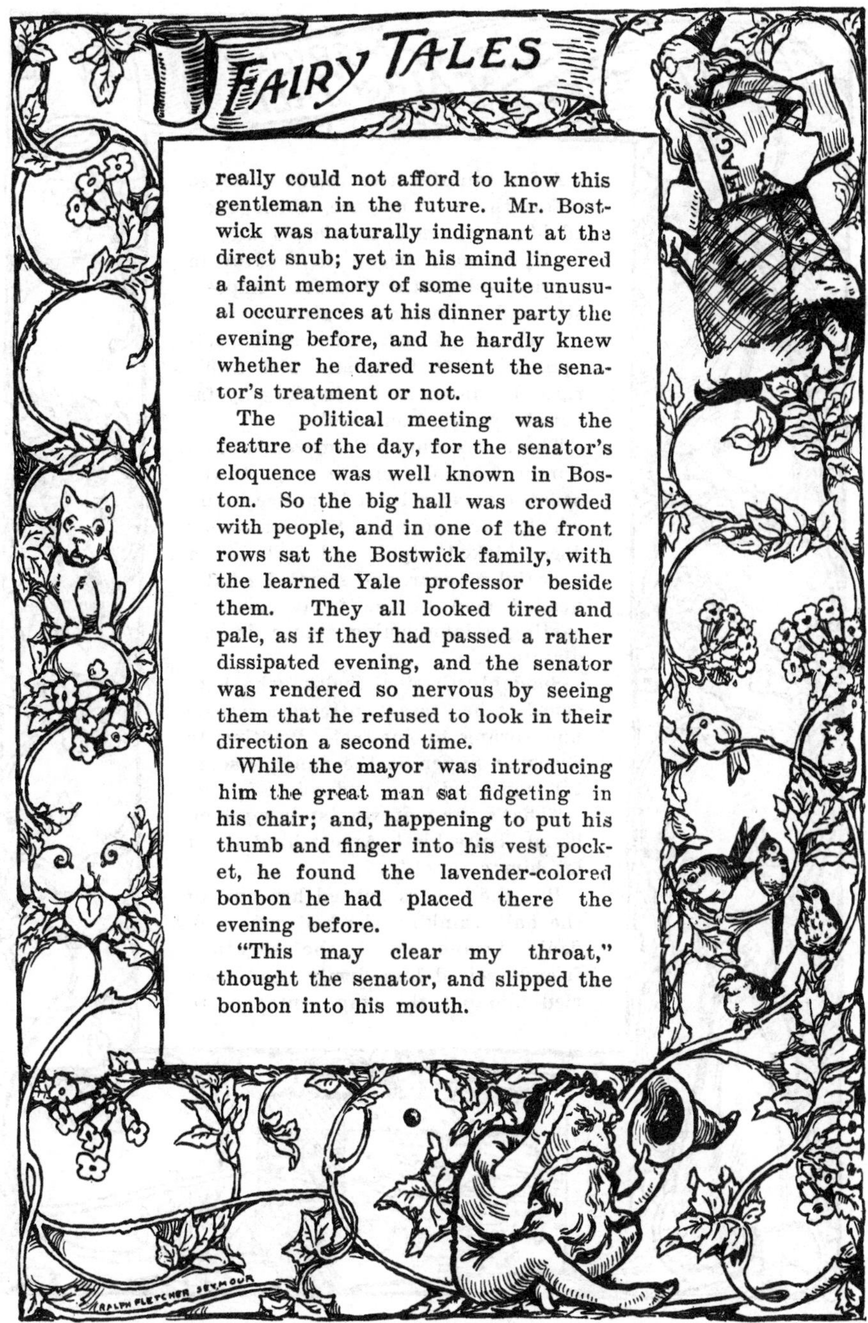

really could not afford to know this gentleman in the future. Mr. Bostwick was naturally indignant at the direct snub; yet in his mind lingered a faint memory of some quite unusual occurrences at his dinner party the evening before, and he hardly knew whether he dared resent the senator's treatment or not.

The political meeting was the feature of the day, for the senator's eloquence was well known in Boston. So the big hall was crowded with people, and in one of the front rows sat the Bostwick family, with the learned Yale professor beside them. They all looked tired and pale, as if they had passed a rather dissipated evening, and the senator was rendered so nervous by seeing them that he refused to look in their direction a second time.

While the mayor was introducing him the great man sat fidgeting in his chair; and, happening to put his thumb and finger into his vest pocket, he found the lavender-colored bonbon he had placed there the evening before.

"This may clear my throat," thought the senator, and slipped the bonbon into his mouth.

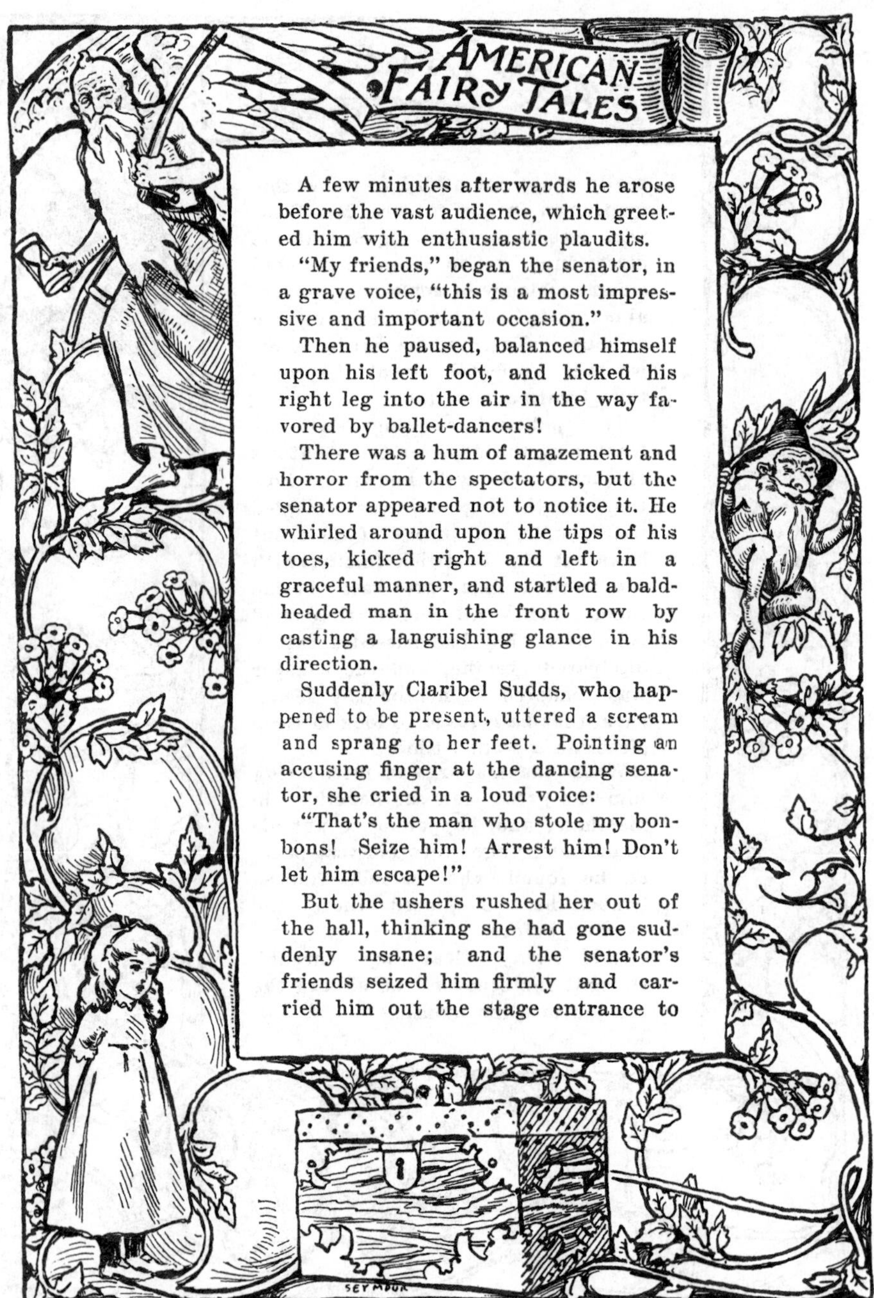

A few minutes afterwards he arose before the vast audience, which greeted him with enthusiastic plaudits.

"My friends," began the senator, in a grave voice, "this is a most impressive and important occasion."

Then he paused, balanced himself upon his left foot, and kicked his right leg into the air in the way favored by ballet-dancers!

There was a hum of amazement and horror from the spectators, but the senator appeared not to notice it. He whirled around upon the tips of his toes, kicked right and left in a graceful manner, and startled a bald-headed man in the front row by casting a languishing glance in his direction.

Suddenly Claribel Sudds, who happened to be present, uttered a scream and sprang to her feet. Pointing an accusing finger at the dancing senator, she cried in a loud voice:

"That's the man who stole my bonbons! Seize him! Arrest him! Don't let him escape!"

But the ushers rushed her out of the hall, thinking she had gone suddenly insane; and the senator's friends seized him firmly and carried him out the stage entrance to

"That's the man who stole my bonbons!"

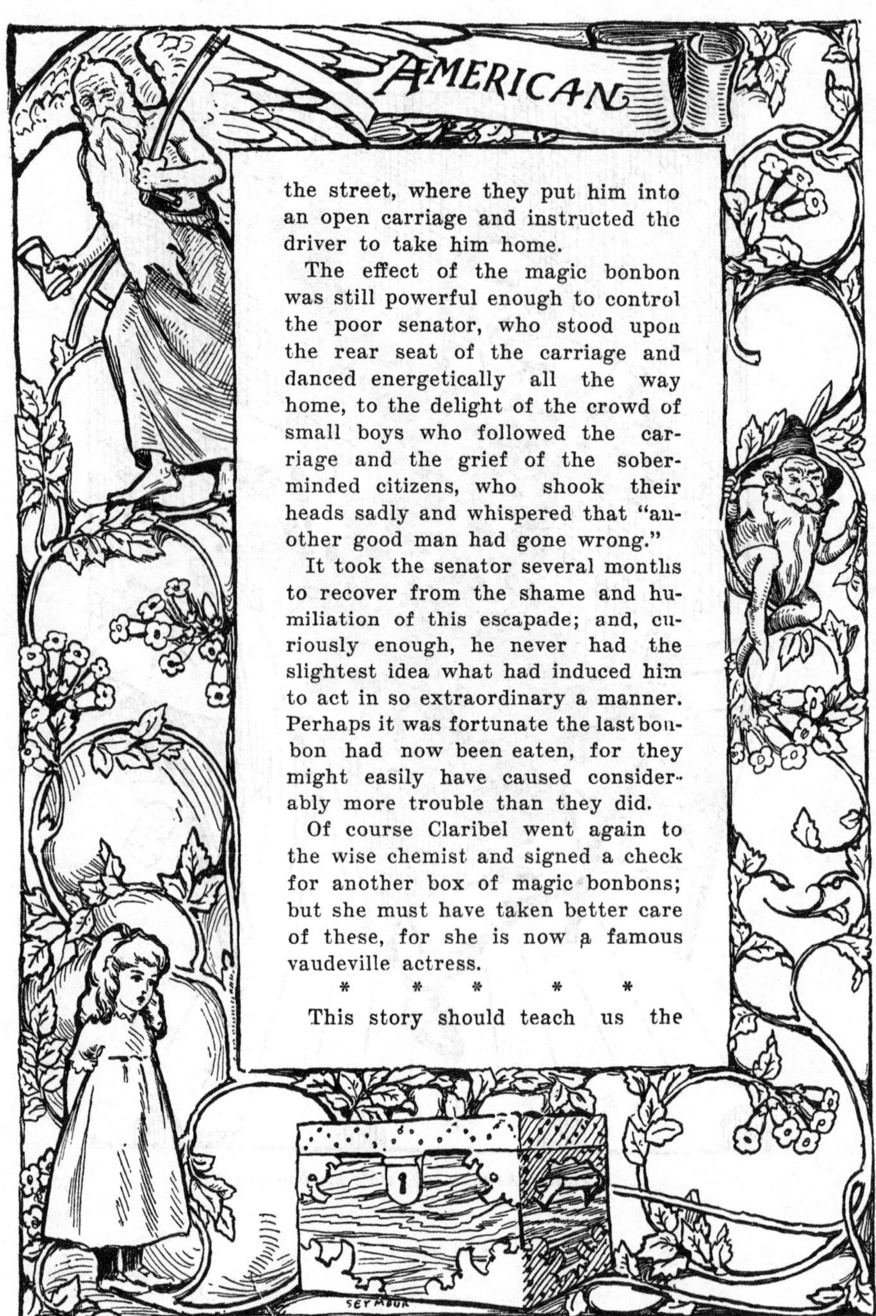

the street, where they put him into an open carriage and instructed the driver to take him home.

The effect of the magic bonbon was still powerful enough to control the poor senator, who stood upon the rear seat of the carriage and danced energetically all the way home, to the delight of the crowd of small boys who followed the carriage and the grief of the soberminded citizens, who shook their heads sadly and whispered that "another good man had gone wrong."

It took the senator several months to recover from the shame and humiliation of this escapade; and, curiously enough, he never had the slightest idea what had induced him to act in so extraordinary a manner. Perhaps it was fortunate the last bonbon had now been eaten, for they might easily have caused considerably more trouble than they did.

Of course Claribel went again to the wise chemist and signed a check for another box of magic bonbons; but she must have taken better care of these, for she is now a famous vaudeville actress.

* * * * *

This story should teach us the

folly of condemning others for actions that we do not understand, for we never know what may happen to ourselves. It may also serve as a hint to be careful about leaving parcels in public places, and, incidentally, to let other people's packages severely alone.

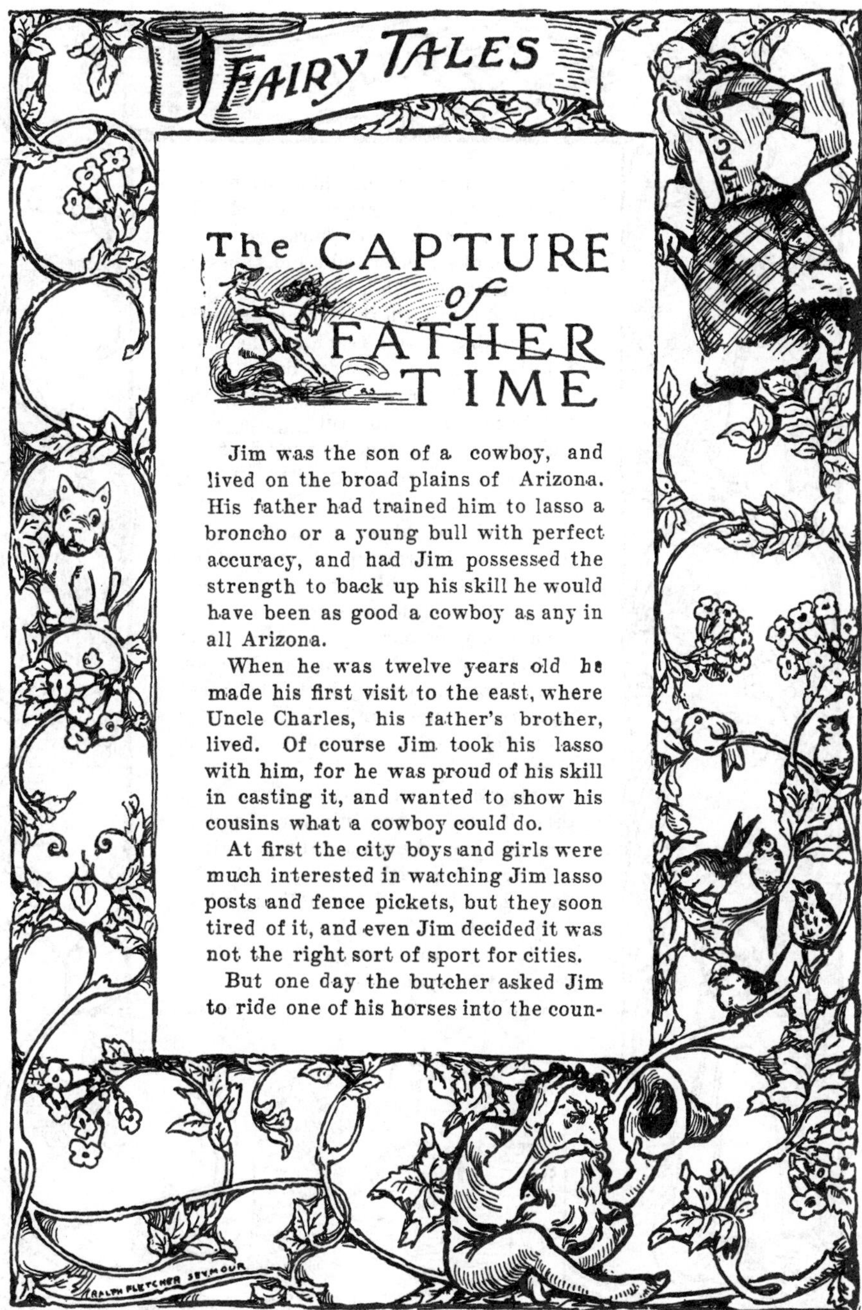

The CAPTURE of FATHER TIME

Jim was the son of a cowboy, and lived on the broad plains of Arizona. His father had trained him to lasso a broncho or a young bull with perfect accuracy, and had Jim possessed the strength to back up his skill he would have been as good a cowboy as any in all Arizona.

When he was twelve years old he made his first visit to the east, where Uncle Charles, his father's brother, lived. Of course Jim took his lasso with him, for he was proud of his skill in casting it, and wanted to show his cousins what a cowboy could do.

At first the city boys and girls were much interested in watching Jim lasso posts and fence pickets, but they soon tired of it, and even Jim decided it was not the right sort of sport for cities.

But one day the butcher asked Jim to ride one of his horses into the coun-

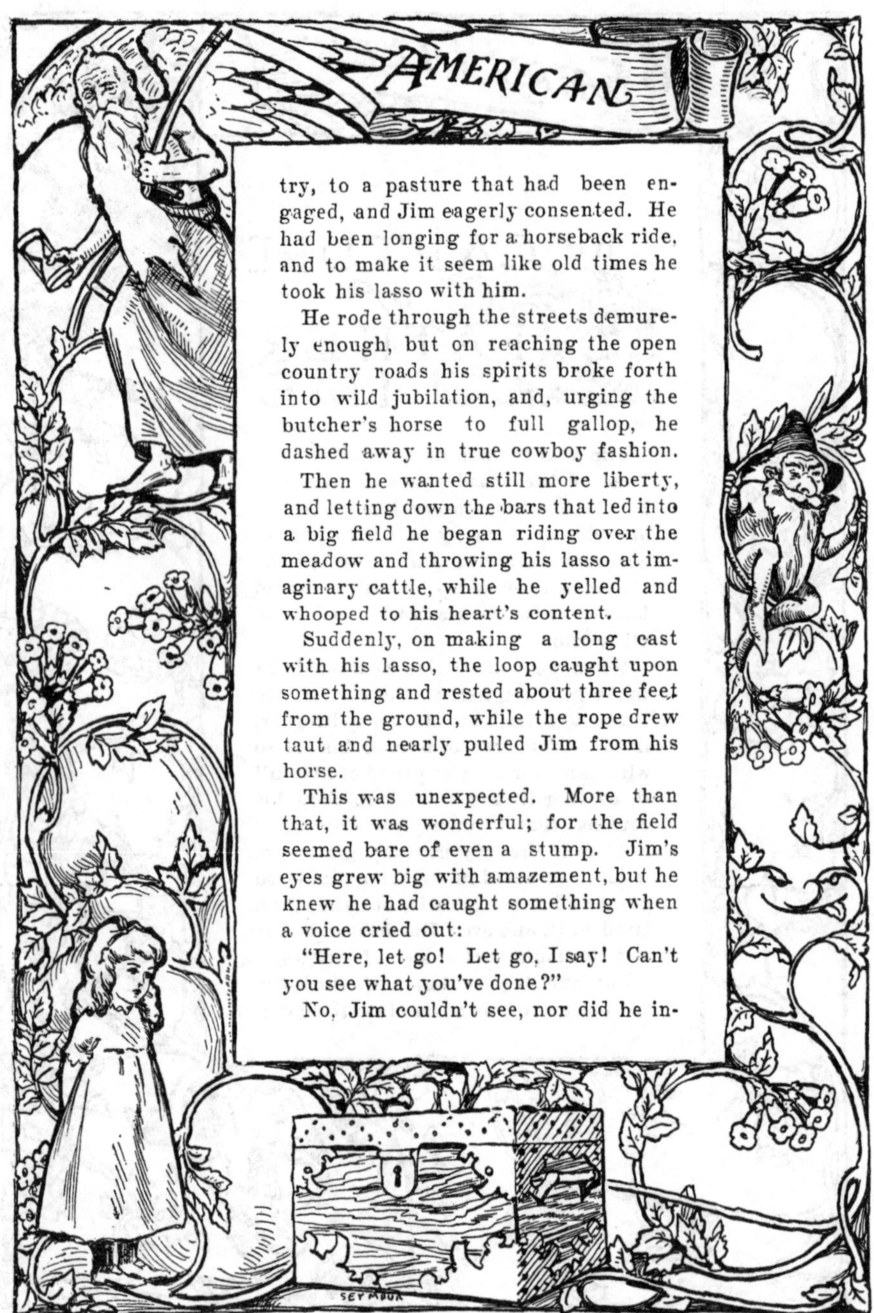

try, to a pasture that had been engaged, and Jim eagerly consented. He had been longing for a horseback ride, and to make it seem like old times he took his lasso with him.

He rode through the streets demurely enough, but on reaching the open country roads his spirits broke forth into wild jubilation, and, urging the butcher's horse to full gallop, he dashed away in true cowboy fashion.

Then he wanted still more liberty, and letting down the bars that led into a big field he began riding over the meadow and throwing his lasso at imaginary cattle, while he yelled and whooped to his heart's content.

Suddenly, on making a long cast with his lasso, the loop caught upon something and rested about three feet from the ground, while the rope drew taut and nearly pulled Jim from his horse.

This was unexpected. More than that, it was wonderful; for the field seemed bare of even a stump. Jim's eyes grew big with amazement, but he knew he had caught something when a voice cried out:

"Here, let go! Let go, I say! Can't you see what you've done?"

No, Jim couldn't see, nor did he in-

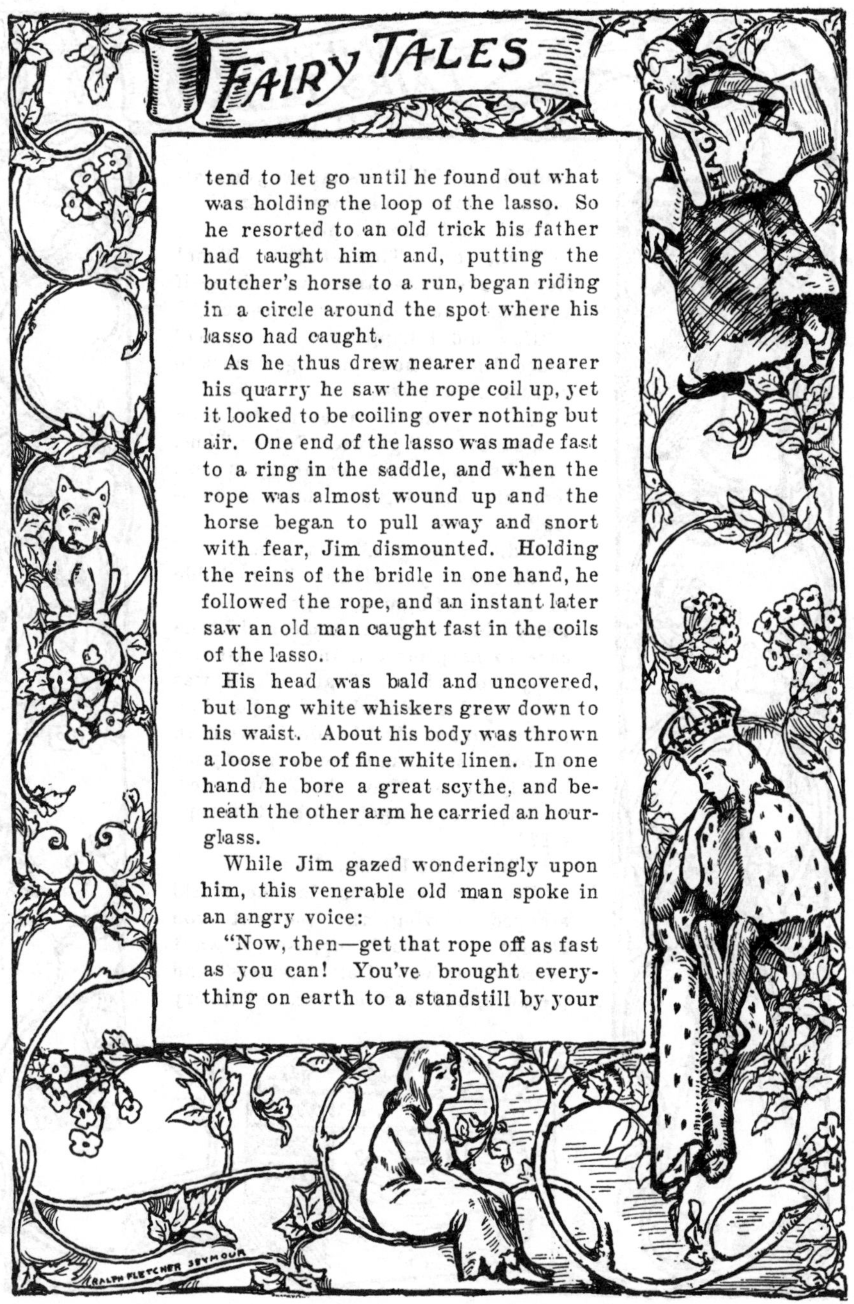

tend to let go until he found out what was holding the loop of the lasso. So he resorted to an old trick his father had taught him and, putting the butcher's horse to a run, began riding in a circle around the spot where his lasso had caught.

As he thus drew nearer and nearer his quarry he saw the rope coil up, yet it looked to be coiling over nothing but air. One end of the lasso was made fast to a ring in the saddle, and when the rope was almost wound up and the horse began to pull away and snort with fear, Jim dismounted. Holding the reins of the bridle in one hand, he followed the rope, and an instant later saw an old man caught fast in the coils of the lasso.

His head was bald and uncovered, but long white whiskers grew down to his waist. About his body was thrown a loose robe of fine white linen. In one hand he bore a great scythe, and beneath the other arm he carried an hourglass.

While Jim gazed wonderingly upon him, this venerable old man spoke in an angry voice:

"Now, then—get that rope off as fast as you can! You've brought everything on earth to a standstill by your

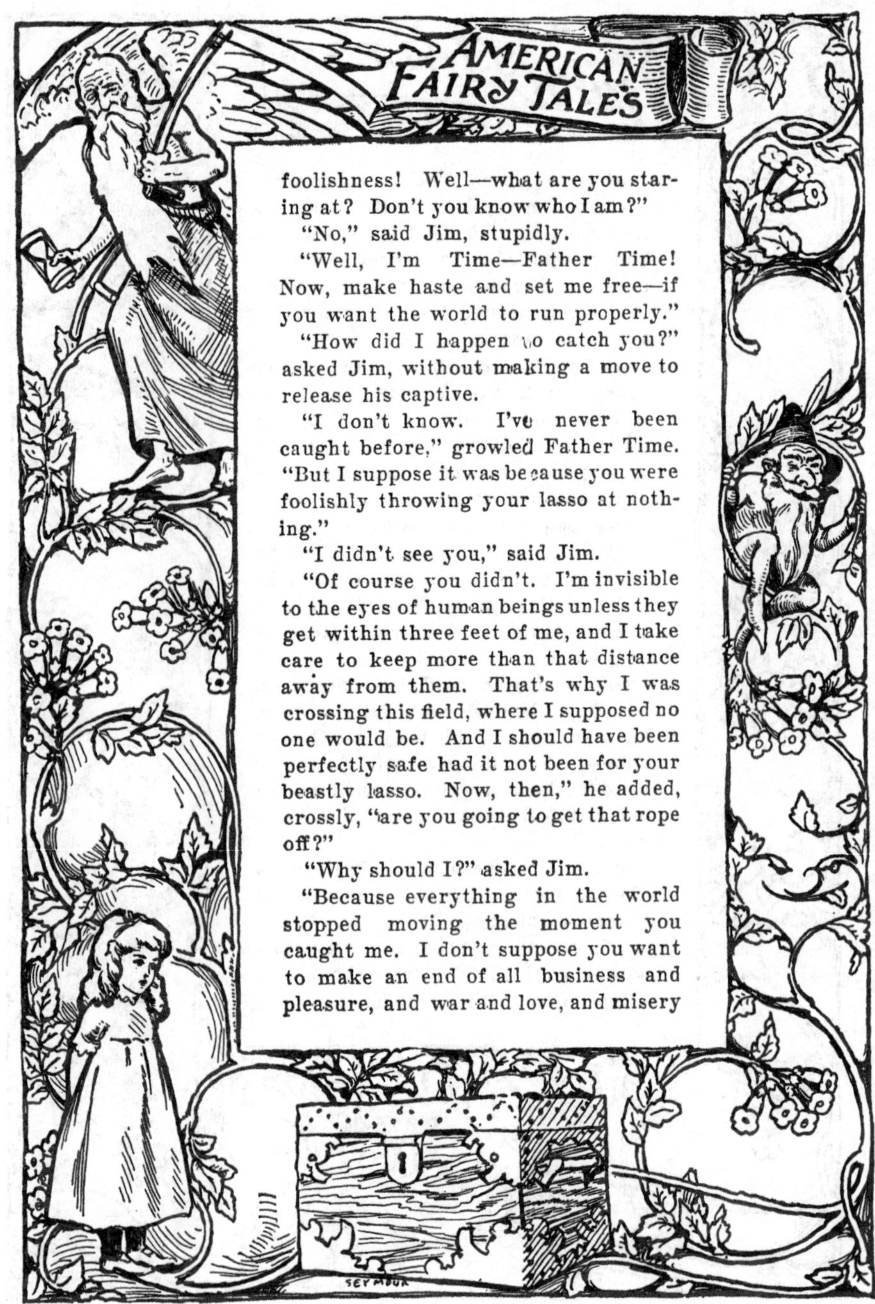

foolishness! Well—what are you staring at? Don't you know who I am?"

"No," said Jim, stupidly.

"Well, I'm Time—Father Time! Now, make haste and set me free—if you want the world to run properly."

"How did I happen to catch you?" asked Jim, without making a move to release his captive.

"I don't know. I've never been caught before," growled Father Time. "But I suppose it was because you were foolishly throwing your lasso at nothing."

"I didn't see you," said Jim.

"Of course you didn't. I'm invisible to the eyes of human beings unless they get within three feet of me, and I take care to keep more than that distance away from them. That's why I was crossing this field, where I supposed no one would be. And I should have been perfectly safe had it not been for your beastly lasso. Now, then," he added, crossly, "are you going to get that rope off?"

"Why should I?" asked Jim.

"Because everything in the world stopped moving the moment you caught me. I don't suppose you want to make an end of all business and pleasure, and war and love, and misery

"You've brought everything on earth to a standstill."

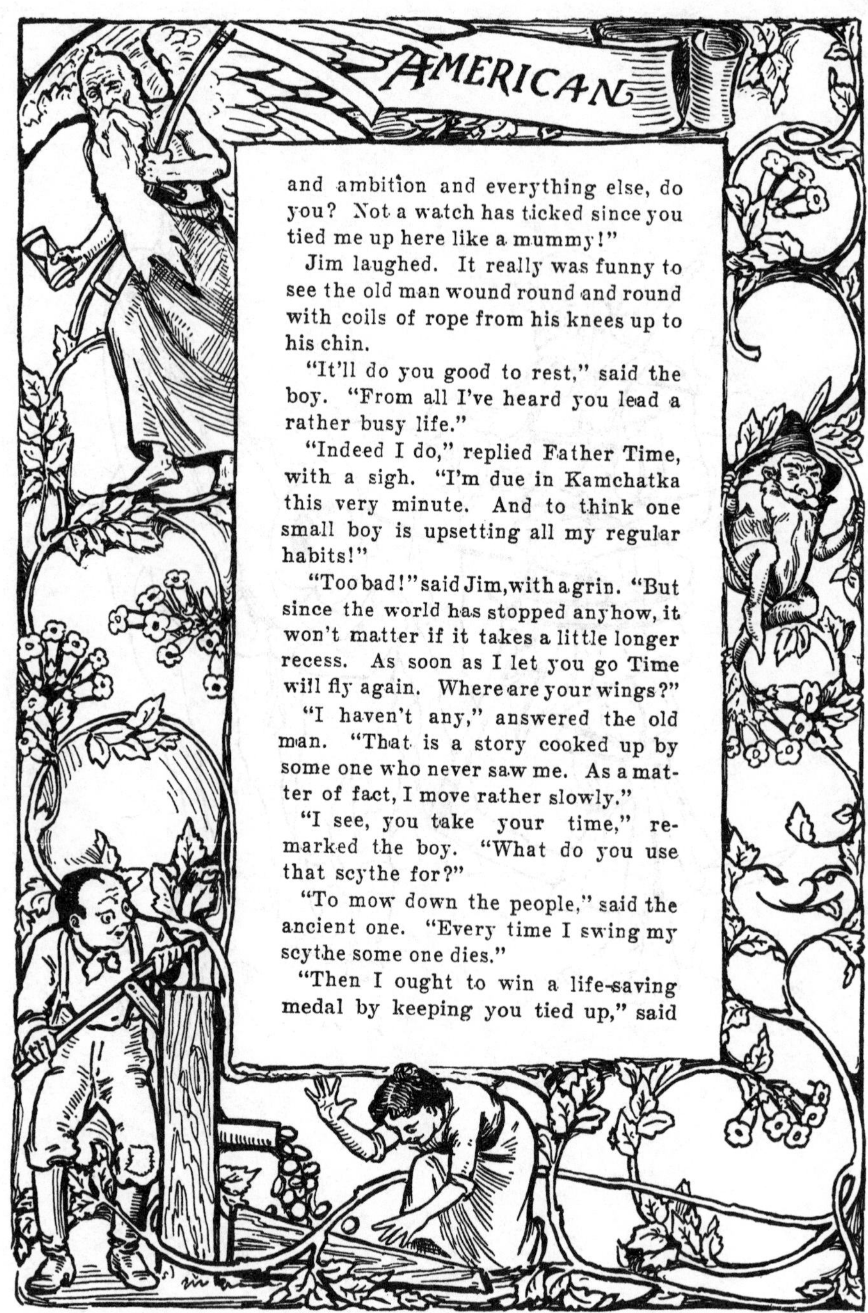

and ambition and everything else, do you? Not a watch has ticked since you tied me up here like a mummy!"

Jim laughed. It really was funny to see the old man wound round and round with coils of rope from his knees up to his chin.

"It'll do you good to rest," said the boy. "From all I've heard you lead a rather busy life."

"Indeed I do," replied Father Time, with a sigh. "I'm due in Kamchatka this very minute. And to think one small boy is upsetting all my regular habits!"

"Too bad!" said Jim, with a grin. "But since the world has stopped anyhow, it won't matter if it takes a little longer recess. As soon as I let you go Time will fly again. Where are your wings?"

"I haven't any," answered the old man. "That is a story cooked up by some one who never saw me. As a matter of fact, I move rather slowly."

"I see, you take your time," remarked the boy. "What do you use that scythe for?"

"To mow down the people," said the ancient one. "Every time I swing my scythe some one dies."

"Then I ought to win a life-saving medal by keeping you tied up," said

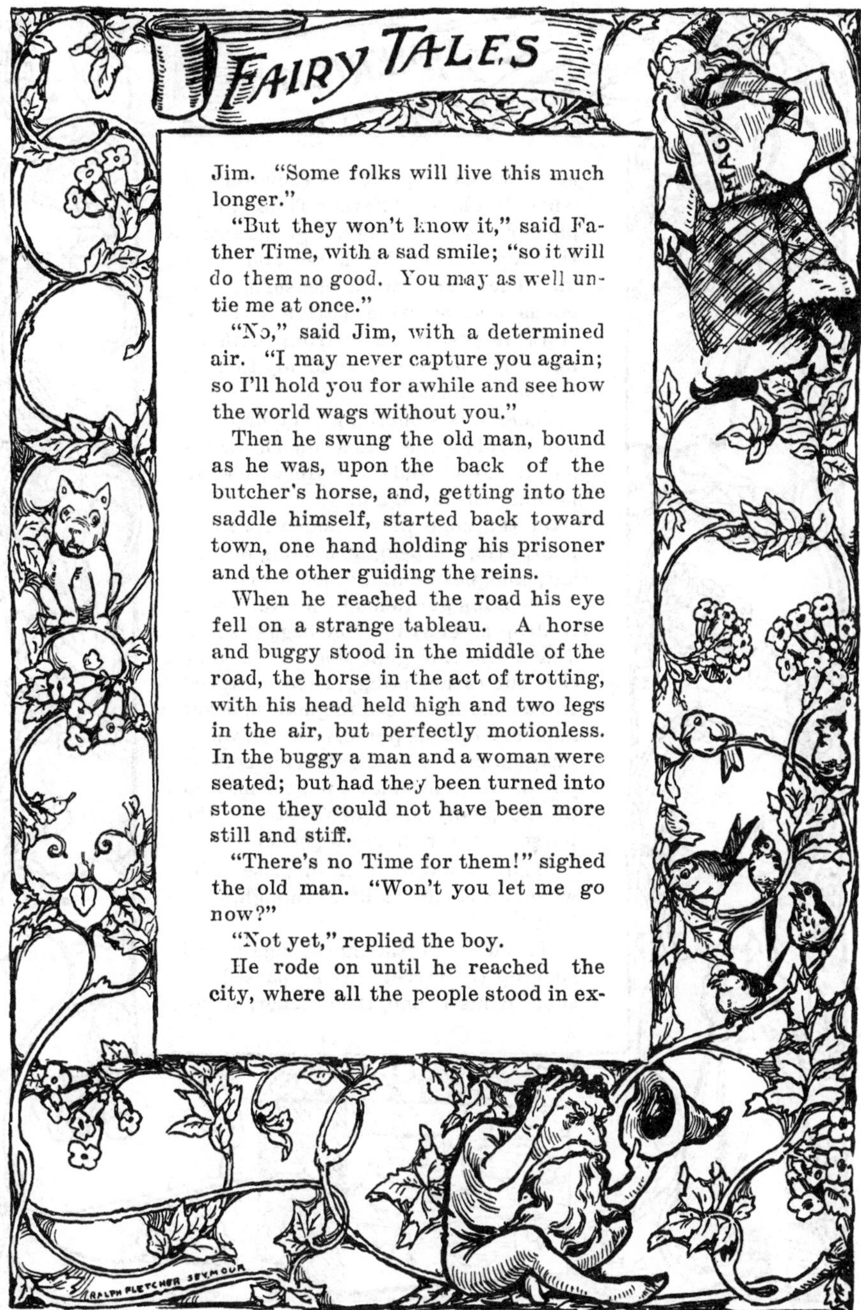

Jim. "Some folks will live this much longer."

"But they won't know it," said Father Time, with a sad smile; "so it will do them no good. You may as well untie me at once."

"No," said Jim, with a determined air. "I may never capture you again; so I'll hold you for awhile and see how the world wags without you."

Then he swung the old man, bound as he was, upon the back of the butcher's horse, and, getting into the saddle himself, started back toward town, one hand holding his prisoner and the other guiding the reins.

When he reached the road his eye fell on a strange tableau. A horse and buggy stood in the middle of the road, the horse in the act of trotting, with his head held high and two legs in the air, but perfectly motionless. In the buggy a man and a woman were seated; but had they been turned into stone they could not have been more still and stiff.

"There's no Time for them!" sighed the old man. "Won't you let me go now?"

"Not yet," replied the boy.

He rode on until he reached the city, where all the people stood in ex-

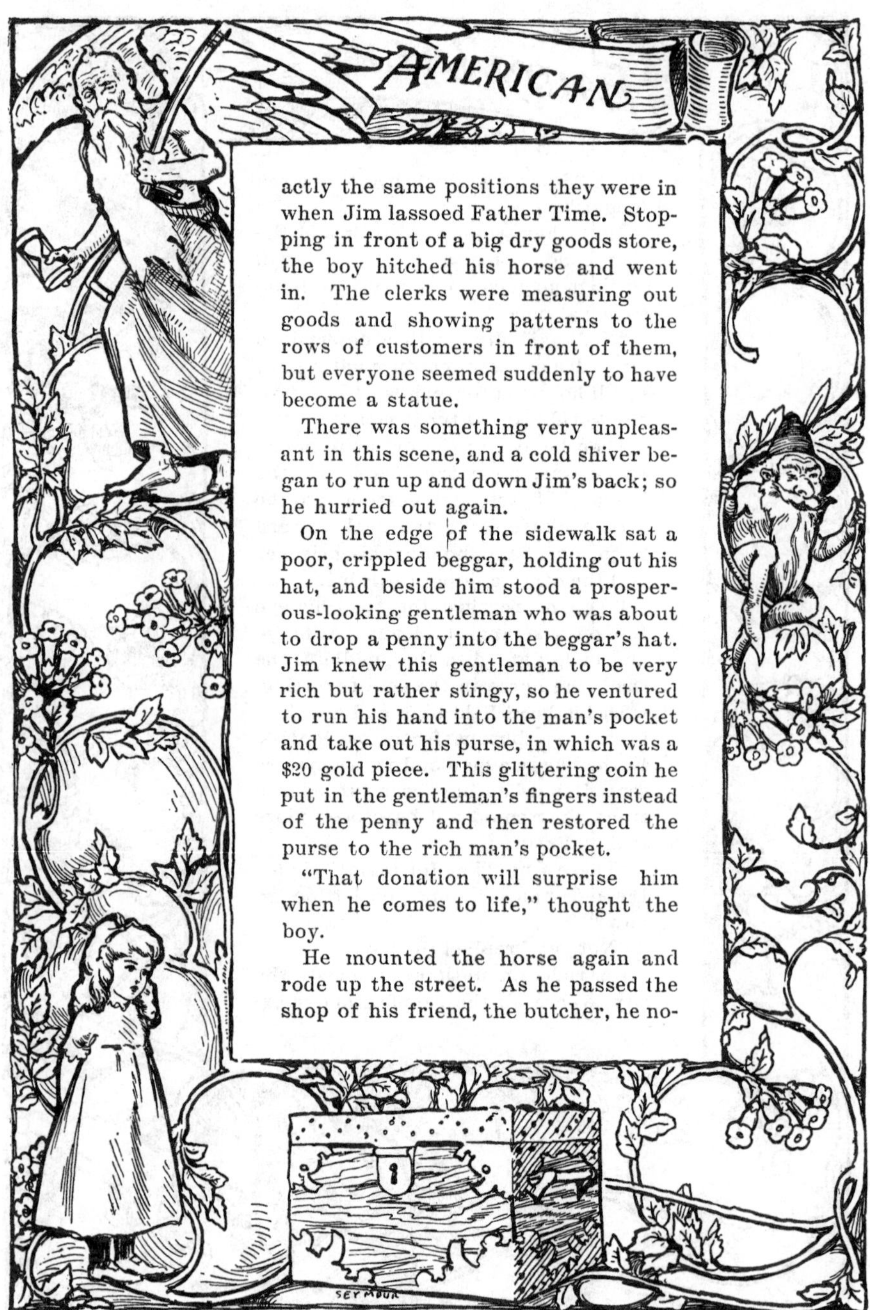

actly the same positions they were in when Jim lassoed Father Time. Stopping in front of a big dry goods store, the boy hitched his horse and went in. The clerks were measuring out goods and showing patterns to the rows of customers in front of them, but everyone seemed suddenly to have become a statue.

There was something very unpleasant in this scene, and a cold shiver began to run up and down Jim's back; so he hurried out again.

On the edge of the sidewalk sat a poor, crippled beggar, holding out his hat, and beside him stood a prosperous-looking gentleman who was about to drop a penny into the beggar's hat. Jim knew this gentleman to be very rich but rather stingy, so he ventured to run his hand into the man's pocket and take out his purse, in which was a $20 gold piece. This glittering coin he put in the gentleman's fingers instead of the penny and then restored the purse to the rich man's pocket.

"That donation will surprise him when he comes to life," thought the boy.

He mounted the horse again and rode up the street. As he passed the shop of his friend, the butcher, he no-

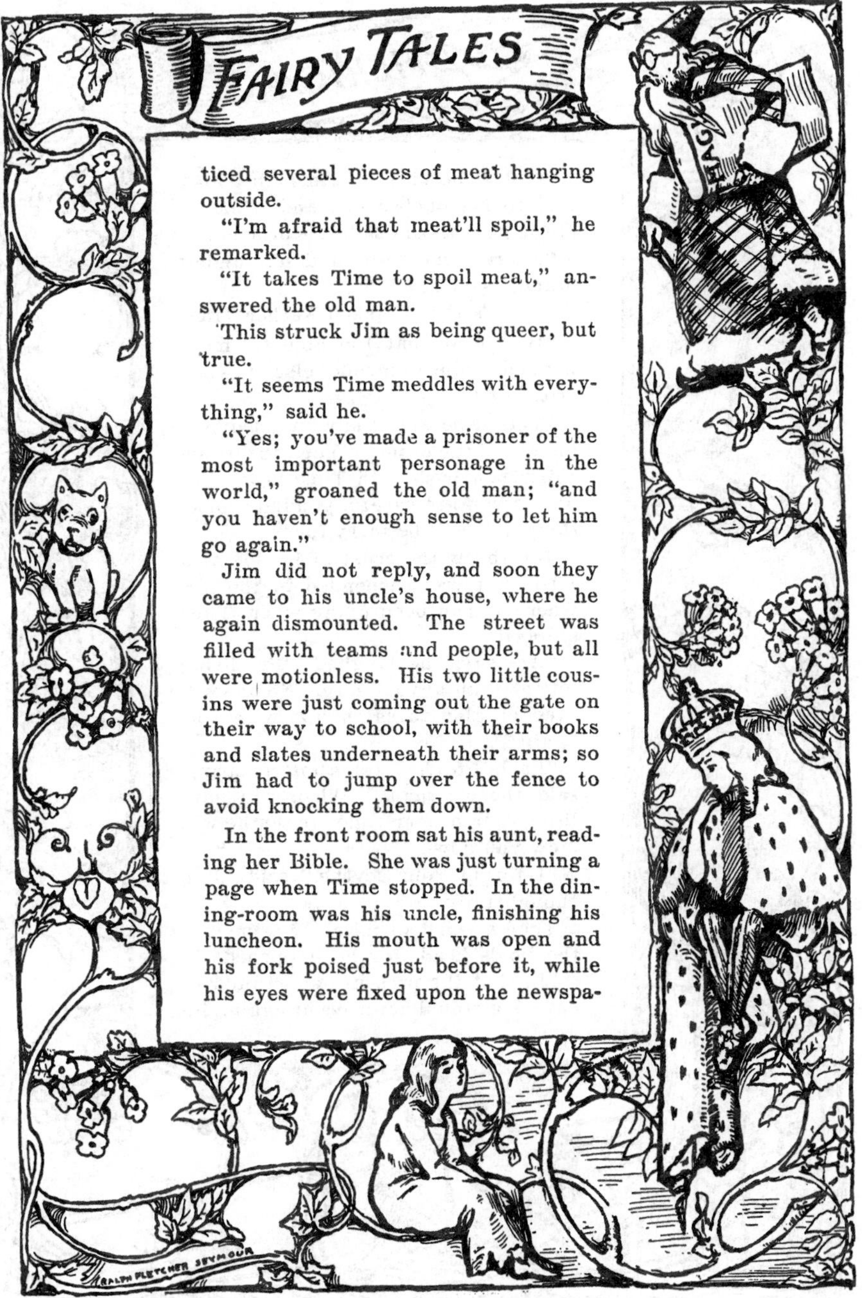

ticed several pieces of meat hanging outside.

"I'm afraid that meat'll spoil," he remarked.

"It takes Time to spoil meat," answered the old man.

This struck Jim as being queer, but true.

"It seems Time meddles with everything," said he.

"Yes; you've made a prisoner of the most important personage in the world," groaned the old man; "and you haven't enough sense to let him go again."

Jim did not reply, and soon they came to his uncle's house, where he again dismounted. The street was filled with teams and people, but all were motionless. His two little cousins were just coming out the gate on their way to school, with their books and slates underneath their arms; so Jim had to jump over the fence to avoid knocking them down.

In the front room sat his aunt, reading her Bible. She was just turning a page when Time stopped. In the dining-room was his uncle, finishing his luncheon. His mouth was open and his fork poised just before it, while his eyes were fixed upon the newspa-

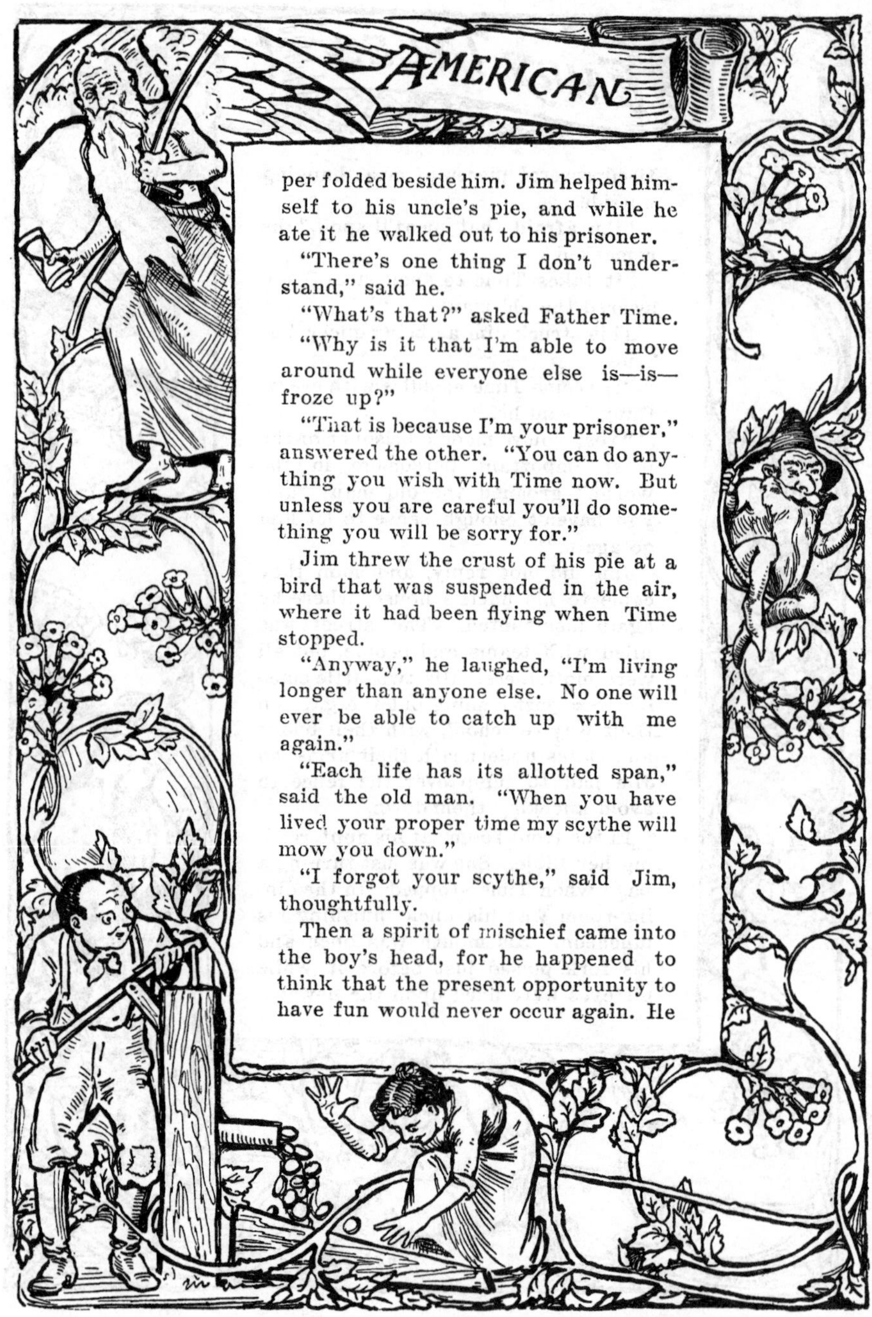

per folded beside him. Jim helped himself to his uncle's pie, and while he ate it he walked out to his prisoner.

"There's one thing I don't understand," said he.

"What's that?" asked Father Time.

"Why is it that I'm able to move around while everyone else is—is—froze up?"

"That is because I'm your prisoner," answered the other. "You can do anything you wish with Time now. But unless you are careful you'll do something you will be sorry for."

Jim threw the crust of his pie at a bird that was suspended in the air, where it had been flying when Time stopped.

"Anyway," he laughed, "I'm living longer than anyone else. No one will ever be able to catch up with me again."

"Each life has its allotted span," said the old man. "When you have lived your proper time my scythe will mow you down."

"I forgot your scythe," said Jim, thoughtfully.

Then a spirit of mischief came into the boy's head, for he happened to think that the present opportunity to have fun would never occur again. He

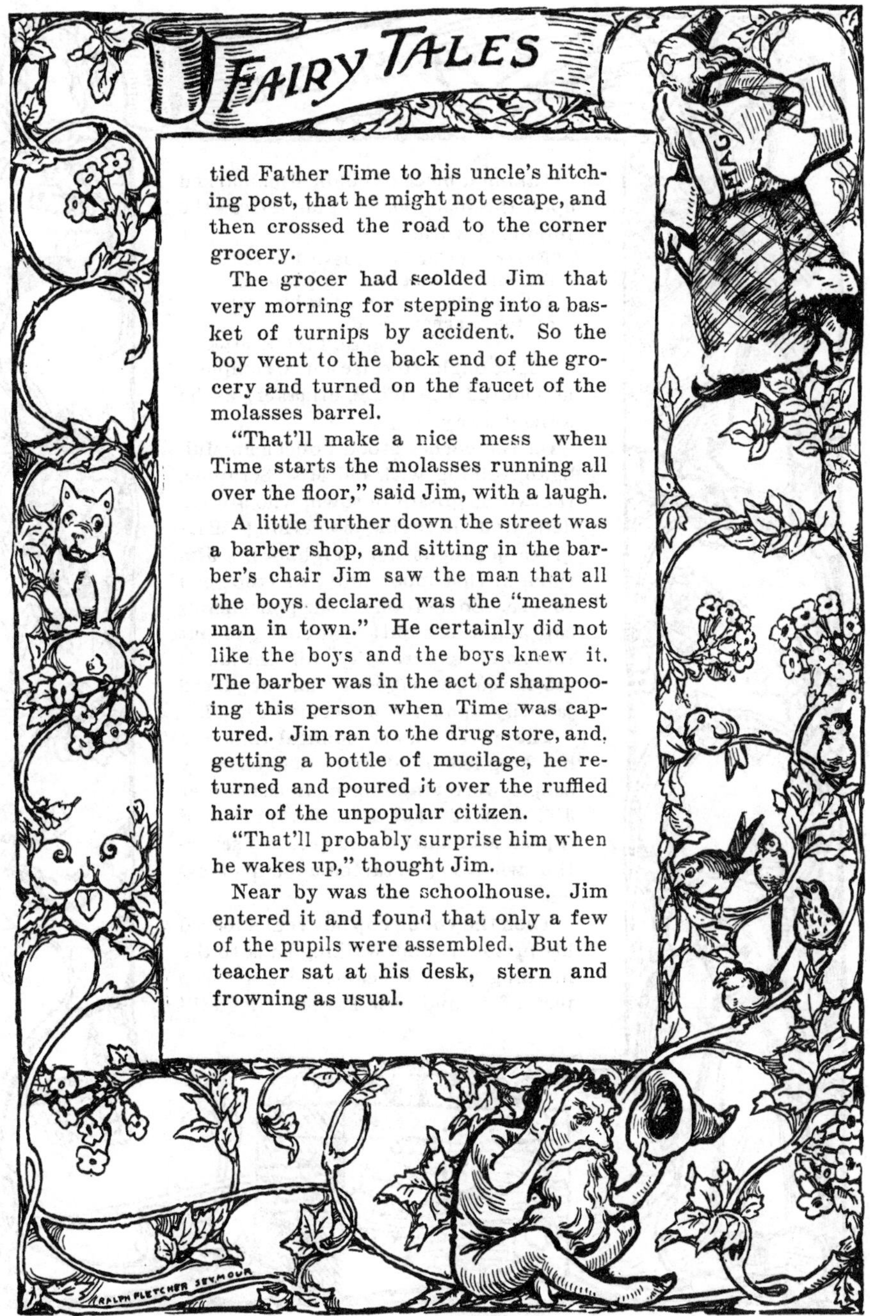

tied Father Time to his uncle's hitching post, that he might not escape, and then crossed the road to the corner grocery.

The grocer had scolded Jim that very morning for stepping into a basket of turnips by accident. So the boy went to the back end of the grocery and turned on the faucet of the molasses barrel.

"That'll make a nice mess when Time starts the molasses running all over the floor," said Jim, with a laugh.

A little further down the street was a barber shop, and sitting in the barber's chair Jim saw the man that all the boys declared was the "meanest man in town." He certainly did not like the boys and the boys knew it. The barber was in the act of shampooing this person when Time was captured. Jim ran to the drug store, and, getting a bottle of mucilage, he returned and poured it over the ruffled hair of the unpopular citizen.

"That'll probably surprise him when he wakes up," thought Jim.

Near by was the schoolhouse. Jim entered it and found that only a few of the pupils were assembled. But the teacher sat at his desk, stern and frowning as usual.

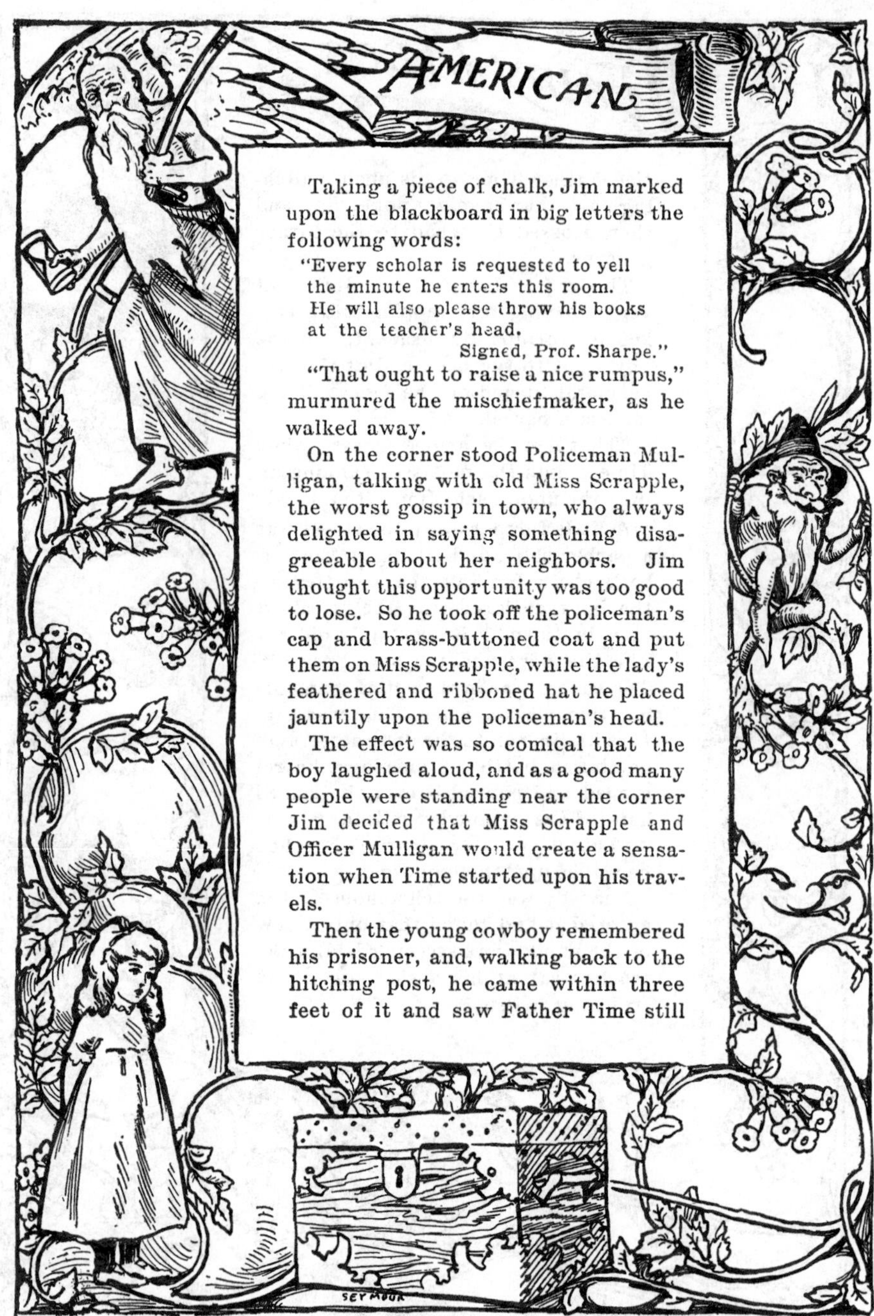

Taking a piece of chalk, Jim marked upon the blackboard in big letters the following words:

"Every scholar is requested to yell
the minute he enters this room.
He will also please throw his books
at the teacher's head.
Signed, Prof. Sharpe."

"That ought to raise a nice rumpus," murmured the mischiefmaker, as he walked away.

On the corner stood Policeman Mulligan, talking with old Miss Scrapple, the worst gossip in town, who always delighted in saying something disagreeable about her neighbors. Jim thought this opportunity was too good to lose. So he took off the policeman's cap and brass-buttoned coat and put them on Miss Scrapple, while the lady's feathered and ribboned hat he placed jauntily upon the policeman's head.

The effect was so comical that the boy laughed aloud, and as a good many people were standing near the corner Jim decided that Miss Scrapple and Officer Mulligan would create a sensation when Time started upon his travels.

Then the young cowboy remembered his prisoner, and, walking back to the hitching post, he came within three feet of it and saw Father Time still

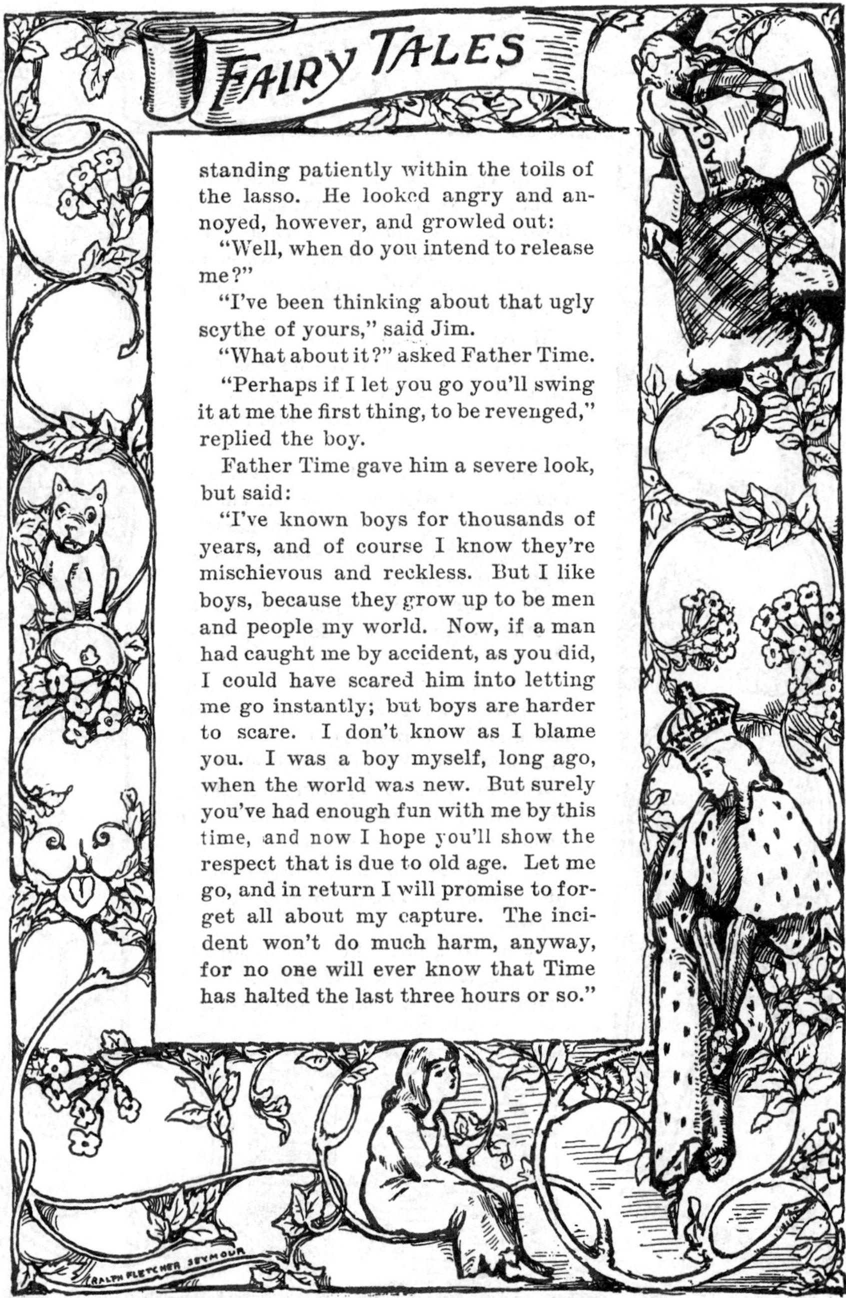

standing patiently within the toils of the lasso. He looked angry and annoyed, however, and growled out:

"Well, when do you intend to release me?"

"I've been thinking about that ugly scythe of yours," said Jim.

"What about it?" asked Father Time.

"Perhaps if I let you go you'll swing it at me the first thing, to be revenged," replied the boy.

Father Time gave him a severe look, but said:

"I've known boys for thousands of years, and of course I know they're mischievous and reckless. But I like boys, because they grow up to be men and people my world. Now, if a man had caught me by accident, as you did, I could have scared him into letting me go instantly; but boys are harder to scare. I don't know as I blame you. I was a boy myself, long ago, when the world was new. But surely you've had enough fun with me by this time, and now I hope you'll show the respect that is due to old age. Let me go, and in return I will promise to forget all about my capture. The incident won't do much harm, anyway, for no one will ever know that Time has halted the last three hours or so."

"All right," said Jim, cheerfully, "since you've promised not to mow me down, I'll let you go." But he had a notion some people in the town would suspect Time had stopped when they returned to life.

He carefully unwound the rope from the old man, who, when he was free, at once shouldered his scythe, re-arranged his white robe and nodded farewell.

The next moment he had disappeared, and with a rustle and rumble and roar of activity the world came to life again and jogged along as it always had before.

Jim wound up his lasso, mounted the butcher's horse and rode slowly down the street.

Loud screams came from the corner, where a great crowd of people quickly assembled. From his seat on the horse Jim saw Miss Scrapple, attired in the policeman's uniform, angrily shaking her fists in Mulligan's face, while the officer was furiously stamping upon the lady's hat, which he had torn from his own head amidst the jeers of the crowd.

As he rode past the schoolhouse he heard a tremendous chorus of yells, and knew Prof. Sharpe was having a

Angrily shaking her fists in Mulligan's face.

hard time to quell the riot caused by the sign on the blackboard.

Through the window of the barber shop he saw the "mean man" frantically belaboring the barber with a hair brush, while his hair stood up stiff as bayonets in all directions. And the grocer ran out of his door and yelled "Fire!" while his shoes left a track of molasses wherever he stepped.

Jim's heart was filled with joy. He was fairly reveling in the excitement he had caused when some one caught his leg and pulled him from the horse.

"What're ye doin' here, ye rascal?" cried the butcher, angrily; "didn't ye promise to put that beast inter Plympton's pasture? An' now I find ye ridin' the poor nag around like a gentleman o' leisure!"

"That's a fact," said Jim, with surprise; "I clean forgot about the horse!"

* * * * *

This story should teach us the supreme importance of Time and the folly of trying to stop it. For should you succeed, as Jim did, in bringing Time to a standstill, the world would soon become a dreary place and life decidedly unpleasant.

The WONDERFUL PUMP

Not many years ago there lived on a stony, barren New England farm a man and his wife. They were sober, honest people, working hard from early morning until dark to enable them to secure a scanty living from their poor land.

Their house, a small, one-storied building, stood upon the side of a steep hill, and the stones lay so thickly about it that scarce anything green could grow from the ground. At the foot of the hill, a quarter of a mile from the house by the winding path, was a small brook, and the woman was obliged to go there for water and to carry it up the hill to the house. This was a tedious task, and with the other hard work that fell to her share had made her gaunt and bent and lean.

Yet she never complained, but

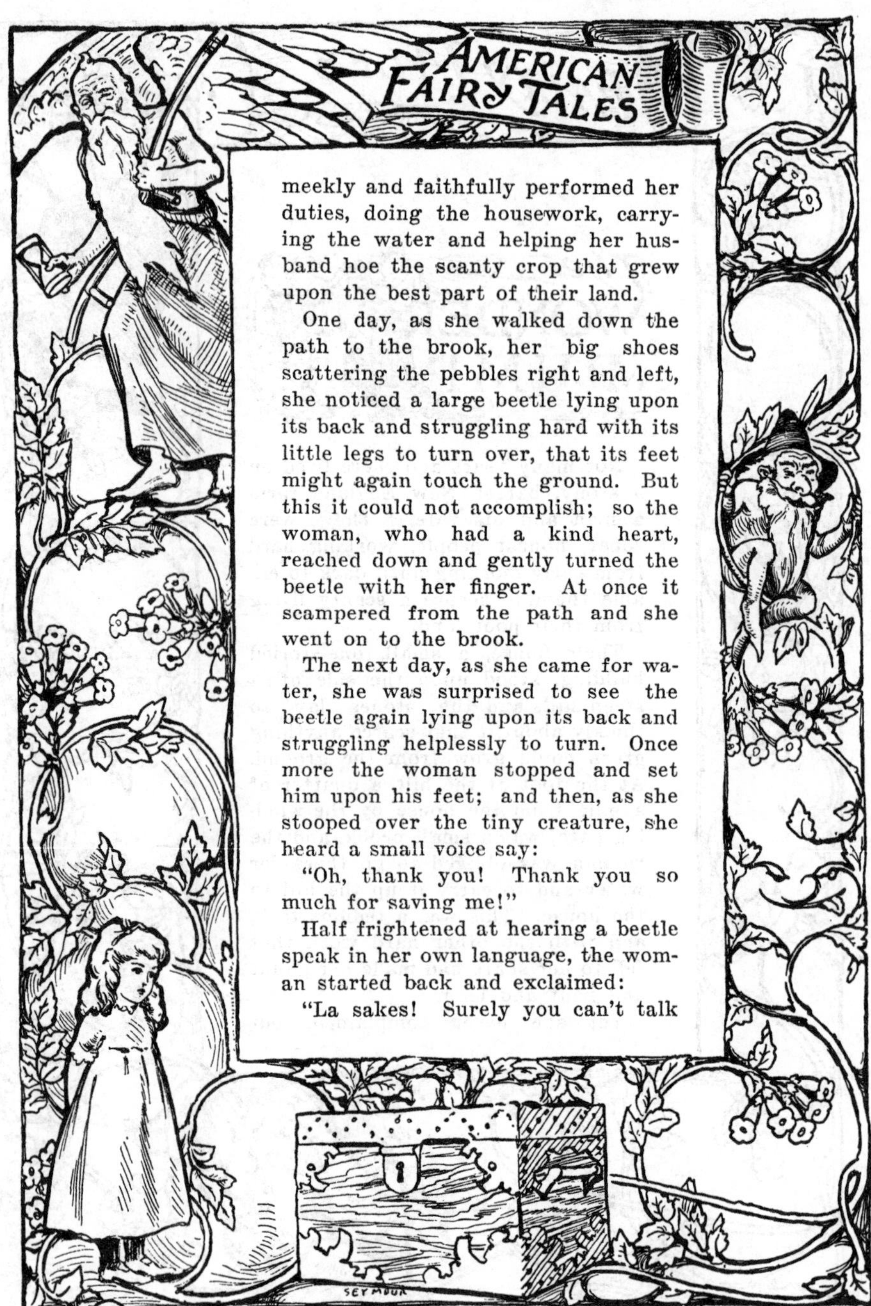

meekly and faithfully performed her duties, doing the housework, carrying the water and helping her husband hoe the scanty crop that grew upon the best part of their land.

One day, as she walked down the path to the brook, her big shoes scattering the pebbles right and left, she noticed a large beetle lying upon its back and struggling hard with its little legs to turn over, that its feet might again touch the ground. But this it could not accomplish; so the woman, who had a kind heart, reached down and gently turned the beetle with her finger. At once it scampered from the path and she went on to the brook.

The next day, as she came for water, she was surprised to see the beetle again lying upon its back and struggling helplessly to turn. Once more the woman stopped and set him upon his feet; and then, as she stooped over the tiny creature, she heard a small voice say:

"Oh, thank you! Thank you so much for saving me!"

Half frightened at hearing a beetle speak in her own language, the woman started back and exclaimed:

"La sakes! Surely you can't talk

"Why shouldn't I talk?" said the beetle.

like humans!" Then, recovering from her alarm, she again bent over the beetle, who answered her:

"Why shouldn't I talk, if I have anything to say?

" 'Cause your a bug," replied the woman.

"That is true; and you saved my life—saved me from my enemies, the sparrows. And this is the second time you have come to my assistance, so I owe you a debt of gratitude. Bugs value their lives as much as human beings, and I am a more important creature than you, in your ignorance, may suppose. But, tell me, why do you come each day to the brook?"

"For water," she answered, staring stupidly down at the talking beetle.

"Isn't it hard work?" the creature inquired.

"Yes; but there's no water on the hill," said she.

"Then dig a well and put a pump in it," replied the beetle.

She shook her head.

"My man tried it once; but there was no water," she said, sadly.

"Try it again," commanded the beetle; "and in return for your kindness to me I will make this promise:

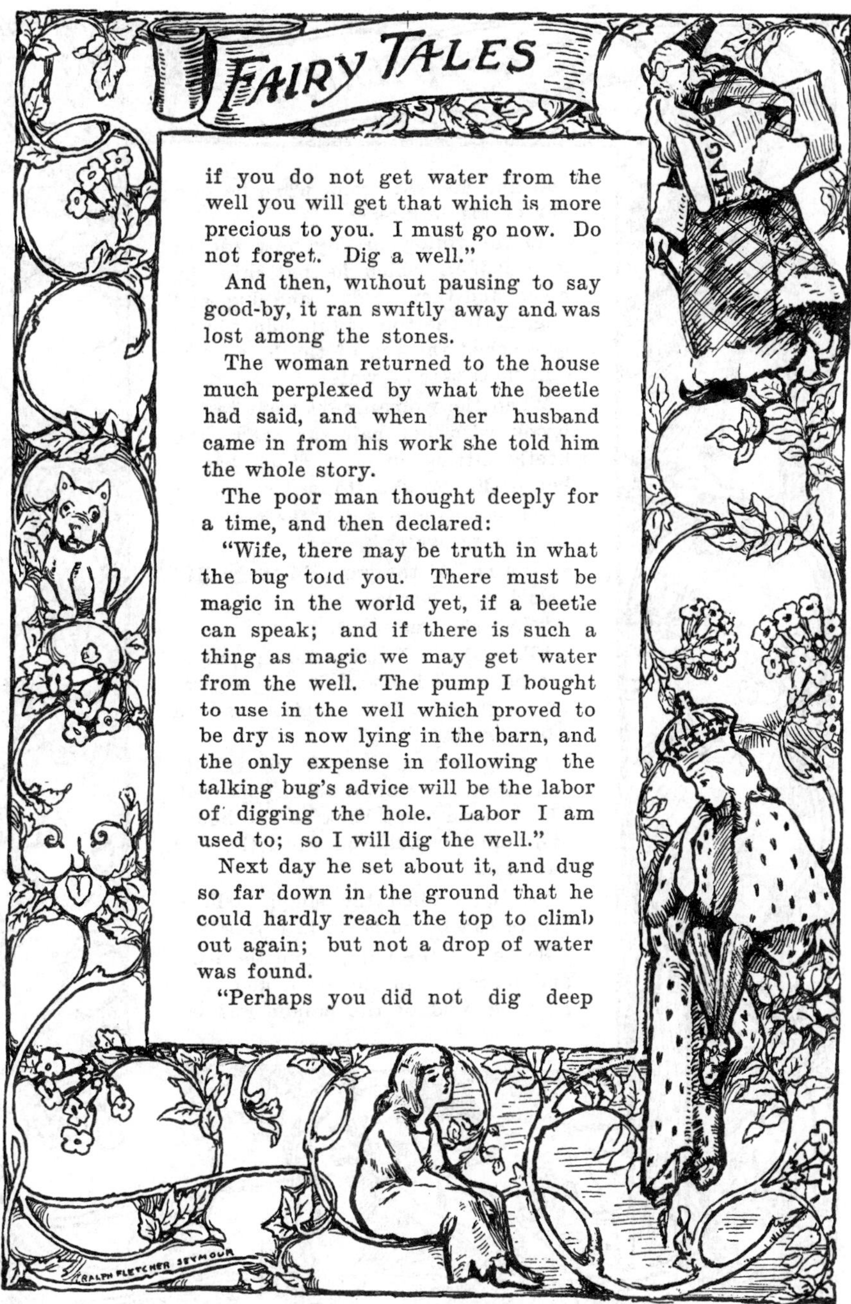

if you do not get water from the well you will get that which is more precious to you. I must go now. Do not forget. Dig a well."

And then, without pausing to say good-by, it ran swiftly away and was lost among the stones.

The woman returned to the house much perplexed by what the beetle had said, and when her husband came in from his work she told him the whole story.

The poor man thought deeply for a time, and then declared:

"Wife, there may be truth in what the bug told you. There must be magic in the world yet, if a beetle can speak; and if there is such a thing as magic we may get water from the well. The pump I bought to use in the well which proved to be dry is now lying in the barn, and the only expense in following the talking bug's advice will be the labor of digging the hole. Labor I am used to; so I will dig the well."

Next day he set about it, and dug so far down in the ground that he could hardly reach the top to climb out again; but not a drop of water was found.

"Perhaps you did not dig deep

enough," his wife said, when he told her of his failure.

So the following day he made a long ladder, which he put into the hole; and then he dug, and dug, and dug, until the top of the ladder barely reached the top of the hole. But still there was no water.

When the woman next went to the brook with her pail she saw the beetle sitting upon a stone beside her path. So she stopped and said:

"My husband has dug the well; but there is no water."

"Did he put the pump in the well?" asked the beetle.

"No," she answered.

"Then do as I commanded; put in the pump, and if you do not get water I promise you something still more precious."

Saying which, the beetle swiftly slid from the stone and disappeared. The woman went back to the house and told her husband what the bug had said.

"Well," replied the simple fellow, "there can be no harm in trying."

So he got the pump from the barn and placed it in the well, and then he took hold of the handle and be-

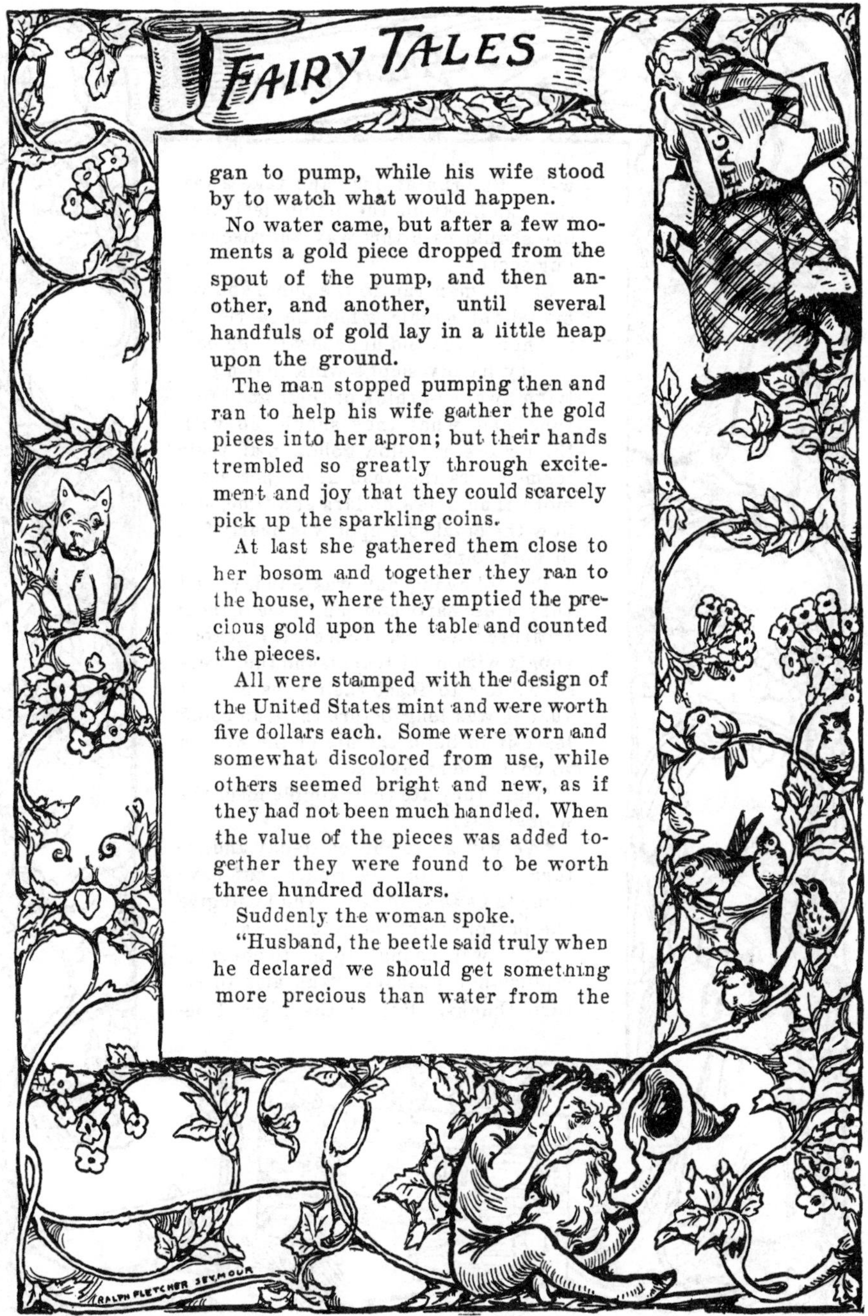

gan to pump, while his wife stood by to watch what would happen.

No water came, but after a few moments a gold piece dropped from the spout of the pump, and then another, and another, until several handfuls of gold lay in a little heap upon the ground.

The man stopped pumping then and ran to help his wife gather the gold pieces into her apron; but their hands trembled so greatly through excitement and joy that they could scarcely pick up the sparkling coins.

At last she gathered them close to her bosom and together they ran to the house, where they emptied the precious gold upon the table and counted the pieces.

All were stamped with the design of the United States mint and were worth five dollars each. Some were worn and somewhat discolored from use, while others seemed bright and new, as if they had not been much handled. When the value of the pieces was added together they were found to be worth three hundred dollars.

Suddenly the woman spoke.

"Husband, the beetle said truly when he declared we should get something more precious than water from the

well. But run at once and take away the handle from the pump, lest anyone should pass this way and discover our secret."

So the man ran to the pump and removed the handle, which he carried to the house and hid underneath the bed.

They hardly slept a wink that night, lying awake to think of their good fortune and what they should do with their store of yellow gold. In all their former lives they had never possessed more than a few dollars at a time, and now the cracked teapot was nearly full of gold coins.

The following day was Sunday, and they arose early and ran to see if their treasure was safe. There it lay, heaped snugly within the teapot, and they were so willing to feast their eyes upon it that it was long before the man could leave it to build the fire or the woman to cook the breakfast.

While they ate their simple meal the woman said:

"We will go to church to-day and return thanks for the riches that have come to us so suddenly. And I will give the pastor one of the gold pieces."

"It is well enough to go to church," replied her husband, "and also to return thanks. But in the night I de-

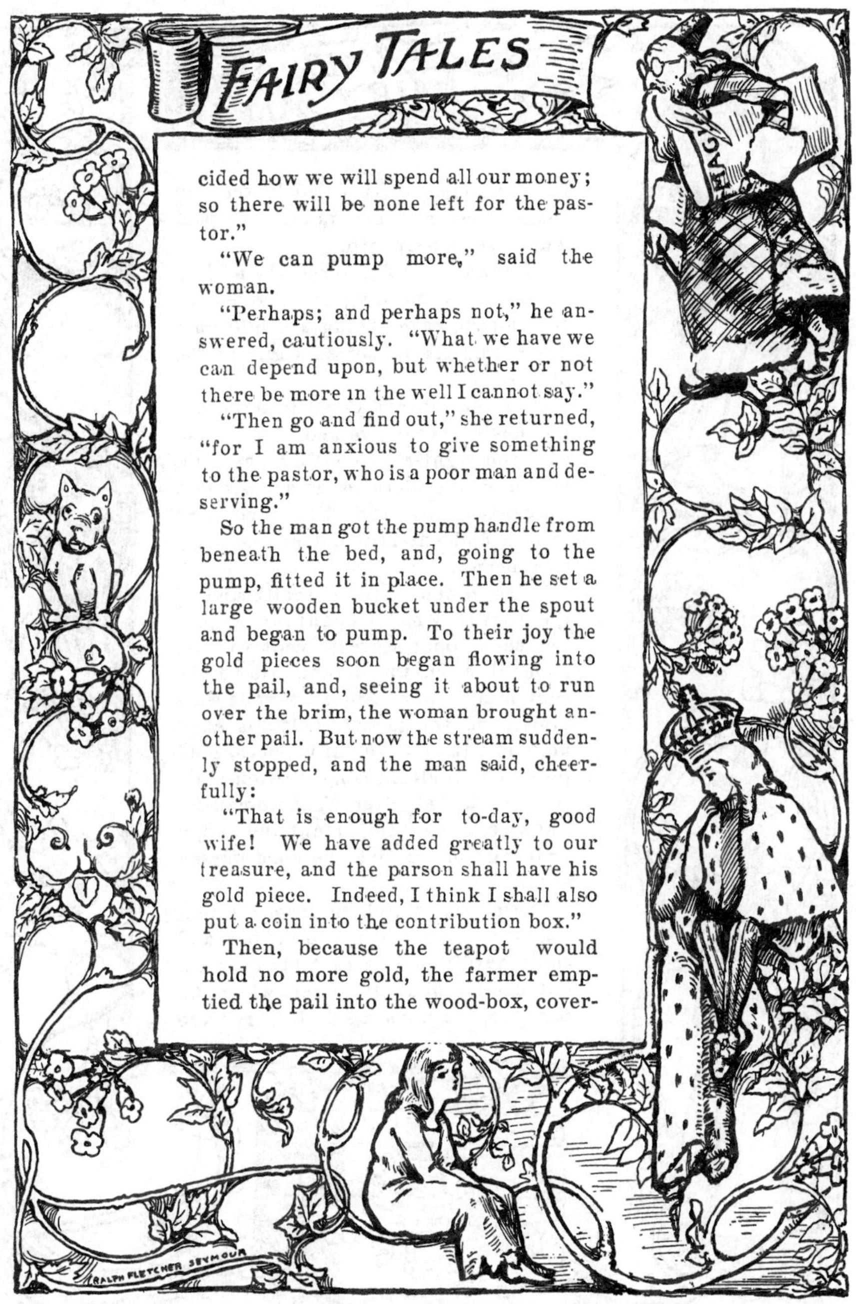

cided how we will spend all our money; so there will be none left for the pastor."

"We can pump more," said the woman.

"Perhaps; and perhaps not," he answered, cautiously. "What we have we can depend upon, but whether or not there be more in the well I cannot say."

"Then go and find out," she returned, "for I am anxious to give something to the pastor, who is a poor man and deserving."

So the man got the pump handle from beneath the bed, and, going to the pump, fitted it in place. Then he set a large wooden bucket under the spout and began to pump. To their joy the gold pieces soon began flowing into the pail, and, seeing it about to run over the brim, the woman brought another pail. But now the stream suddenly stopped, and the man said, cheerfully:

"That is enough for to-day, good wife! We have added greatly to our treasure, and the parson shall have his gold piece. Indeed, I think I shall also put a coin into the contribution box."

Then, because the teapot would hold no more gold, the farmer emptied the pail into the wood-box, cover-

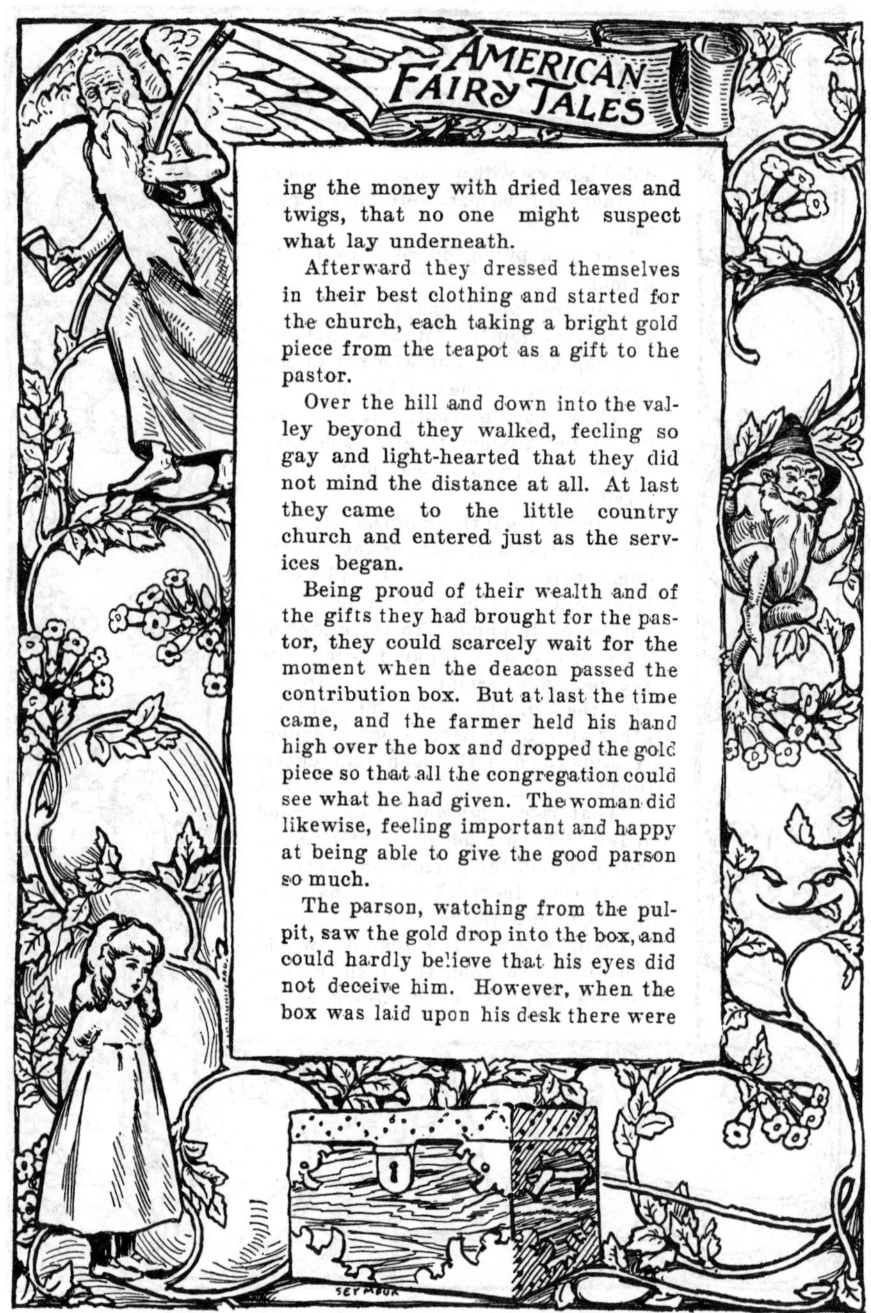

ing the money with dried leaves and twigs, that no one might suspect what lay underneath.

Afterward they dressed themselves in their best clothing and started for the church, each taking a bright gold piece from the teapot as a gift to the pastor.

Over the hill and down into the valley beyond they walked, feeling so gay and light-hearted that they did not mind the distance at all. At last they came to the little country church and entered just as the services began.

Being proud of their wealth and of the gifts they had brought for the pastor, they could scarcely wait for the moment when the deacon passed the contribution box. But at last the time came, and the farmer held his hand high over the box and dropped the gold piece so that all the congregation could see what he had given. The woman did likewise, feeling important and happy at being able to give the good parson so much.

The parson, watching from the pulpit, saw the gold drop into the box, and could hardly believe that his eyes did not deceive him. However, when the box was laid upon his desk there were

No water came, but gold pieces.

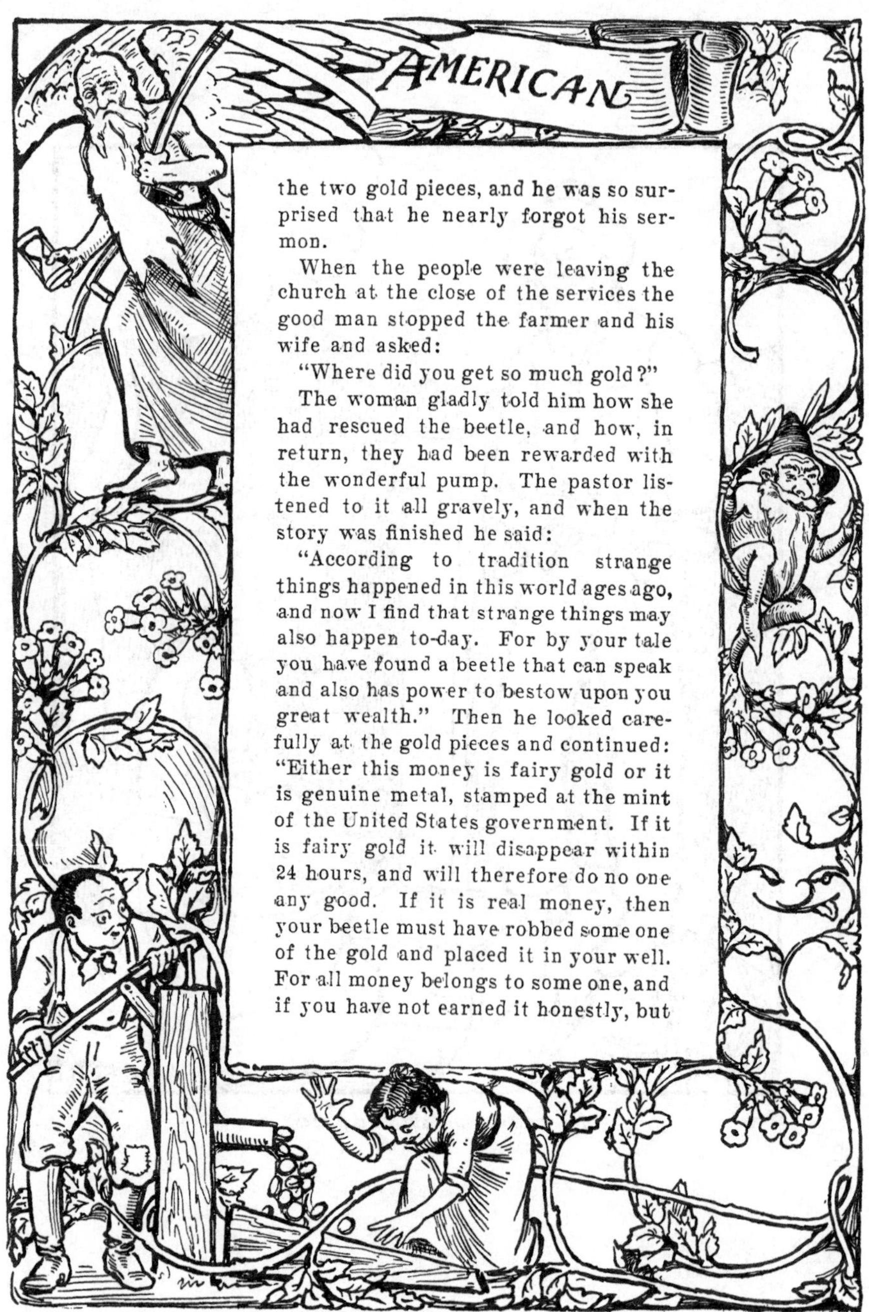

the two gold pieces, and he was so surprised that he nearly forgot his sermon.

When the people were leaving the church at the close of the services the good man stopped the farmer and his wife and asked:

"Where did you get so much gold?"

The woman gladly told him how she had rescued the beetle, and how, in return, they had been rewarded with the wonderful pump. The pastor listened to it all gravely, and when the story was finished he said:

"According to tradition strange things happened in this world ages ago, and now I find that strange things may also happen to-day. For by your tale you have found a beetle that can speak and also has power to bestow upon you great wealth." Then he looked carefully at the gold pieces and continued: "Either this money is fairy gold or it is genuine metal, stamped at the mint of the United States government. If it is fairy gold it will disappear within 24 hours, and will therefore do no one any good. If it is real money, then your beetle must have robbed some one of the gold and placed it in your well. For all money belongs to some one, and if you have not earned it honestly, but

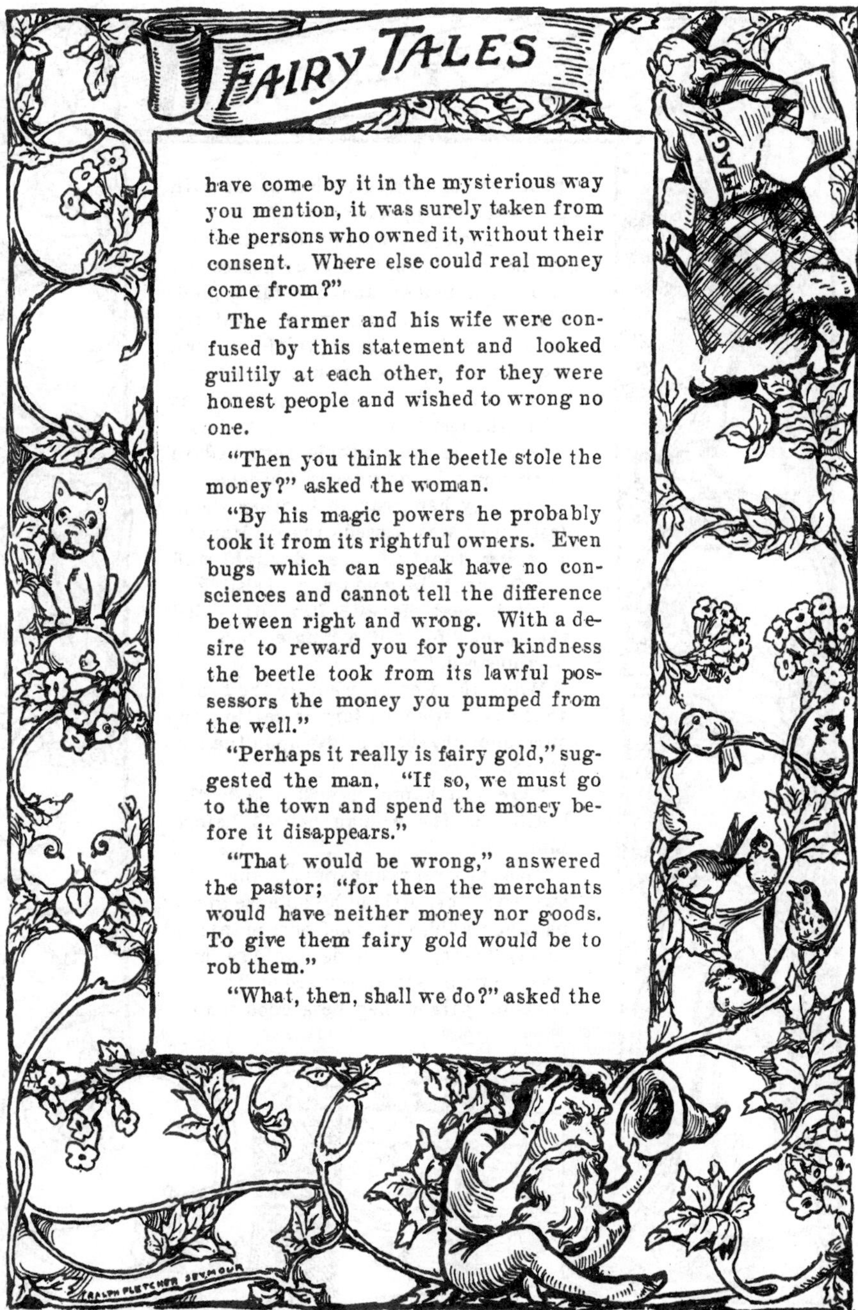

have come by it in the mysterious way you mention, it was surely taken from the persons who owned it, without their consent. Where else could real money come from?"

The farmer and his wife were confused by this statement and looked guiltily at each other, for they were honest people and wished to wrong no one.

"Then you think the beetle stole the money?" asked the woman.

"By his magic powers he probably took it from its rightful owners. Even bugs which can speak have no consciences and cannot tell the difference between right and wrong. With a desire to reward you for your kindness the beetle took from its lawful possessors the money you pumped from the well."

"Perhaps it really is fairy gold," suggested the man. "If so, we must go to the town and spend the money before it disappears."

"That would be wrong," answered the pastor; "for then the merchants would have neither money nor goods. To give them fairy gold would be to rob them."

"What, then, shall we do?" asked the

poor woman, wringing her hands with grief and disappointment.

"Go home and wait until to-morrow. If the gold is then in your possession it is real money and not fairy gold. But if it is real money you must try to restore it to its rightful owners. Take, also, these pieces which you have given me, for I cannot accept gold that is not honestly come by."

Sadly the poor people returned to their home, being greatly disturbed by what they had heard. Another sleepless night was passed, and on Monday morning they arose at daylight and ran to see if the gold was still visible.

"It is real money, after all!" cried the man; "for not a single piece has disappeared."

When the woman went to the brook that day she looked for the beetle, and, sure enough, there he sat upon the flat stone.

"Are you happy now?" asked the beetle, as the woman paused before him.

"We are very unhappy," she answered; "for, although you have given us much gold, our good parson says it surely belongs to some one else, and was stolen by you to reward us."

"Your parson may be a good man,"

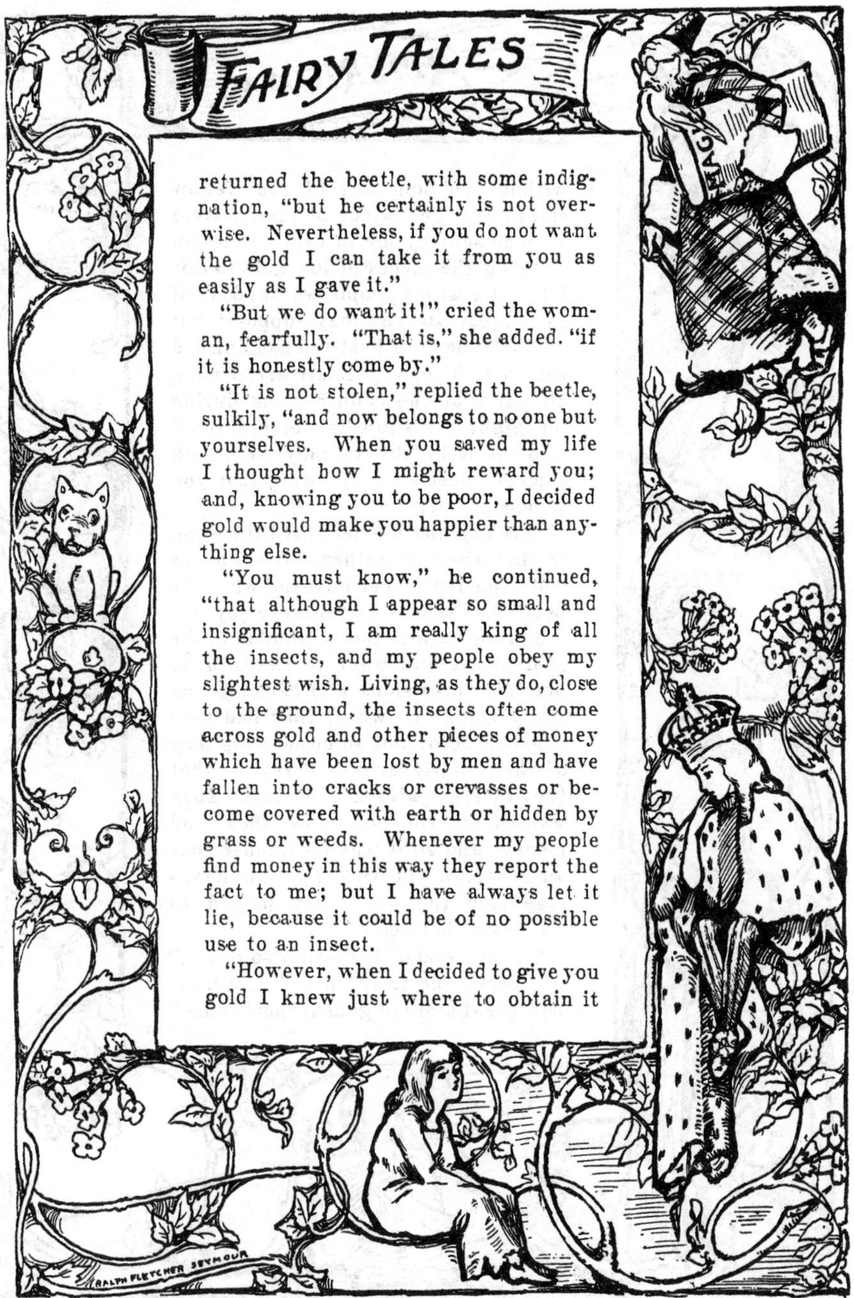

returned the beetle, with some indignation, "but he certainly is not overwise. Nevertheless, if you do not want the gold I can take it from you as easily as I gave it."

"But we do want it!" cried the woman, fearfully. "That is," she added. "if it is honestly come by."

"It is not stolen," replied the beetle, sulkily, "and now belongs to no one but yourselves. When you saved my life I thought how I might reward you; and, knowing you to be poor, I decided gold would make you happier than anything else.

"You must know," he continued, "that although I appear so small and insignificant, I am really king of all the insects, and my people obey my slightest wish. Living, as they do, close to the ground, the insects often come across gold and other pieces of money which have been lost by men and have fallen into cracks or crevasses or become covered with earth or hidden by grass or weeds. Whenever my people find money in this way they report the fact to me; but I have always let it lie, because it could be of no possible use to an insect.

"However, when I decided to give you gold I knew just where to obtain it

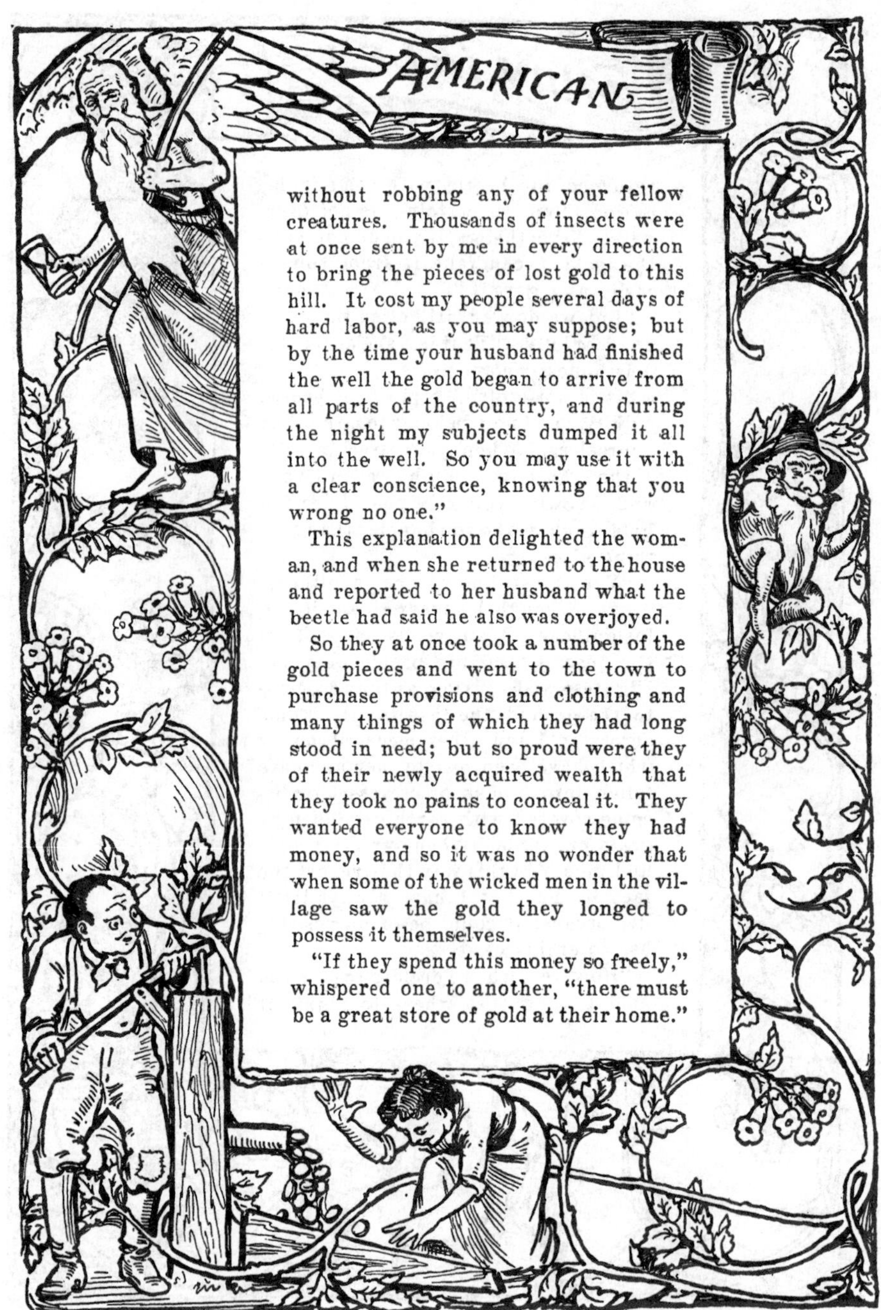

without robbing any of your fellow creatures. Thousands of insects were at once sent by me in every direction to bring the pieces of lost gold to this hill. It cost my people several days of hard labor, as you may suppose; but by the time your husband had finished the well the gold began to arrive from all parts of the country, and during the night my subjects dumped it all into the well. So you may use it with a clear conscience, knowing that you wrong no one."

This explanation delighted the woman, and when she returned to the house and reported to her husband what the beetle had said he also was overjoyed.

So they at once took a number of the gold pieces and went to the town to purchase provisions and clothing and many things of which they had long stood in need; but so proud were they of their newly acquired wealth that they took no pains to conceal it. They wanted everyone to know they had money, and so it was no wonder that when some of the wicked men in the village saw the gold they longed to possess it themselves.

"If they spend this money so freely," whispered one to another, "there must be a great store of gold at their home."

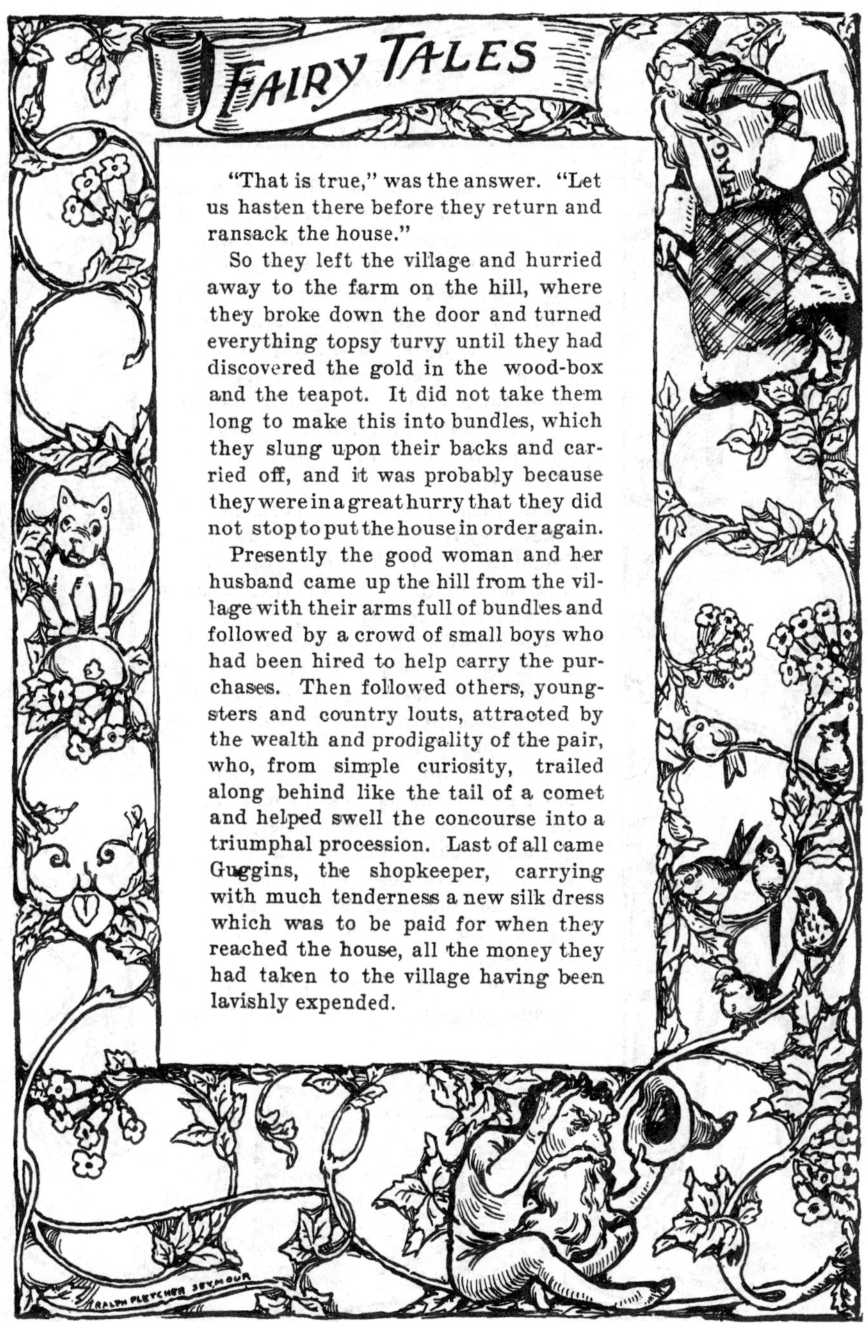

"That is true," was the answer. "Let us hasten there before they return and ransack the house."

So they left the village and hurried away to the farm on the hill, where they broke down the door and turned everything topsy turvy until they had discovered the gold in the wood-box and the teapot. It did not take them long to make this into bundles, which they slung upon their backs and carried off, and it was probably because they were in a great hurry that they did not stop to put the house in order again.

Presently the good woman and her husband came up the hill from the village with their arms full of bundles and followed by a crowd of small boys who had been hired to help carry the purchases. Then followed others, youngsters and country louts, attracted by the wealth and prodigality of the pair, who, from simple curiosity, trailed along behind like the tail of a comet and helped swell the concourse into a triumphal procession. Last of all came Guggins, the shopkeeper, carrying with much tenderness a new silk dress which was to be paid for when they reached the house, all the money they had taken to the village having been lavishly expended.

The farmer, who had formerly been a modest man, was now so swelled with pride that he tipped the rim of his hat over his left ear and smoked a big cigar that was fast making him ill. His wife strutted along beside him like a peacock, enjoying to the full the homage and respect her wealth had won from those who formerly deigned not to notice her, and glancing from time to time at the admiring procession in the rear.

But, alas for their new-born pride! when they reached the farmhouse they found the door broken in, the furniture strewn in all directions and their treasure stolen to the very last gold piece.

The crowd grinned and made slighting remarks of a personal nature, and Guggins, the shopkeeper, demanded in a loud voice the money for the silk dress he had brought.

Then the woman whispered her husband to run and pump some more gold while she kept the crowd quiet, and he obeyed quickly. But after a few moments he returned with a white face to tell her the pump was dry, and not a gold piece could now be coaxed from the spout.

The procession marched back to the village laughing and jeering at the

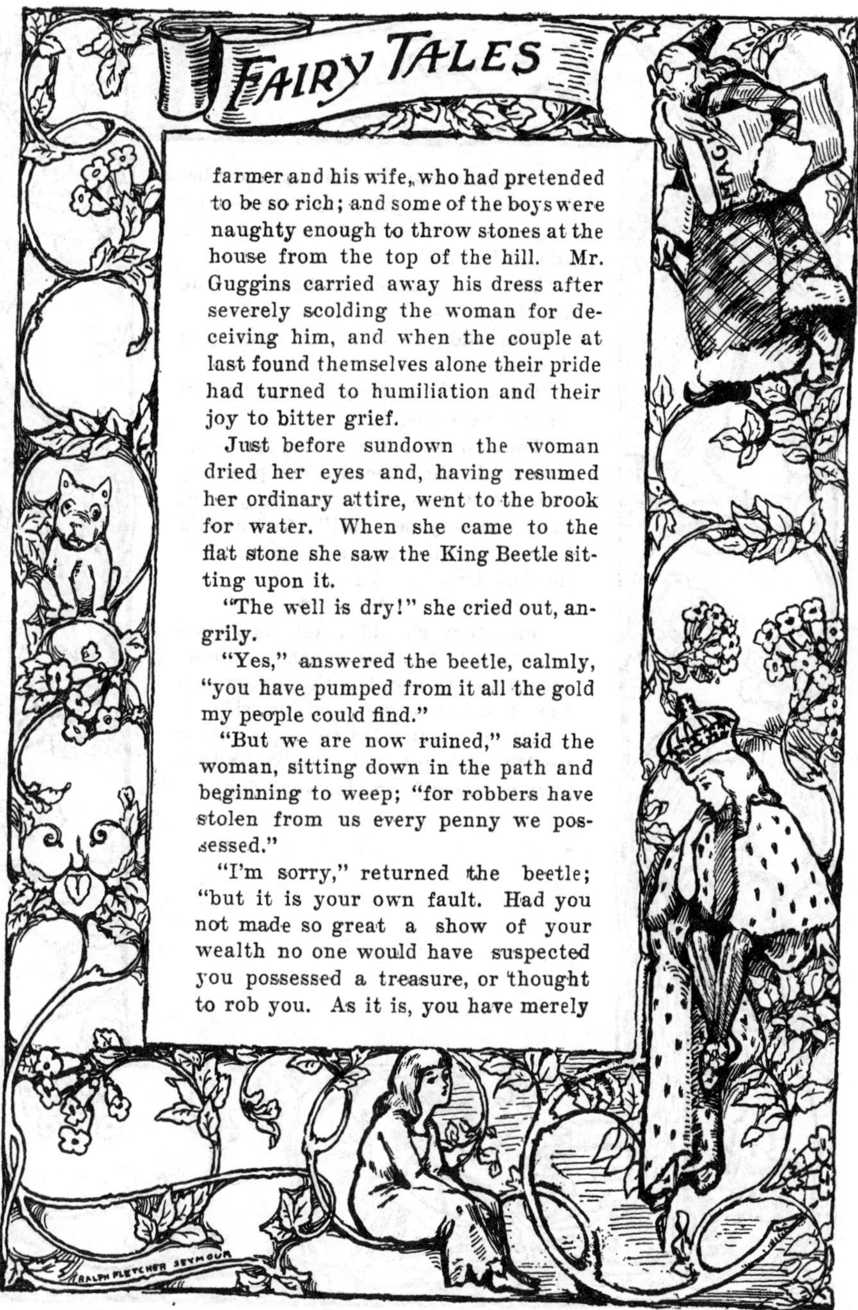

farmer and his wife, who had pretended to be so rich; and some of the boys were naughty enough to throw stones at the house from the top of the hill. Mr. Guggins carried away his dress after severely scolding the woman for deceiving him, and when the couple at last found themselves alone their pride had turned to humiliation and their joy to bitter grief.

Just before sundown the woman dried her eyes and, having resumed her ordinary attire, went to the brook for water. When she came to the flat stone she saw the King Beetle sitting upon it.

"The well is dry!" she cried out, angrily.

"Yes," answered the beetle, calmly, "you have pumped from it all the gold my people could find."

"But we are now ruined," said the woman, sitting down in the path and beginning to weep; "for robbers have stolen from us every penny we possessed."

"I'm sorry," returned the beetle; "but it is your own fault. Had you not made so great a show of your wealth no one would have suspected you possessed a treasure, or thought to rob you. As it is, you have merely

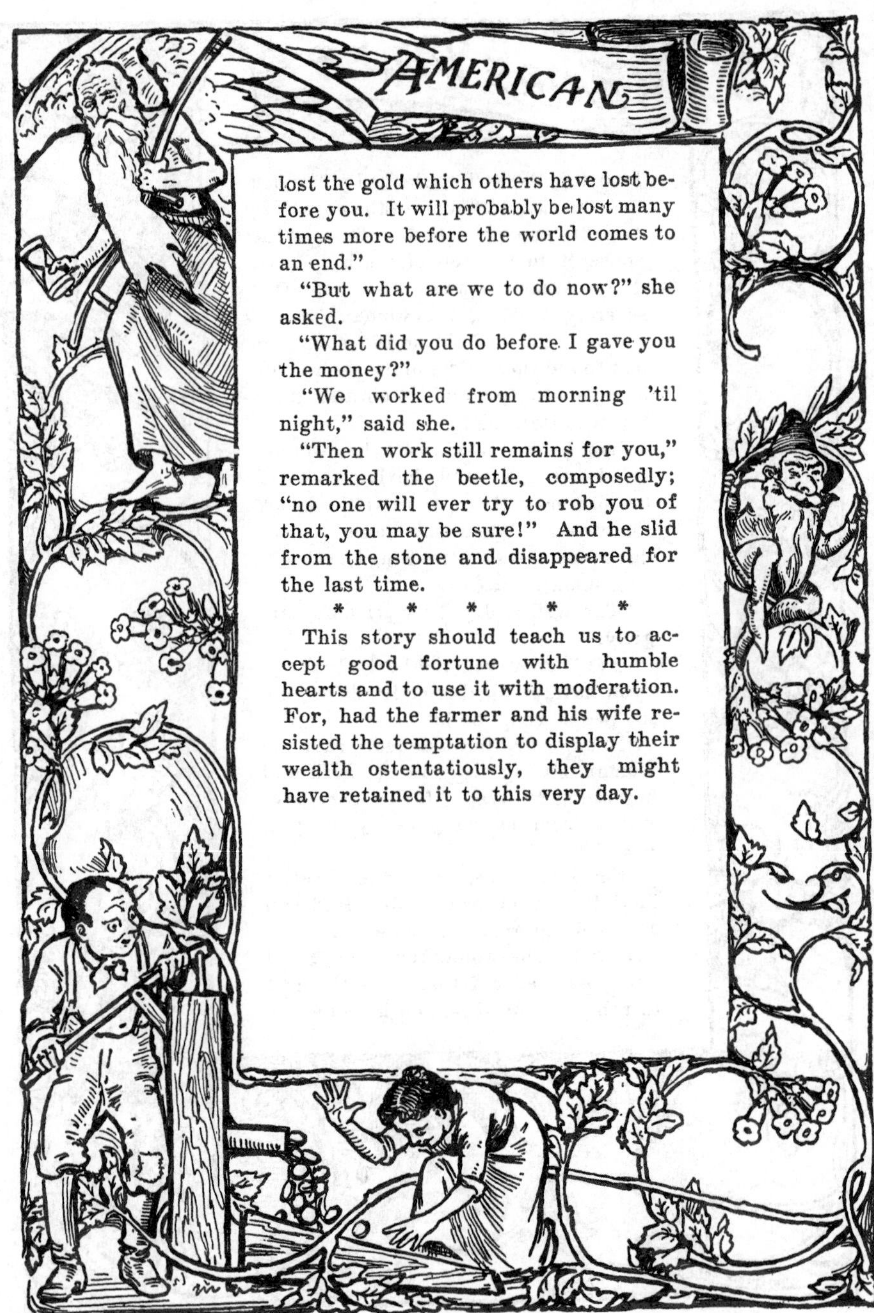

lost the gold which others have lost before you. It will probably be lost many times more before the world comes to an end."

"But what are we to do now?" she asked.

"What did you do before I gave you the money?"

"We worked from morning 'til night," said she.

"Then work still remains for you," remarked the beetle, composedly; "no one will ever try to rob you of that, you may be sure!" And he slid from the stone and disappeared for the last time.

* * * * *

This story should teach us to accept good fortune with humble hearts and to use it with moderation. For, had the farmer and his wife resisted the temptation to display their wealth ostentatiously, they might have retained it to this very day.

THE DUMMY THAT LIVED

In all Fairyland there is no more mischievous a person than Tanko-Mankie the Yellow Ryl. He flew through the city one afternoon—quite invisible to mortal eyes, but seeing everything himself—and noticed a figure of a wax lady standing behind the big plate glass window of Mr. Floman's department store.

The wax lady was beautifully dressed, and extended in her stiff left hand was a card bearing the words:

"RARE BARGAIN!
This Stylish Costume
(Imported from Paris)
Former Price, $20,
REDUCED TO ONLY $19.98."

This impressive announcement had drawn before the window a crowd of women shoppers, who stood looking at the wax lady with critical eyes.

Tanko-Mankie laughed to himself

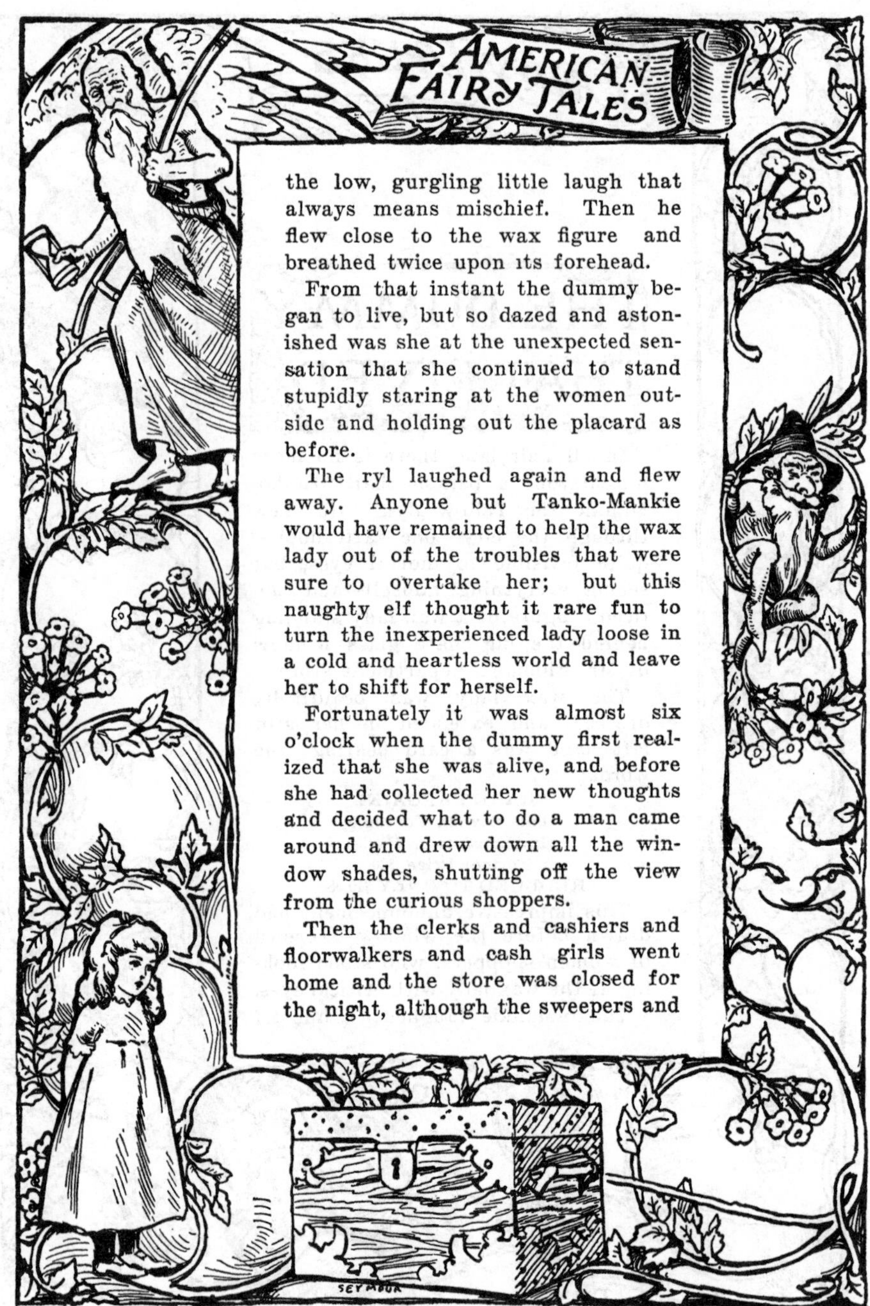

the low, gurgling little laugh that always means mischief. Then he flew close to the wax figure and breathed twice upon its forehead.

From that instant the dummy began to live, but so dazed and astonished was she at the unexpected sensation that she continued to stand stupidly staring at the women outside and holding out the placard as before.

The ryl laughed again and flew away. Anyone but Tanko-Mankie would have remained to help the wax lady out of the troubles that were sure to overtake her; but this naughty elf thought it rare fun to turn the inexperienced lady loose in a cold and heartless world and leave her to shift for herself.

Fortunately it was almost six o'clock when the dummy first realized that she was alive, and before she had collected her new thoughts and decided what to do a man came around and drew down all the window shades, shutting off the view from the curious shoppers.

Then the clerks and cashiers and floorwalkers and cash girls went home and the store was closed for the night, although the sweepers and

From that instant the dummy began to live.

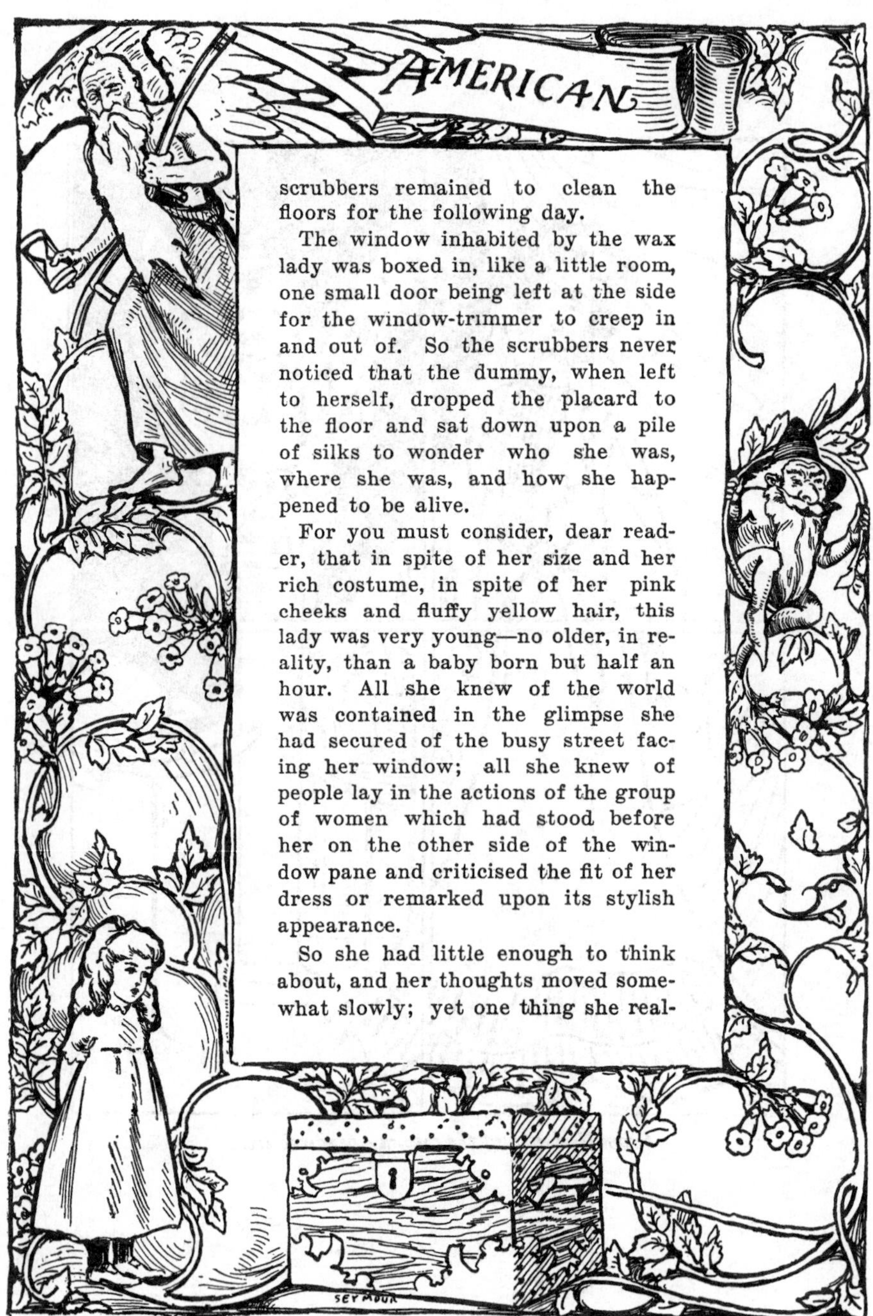

scrubbers remained to clean the floors for the following day.

The window inhabited by the wax lady was boxed in, like a little room, one small door being left at the side for the window-trimmer to creep in and out of. So the scrubbers never noticed that the dummy, when left to herself, dropped the placard to the floor and sat down upon a pile of silks to wonder who she was, where she was, and how she happened to be alive.

For you must consider, dear reader, that in spite of her size and her rich costume, in spite of her pink cheeks and fluffy yellow hair, this lady was very young—no older, in reality, than a baby born but half an hour. All she knew of the world was contained in the glimpse she had secured of the busy street facing her window; all she knew of people lay in the actions of the group of women which had stood before her on the other side of the window pane and criticised the fit of her dress or remarked upon its stylish appearance.

So she had little enough to think about, and her thoughts moved somewhat slowly; yet one thing she real-

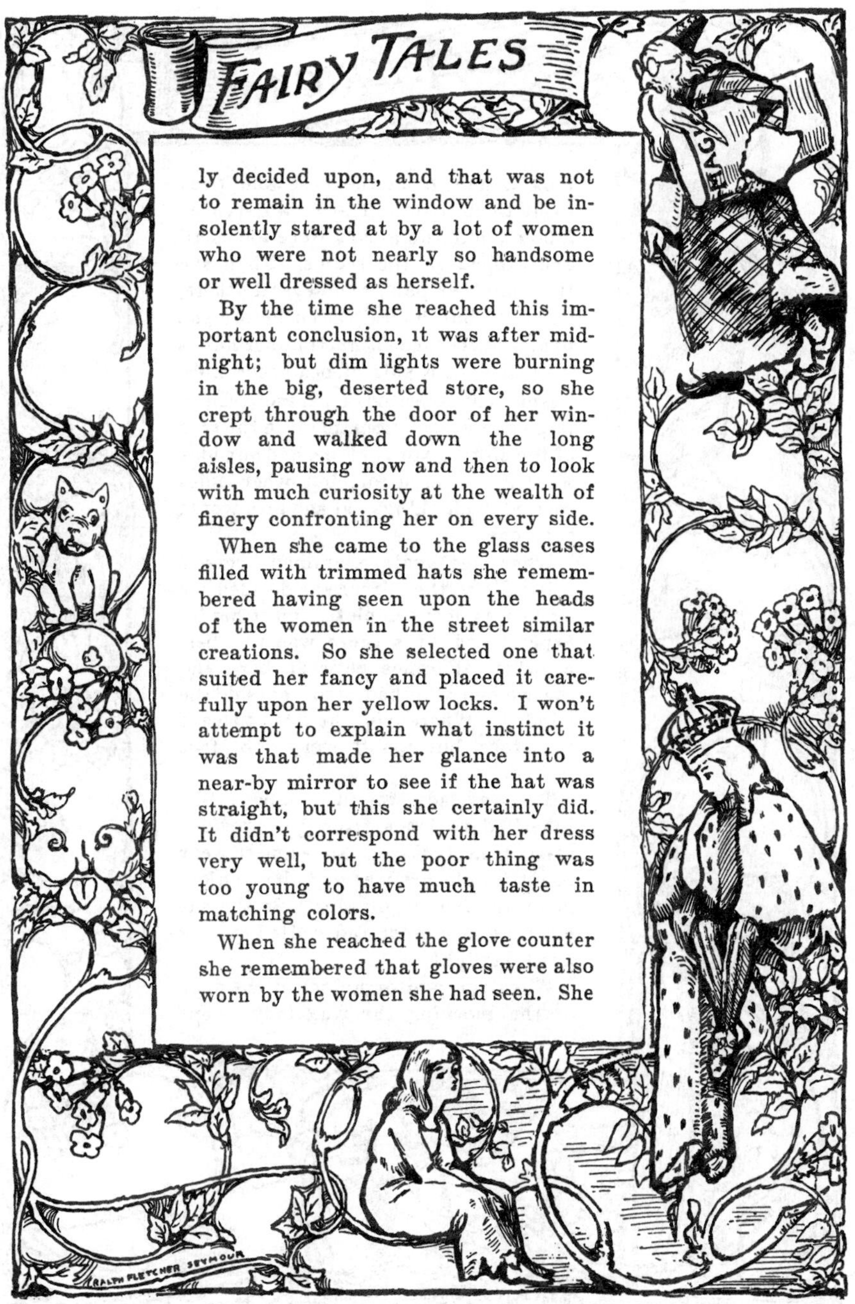

ly decided upon, and that was not to remain in the window and be insolently stared at by a lot of women who were not nearly so handsome or well dressed as herself.

By the time she reached this important conclusion, it was after midnight; but dim lights were burning in the big, deserted store, so she crept through the door of her window and walked down the long aisles, pausing now and then to look with much curiosity at the wealth of finery confronting her on every side.

When she came to the glass cases filled with trimmed hats she remembered having seen upon the heads of the women in the street similar creations. So she selected one that suited her fancy and placed it carefully upon her yellow locks. I won't attempt to explain what instinct it was that made her glance into a near-by mirror to see if the hat was straight, but this she certainly did. It didn't correspond with her dress very well, but the poor thing was too young to have much taste in matching colors.

When she reached the glove counter she remembered that gloves were also worn by the women she had seen. She

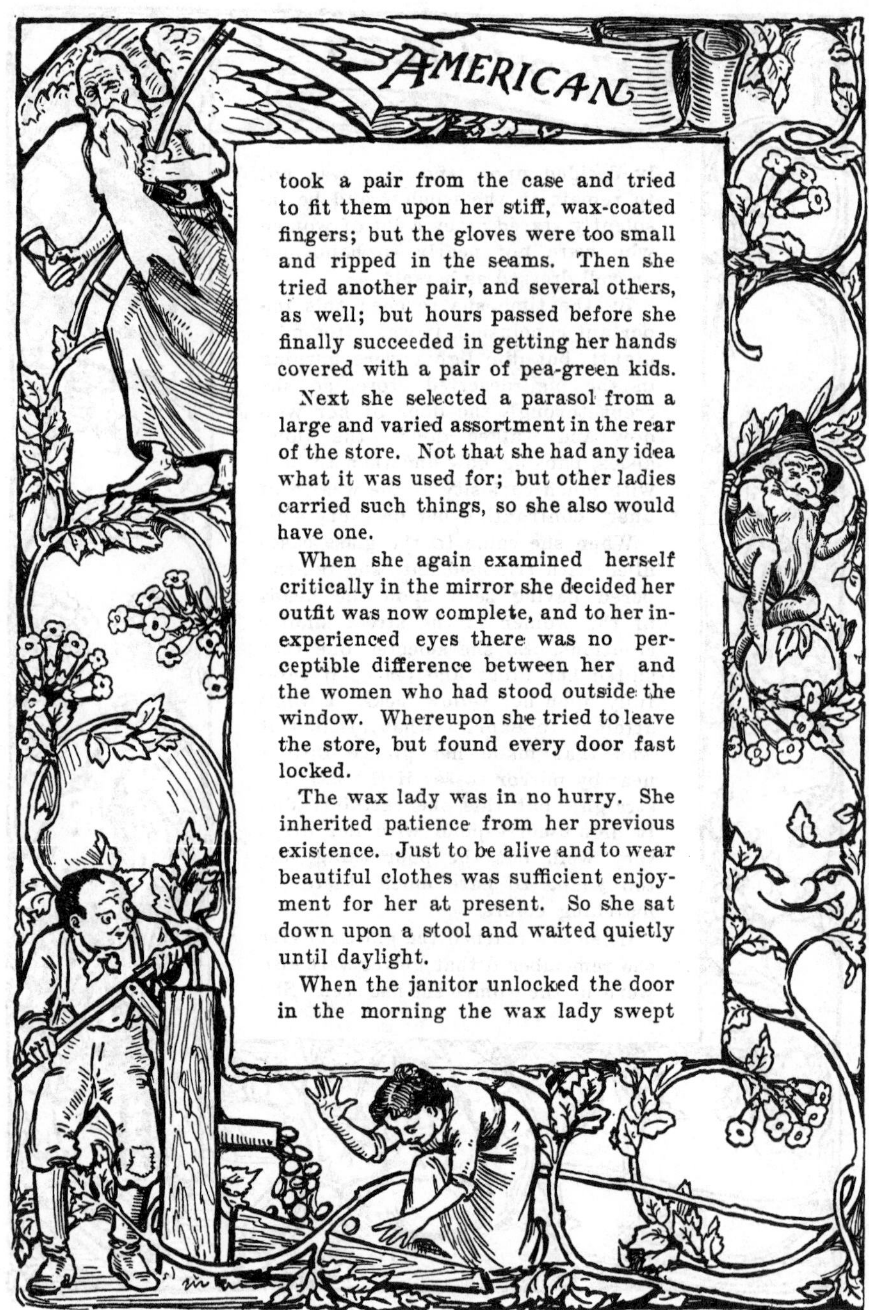

took a pair from the case and tried to fit them upon her stiff, wax-coated fingers; but the gloves were too small and ripped in the seams. Then she tried another pair, and several others, as well; but hours passed before she finally succeeded in getting her hands covered with a pair of pea-green kids.

Next she selected a parasol from a large and varied assortment in the rear of the store. Not that she had any idea what it was used for; but other ladies carried such things, so she also would have one.

When she again examined herself critically in the mirror she decided her outfit was now complete, and to her inexperienced eyes there was no perceptible difference between her and the women who had stood outside the window. Whereupon she tried to leave the store, but found every door fast locked.

The wax lady was in no hurry. She inherited patience from her previous existence. Just to be alive and to wear beautiful clothes was sufficient enjoyment for her at present. So she sat down upon a stool and waited quietly until daylight.

When the janitor unlocked the door in the morning the wax lady swept

past him and walked with stiff but stately strides down the street. The poor fellow was so completely whuckered at seeing the well-known wax lady leave her window and march away from the store that he fell over in a heap and only saved himself from fainting by striking his funny bone against the doorstep. When he recovered his wits she had turned the corner and disappeared.

The wax lady's immature mind had reasoned that, since she had come to life, her evident duty was to mix with the world and do whatever other folks did. She could not realize how different she was from people of flesh and blood; nor did she know she was the first dummy that had ever lived, or that she owed her unique experience to Tanko-Mankie's love of mischief. So ignorance gave her a confidence in herself that she was not justly entitled to.

It was yet early in the day, and the few people she met were hurrying along the streets. Many of them turned into restaurants and eating houses, and following their example the wax lady also entered one and sat upon a stool before a lunch counter.

"Coffee 'n' rolls!" said a shop girl on the next stool.

"Coffee 'n' rolls!" repeated the dummy, and soon the waiter placed them before her. Of course she had no appetite, as her constitution, being mostly wood, did not require food; but she watched the shop girl, and saw her put the coffee to her mouth and drink it. Therefore the wax lady did the same, and the next instant was surprised to feel the hot liquid trickling out between her wooden ribs. The coffee also blistered her wax lips, and so disagreeable was the experience that she arose and left the restaurant, paying no attention to the demands of the waiter for "20 cents, mum." Not that she intended to defraud him, but the poor creature had no idea what he meant by "20 cents, mum."

As she came out she met the window trimmer at Floman's store. The man was rather near-sighted, but seeing something familiar in the lady's features he politely raised his hat. The wax lady also raised her hat, thinking it the proper thing to do, and the man hurried away with a horrified face.

Then a woman touched her arm and said:

"Beg pardon, ma'am; but there's a price-mark hanging on your dress behind."

"Yes, I know," replied the wax lady, stiffly; "it was originally $20, but it's been reduced to $19.98."

The woman looked surprised at such indifference and walked on. Some carriages were standing at the edge of the sidewalk, and seeing the dummy hesitate a driver approached her and touched his cap.

"Cab, ma'am?" he asked.

"No," said she, misunderstanding him; "I'm wax."

"Oh!" he exclaimed, and looked after her wonderingly.

"Here's yer mornin' paper!" yelled a newsboy.

"Mine, did you say?" she asked.

"Sure! Chronicle, 'Quirer, R'public 'n' 'Spatch! Wot'll ye 'ave?"

"What are they for?" inquired the wax lady, simply.

"W'y, ter read, o' course All the news, you know."

She shook her head and glanced at a paper.

"It looks all speckled and mixed up," she said. "I'm afraid I can't read."

"Ever ben to school?" asked the boy, becoming interested.

"No; what's school?" she inquired.

The boy gave her an indignant look.

"Say!" he cried, "ye'r just a dummy,

12

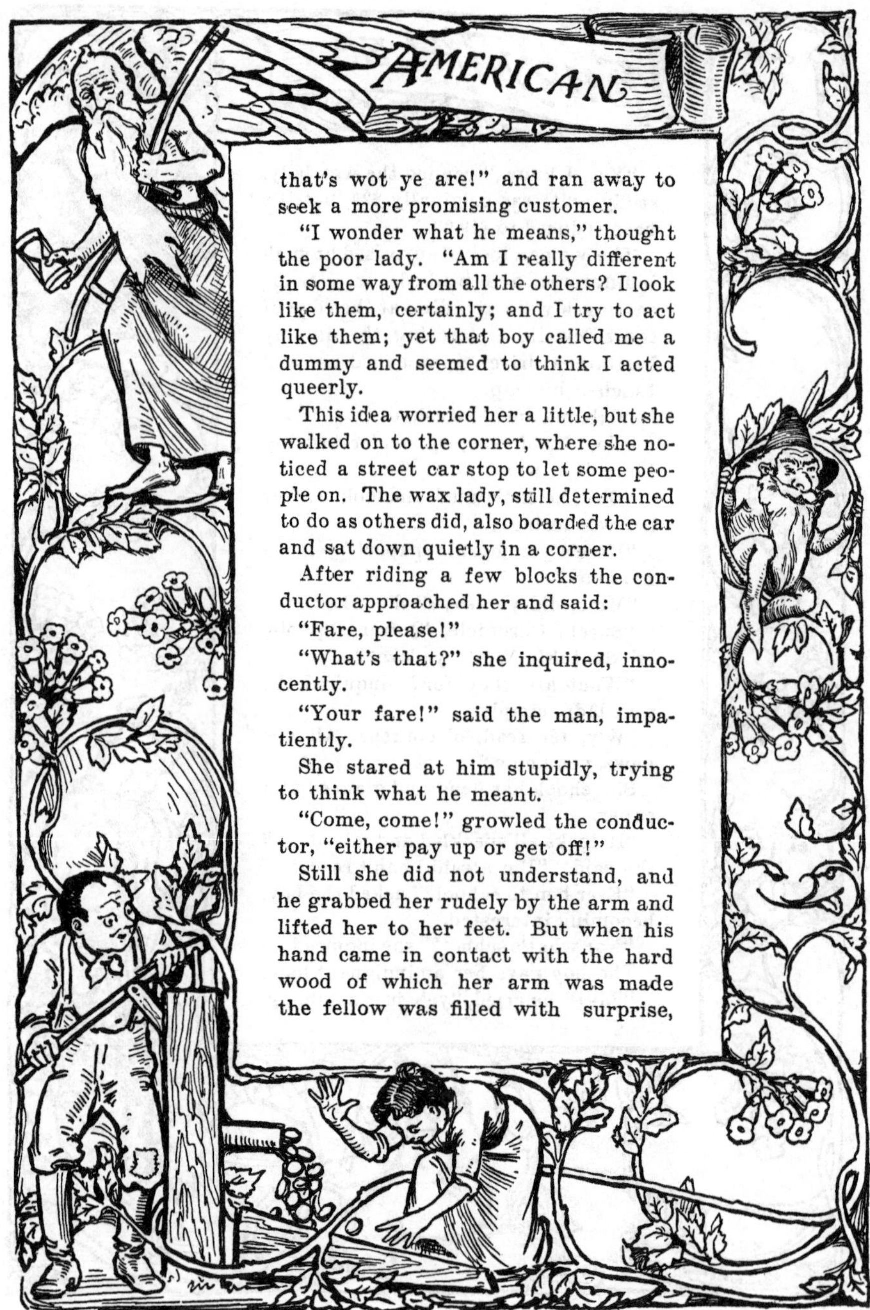

that's wot ye are!" and ran away to seek a more promising customer.

"I wonder what he means," thought the poor lady. "Am I really different in some way from all the others? I look like them, certainly; and I try to act like them; yet that boy called me a dummy and seemed to think I acted queerly.

This idea worried her a little, but she walked on to the corner, where she noticed a street car stop to let some people on. The wax lady, still determined to do as others did, also boarded the car and sat down quietly in a corner.

After riding a few blocks the conductor approached her and said:

"Fare, please!"

"What's that?" she inquired, innocently.

"Your fare!" said the man, impatiently.

She stared at him stupidly, trying to think what he meant.

"Come, come!" growled the conductor, "either pay up or get off!"

Still she did not understand, and he grabbed her rudely by the arm and lifted her to her feet. But when his hand came in contact with the hard wood of which her arm was made the fellow was filled with surprise,

He stooped down and peered into her face, and, seeing it was wax instead of flesh, he gave a yell of fear and jumped from the car, running as if he had seen a ghost.

At this the other passengers also yelled and sprang from the car, fearing a collision; and the motorman, knowing something was wrong, followed suit. The wax lady, seeing the others run, jumped from the car last of all, and stepped in front of another car coming at full speed from the opposite direction.

She heard cries of fear and of warning on all sides, but before she understood her danger she was knocked down and dragged for half a block.

When the car was brought to a stop a policeman reached down and pulled her from under the wheels. Her dress was badly torn and soiled, her left ear was entirely gone, and the left side of her head was caved in; but she quickly scrambled to her feet and asked for her hat. This a gentleman had already picked up, and when the policeman handed it to her and noticed the great hole in her head and the hollow place it disclosed, the poor fellow trembled so

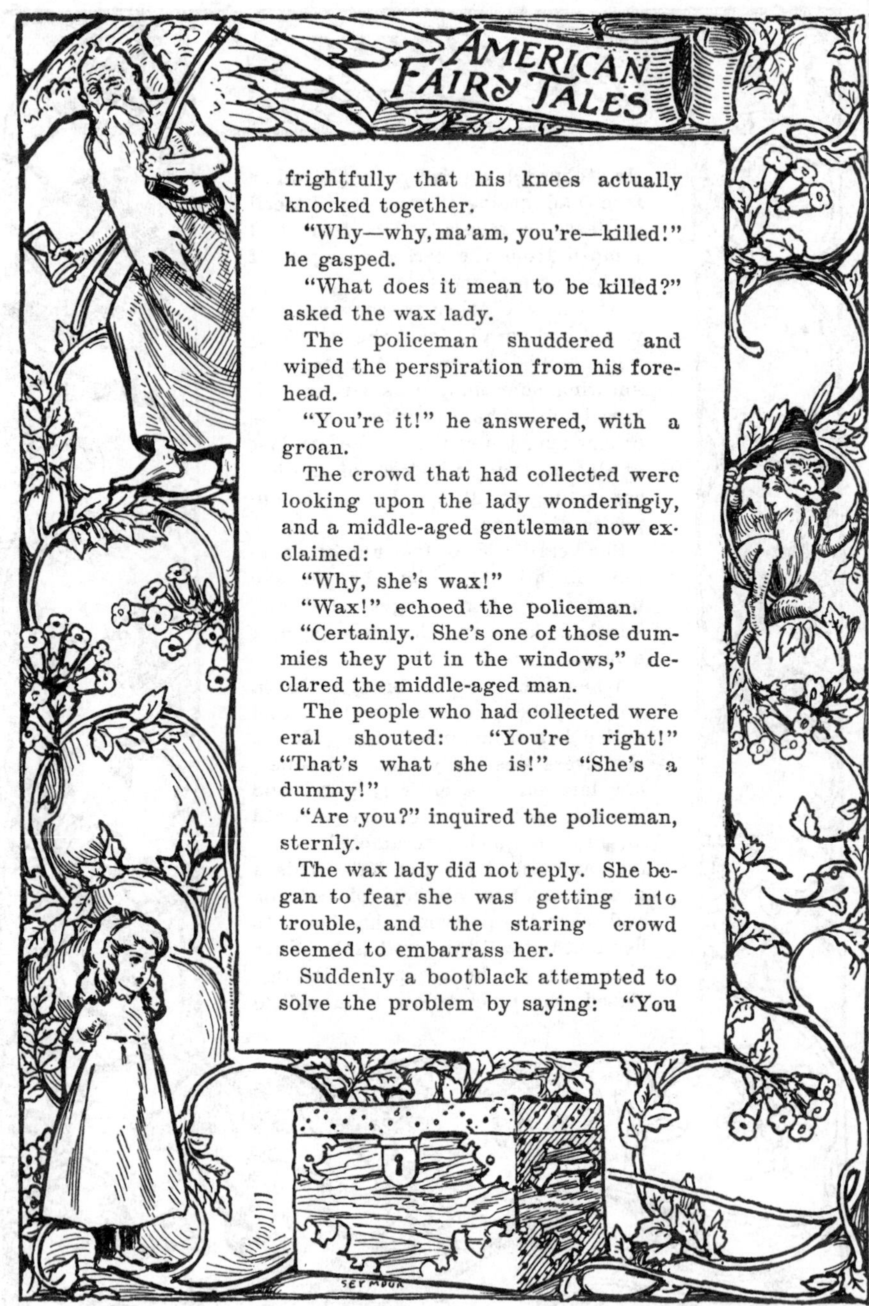

frightfully that his knees actually knocked together.

"Why—why, ma'am, you're—killed!" he gasped.

"What does it mean to be killed?" asked the wax lady.

The policeman shuddered and wiped the perspiration from his forehead.

"You're it!" he answered, with a groan.

The crowd that had collected were looking upon the lady wonderingly, and a middle-aged gentleman now exclaimed:

"Why, she's wax!"

"Wax!" echoed the policeman.

"Certainly. She's one of those dummies they put in the windows," declared the middle-aged man.

The people who had collected were eral shouted: "You're right!" "That's what she is!" "She's a dummy!"

"Are you?" inquired the policeman, sternly.

The wax lady did not reply. She began to fear she was getting into trouble, and the staring crowd seemed to embarrass her.

Suddenly a bootblack attempted to solve the problem by saying: "You

"You're it," he answered, with a groan.

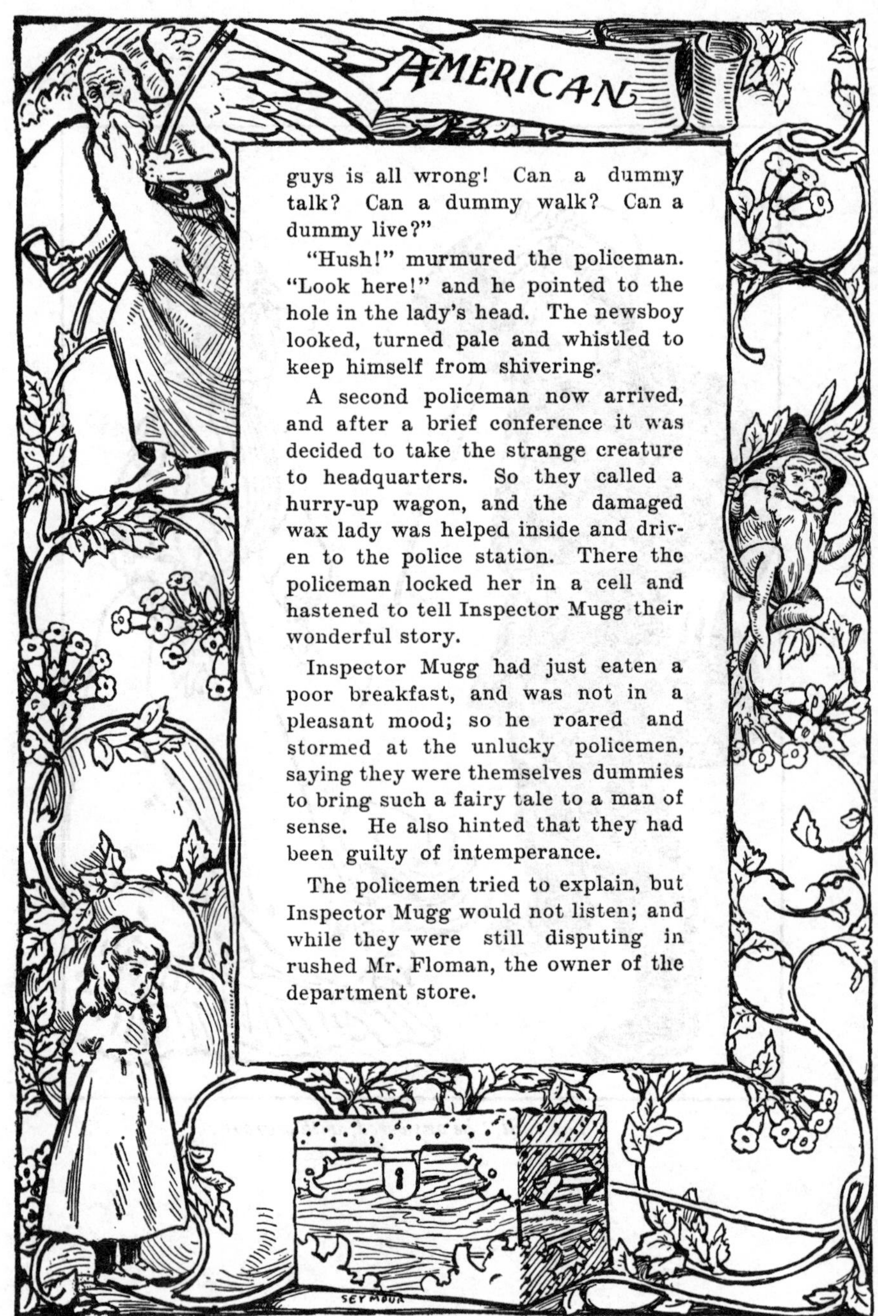

guys is all wrong! Can a dummy talk? Can a dummy walk? Can a dummy live?"

"Hush!" murmured the policeman. "Look here!" and he pointed to the hole in the lady's head. The newsboy looked, turned pale and whistled to keep himself from shivering.

A second policeman now arrived, and after a brief conference it was decided to take the strange creature to headquarters. So they called a hurry-up wagon, and the damaged wax lady was helped inside and driven to the police station. There the policeman locked her in a cell and hastened to tell Inspector Mugg their wonderful story.

Inspector Mugg had just eaten a poor breakfast, and was not in a pleasant mood; so he roared and stormed at the unlucky policemen, saying they were themselves dummies to bring such a fairy tale to a man of sense. He also hinted that they had been guilty of intemperance.

The policemen tried to explain, but Inspector Mugg would not listen; and while they were still disputing in rushed Mr. Floman, the owner of the department store.

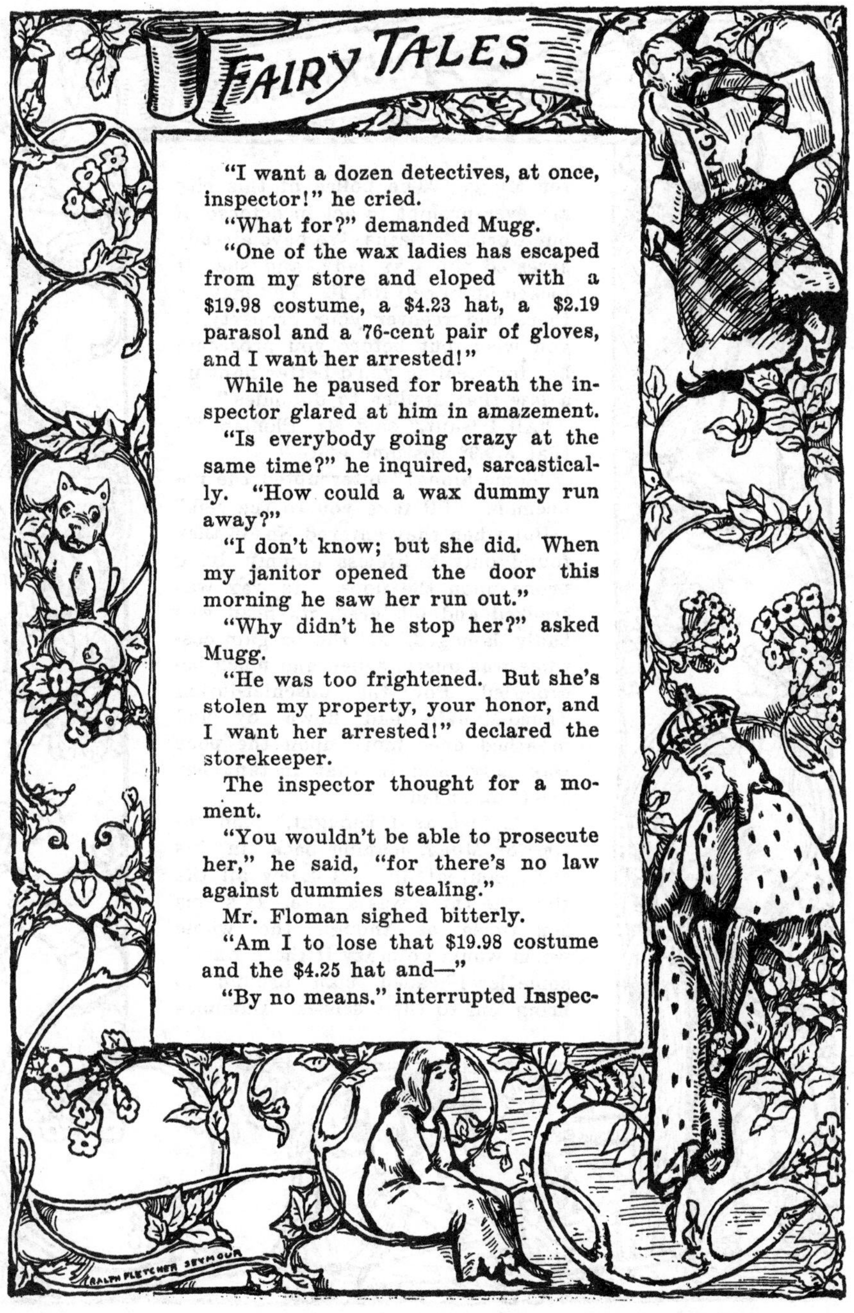

"I want a dozen detectives, at once, inspector!" he cried.

"What for?" demanded Mugg.

"One of the wax ladies has escaped from my store and eloped with a $19.98 costume, a $4.23 hat, a $2.19 parasol and a 76-cent pair of gloves, and I want her arrested!"

While he paused for breath the inspector glared at him in amazement.

"Is everybody going crazy at the same time?" he inquired, sarcastically. "How could a wax dummy run away?"

"I don't know; but she did. When my janitor opened the door this morning he saw her run out."

"Why didn't he stop her?" asked Mugg.

"He was too frightened. But she's stolen my property, your honor, and I want her arrested!" declared the storekeeper.

The inspector thought for a moment.

"You wouldn't be able to prosecute her," he said, "for there's no law against dummies stealing."

Mr. Floman sighed bitterly.

"Am I to lose that $19.98 costume and the $4.25 hat and—"

"By no means." interrupted Inspec-

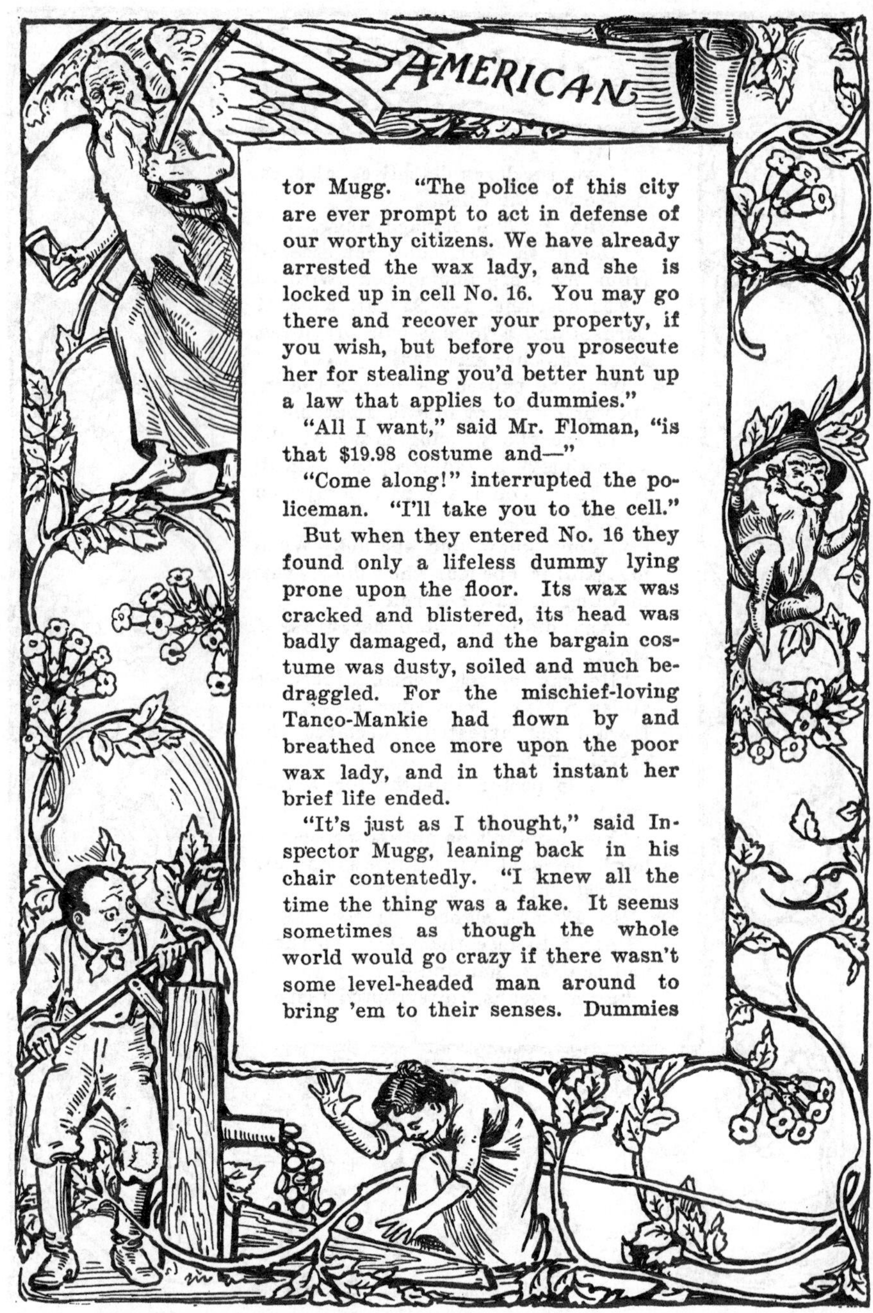

tor Mugg. "The police of this city are ever prompt to act in defense of our worthy citizens. We have already arrested the wax lady, and she is locked up in cell No. 16. You may go there and recover your property, if you wish, but before you prosecute her for stealing you'd better hunt up a law that applies to dummies."

"All I want," said Mr. Floman, "is that $19.98 costume and—"

"Come along!" interrupted the policeman. "I'll take you to the cell."

But when they entered No. 16 they found only a lifeless dummy lying prone upon the floor. Its wax was cracked and blistered, its head was badly damaged, and the bargain costume was dusty, soiled and much bedraggled. For the mischief-loving Tanco-Mankie had flown by and breathed once more upon the poor wax lady, and in that instant her brief life ended.

"It's just as I thought," said Inspector Mugg, leaning back in his chair contentedly. "I knew all the time the thing was a fake. It seems sometimes as though the whole world would go crazy if there wasn't some level-headed man around to bring 'em to their senses. Dummies

are wood an' wax, an' that's all there is of 'em."

"That may be the rule," whispered the policeman to himself, "but this one were a dummy as lived!"

THE KING of the POLAR BEARS

The King of the Polar Bears lived among the icebergs in the far north country. He was old and monstrous big; he was wise and friendly to all who knew him. His body was thickly covered with long, white hair that glistened like silver under the rays of the midnight sun. His claws were strong and sharp, that he might walk safely over the smooth ice or grasp and tear the fishes and seals upon which he fed.

The seals were afraid when he drew near, and tried to avoid him; but the gulls, both white and gray, loved him because he left the remnants of his feasts for them to devour.

Often his subjects, the polar bears, came to him for advice when ill or in trouble; but they wisely kept away from his hunting grounds, lest they

might interfere with his sport and arouse his anger.

The wolves, who sometimes came as far north as the icebergs, whispered among themselves that the King of the Polar Bears was either a magician or under the protection of a powerful fairy. For no earthly thing seemed able to harm him; he never failed to secure plenty of food, and he grew bigger and stronger day by day and year by year.

Yet the time came when this monarch of the north met man, and his wisdom failed him.

He came out of his cave among the icebergs one day and saw a boat moving through the strip of water which had been uncovered by the shifting of the summer ice. In the boat were men.

The great bear had never seen such creatures before, and therefore advanced toward the boat, sniffing the strange scent with aroused curiosity and wondering whether he might take them for friends or foes, food or carrion.

When the king came near the water's edge a man stood up in the boat and with a queer instrument made a loud "bang!" The polar bear

A queer instrument made a loud "bang."

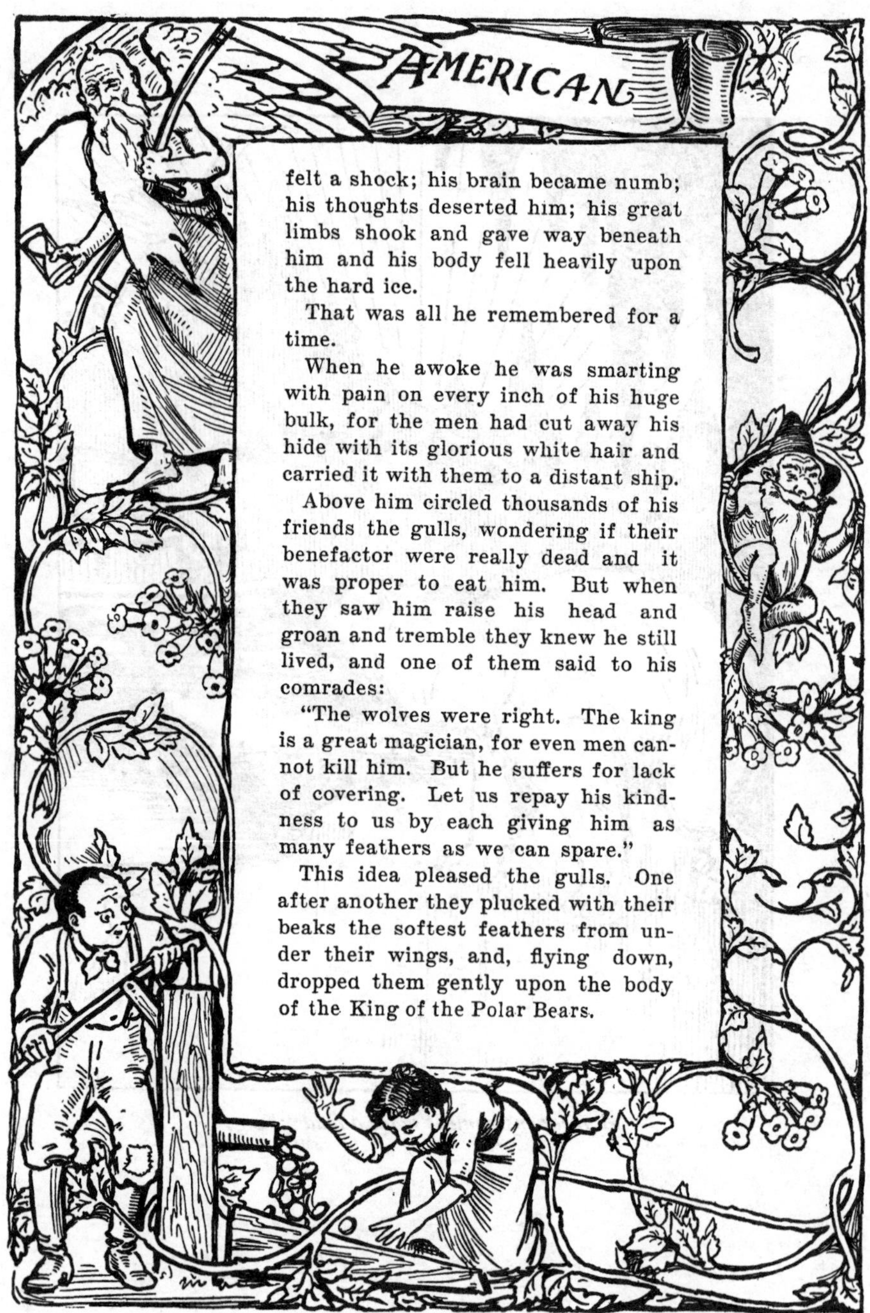

felt a shock; his brain became numb; his thoughts deserted him; his great limbs shook and gave way beneath him and his body fell heavily upon the hard ice.

That was all he remembered for a time.

When he awoke he was smarting with pain on every inch of his huge bulk, for the men had cut away his hide with its glorious white hair and carried it with them to a distant ship.

Above him circled thousands of his friends the gulls, wondering if their benefactor were really dead and it was proper to eat him. But when they saw him raise his head and groan and tremble they knew he still lived, and one of them said to his comrades:

"The wolves were right. The king is a great magician, for even men cannot kill him. But he suffers for lack of covering. Let us repay his kindness to us by each giving him as many feathers as we can spare."

This idea pleased the gulls. One after another they plucked with their beaks the softest feathers from under their wings, and, flying down, dropped them gently upon the body of the King of the Polar Bears.

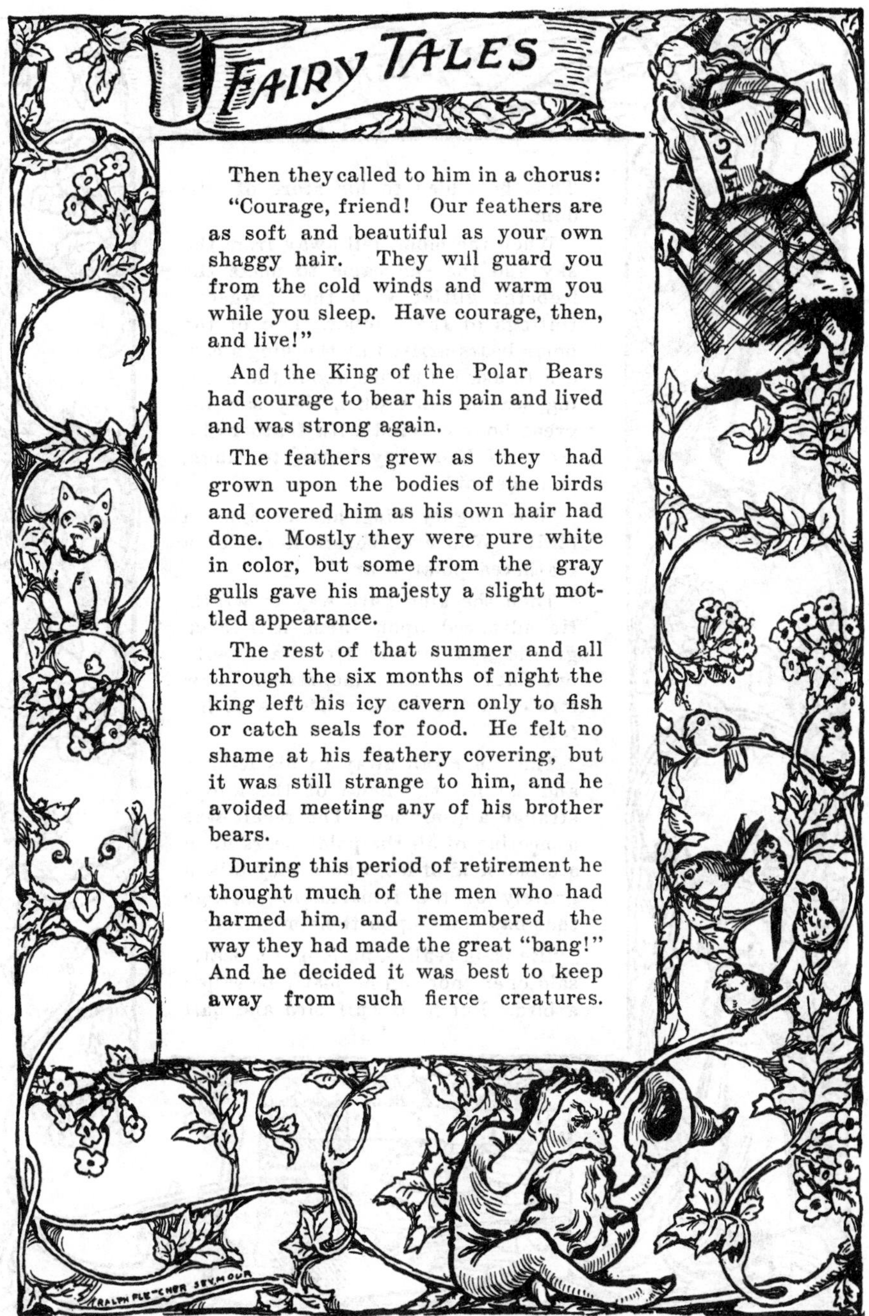

Then they called to him in a chorus: "Courage, friend! Our feathers are as soft and beautiful as your own shaggy hair. They will guard you from the cold winds and warm you while you sleep. Have courage, then, and live!"

And the King of the Polar Bears had courage to bear his pain and lived and was strong again.

The feathers grew as they had grown upon the bodies of the birds and covered him as his own hair had done. Mostly they were pure white in color, but some from the gray gulls gave his majesty a slight mottled appearance.

The rest of that summer and all through the six months of night the king left his icy cavern only to fish or catch seals for food. He felt no shame at his feathery covering, but it was still strange to him, and he avoided meeting any of his brother bears.

During this period of retirement he thought much of the men who had harmed him, and remembered the way they had made the great "bang!" And he decided it was best to keep away from such fierce creatures.

Thus he added to his store of wisdom.

When the moon fell away from the sky and the sun came to make the icebergs glitter with the gorgeous tintings of the rainbow, two of the polar bears arrived at the king's cavern to ask his advice about the hunting season. But when they saw his great body covered with feathers instead of hair they began to laugh, and one said:

"Our mighty king has become a bird! Who ever before heard of a feathered polar bear?"

Then the king gave way to wrath. He advanced upon them with deep growls and stately tread and with one blow of his monstrous paw stretched the mocker lifeless at his feet.

The other ran away to his fellows and carried the news of the king's strange appearance. The result was a meeting of all the polar bears upon a broad field of ice, where they talked gravely of the remarkable change that had come upon their monarch.

"He is, in reality, no longer a bear," said one; "nor can he justly be called a bird. But he is half bird and half

bear, and so unfitted to remain our king."

"Then who shall take his place?" asked another.

"He who can fight the bird-bear and overcome him," answered an aged member of the group. "Only the strongest is fit to rule our race."

There was silence for a time, but at length a great bear moved to the front and said:

"I will fight him; I—Woof—the strongest of our race! And I will be King of the Polar Bears."

The others nodded assent, and dispatched a messenger to the king to say he must fight the great Woof and master him or resign his sovereignty.

"For a bear with feathers," added the messenger, "is no bear at all, and the king we obey must resemble the rest of us."

"I wear feathers because it pleases me," growled the king. "Am I not a great magician? But I will fight, nevertheless, and if Woof masters me he shall be king in my stead."

Then he visited his friends, the gulls, who were even then feasting upon the dead bear, and told them of the coming battle.

"I shall conquer," he said, proudly.

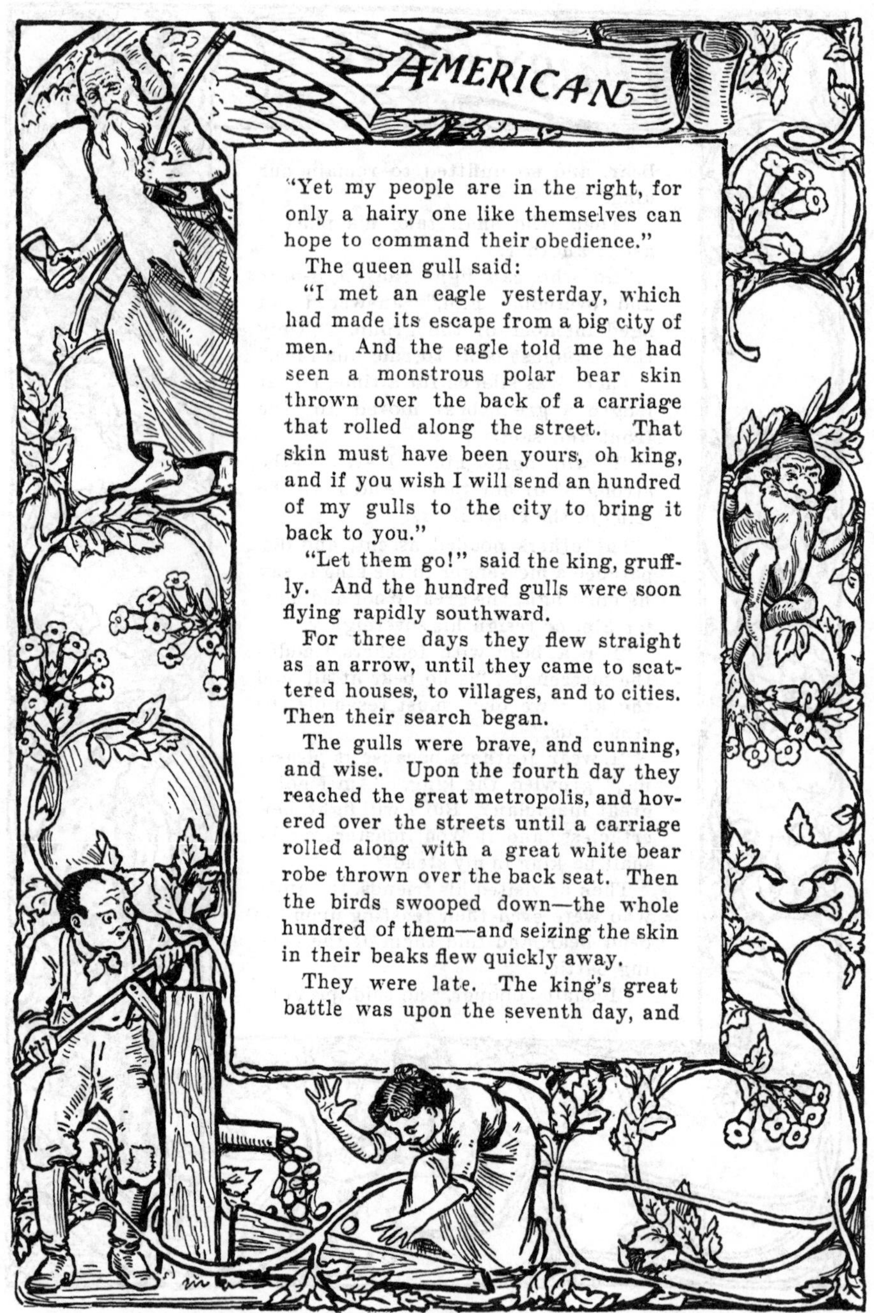

"Yet my people are in the right, for only a hairy one like themselves can hope to command their obedience."

The queen gull said:

"I met an eagle yesterday, which had made its escape from a big city of men. And the eagle told me he had seen a monstrous polar bear skin thrown over the back of a carriage that rolled along the street. That skin must have been yours, oh king, and if you wish I will send an hundred of my gulls to the city to bring it back to you."

"Let them go!" said the king, gruffly. And the hundred gulls were soon flying rapidly southward.

For three days they flew straight as an arrow, until they came to scattered houses, to villages, and to cities. Then their search began.

The gulls were brave, and cunning, and wise. Upon the fourth day they reached the great metropolis, and hovered over the streets until a carriage rolled along with a great white bear robe thrown over the back seat. Then the birds swooped down—the whole hundred of them—and seizing the skin in their beaks flew quickly away.

They were late. The king's great battle was upon the seventh day, and

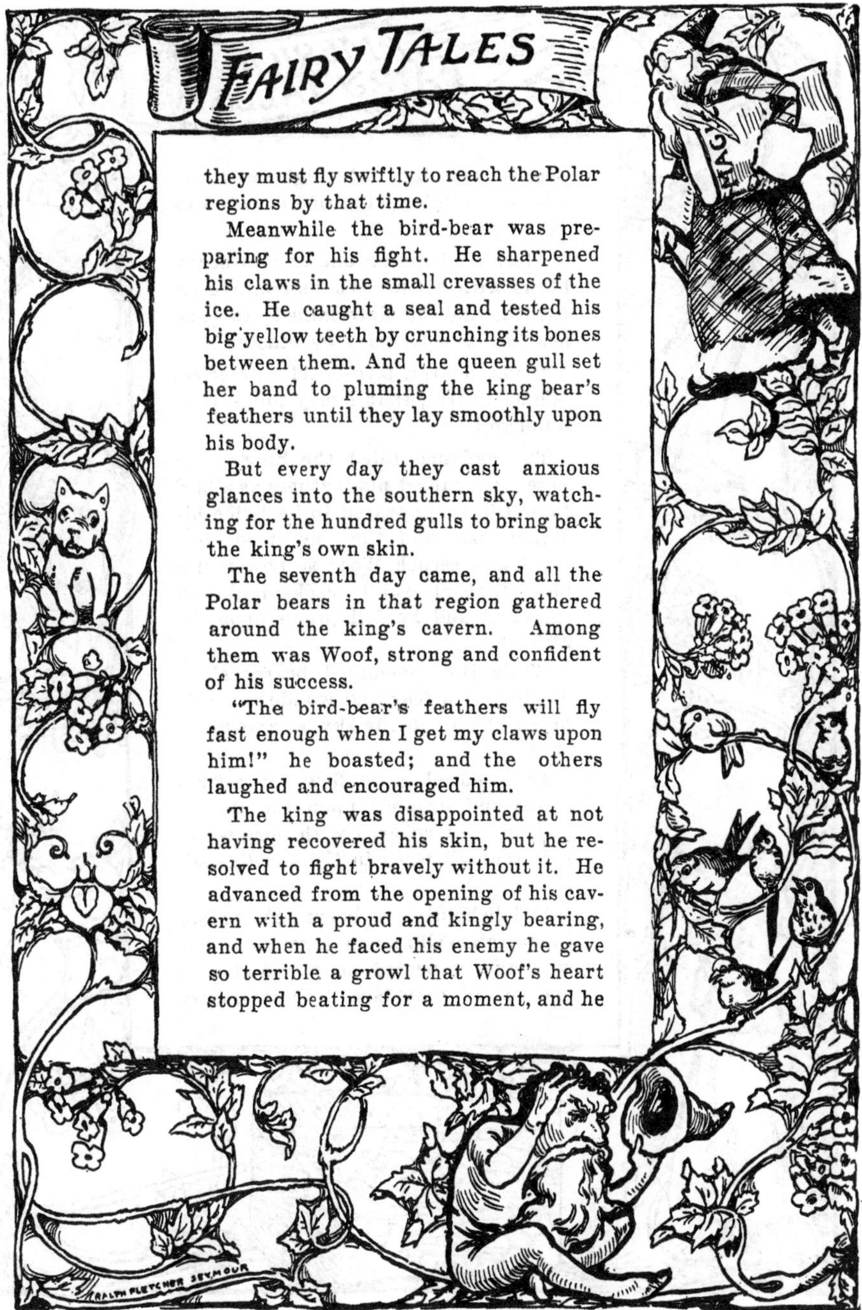

they must fly swiftly to reach the Polar regions by that time.

Meanwhile the bird-bear was preparing for his fight. He sharpened his claws in the small crevasses of the ice. He caught a seal and tested his big yellow teeth by crunching its bones between them. And the queen gull set her band to pluming the king bear's feathers until they lay smoothly upon his body.

But every day they cast anxious glances into the southern sky, watching for the hundred gulls to bring back the king's own skin.

The seventh day came, and all the Polar bears in that region gathered around the king's cavern. Among them was Woof, strong and confident of his success.

"The bird-bear's feathers will fly fast enough when I get my claws upon him!" he boasted; and the others laughed and encouraged him.

The king was disappointed at not having recovered his skin, but he resolved to fight bravely without it. He advanced from the opening of his cavern with a proud and kingly bearing, and when he faced his enemy he gave so terrible a growl that Woof's heart stopped beating for a moment, and he

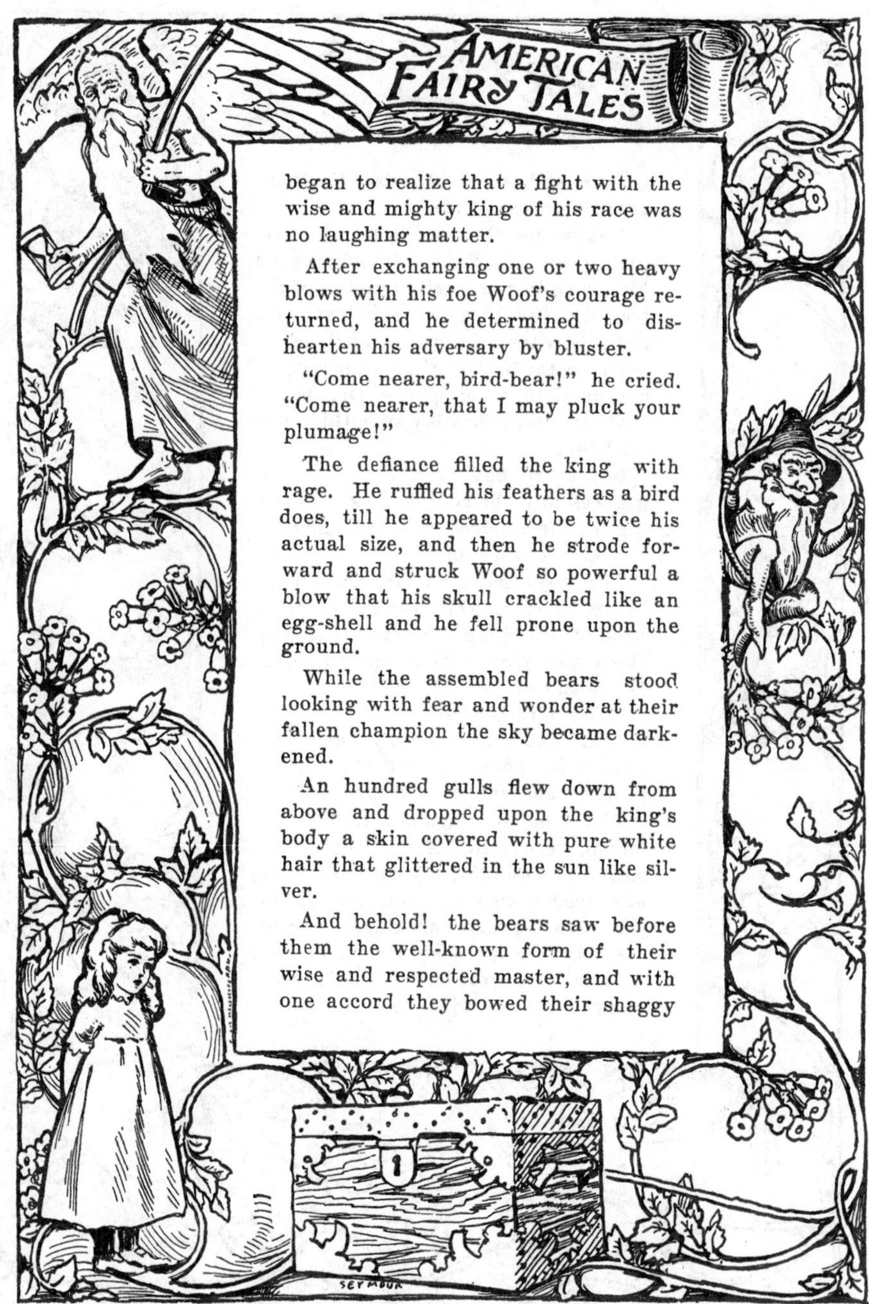

began to realize that a fight with the wise and mighty king of his race was no laughing matter.

After exchanging one or two heavy blows with his foe Woof's courage returned, and he determined to dishearten his adversary by bluster.

"Come nearer, bird-bear!" he cried. "Come nearer, that I may pluck your plumage!"

The defiance filled the king with rage. He ruffled his feathers as a bird does, till he appeared to be twice his actual size, and then he strode forward and struck Woof so powerful a blow that his skull crackled like an egg-shell and he fell prone upon the ground.

While the assembled bears stood looking with fear and wonder at their fallen champion the sky became darkened.

An hundred gulls flew down from above and dropped upon the king's body a skin covered with pure white hair that glittered in the sun like silver.

And behold! the bears saw before them the well-known form of their wise and respected master, and with one accord they bowed their shaggy

He ruffled his feathers as a bird does and struck Woof a powerful blow.

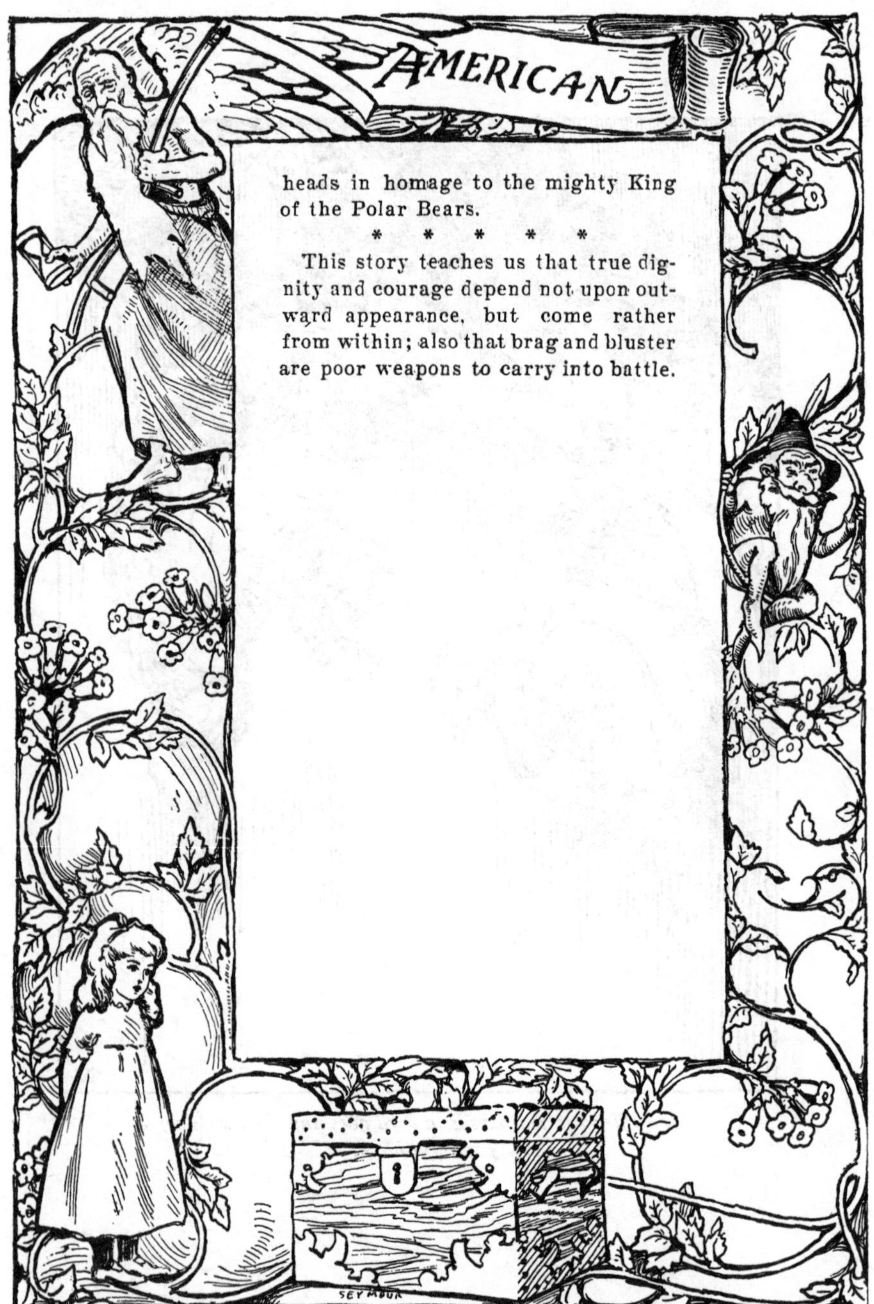

heads in homage to the mighty King of the Polar Bears.

* * * * *

This story teaches us that true dignity and courage depend not upon outward appearance, but come rather from within; also that brag and bluster are poor weapons to carry into battle.

The MANDARIN and the BUTTERFLY

A mandarin once lived in Kiang-ho who was so exceedingly cross and disagreeable that everyone hated him. He snarled and stormed at every person he met and was never known to laugh or be merry under any circumstances. Especially he hated boys and girls; for the boys jeered at him, which aroused his wrath, and the girls made fun of him, which hurt his pride.

When he had become so unpopular that no one would speak to him, the emperor heard about it and commanded him to emigrate to America. This suited the mandarin very well; but before he left China he stole the Great Book of Magic that belonged to the wise magician Haot-sai. Then, gathering up his little store of money, he took ship for America.

He settled in a city of the middle west and of course started a laundry,

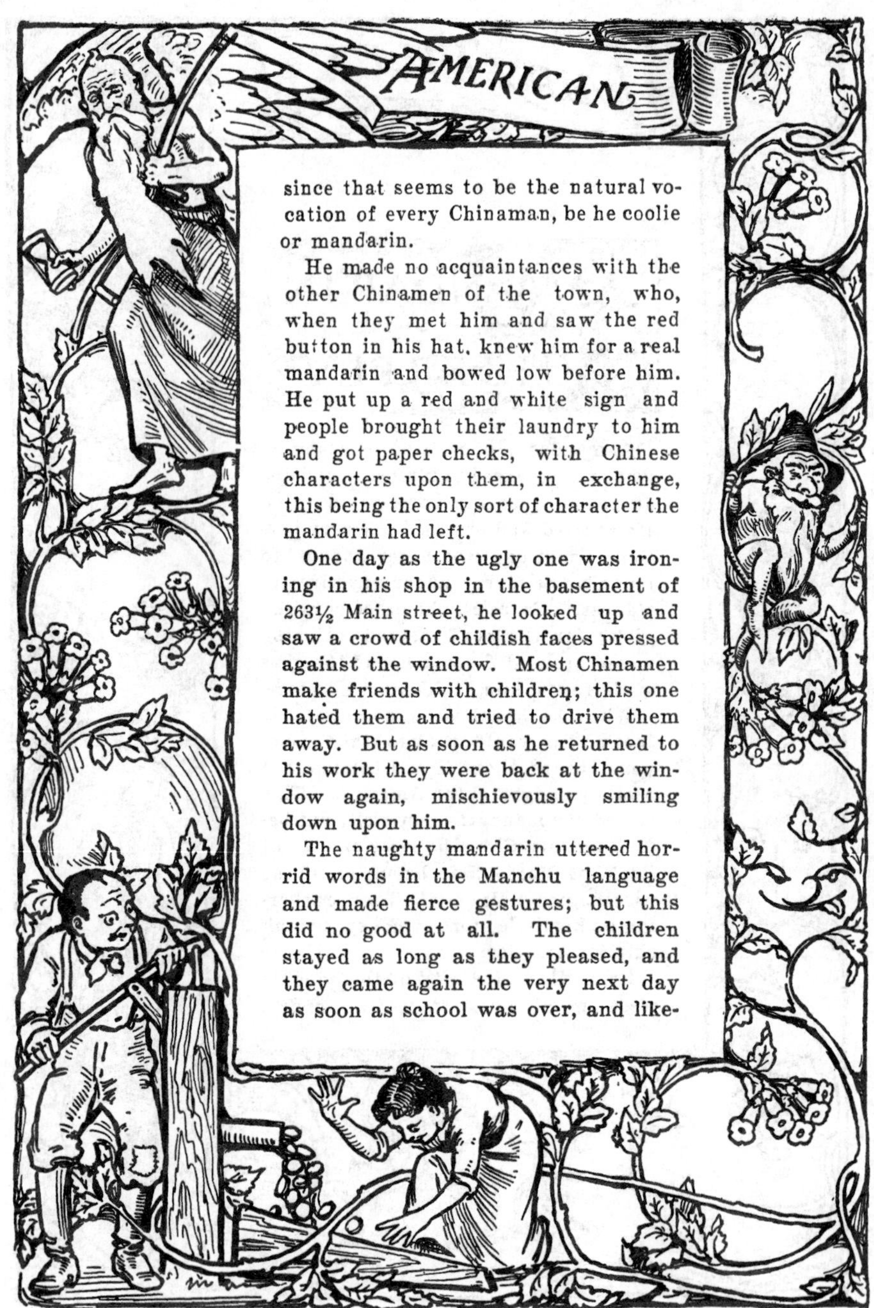

since that seems to be the natural vocation of every Chinaman, be he coolie or mandarin.

He made no acquaintances with the other Chinamen of the town, who, when they met him and saw the red button in his hat, knew him for a real mandarin and bowed low before him. He put up a red and white sign and people brought their laundry to him and got paper checks, with Chinese characters upon them, in exchange, this being the only sort of character the mandarin had left.

One day as the ugly one was ironing in his shop in the basement of 263½ Main street, he looked up and saw a crowd of childish faces pressed against the window. Most Chinamen make friends with children; this one hated them and tried to drive them away. But as soon as he returned to his work they were back at the window again, mischievously smiling down upon him.

The naughty mandarin uttered horrid words in the Manchu language and made fierce gestures; but this did no good at all. The children stayed as long as they pleased, and they came again the very next day as soon as school was over, and like-

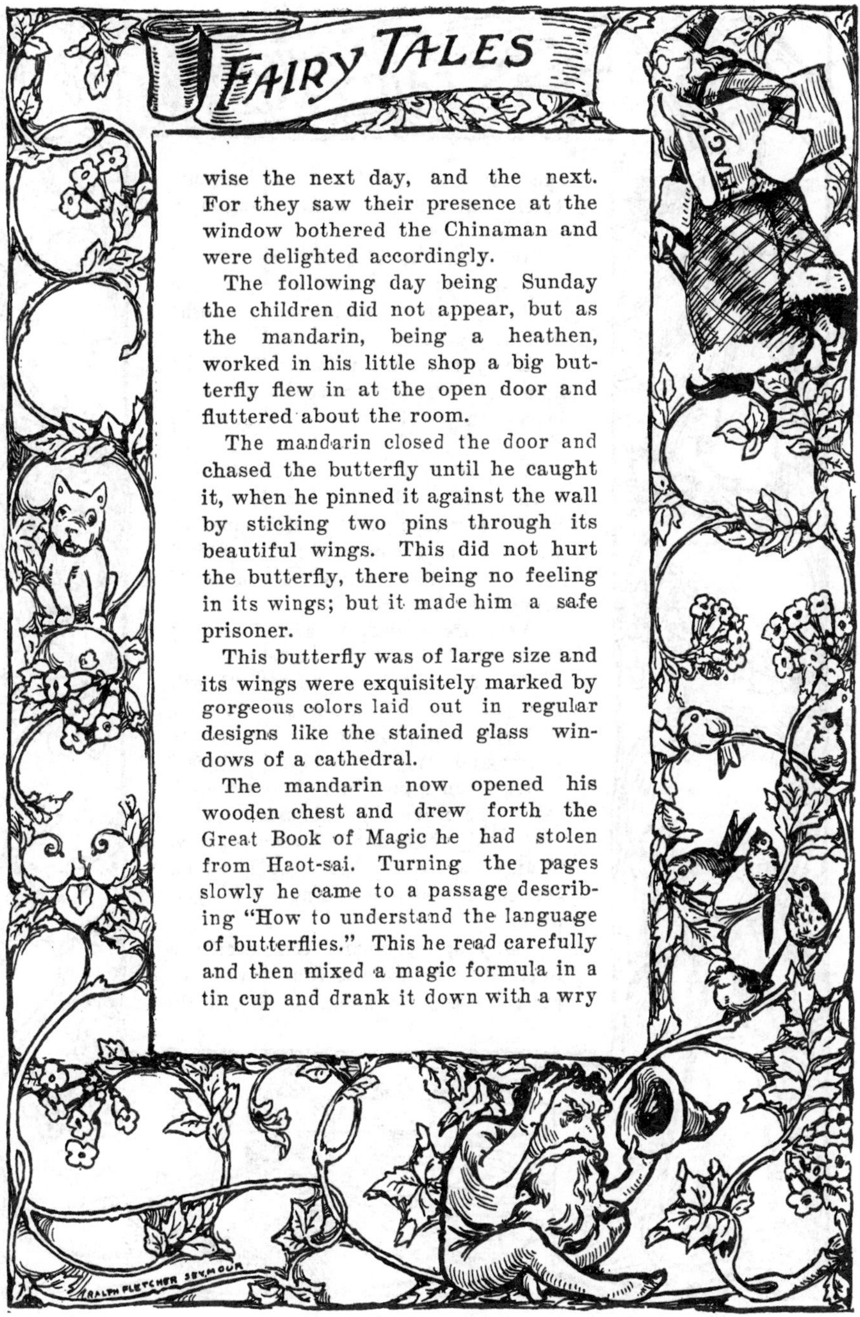

wise the next day, and the next. For they saw their presence at the window bothered the Chinaman and were delighted accordingly.

The following day being Sunday the children did not appear, but as the mandarin, being a heathen, worked in his little shop a big butterfly flew in at the open door and fluttered about the room.

The mandarin closed the door and chased the butterfly until he caught it, when he pinned it against the wall by sticking two pins through its beautiful wings. This did not hurt the butterfly, there being no feeling in its wings; but it made him a safe prisoner.

This butterfly was of large size and its wings were exquisitely marked by gorgeous colors laid out in regular designs like the stained glass windows of a cathedral.

The mandarin now opened his wooden chest and drew forth the Great Book of Magic he had stolen from Haot-sai. Turning the pages slowly he came to a passage describing "How to understand the language of butterflies." This he read carefully and then mixed a magic formula in a tin cup and drank it down with a wry

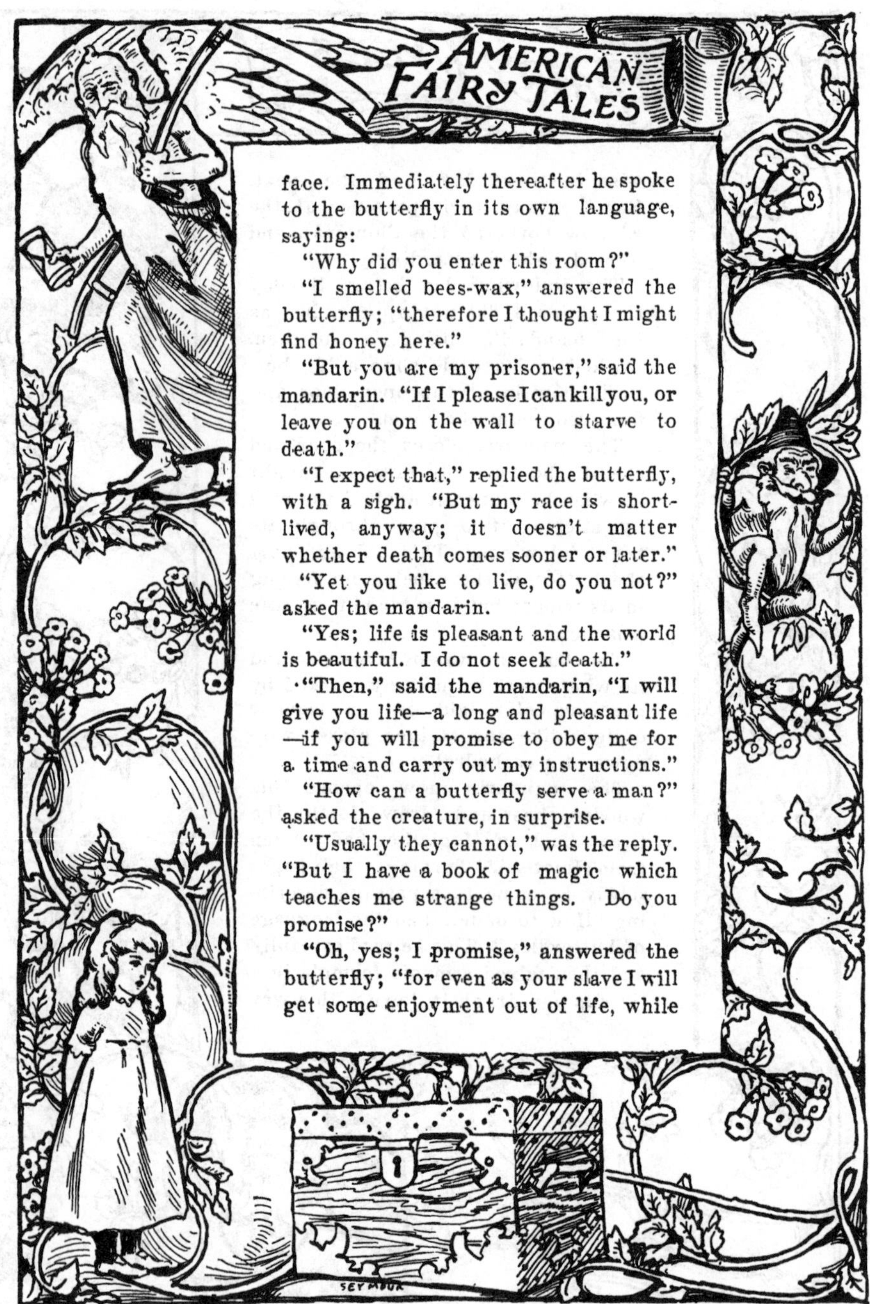

face. Immediately thereafter he spoke to the butterfly in its own language, saying:

"Why did you enter this room?"

"I smelled bees-wax," answered the butterfly; "therefore I thought I might find honey here."

"But you are my prisoner," said the mandarin. "If I please I can kill you, or leave you on the wall to starve to death."

"I expect that," replied the butterfly, with a sigh. "But my race is short-lived, anyway; it doesn't matter whether death comes sooner or later."

"Yet you like to live, do you not?" asked the mandarin.

"Yes; life is pleasant and the world is beautiful. I do not seek death."

"Then," said the mandarin, "I will give you life—a long and pleasant life—if you will promise to obey me for a time and carry out my instructions."

"How can a butterfly serve a man?" asked the creature, in surprise.

"Usually they cannot," was the reply. "But I have a book of magic which teaches me strange things. Do you promise?"

"Oh, yes; I promise," answered the butterfly; "for even as your slave I will get some enjoyment out of life, while

"You are my prisoner," said the mandarin.

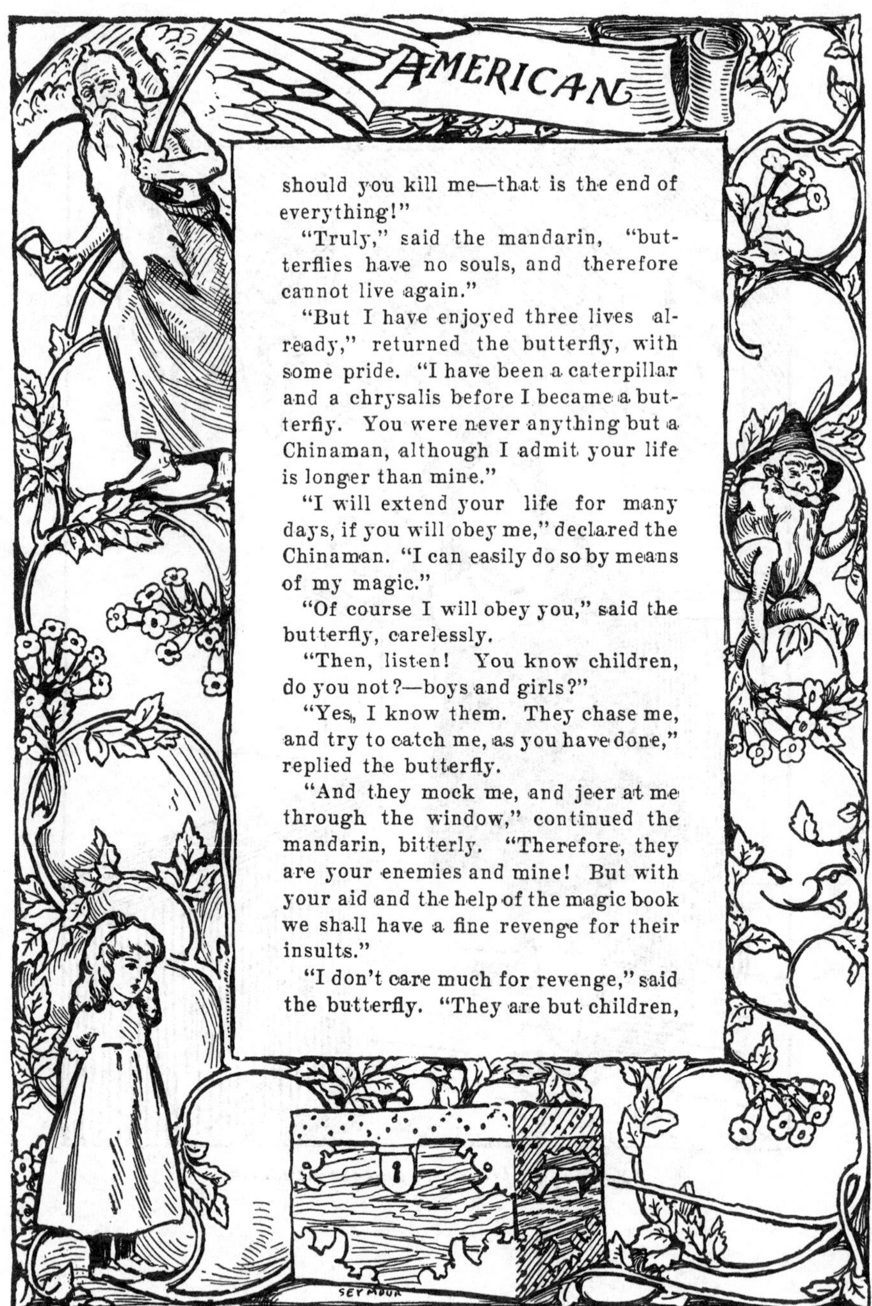

should you kill me—that is the end of everything!"

"Truly," said the mandarin, "butterflies have no souls, and therefore cannot live again."

"But I have enjoyed three lives already," returned the butterfly, with some pride. "I have been a caterpillar and a chrysalis before I became a butterfly. You were never anything but a Chinaman, although I admit your life is longer than mine."

"I will extend your life for many days, if you will obey me," declared the Chinaman. "I can easily do so by means of my magic."

"Of course I will obey you," said the butterfly, carelessly.

"Then, listen! You know children, do you not?—boys and girls?"

"Yes, I know them. They chase me, and try to catch me, as you have done," replied the butterfly.

"And they mock me, and jeer at me through the window," continued the mandarin, bitterly. "Therefore, they are your enemies and mine! But with your aid and the help of the magic book we shall have a fine revenge for their insults."

"I don't care much for revenge," said the butterfly. "They are but children,

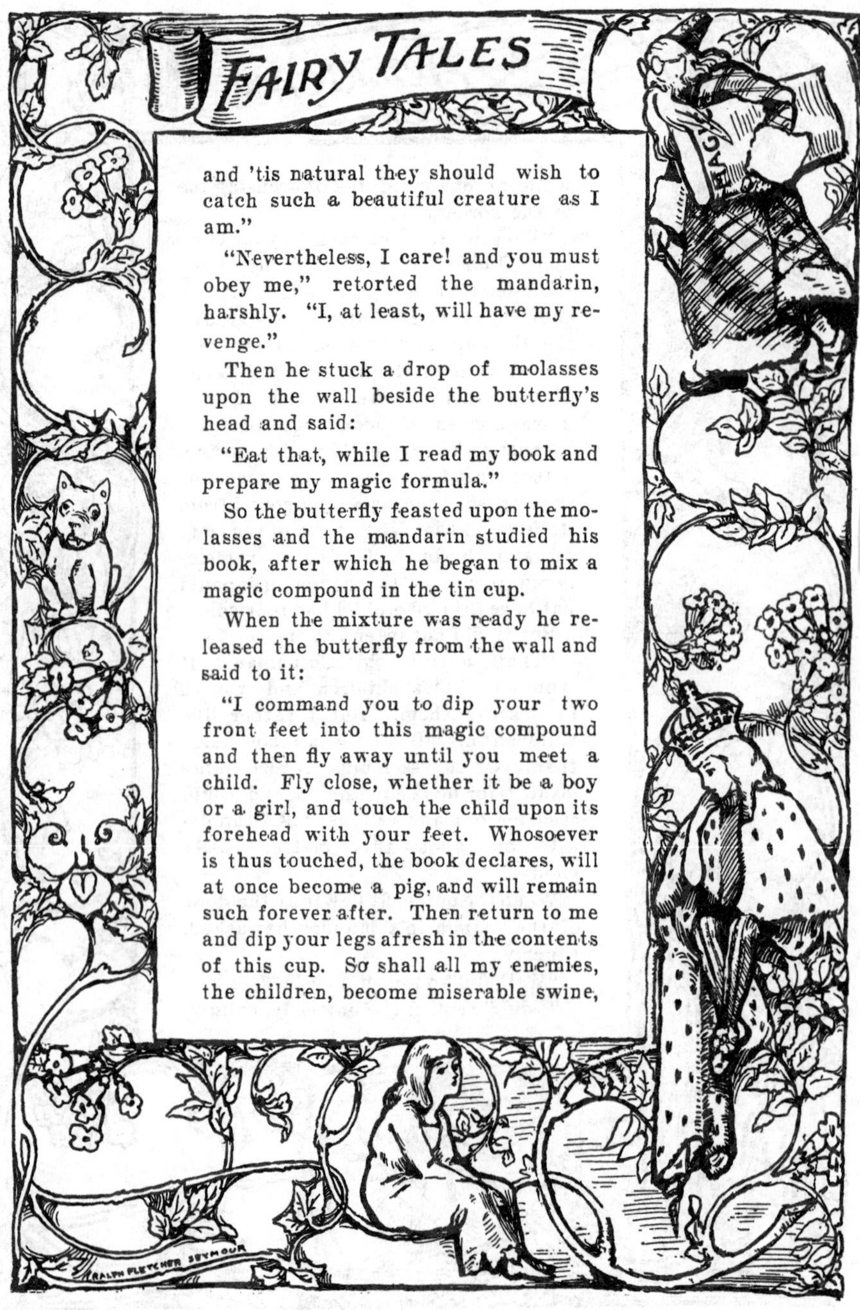

and 'tis natural they should wish to catch such a beautiful creature as I am."

"Nevertheless, I care! and you must obey me," retorted the mandarin, harshly. "I, at least, will have my revenge."

Then he stuck a drop of molasses upon the wall beside the butterfly's head and said:

"Eat that, while I read my book and prepare my magic formula."

So the butterfly feasted upon the molasses and the mandarin studied his book, after which he began to mix a magic compound in the tin cup.

When the mixture was ready he released the butterfly from the wall and said to it:

"I command you to dip your two front feet into this magic compound and then fly away until you meet a child. Fly close, whether it be a boy or a girl, and touch the child upon its forehead with your feet. Whosoever is thus touched, the book declares, will at once become a pig, and will remain such forever after. Then return to me and dip your legs afresh in the contents of this cup. So shall all my enemies, the children, become miserable swine,

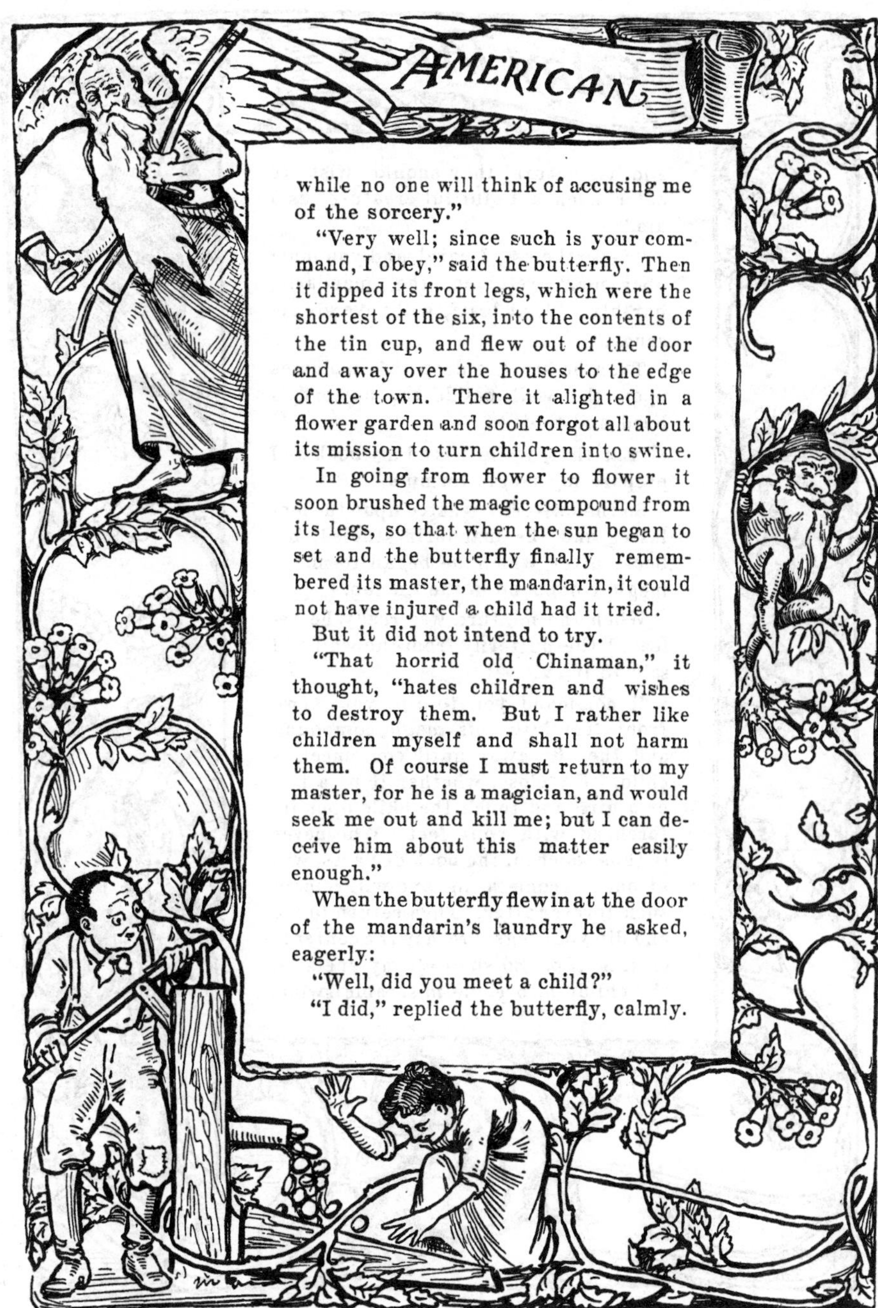

while no one will think of accusing me of the sorcery."

"Very well; since such is your command, I obey," said the butterfly. Then it dipped its front legs, which were the shortest of the six, into the contents of the tin cup, and flew out of the door and away over the houses to the edge of the town. There it alighted in a flower garden and soon forgot all about its mission to turn children into swine.

In going from flower to flower it soon brushed the magic compound from its legs, so that when the sun began to set and the butterfly finally remembered its master, the mandarin, it could not have injured a child had it tried.

But it did not intend to try.

"That horrid old Chinaman," it thought, "hates children and wishes to destroy them. But I rather like children myself and shall not harm them. Of course I must return to my master, for he is a magician, and would seek me out and kill me; but I can deceive him about this matter easily enough."

When the butterfly flew in at the door of the mandarin's laundry he asked, eagerly:

"Well, did you meet a child?"

"I did," replied the butterfly, calmly.

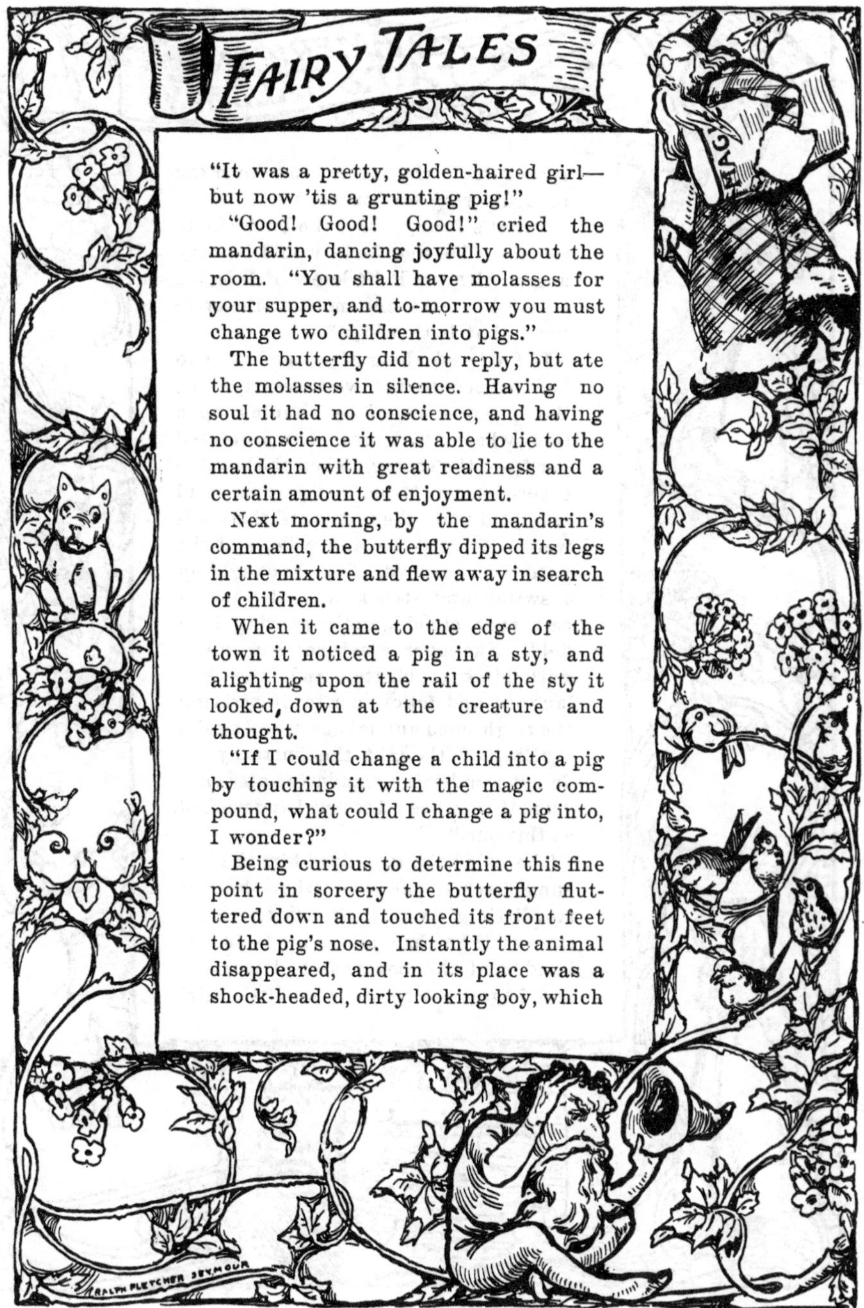

"It was a pretty, golden-haired girl—but now 'tis a grunting pig!"

"Good! Good! Good!" cried the mandarin, dancing joyfully about the room. "You shall have molasses for your supper, and to-morrow you must change two children into pigs."

The butterfly did not reply, but ate the molasses in silence. Having no soul it had no conscience, and having no conscience it was able to lie to the mandarin with great readiness and a certain amount of enjoyment.

Next morning, by the mandarin's command, the butterfly dipped its legs in the mixture and flew away in search of children.

When it came to the edge of the town it noticed a pig in a sty, and alighting upon the rail of the sty it looked, down at the creature and thought.

"If I could change a child into a pig by touching it with the magic compound, what could I change a pig into, I wonder?"

Being curious to determine this fine point in sorcery the butterfly fluttered down and touched its front feet to the pig's nose. Instantly the animal disappeared, and in its place was a shock-headed, dirty looking boy, which

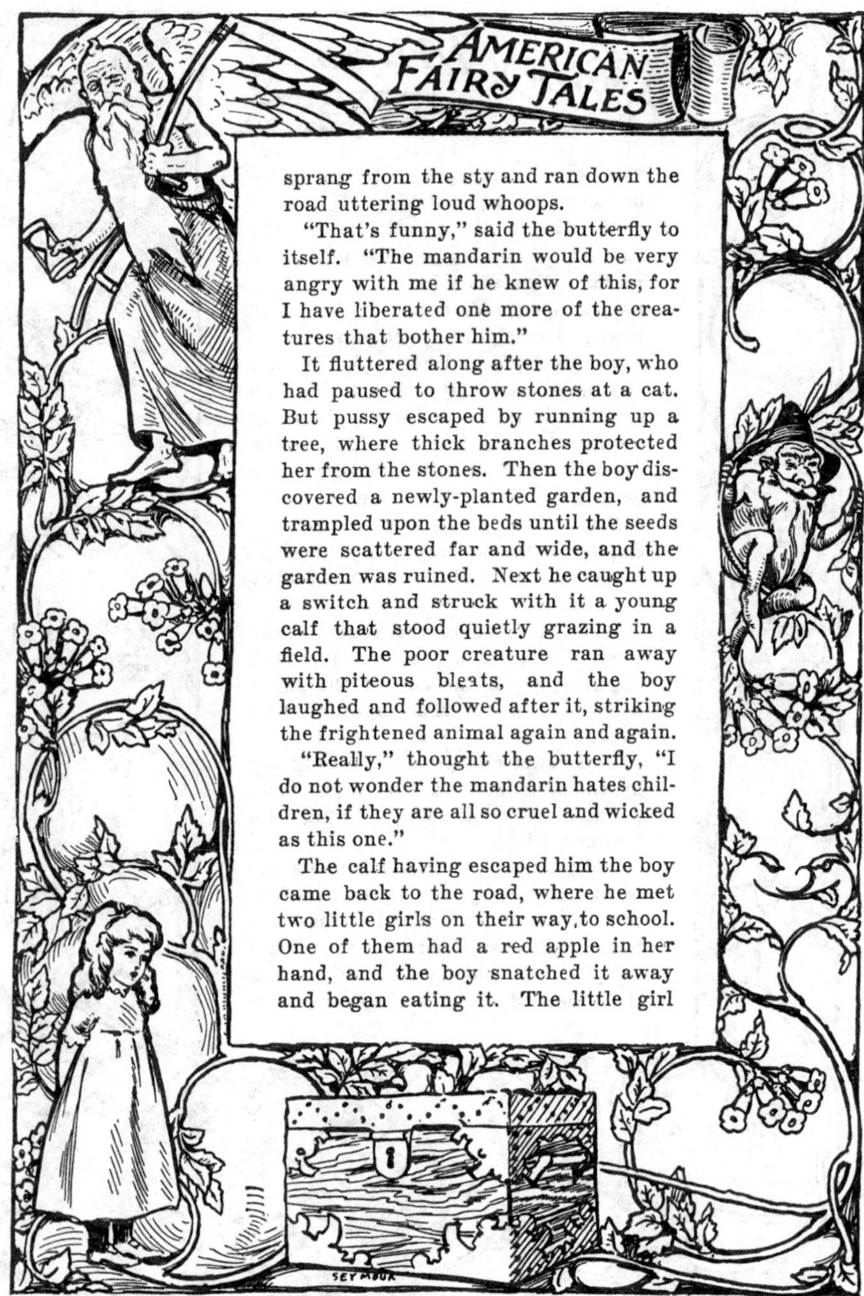

sprang from the sty and ran down the road uttering loud whoops.

"That's funny," said the butterfly to itself. "The mandarin would be very angry with me if he knew of this, for I have liberated one more of the creatures that bother him."

It fluttered along after the boy, who had paused to throw stones at a cat. But pussy escaped by running up a tree, where thick branches protected her from the stones. Then the boy discovered a newly-planted garden, and trampled upon the beds until the seeds were scattered far and wide, and the garden was ruined. Next he caught up a switch and struck with it a young calf that stood quietly grazing in a field. The poor creature ran away with piteous bleats, and the boy laughed and followed after it, striking the frightened animal again and again.

"Really," thought the butterfly, "I do not wonder the mandarin hates children, if they are all so cruel and wicked as this one."

The calf having escaped him the boy came back to the road, where he met two little girls on their way to school. One of them had a red apple in her hand, and the boy snatched it away and began eating it. The little girl

A gentleman came into the room for his laundry.

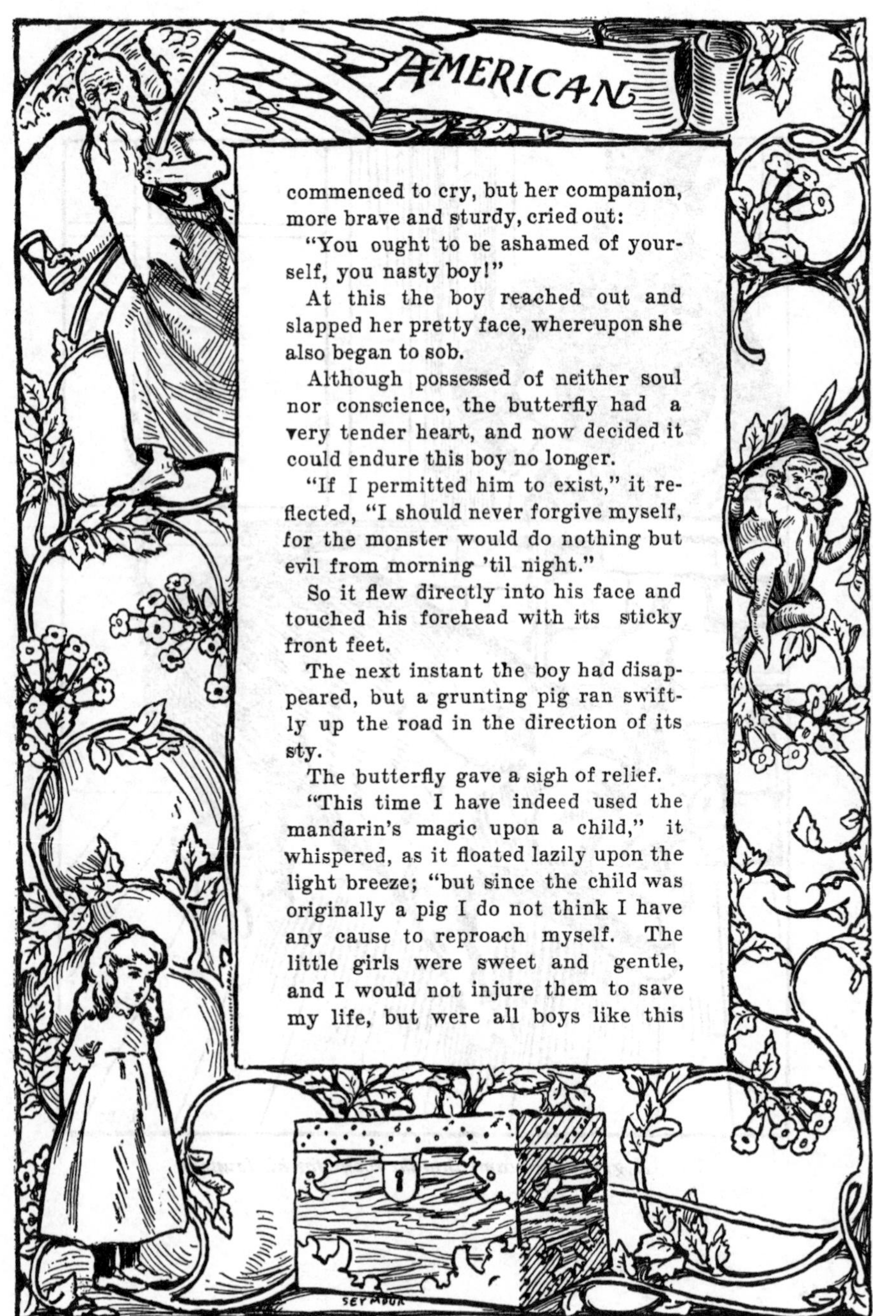

commenced to cry, but her companion, more brave and sturdy, cried out:

"You ought to be ashamed of yourself, you nasty boy!"

At this the boy reached out and slapped her pretty face, whereupon she also began to sob.

Although possessed of neither soul nor conscience, the butterfly had a very tender heart, and now decided it could endure this boy no longer.

"If I permitted him to exist," it reflected, "I should never forgive myself, for the monster would do nothing but evil from morning 'til night."

So it flew directly into his face and touched his forehead with its sticky front feet.

The next instant the boy had disappeared, but a grunting pig ran swiftly up the road in the direction of its sty.

The butterfly gave a sigh of relief.

"This time I have indeed used the mandarin's magic upon a child," it whispered, as it floated lazily upon the light breeze; "but since the child was originally a pig I do not think I have any cause to reproach myself. The little girls were sweet and gentle, and I would not injure them to save my life, but were all boys like this

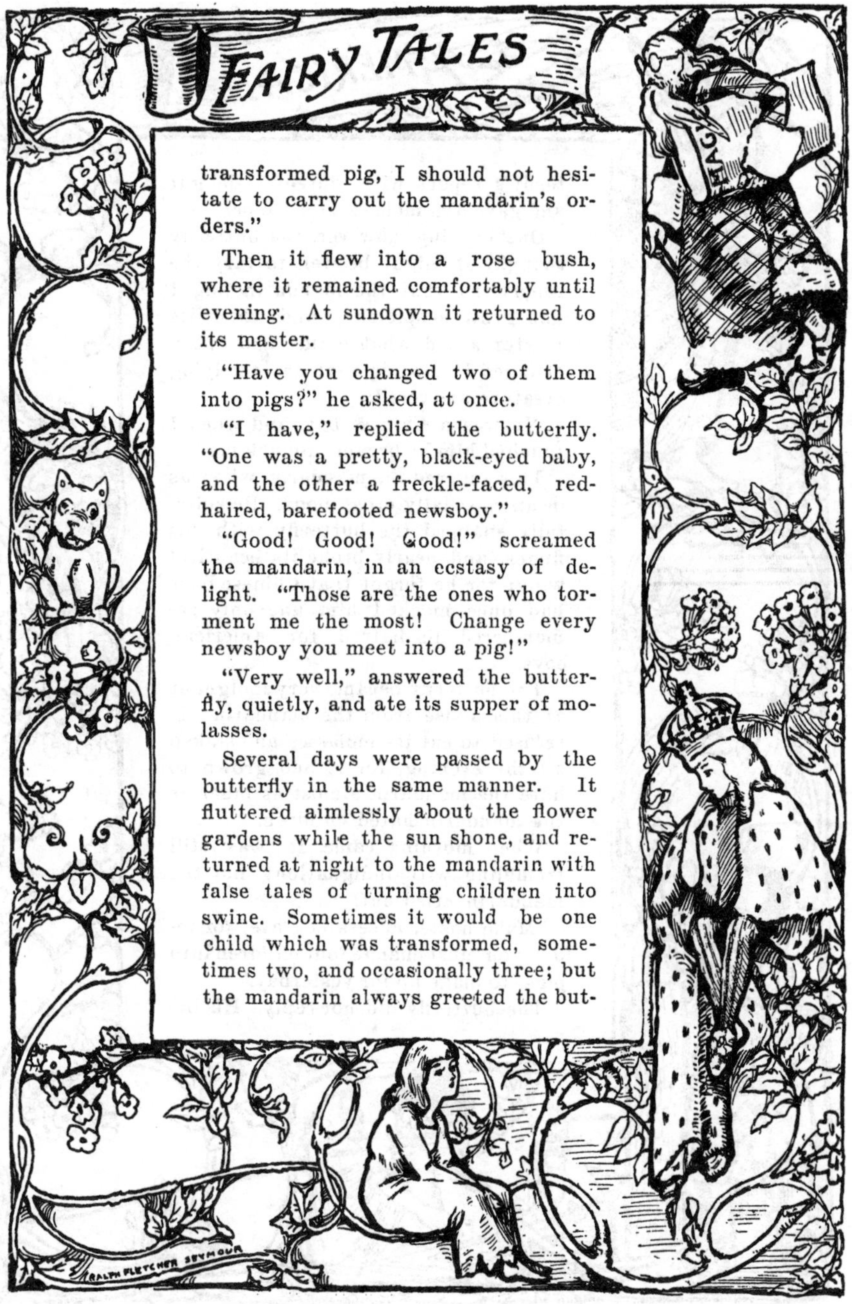

transformed pig, I should not hesitate to carry out the mandarin's orders."

Then it flew into a rose bush, where it remained comfortably until evening. At sundown it returned to its master.

"Have you changed two of them into pigs?" he asked, at once.

"I have," replied the butterfly. "One was a pretty, black-eyed baby, and the other a freckle-faced, red-haired, barefooted newsboy."

"Good! Good! Good!" screamed the mandarin, in an ecstasy of delight. "Those are the ones who torment me the most! Change every newsboy you meet into a pig!"

"Very well," answered the butterfly, quietly, and ate its supper of molasses.

Several days were passed by the butterfly in the same manner. It fluttered aimlessly about the flower gardens while the sun shone, and returned at night to the mandarin with false tales of turning children into swine. Sometimes it would be one child which was transformed, sometimes two, and occasionally three; but the mandarin always greeted the but-

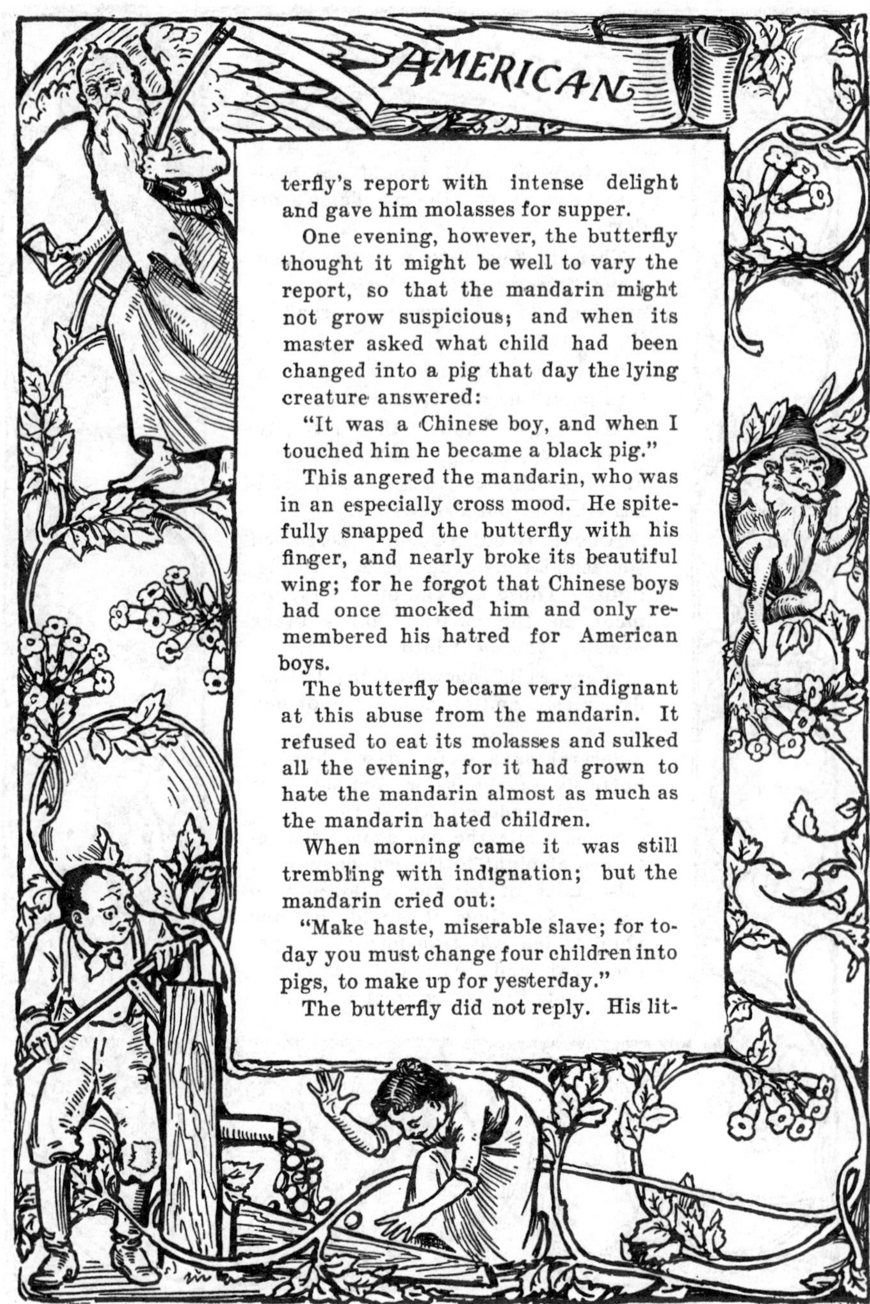

terfly's report with intense delight and gave him molasses for supper.

One evening, however, the butterfly thought it might be well to vary the report, so that the mandarin might not grow suspicious; and when its master asked what child had been changed into a pig that day the lying creature answered:

"It was a Chinese boy, and when I touched him he became a black pig."

This angered the mandarin, who was in an especially cross mood. He spitefully snapped the butterfly with his finger, and nearly broke its beautiful wing; for he forgot that Chinese boys had once mocked him and only remembered his hatred for American boys.

The butterfly became very indignant at this abuse from the mandarin. It refused to eat its molasses and sulked all the evening, for it had grown to hate the mandarin almost as much as the mandarin hated children.

When morning came it was still trembling with indignation; but the mandarin cried out:

"Make haste, miserable slave; for today you must change four children into pigs, to make up for yesterday."

The butterfly did not reply. His lit-

tle black eyes were sparkling wickedly, and no sooner had he dipped his feet into the magic compound than he flew full in the mandarin's face, and touched him upon his ugly, flat forehead.

Soon after a gentleman came into the room for his laundry. The mandarin was not there, but running around the place was a repulsive, scrawny pig, which squealed most miserably.

The butterfly flew away to a brook and washed from its feet all traces of the magic compound. When night came it slept in a rose bush.

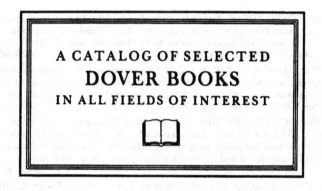

A CATALOG OF SELECTED

DOVER BOOKS

IN ALL FIELDS OF INTEREST

A CATALOG OF SELECTED DOVER BOOKS IN ALL FIELDS OF INTEREST

ALICE'S ADVENTURES IN WONDERLAND, Lewis Carroll. Beloved classic about a little girl lost in a topsy-turvy land and her encounters with the White Rabbit, March Hare, Mad Hatter, Cheshire Cat, and other delightfully improbable characters. 42 illustrations by Sir John Tenniel. 96pp. 5$\frac{3}{16}$ x 8¼. 0-486-27543-4

AMERICA'S LIGHTHOUSES: An Illustrated History, Francis Ross Holland. Profusely illustrated fact-filled survey of American lighthouses since 1716. Over 200 stations — East, Gulf, and West coasts, Great Lakes, Hawaii, Alaska, Puerto Rico, the Virgin Islands, and the Mississippi and St. Lawrence Rivers. 240pp. 8 x 10¾. 0-486-25576-X

AN ENCYCLOPEDIA OF THE VIOLIN, Alberto Bachmann. Translated by Frederick H. Martens. Introduction by Eugene Ysaye. First published in 1925, this renowned reference remains unsurpassed as a source of essential information, from construction and evolution to repertoire and technique. Includes a glossary and 73 illustrations. 496pp. 6⅛ x 9¼. 0-486-46618-3

ANIMALS: 1,419 Copyright-Free Illustrations of Mammals, Birds, Fish, Insects, etc., Selected by Jim Harter. Selected for its visual impact and ease of use, this outstanding collection of wood engravings presents over 1,000 species of animals in extremely lifelike poses. Includes mammals, birds, reptiles, amphibians, fish, insects, and other invertebrates. 284pp. 9 x 12. 0-486-23766-4

THE ANNALS, Tacitus. Translated by Alfred John Church and William Jackson Brodribb. This vital chronicle of Imperial Rome, written by the era's great historian, spans A.D. 14-68 and paints incisive psychological portraits of major figures, from Tiberius to Nero. 416pp. 5$\frac{3}{16}$ x 8¼. 0-486-45236-0

ANTIGONE, Sophocles. Filled with passionate speeches and sensitive probing of moral and philosophical issues, this powerful and often-performed Greek drama reveals the grim fate that befalls the children of Oedipus. Footnotes. 64pp. 5$\frac{3}{16}$ x 8 ¼. 0-486-27804-2

ART DECO DECORATIVE PATTERNS IN FULL COLOR, Christian Stoll. Reprinted from a rare 1910 portfolio, 160 sensuous and exotic images depict a breathtaking array of florals, geometrics, and abstracts — all elegant in their stark simplicity. 64pp. 8⅜ x 11. 0-486-44862-2

THE ARTHUR RACKHAM TREASURY: 86 Full-Color Illustrations, Arthur Rackham. Selected and Edited by Jeff A. Menges. A stunning treasury of 86 full-page plates span the famed English artist's career, from *Rip Van Winkle* (1905) to masterworks such as *Undine, A Midsummer Night's Dream,* and *Wind in the Willows* (1939). 96pp. 8⅜ x 11. 0-486-44685-9

THE AUTHENTIC GILBERT & SULLIVAN SONGBOOK, W. S. Gilbert and A. S. Sullivan. The most comprehensive collection available, this songbook includes selections from every one of Gilbert and Sullivan's light operas. Ninety-two numbers are presented uncut and unedited, and in their original keys. 410pp. 9 x 12. 0-486-23482-7

THE AWAKENING, Kate Chopin. First published in 1899, this controversial novel of a New Orleans wife's search for love outside a stifling marriage shocked readers. Today, it remains a first-rate narrative with superb characterization. New introductory Note. 128pp. 5$\frac{3}{16}$ x 8¼. 0-486-27786-0

BASIC DRAWING, Louis Priscilla. Beginning with perspective, this commonsense manual progresses to the figure in movement, light and shade, anatomy, drapery, composition, trees and landscape, and outdoor sketching. Black-and-white illustrations throughout. 128pp. 8⅜ x 11. 0-486-45815-6

THE BATTLES THAT CHANGED HISTORY, Fletcher Pratt. Historian profiles 16 crucial conflicts, ancient to modern, that changed the course of Western civilization. Gripping accounts of battles led by Alexander the Great, Joan of Arc, Ulysses S. Grant, other commanders. 27 maps. 352pp. 5⅜ x 8½. 0-486-41129-X

BEETHOVEN'S LETTERS, Ludwig van Beethoven. Edited by Dr. A. C. Kalischer. Features 457 letters to fellow musicians, friends, greats, patrons, and literary men. Reveals musical thoughts, quirks of personality, insights, and daily events. Includes 15 plates. 410pp. 5⅜ x 8½. 0-486-22769-3

BERNICE BOBS HER HAIR AND OTHER STORIES, F. Scott Fitzgerald. This brilliant anthology includes 6 of Fitzgerald's most popular stories: "The Diamond as Big as the Ritz," the title tale, "The Offshore Pirate," "The Ice Palace," "The Jelly Bean," and "May Day." 176pp. 5⅜ x 8½. 0-486-47049-0

BESLER'S BOOK OF FLOWERS AND PLANTS: 73 Full-Color Plates from Hortus Eystettensis, 1613, Basilius Besler. Here is a selection of magnificent plates from the *Hortus Eystettensis,* which vividly illustrated and identified the plants, flowers, and trees that thrived in the legendary German garden at Eichstätt. 80pp. 8⅜ x 11. 0-486-46005-3

THE BOOK OF KELLS, Edited by Blanche Cirker. Painstakingly reproduced from a rare facsimile edition, this volume contains full-page decorations, portraits, illustrations, plus a sampling of textual leaves with exquisite calligraphy and ornamentation. 32 full-color illustrations. 32pp. 9⅜ x 12¼. 0-486-24345-1

THE BOOK OF THE CROSSBOW: With an Additional Section on Catapults and Other Siege Engines, Ralph Payne-Gallwey. Fascinating study traces history and use of crossbow as military and sporting weapon, from Middle Ages to modern times. Also covers related weapons: balistas, catapults, Turkish bows, more. Over 240 illustrations. 400pp. 7¼ x 10⅝. 0-486-28720-3

THE BUNGALOW BOOK: Floor Plans and Photos of 112 Houses, 1910, Henry L. Wilson. Here are 112 of the most popular and economic blueprints of the early 20th century — plus an illustration or photograph of each completed house. A wonderful time capsule that still offers a wealth of valuable insights. 160pp. 8⅜ x 11. 0-486-45104-6

THE CALL OF THE WILD, Jack London. A classic novel of adventure, drawn from London's own experiences as a Klondike adventurer, relating the story of a heroic dog caught in the brutal life of the Alaska Gold Rush. Note. 64pp. 5$\frac{3}{16}$ x 8¼. 0-486-26472-6

CANDIDE, Voltaire. Edited by Francois-Marie Arouet. One of the world's great satires since its first publication in 1759. Witty, caustic skewering of romance, science, philosophy, religion, government — nearly all human ideals and institutions. 112pp. 5$\frac{3}{16}$ x 8¼. 0-486-26689-3

CELEBRATED IN THEIR TIME: Photographic Portraits from the George Grantham Bain Collection, Edited by Amy Pastan. With an Introduction by Michael Carlebach. Remarkable portrait gallery features 112 rare images of Albert Einstein, Charlie Chaplin, the Wright Brothers, Henry Ford, and other luminaries from the worlds of politics, art, entertainment, and industry. 128pp. 8⅜ x 11. 0-486-46754-6

CHARIOTS FOR APOLLO: The NASA History of Manned Lunar Spacecraft to 1969, Courtney G. Brooks, James M. Grimwood, and Loyd S. Swenson, Jr. This illustrated history by a trio of experts is the definitive reference on the Apollo spacecraft and lunar modules. It traces the vehicles' design, development, and operation in space. More than 100 photographs and illustrations. 576pp. 6¾ x 9¼. 0-486-46756-2

DOOMED SHIPS: Great Ocean Liner Disasters, William H. Miller, Jr. Nearly 200 photographs, many from private collections, highlight tales of some of the vessels whose pleasure cruises ended in catastrophe: the *Morro Castle, Normandie, Andrea Doria, Europa,* and many others. 128pp. 8⅞ x 11¾. 0-486-45366-9

THE DORÉ BIBLE ILLUSTRATIONS, Gustave Doré. Detailed plates from the Bible: the Creation scenes, Adam and Eve, horrifying visions of the Flood, the battle sequences with their monumental crowds, depictions of the life of Jesus, 241 plates in all. 241pp. 9 x 12. 0-486-23004-X

DRAWING DRAPERY FROM HEAD TO TOE, Cliff Young. Expert guidance on how to draw shirts, pants, skirts, gloves, hats, and coats on the human figure, including folds in relation to the body, pull and crush, action folds, creases, more. Over 200 drawings. 48pp. 8¼ x 11. 0-486-45591-2

DUBLINERS, James Joyce. A fine and accessible introduction to the work of one of the 20th century's most influential writers, this collection features 15 tales, including a masterpiece of the short-story genre, "The Dead." 160pp. 5³⁄₁₆ x 8¼. 0-486-26870-5

EASY-TO-MAKE POP-UPS, Joan Irvine. Illustrated by Barbara Reid. Dozens of wonderful ideas for three-dimensional paper fun — from holiday greeting cards with moving parts to a pop-up menagerie. Easy-to-follow, illustrated instructions for more than 30 projects. 299 black-and-white illustrations. 96pp. 8⅜ x 11. 0-486-44622-0

EASY-TO-MAKE STORYBOOK DOLLS: A "Novel" Approach to Cloth Dollmaking, Sherralyn St. Clair. Favorite fictional characters come alive in this unique beginner's dollmaking guide. Includes patterns for Pollyanna, Dorothy from *The Wonderful Wizard of Oz,* Mary of *The Secret Garden,* plus easy-to-follow instructions, 263 black-and-white illustrations, and an 8-page color insert. 112pp. 8¼ x 11. 0-486-47360-0

EINSTEIN'S ESSAYS IN SCIENCE, Albert Einstein. Speeches and essays in accessible, everyday language profile influential physicists such as Niels Bohr and Isaac Newton. They also explore areas of physics to which the author made major contributions. 128pp. 5 x 8. 0-486-47011-3

EL DORADO: Further Adventures of the Scarlet Pimpernel, Baroness Orczy. A popular sequel to *The Scarlet Pimpernel,* this suspenseful story recounts the Pimpernel's attempts to rescue the Dauphin from imprisonment during the French Revolution. An irresistible blend of intrigue, period detail, and vibrant characterizations. 352pp. 5³⁄₁₆ x 8¼. 0-486-44026-5

ELEGANT SMALL HOMES OF THE TWENTIES: 99 Designs from a Competition, Chicago Tribune. Nearly 100 designs for five- and six-room houses feature New England and Southern colonials, Normandy cottages, stately Italianate dwellings, and other fascinating snapshots of American domestic architecture of the 1920s. 112pp. 9 x 12. 0-486-46910-7

THE ELEMENTS OF STYLE: The Original Edition, William Strunk, Jr. This is the book that generations of writers have relied upon for timeless advice on grammar, diction, syntax, and other essentials. In concise terms, it identifies the principal requirements of proper style and common errors. 64pp. 5⅜ x 8½. 0-486-44798-7

THE ELUSIVE PIMPERNEL, Baroness Orczy. Robespierre's revolutionaries find their wicked schemes thwarted by the heroic Pimpernel — Sir Percival Blakeney. In this thrilling sequel, Chauvelin devises a plot to eliminate the Pimpernel and his wife. 272pp. 5³⁄₁₆ x 8¼. 0-486-45464-9

AN ENCYCLOPEDIA OF BATTLES: Accounts of Over 1,560 Battles from 1479 B.C. to the Present, David Eggenberger. Essential details of every major battle in recorded history from the first battle of Megiddo in 1479 B.C. to Grenada in 1984. List of battle maps. 99 illustrations. 544pp. 6½ x 9¼. 0-486-24913-1

ENCYCLOPEDIA OF EMBROIDERY STITCHES, INCLUDING CREWEL, Marion Nichols. Precise explanations and instructions, clearly illustrated, on how to work chain, back, cross, knotted, woven stitches, and many more — 178 in all, including Cable Outline, Whipped Satin, and Eyelet Buttonhole. Over 1400 illustrations. 219pp. 8⅜ x 11¼. 0-486-22929-7

ENTER JEEVES: 15 Early Stories, P. G. Wodehouse. Splendid collection contains first 8 stories featuring Bertie Wooster, the deliciously dim aristocrat and Jeeves, his brainy, imperturbable manservant. Also, the complete Reggie Pepper (Bertie's prototype) series. 288pp. 5⅜ x 8½. 0-486-29717-9

ERIC SLOANE'S AMERICA: Paintings in Oil, Michael Wigley. With a Foreword by Mimi Sloane. Eric Sloane's evocative oils of America's landscape and material culture shimmer with immense historical and nostalgic appeal. This original hardcover collection gathers nearly a hundred of his finest paintings, with subjects ranging from New England to the American Southwest. 128pp. 10⅝ x 9. 0-486-46525-X

ETHAN FROME, Edith Wharton. Classic story of wasted lives, set against a bleak New England background. Superbly delineated characters in a hauntingly grim tale of thwarted love. Considered by many to be Wharton's masterpiece. 96pp. 5³⁄₁₆ x 8 ¼. 0-486-26690-7

THE EVERLASTING MAN, G. K. Chesterton. Chesterton's view of Christianity — as a blend of philosophy and mythology, satisfying intellect and spirit — applies to his brilliant book, which appeals to readers' heads as well as their hearts. 288pp. 5⅜ x 8½. 0-486-46036-3

THE FIELD AND FOREST HANDY BOOK, Daniel Beard. Written by a co-founder of the Boy Scouts, this appealing guide offers illustrated instructions for building kites, birdhouses, boats, igloos, and other fun projects, plus numerous helpful tips for campers. 448pp. 5³⁄₁₆ x 8¼. 0-486-46191-2

FINDING YOUR WAY WITHOUT MAP OR COMPASS, Harold Gatty. Useful, instructive manual shows would-be explorers, hikers, bikers, scouts, sailors, and survivalists how to find their way outdoors by observing animals, weather patterns, shifting sands, and other elements of nature. 288pp. 5⅜ x 8½. 0-486-40613-X

FIRST FRENCH READER: A Beginner's Dual-Language Book, Edited and Translated by Stanley Appelbaum. This anthology introduces 50 legendary writers — Voltaire, Balzac, Baudelaire, Proust, more — through passages from *The Red and the Black, Les Misérables, Madame Bovary,* and other classics. Original French text plus English translation on facing pages. 240pp. 5⅜ x 8½. 0-486-46178-5

FIRST GERMAN READER: A Beginner's Dual-Language Book, Edited by Harry Steinhauer. Specially chosen for their power to evoke German life and culture, these short, simple readings include poems, stories, essays, and anecdotes by Goethe, Hesse, Heine, Schiller, and others. 224pp. 5⅜ x 8½. 0-486-46179-3

FIRST SPANISH READER: A Beginner's Dual-Language Book, Angel Flores. Delightful stories, other material based on works of Don Juan Manuel, Luis Taboada, Ricardo Palma, other noted writers. Complete faithful English translations on facing pages. Exercises. 176pp. 5⅜ x 8½. 0-486-25810-6

FIVE ACRES AND INDEPENDENCE, Maurice G. Kains. Great back-to-the-land classic explains basics of self-sufficient farming. The one book to get. 95 illustrations. 397pp. 5⅜ x 8½. 0-486-20974-1

FLAGG'S SMALL HOUSES: Their Economic Design and Construction, 1922, Ernest Flagg. Although most famous for his skyscrapers, Flagg was also a proponent of the well-designed single-family dwelling. His classic treatise features innovations that save space, materials, and cost. 526 illustrations. 160pp. 9⅜ x 12¼. 0-486-45197-6

FLATLAND: A Romance of Many Dimensions, Edwin A. Abbott. Classic of science (and mathematical) fiction — charmingly illustrated by the author — describes the adventures of A. Square, a resident of Flatland, in Spaceland (three dimensions), Lineland (one dimension), and Pointland (no dimensions). 96pp. 5³⁄₁₆ x 8¼. 0-486-27263-X

FRANKENSTEIN, Mary Shelley. The story of Victor Frankenstein's monstrous creation and the havoc it caused has enthralled generations of readers and inspired countless writers of horror and suspense. With the author's own 1831 introduction. 176pp. 5³⁄₁₆ x 8¼. 0-486-28211-2

THE GARGOYLE BOOK: 572 Examples from Gothic Architecture, Lester Burbank Bridaham. Dispelling the conventional wisdom that French Gothic architectural flourishes were born of despair or gloom, Bridaham reveals the whimsical nature of these creations and the ingenious artisans who made them. 572 illustrations. 224pp. 8⅜ x 11. 0-486-44754-5

THE GIFT OF THE MAGI AND OTHER SHORT STORIES, O. Henry. Sixteen captivating stories by one of America's most popular storytellers. Included are such classics as "The Gift of the Magi," "The Last Leaf," and "The Ransom of Red Chief." Publisher's Note. 96pp. 5³⁄₁₆ x 8¼. 0-486-27061-0

THE GOETHE TREASURY: Selected Prose and Poetry, Johann Wolfgang von Goethe. Edited, Selected, and with an Introduction by Thomas Mann. In addition to his lyric poetry, Goethe wrote travel sketches, autobiographical studies, essays, letters, and proverbs in rhyme and prose. This collection presents outstanding examples from each genre. 368pp. 5⅜ x 8½. 0-486-44780-4

GREAT EXPECTATIONS, Charles Dickens. Orphaned Pip is apprenticed to the dirty work of the forge but dreams of becoming a gentleman — and one day finds himself in possession of "great expectations." Dickens' finest novel. 400pp. 5³⁄₁₆ x 8¼. 0-486-41586-4

GREAT WRITERS ON THE ART OF FICTION: From Mark Twain to Joyce Carol Oates, Edited by James Daley. An indispensable source of advice and inspiration, this anthology features essays by Henry James, Kate Chopin, Willa Cather, Sinclair Lewis, Jack London, Raymond Chandler, Raymond Carver, Eudora Welty, and Kurt Vonnegut, Jr. 192pp. 5⅜ x 8½. 0-486-45128-3

HAMLET, William Shakespeare. The quintessential Shakespearean tragedy, whose highly charged confrontations and anguished soliloquies probe depths of human feeling rarely sounded in any art. Reprinted from an authoritative British edition complete with illuminating footnotes. 128pp. 5³⁄₁₆ x 8¼. 0-486-27278-8

THE HAUNTED HOUSE, Charles Dickens. A Yuletide gathering in an eerie country retreat provides the backdrop for Dickens and his friends — including Elizabeth Gaskell and Wilkie Collins — who take turns spinning supernatural yarns. 144pp. 5⅜ x 8½. 0-486-46309-5

HEART OF DARKNESS, Joseph Conrad. Dark allegory of a journey up the Congo River and the narrator's encounter with the mysterious Mr. Kurtz. Masterly blend of adventure, character study, psychological penetration. For many, Conrad's finest, most enigmatic story. 80pp. 5³⁄₁₆ x 8¼. 0-486-26464-5

HENSON AT THE NORTH POLE, Matthew A. Henson. This thrilling memoir by the heroic African-American who was Peary's companion through two decades of Arctic exploration recounts a tale of danger, courage, and determination. "Fascinating and exciting." — *Commonweal*. 128pp. 5⅜ x 8½. 0-486-45472-X

HISTORIC COSTUMES AND HOW TO MAKE THEM, Mary Fernald and E. Shenton. Practical, informative guidebook shows how to create everything from short tunics worn by Saxon men in the fifth century to a lady's bustle dress of the late 1800s. 81 illustrations. 176pp. 5⅜ x 8½. 0-486-44906-8

THE HOUND OF THE BASKERVILLES, Arthur Conan Doyle. A deadly curse in the form of a legendary ferocious beast continues to claim its victims from the Baskerville family until Holmes and Watson intervene. Often called the best detective story ever written. 128pp. 5³⁄₁₆ x 8¼. 0-486-28214-7

THE HOUSE BEHIND THE CEDARS, Charles W. Chesnutt. Originally published in 1900, this groundbreaking novel by a distinguished African-American author recounts the drama of a brother and sister who "pass for white" during the dangerous days of Reconstruction. 208pp. 5⅜ x 8½. 0-486-46144-0

THE HUMAN FIGURE IN MOTION, Eadweard Muybridge. The 4,789 photographs in this definitive selection show the human figure — models almost all undraped — engaged in over 160 different types of action: running, climbing stairs, etc. 390pp. 7⅞ x 10⅝. 0-486-20204-6

THE IMPORTANCE OF BEING EARNEST, Oscar Wilde. Wilde's witty and buoyant comedy of manners, filled with some of literature's most famous epigrams, reprinted from an authoritative British edition. Considered Wilde's most perfect work. 64pp. 5³⁄₁₆ x 8¼. 0-486-26478-5

THE INFERNO, Dante Alighieri. Translated and with notes by Henry Wadsworth Longfellow. The first stop on Dante's famous journey from Hell to Purgatory to Paradise, this 14th-century allegorical poem blends vivid and shocking imagery with graceful lyricism. Translated by the beloved 19th-century poet, Henry Wadsworth Longfellow. 256pp. 5³⁄₁₆ x 8¼. 0-486-44288-8

JANE EYRE, Charlotte Brontë. Written in 1847, *Jane Eyre* tells the tale of an orphan girl's progress from the custody of cruel relatives to an oppressive boarding school and its culmination in a troubled career as a governess. 448pp. 5³⁄₁₆ x 8¼. 0-486-42449-9

JAPANESE WOODBLOCK FLOWER PRINTS, Tanigami Kônan. Extraordinary collection of Japanese woodblock prints by a well-known artist features 120 plates in brilliant color. Realistic images from a rare edition include daffodils, tulips, and other familiar and unusual flowers. 128pp. 11 x 8¼. 0-486-46442-3

JEWELRY MAKING AND DESIGN, Augustus F. Rose and Antonio Cirino. Professional secrets of jewelry making are revealed in a thorough, practical guide. Over 200 illustrations. 306pp. 5⅜ x 8½. 0-486-21750-7

JULIUS CAESAR, William Shakespeare. Great tragedy based on Plutarch's account of the lives of Brutus, Julius Caesar and Mark Antony. Evil plotting, ringing oratory, high tragedy with Shakespeare's incomparable insight, dramatic power. Explanatory footnotes. 96pp. 5³⁄₁₆ x 8¼. 0-486-26876-4

THE JUNGLE, Upton Sinclair. 1906 bestseller shockingly reveals intolerable labor practices and working conditions in the Chicago stockyards as it tells the grim story of a Slavic family that emigrates to America full of optimism but soon faces despair. 320pp. 5$\frac{3}{16}$ x 8¼. 0-486-41923-1

THE KINGDOM OF GOD IS WITHIN YOU, Leo Tolstoy. The soul-searching book that inspired Gandhi to embrace the concept of passive resistance, Tolstoy's 1894 polemic clearly outlines a radical, well-reasoned revision of traditional Christian thinking. 352pp. 5$\frac{3}{16}$ x 8¼. 0-486-45138-0

THE LADY OR THE TIGER?: and Other Logic Puzzles, Raymond M. Smullyan. Created by a renowned puzzle master, these whimsically themed challenges involve paradoxes about probability, time, and change; metapuzzles; and self-referentiality. Nineteen chapters advance in difficulty from relatively simple to highly complex. 1982 edition. 240pp. 5⅜ x 8½. 0-486-47027-X

LEAVES OF GRASS: The Original 1855 Edition, Walt Whitman. Whitman's immortal collection includes some of the greatest poems of modern times, including his masterpiece, "Song of Myself." Shattering standard conventions, it stands as an unabashed celebration of body and nature. 128pp. 5$\frac{3}{16}$ x 8¼. 0-486-45676-5

LES MISÉRABLES, Victor Hugo. Translated by Charles E. Wilbour. Abridged by James K. Robinson. A convict's heroic struggle for justice and redemption plays out against a fiery backdrop of the Napoleonic wars. This edition features the excellent original translation and a sensitive abridgment. 304pp. 6⅛ x 9¼. 0-486-45789-3

LILITH: A Romance, George MacDonald. In this novel by the father of fantasy literature, a man travels through time to meet Adam and Eve and to explore humanity's fall from grace and ultimate redemption. 240pp. 5⅜ x 8½. 0-486-46818-6

THE LOST LANGUAGE OF SYMBOLISM, Harold Bayley. This remarkable book reveals the hidden meaning behind familiar images and words, from the origins of Santa Claus to the fleur-de-lys, drawing from mythology, folklore, religious texts, and fairy tales. 1,418 illustrations. 784pp. 5⅜ x 8½. 0-486-44787-1

MACBETH, William Shakespeare. A Scottish nobleman murders the king in order to succeed to the throne. Tortured by his conscience and fearful of discovery, he becomes tangled in a web of treachery and deceit that ultimately spells his doom. 96pp. 5$\frac{3}{16}$ x 8¼. 0-486-27802-6

MAKING AUTHENTIC CRAFTSMAN FURNITURE: Instructions and Plans for 62 Projects, Gustav Stickley. Make authentic reproductions of handsome, functional, durable furniture: tables, chairs, wall cabinets, desks, a hall tree, and more. Construction plans with drawings, schematics, dimensions, and lumber specs reprinted from 1900s *The Craftsman* magazine. 128pp. 8⅛ x 11. 0-486-25000-8

MATHEMATICS FOR THE NONMATHEMATICIAN, Morris Kline. Erudite and entertaining overview follows development of mathematics from ancient Greeks to present. Topics include logic and mathematics, the fundamental concept, differential calculus, probability theory, much more. Exercises and problems. 641pp. 5⅜ x 8½. 0-486-24823-2

MEMOIRS OF AN ARABIAN PRINCESS FROM ZANZIBAR, Emily Ruete. This 19th-century autobiography offers a rare inside look at the society surrounding a sultan's palace. A real-life princess in exile recalls her vanished world of harems, slave trading, and court intrigues. 288pp. 5⅜ x 8½. 0-486-47121-7

THE METAMORPHOSIS AND OTHER STORIES, Franz Kafka. Excellent new English translations of title story (considered by many critics Kafka's most perfect work), plus "The Judgment," "In the Penal Colony," "A Country Doctor," and "A Report to an Academy." Note. 96pp. 5$\frac{3}{16}$ x 8$\frac{1}{4}$. 0-486-29030-1

MICROSCOPIC ART FORMS FROM THE PLANT WORLD, R. Anheisser. From undulating curves to complex geometrics, a world of fascinating images abound in this classic, illustrated survey of microscopic plants. Features 400 detailed illustrations of nature's minute but magnificent handiwork. The accompanying CD-ROM includes all of the images in the book. 128pp. 9 x 9. 0-486-46013-4

A MIDSUMMER NIGHT'S DREAM, William Shakespeare. Among the most popular of Shakespeare's comedies, this enchanting play humorously celebrates the vagaries of love as it focuses upon the intertwined romances of several pairs of lovers. Explanatory footnotes. 80pp. 5$\frac{3}{16}$ x 8$\frac{1}{4}$. 0-486-27067-X

THE MONEY CHANGERS, Upton Sinclair. Originally published in 1908, this cautionary novel from the author of *The Jungle* explores corruption within the American system as a group of power brokers joins forces for personal gain, triggering a crash on Wall Street. 192pp. 5$\frac{3}{8}$ x 8$\frac{1}{2}$. 0-486-46917-4

THE MOST POPULAR HOMES OF THE TWENTIES, William A. Radford. With a New Introduction by Daniel D. Reiff. Based on a rare 1925 catalog, this architectural showcase features floor plans, construction details, and photos of 26 homes, plus articles on entrances, porches, garages, and more. 250 illustrations, 21 color plates. 176pp. 8$\frac{3}{8}$ x 11. 0-486-47028-8

MY 66 YEARS IN THE BIG LEAGUES, Connie Mack. With a New Introduction by Rich Westcott. A Founding Father of modern baseball, Mack holds the record for most wins — and losses — by a major league manager. Enhanced by 70 photographs, his warmhearted autobiography is populated by many legends of the game. 288pp. 5$\frac{3}{8}$ x 8$\frac{1}{2}$. 0-486-47184-5

NARRATIVE OF THE LIFE OF FREDERICK DOUGLASS, Frederick Douglass. Douglass's graphic depictions of slavery, harrowing escape to freedom, and life as a newspaper editor, eloquent orator, and impassioned abolitionist. 96pp. 5$\frac{3}{16}$ x 8$\frac{1}{4}$. 0-486-28499-9

THE NIGHTLESS CITY: Geisha and Courtesan Life in Old Tokyo, J. E. de Becker. This unsurpassed study from 100 years ago ventured into Tokyo's red-light district to survey geisha and courtesan life and offer meticulous descriptions of training, dress, social hierarchy, and erotic practices. 49 black-and-white illustrations; 2 maps. 496pp. 5$\frac{3}{8}$ x 8$\frac{1}{2}$. 0-486-45563-7

THE ODYSSEY, Homer. Excellent prose translation of ancient epic recounts adventures of the homeward-bound Odysseus. Fantastic cast of gods, giants, cannibals, sirens, other supernatural creatures — true classic of Western literature. 256pp. 5$\frac{3}{16}$ x 8$\frac{1}{4}$. 0-486-40654-7

OEDIPUS REX, Sophocles. Landmark of Western drama concerns the catastrophe that ensues when King Oedipus discovers he has inadvertently killed his father and married his mother. Masterly construction, dramatic irony. Explanatory footnotes. 64pp. 5$\frac{3}{16}$ x 8$\frac{1}{4}$. 0-486-26877-2

ONCE UPON A TIME: The Way America Was, Eric Sloane. Nostalgic text and drawings brim with gentle philosophies and descriptions of how we used to live — self-sufficiently — on the land, in homes, and among the things built by hand. 44 line illustrations. 64pp. 8$\frac{3}{8}$ x 11. 0-486-44411-2

ONE OF OURS, Willa Cather. The Pulitzer Prize–winning novel about a young Nebraskan looking for something to believe in. Alienated from his parents, rejected by his wife, he finds his destiny on the bloody battlefields of World War I. 352pp. 5³⁄₁₆ x 8¼. 0-486-45599-8

ORIGAMI YOU CAN USE: 27 Practical Projects, Rick Beech. Origami models can be more than decorative, and this unique volume shows how! The 27 practical projects include a CD case, frame, napkin ring, and dish. Easy instructions feature 400 two-color illustrations. 96pp. 8¼ x 11. 0-486-47057-1

OTHELLO, William Shakespeare. Towering tragedy tells the story of a Moorish general who earns the enmity of his ensign Iago when he passes him over for a promotion. Masterly portrait of an archvillain. Explanatory footnotes. 112pp. 5³⁄₁₆ x 8¼. 0-486-29097-2

PARADISE LOST, John Milton. Notes by John A. Himes. First published in 1667, *Paradise Lost* ranks among the greatest of English literature's epic poems. It's a sublime retelling of Adam and Eve's fall from grace and expulsion from Eden. Notes by John A. Himes. 480pp. 5³⁄₁₆ x 8¼. 0-486-44287-X

PASSING, Nella Larsen. Married to a successful physician and prominently ensconced in society, Irene Redfield leads a charmed existence — until a chance encounter with a childhood friend who has been "passing for white." 112pp. 5⅜ x 8½. 0-486-43713-2

PERSPECTIVE DRAWING FOR BEGINNERS, Len A. Doust. Doust carefully explains the roles of lines, boxes, and circles, and shows how visualizing shapes and forms can be used in accurate depictions of perspective. One of the most concise introductions available. 33 illustrations. 64pp. 5⅜ x 8½. 0-486-45149-6

PERSPECTIVE MADE EASY, Ernest R. Norling. Perspective is easy; yet, surprisingly few artists know the simple rules that make it so. Remedy that situation with this simple, step-by-step book, the first devoted entirely to the topic. 256 illustrations. 224pp. 5⅜ x 8½. 0-486-40473-0

THE PICTURE OF DORIAN GRAY, Oscar Wilde. Celebrated novel involves a handsome young Londoner who sinks into a life of depravity. His body retains perfect youth and vigor while his recent portrait reflects the ravages of his crime and sensuality. 176pp. 5³⁄₁₆ x 8¼. 0-486-27807-7

PRIDE AND PREJUDICE, Jane Austen. One of the most universally loved and admired English novels, an effervescent tale of rural romance transformed by Jane Austen's art into a witty, shrewdly observed satire of English country life. 272pp. 5³⁄₁₆ x 8¼. 0-486-28473-5

THE PRINCE, Niccolò Machiavelli. Classic, Renaissance-era guide to acquiring and maintaining political power. Today, nearly 500 years after it was written, this calculating prescription for autocratic rule continues to be much read and studied. 80pp. 5³⁄₁₆ x 8¼. 0-486-27274-5

QUICK SKETCHING, Carl Cheek. A perfect introduction to the technique of "quick sketching." Drawing upon an artist's immediate emotional responses, this is an extremely effective means of capturing the essential form and features of a subject. More than 100 black-and-white illustrations throughout. 48pp. 11 x 8¼. 0-486-46608-6

RANCH LIFE AND THE HUNTING TRAIL, Theodore Roosevelt. Illustrated by Frederic Remington. Beautifully illustrated by Remington, Roosevelt's celebration of the Old West recounts his adventures in the Dakota Badlands of the 1880s, from roundups to Indian encounters to hunting bighorn sheep. 208pp. 6¼ x 9¼. 0-486-47340-6

THE RED BADGE OF COURAGE, Stephen Crane. Amid the nightmarish chaos of a Civil War battle, a young soldier discovers courage, humility, and, perhaps, wisdom. Uncanny re-creation of actual combat. Enduring landmark of American fiction. 112pp. $5\frac{3}{16}$ x $8\frac{1}{4}$. 0-486-26465-3

RELATIVITY SIMPLY EXPLAINED, Martin Gardner. One of the subject's clearest, most entertaining introductions offers lucid explanations of special and general theories of relativity, gravity, and spacetime, models of the universe, and more. 100 illustrations. 224pp. $5\frac{3}{8}$ x $8\frac{1}{2}$. 0-486-29315-7

REMBRANDT DRAWINGS: 116 Masterpieces in Original Color, Rembrandt van Rijn. This deluxe hardcover edition features drawings from throughout the Dutch master's prolific career. Informative captions accompany these beautifully reproduced landscapes, biblical vignettes, figure studies, animal sketches, and portraits. 128pp. $8\frac{3}{8}$ x 11. 0-486-46149-1

THE ROAD NOT TAKEN AND OTHER POEMS, Robert Frost. A treasury of Frost's most expressive verse. In addition to the title poem: "An Old Man's Winter Night," "In the Home Stretch," "Meeting and Passing," "Putting in the Seed," many more. All complete and unabridged. 64pp. $5\frac{3}{16}$ x $8\frac{1}{4}$. 0-486-27550-7

ROMEO AND JULIET, William Shakespeare. Tragic tale of star-crossed lovers, feuding families and timeless passion contains some of Shakespeare's most beautiful and lyrical love poetry. Complete, unabridged text with explanatory footnotes. 96pp. $5\frac{3}{16}$ x $8\frac{1}{4}$. 0-486-27557-4

SANDITON AND THE WATSONS: Austen's Unfinished Novels, Jane Austen. Two tantalizing incomplete stories revisit Austen's customary milieu of courtship and venture into new territory, amid guests at a seaside resort. Both are worth reading for pleasure and study. 112pp. $5\frac{3}{8}$ x $8\frac{1}{2}$. 0-486-45793-1

THE SCARLET LETTER, Nathaniel Hawthorne. With stark power and emotional depth, Hawthorne's masterpiece explores sin, guilt, and redemption in a story of adultery in the early days of the Massachusetts Colony. 192pp. $5\frac{3}{16}$ x $8\frac{1}{4}$. 0-486-28048-9

THE SEASONS OF AMERICA PAST, Eric Sloane. Seventy-five illustrations depict cider mills and presses, sleds, pumps, stump-pulling equipment, plows, and other elements of America's rural heritage. A section of old recipes and household hints adds additional color. 160pp. $8\frac{3}{8}$ x 11. 0-486-44220-9

SELECTED CANTERBURY TALES, Geoffrey Chaucer. Delightful collection includes the General Prologue plus three of the most popular tales: "The Knight's Tale," "The Miller's Prologue and Tale," and "The Wife of Bath's Prologue and Tale." In modern English. 144pp. $5\frac{3}{16}$ x $8\frac{1}{4}$. 0-486-28241-4

SELECTED POEMS, Emily Dickinson. Over 100 best-known, best-loved poems by one of America's foremost poets, reprinted from authoritative early editions. No comparable edition at this price. Index of first lines. 64pp. $5\frac{3}{16}$ x $8\frac{1}{4}$. 0-486-26466-1

SIDDHARTHA, Hermann Hesse. Classic novel that has inspired generations of seekers. Blending Eastern mysticism and psychoanalysis, Hesse presents a strikingly original view of man and culture and the arduous process of self-discovery, reconciliation, harmony, and peace. 112pp. $5\frac{3}{16}$ x $8\frac{1}{4}$. 0-486-40653-9

SKETCHING OUTDOORS, Leonard Richmond. This guide offers beginners step-by-step demonstrations of how to depict clouds, trees, buildings, and other outdoor sights. Explanations of a variety of techniques include shading and constructional drawing. 48pp. 11 x $8\frac{1}{4}$. 0-486-46922-0

SMALL HOUSES OF THE FORTIES: With Illustrations and Floor Plans, Harold E. Group. 56 floor plans and elevations of houses that originally cost less than $15,000 to build. Recommended by financial institutions of the era, they range from Colonials to Cape Cods. 144pp. 8⅜ x 11. 0-486-45598-X

SOME CHINESE GHOSTS, Lafcadio Hearn. Rooted in ancient Chinese legends, these richly atmospheric supernatural tales are recounted by an expert in Oriental lore. Their originality, power, and literary charm will captivate readers of all ages. 96pp. 5⅜ x 8½. 0-486-46306-0

SONGS FOR THE OPEN ROAD: Poems of Travel and Adventure, Edited by The American Poetry & Literacy Project. More than 80 poems by 50 American and British masters celebrate real and metaphorical journeys. Poems by Whitman, Byron, Millay, Sandburg, Langston Hughes, Emily Dickinson, Robert Frost, Shelley, Tennyson, Yeats, many others. Note. 80pp. 5³⁄₁₆ x 8¼. 0-486-40646-6

SPOON RIVER ANTHOLOGY, Edgar Lee Masters. An American poetry classic, in which former citizens of a mythical midwestern town speak touchingly from the grave of the thwarted hopes and dreams of their lives. 144pp. 5³⁄₁₆ x 8¼. 0-486-27275-3

STAR LORE: Myths, Legends, and Facts, William Tyler Olcott. Captivating retellings of the origins and histories of ancient star groups include Pegasus, Ursa Major, Pleiades, signs of the zodiac, and other constellations. "Classic." — *Sky & Telescope.* 58 illustrations. 544pp. 5⅜ x 8½. 0-486-43581-4

THE STRANGE CASE OF DR. JEKYLL AND MR. HYDE, Robert Louis Stevenson. This intriguing novel, both fantasy thriller and moral allegory, depicts the struggle of two opposing personalities — one essentially good, the other evil — for the soul of one man. 64pp. 5³⁄₁₆ x 8¼. 0-486-26688-5

SURVIVAL HANDBOOK: The Official U.S. Army Guide, Department of the Army. This special edition of the Army field manual is geared toward civilians. An essential companion for campers and all lovers of the outdoors, it constitutes the most authoritative wilderness guide. 288pp. 5³⁄₁₆ x 8¼. 0-486-46184-X

A TALE OF TWO CITIES, Charles Dickens. Against the backdrop of the French Revolution, Dickens unfolds his masterpiece of drama, adventure, and romance about a man falsely accused of treason. Excitement and derring-do in the shadow of the guillotine. 304pp. 5³⁄₁₆ x 8¼. 0-486-40651-2

TEN PLAYS, Anton Chekhov. *The Sea Gull, Uncle Vanya, The Three Sisters, The Cherry Orchard,* and *Ivanov,* plus 5 one-act comedies: *The Anniversary, An Unwilling Martyr, The Wedding, The Bear,* and *The Proposal.* 336pp. 5³⁄₁₆ x 8¼. 0-486-46560-8

THE FLYING INN, G. K. Chesterton. Hilarious romp in which pub owner Humphrey Hump and friend take to the road in a donkey cart filled with rum and cheese, inveighing against Prohibition and other "oppressive forms of modernity." 320pp. 5⅜ x 8½. 0-486-41910-X

THIRTY YEARS THAT SHOOK PHYSICS: The Story of Quantum Theory, George Gamow. Lucid, accessible introduction to the influential theory of energy and matter features careful explanations of Dirac's anti-particles, Bohr's model of the atom, and much more. Numerous drawings. 1966 edition. 240pp. 5⅜ x 8½. 0-486-24895-X

TREASURE ISLAND, Robert Louis Stevenson. Classic adventure story of a perilous sea journey, a mutiny led by the infamous Long John Silver, and a lethal scramble for buried treasure — seen through the eyes of cabin boy Jim Hawkins. 160pp. 5³⁄₁₆ x 8¼. 0-486-27559-0

THE TRIAL, Franz Kafka. Translated by David Wyllie. From its gripping first sentence onward, this novel exemplifies the term "Kafkaesque." Its darkly humorous narrative recounts a bank clerk's entrapment in a bureaucratic maze, based on an undisclosed charge. 176pp. 5³⁄₁₆ x 8¼. 0-486-47061-X

THE TURN OF THE SCREW, Henry James. Gripping ghost story by great novelist depicts the sinister transformation of 2 innocent children into flagrant liars and hypocrites. An elegantly told tale of unspoken horror and psychological terror. 96pp. 5³⁄₁₆ x 8¼. 0-486-26684-2

UP FROM SLAVERY, Booker T. Washington. Washington (1856-1915) rose to become the most influential spokesman for African-Americans of his day. In this eloquently written book, he describes events in a remarkable life that began in bondage and culminated in worldwide recognition. 160pp. 5³⁄₁₆ x 8¼. 0-486-28738-6

VICTORIAN HOUSE DESIGNS IN AUTHENTIC FULL COLOR: 75 Plates from the "Scientific American – Architects and Builders Edition," 1885-1894, Edited by Blanche Cirker. Exquisitely detailed, exceptionally handsome designs for an enormous variety of attractive city dwellings, spacious suburban and country homes, charming "cottages" and other structures — all accompanied by perspective views and floor plans. 80pp. 9¼ x 12¼. 0-486-29438-2

VILLETTE, Charlotte Brontë. Acclaimed by Virginia Woolf as "Brontë's finest novel," this moving psychological study features a remarkably modern heroine who abandons her native England for a new life as a schoolteacher in Belgium. 480pp. 5³⁄₁₆ x 8¼. 0-486-45557-2

THE VOYAGE OUT, Virginia Woolf. A moving depiction of the thrills and confusion of youth, Woolf's acclaimed first novel traces a shipboard journey to South America for a captivating exploration of a woman's growing self-awareness. 288pp. 5³⁄₁₆ x 8¼. 0-486-45005-8

WALDEN; OR, LIFE IN THE WOODS, Henry David Thoreau. Accounts of Thoreau's daily life on the shores of Walden Pond outside Concord, Massachusetts, are interwoven with musings on the virtues of self-reliance and individual freedom, on society, government, and other topics. 224pp. 5³⁄₁₆ x 8¼. 0-486-28495-6

WILD PILGRIMAGE: A Novel in Woodcuts, Lynd Ward. Through startling engravings shaded in black and red, Ward wordlessly tells the story of a man trapped in an industrial world, struggling between the grim reality around him and the fantasies his imagination creates. 112pp. 6⅛ x 9¼. 0-486-46583-7

WILLY POGÁNY REDISCOVERED, Willy Pogány. Selected and Edited by Jeff A. Menges. More than 100 color and black-and-white Art Nouveau–style illustrations from fairy tales and adventure stories include scenes from Wagner's "Ring" cycle, *The Rime of the Ancient Mariner, Gulliver's Travels,* and *Faust.* 144pp. 8⅜ x 11. 0-486-47046-6

WOOLLY THOUGHTS: Unlock Your Creative Genius with Modular Knitting, Pat Ashforth and Steve Plummer. Here's the revolutionary way to knit — easy, fun, and foolproof! Beginners and experienced knitters need only master a single stitch to create their own designs with patchwork squares. More than 100 illustrations. 128pp. 6½ x 9¼. 0-486-46084-3

WUTHERING HEIGHTS, Emily Brontë. Somber tale of consuming passions and vengeance — played out amid the lonely English moors — recounts the turbulent and tempestuous love story of Cathy and Heathcliff. Poignant and compelling. 256pp. 5³⁄₁₆ x 8¼. 0-486-29256-8